GUNS & GOD

LINES IN THE SAND

BY

RAIN STORY

Published by:
Light Switch Press
PO Box 272847
Fort Collins, CO 80527

TABLE OF CONTENTS

"No one is born hating another person because of the color of his skin or his background or his religion. People must learn to hate, and if they can learn to hate, they can be taught to love, for love comes more naturally to the human heart than its opposite."

~ Nelson Mandela

DEEP-RUNNIN' ROOTS

CHAPTER 1

Thursday, April 4, 2013. Dressed in his best navy-blue suit and red tie, Henry emerged from his polished black limo and stepped onto the Capitol lawn at 500 Woodlane Street.

A crowd of activists clapped, whistled, and cheered, "Little Rock loves you, Henry Shoemaker! Arkansas loves you! God loves you!"

The nasal-cleansing aroma of freshly-cut grass, honeysuckle dew, and mudcat river water wafted through the downtown concrete canyons surrounded by semi-tall buildings.

The early morning sunshine glistened across the tops of the City's taller buildings and lit up the Capitol building dome with a glowing, golden semblance that would rival mosques around the world. However, a mosque, this surely was not.

On the lawn, activists sauntered back and forth while they carried Holy Bibles heavily laden with sticky tabs and waved signs that read: *Republican for Life*; *Less Government, More Jobs*; *Second Amendment, Our God-Given Right*; *Abortion is Murder*; and, *Pry my guns from my cold dead hands*.

2.

Henry's middle-aged smile exaggerated the deep crevices carved around his gap-toothed grin and shadowy hazel eyes. His longer classic crew cut flittered in the breeze as his tall lanky frame climbed the steps. He waved to the crowd and made his way toward the door.

A young, admiring professionally dressed intern, Lisa Turner, attempted to open the door for Henry.

Just as he approached, he lifted his arm sharply and pushed her aside with his elbow. "Move. I don't have time for this."

Her face quickly changed to disgust.

Henry did an about-face before entering the doorway, forced a smile, and waved to his constituents once more. "Today, the governor will sign constitutional carry into law! We thank you! Thank you all! God bless!"

***

Sunday, July 7, 2013. In Beebe, Arkansas, daylight sparkled off the dew-covered grass like tiny shimmering diamonds. This ocean of gems covered a spacious subdivision of carefully landscaped yards belonging to upper-middle-class homes.

Catherine and Willie Rose stretched, yawned, and beamed lovingly at each other as the early morning splendor peeked through the bedroom window. He stared at her natural beauty as he gently moved her hair with his finger. The tranquil expression on her face kept him entranced. She gazed into his eyes. Her spirit seeped into his soul.

Then her smile grew big as she stuck her finger into his burly-looking beard, gave him a jab, and rolled out of the bed in a flash. "Somebody needs to shave!"

He reached out to grab her and missed. "Hey, you!" He lunged again.

She squealed as he caught her by the arm and pulled her back onto the bed.

After a few seconds of petting, they kissed with a strong lust for one another. Willie, with a talented pair of hands, slipped her lingerie up around her neck without ceasing his kisses for more than a second or two.

Catherine assisted him and pulled the gown off her head. She stood to her feet and tossed it on the dresser.

Willie—still entranced—looked on as the sun glimmered off her silky skin, her hips, her legs, her back, her arms, neck, and breasts. Her long blonde hair, though bedraggled, cascaded down to touch the small of her back. As she crawled into bed, he whispered, "I am a damned lucky man."

"Yes, you are, Willie Rose." She kissed his neck.

He smiled in ecstasy. He pushed her back, laying his larger body on top of hers and kissing her neck and breasts with the excitement of a teenage boy.

They made love for almost an hour. Then, after they caught their breath, they held each other tight.

"I love you, Willie."

"I love you too, baby girl."

***

In the next room, their 5-year-old son, Colton, awoke and rubbed his eyes. He stretched and yawned. He patted his blanket, kicked the covers, and patted some more. He searched the blankets all around and became panicked. "No. No. No. Where is it?"

He lifted his pillow, and there it was: his G.I. Joe action figure. He picked it up and held it to his chest. "I don't ever want to lose you again. You hear me?"

***

Later in the morning, Catherine stood by the kitchen window as she sipped her morning coffee. Her long hair was partly pulled away from her face as the rest flowed down the back of her pure, white cotton robe. She sorted her thoughts as she looked out across the yard where colorful butterflies fluttered around.

Suddenly, her peaceful moment of meditation was broken by Willie's voice shouting, "Damned straight!"

In the living room, Willie turned up the volume on the computer.

Radical radio host Conrad Davis spewed conspiracy theories across the airwaves and growled, "Don't be stupid folks! They're comin' for you! Mark my words! That's their agenda! They're gonna take all of our guns so we can't defend ourselves, and then they're gonna haul our asses to the North where they have concentration camps waitin'!"

Willie chimed in, "They're not gettin' my guns! Hell no!"

Colton scooted into the kitchen to his mother's side as he held his G.I. Joe and rubbed his eyes. "Momma, I'm scared."

Catherine gently picked up her son. "Aw, Colton, there's nothing to be afraid of, honey. Daddy's just a little bit excited this morning. Everything is okay."

A sharp knock on the front door drew everyone's attention.

Catherine swayed back and forth, comforting her son. "Willie, will you get the door?"

Clearly irritated, Willie—dressed in faded blue jeans, a western button-down shirt, and worn-out cowboy boots—stomped toward the front door. "Dammit, woman," he mumbled.

Within Catherine's line of sight from the kitchen, Willie abruptly opened the door. The irritation on his face morphed to horror as he looked five heavily armed special ops soldiers in the eye.

He slowly turned and looked at Catherine with fear.

Wide-eyed, she stared at his face and tightly gripped her son in her arms. She pressed his head to her shoulder.

Her coffee cup dropped to the floor. It was a moment so absolutely terrifying that it seemed to play out in slow motion.

The soldiers—dressed in black with ski masks—burst through the front door so hard that it knocked Willie to the floor. They rushed inside.

With assault rifles aimed at Willie, one soldier brutally smashed his face to the floor with his boot heel while another forced his arms behind his back and handcuffed him with a zip tie.

As the soldiers viciously lifted Willie from the floor and pressed him against the wall, Catherine screamed. She set Colton down and tried to go to Willie. She reached her arm out toward her husband, but a tall muscular soldier blocked her way.

Her eyes met his. She glared at him with hatred.

Colton screamed, "Mommy! Mommy!"

She quickly turned back and picked up her terrified son. Her body convulsed with fear. She looked back at Willie again.

He silently mouthed to her, "I love you."

The tall muscular soldier ripped Colton from her arms. He then roughly twisted her wrists behind her back, handcuffed her, and shoved her into the hallway.

In the adjoining living room, a smaller thin-framed soldier smashed the glass on the gun cabinet. The soldier pulled her mask off, revealing the silhouette of her face and ponytail that eerily resembled Catherine herself.

She removed all of Willie's guns and assault weapons from the cabinet and carefully placed them in a black bag on the floor. The bag had a sizeable tag on it that read: *Confiscated from Willie Rose.*

***

The special ops soldiers escorted the stunned family outside near a line of massive black buses where many shocked and fearful, yet familiar, folks from all over the neighborhood stood in line—handcuffed—waiting to board.

Catherine and Willie waited together. They stooped and sobbed as a soldier held Colton away from them at the end of the line.

The young boy kicked and screamed. "Mommy! Daddy! Help me!"

Willie—beaten, bruised, and bleeding—tried to charge the soldier who held his son, but his knees were knocked out from under him by another soldier who monitored the crowd. Willie fell to the ground. Blood oozed from the tight zip tie that restrained him. He gasped for breath and moaned in pain.

Catherine shrieked, "Willie!"

Colton's screams grew louder. Yet there was nothing that either of his parents could do to comfort him. Their agony was overwhelming.

Moans and sorrow pulsed through the air from the entire subdivision. From the bus windows, horrified faces gaped outward in disbelief and shock.

Once boarded, Catherine sat next to Willie. She softly kissed his battered face. He bowed his head in defeat.

The entire bus vibrated with misery.

Finally, Colton broke free from the soldier's grasp at the door of the bus, raced toward his mother, and clung tightly to her neck. "Mommy! Mommy!"

"Baby boy! Hang on to me! Don't leave me!" she pleaded.

Willie lifted his head and looked out the window as soldiers carried firearms from his home and loaded them onto a military Humvee. His eyes twitched uncontrollably as tears rolled down his face. He prayed, "Dear God. Help us all."

***

In the kitchen of Willie and Catherine's home, Colton's G.I. Joe action figure rested on the floor. Its arms and legs were twisted. The gun was ripped from its hands.

From the living room, Conrad warned with a low, gruff voice, "You believe whatever you want to, but I'm tellin' you people, this stuff is real! I feel it in my gut, and my gut don't lie! It is the end of life as we know it as God-fearin', Constitution-abidin' American citizens! You can call it whatever you like, but I'm tellin' you now, it's called Communism! And it's comin'! It's comin' for each one of you!"

***

Catherine's eyes popped open. She sat up in bed and panted. Her body was saturated with sweat. She wiped her face with her hand and looked around the room to get her bearings. "My bedroom," she sighed.

Her body wilted back onto the bed. She rolled over and observed Colton, sleeping in Willie's place. She kissed his head and put her face against his.

Suddenly, the stillness was shattered. "Damned straight!"

***

In the living room, Willie turned up the volume on the computer.

Conrad erupted. "Don't be stupid folks! They're comin' for you! Mark my words! That's their agenda! They're gonna take all our guns so we can't defend ourselves, and then they are gonna haul our asses to the North where they have concentration camps waitin'!"

Willie chimed in, "They're not gettin' my guns! Hell no!" He paced back and forth across the floor as he nervously shoved his hands in his jeans pockets then jerked them out and waved them around. He rubbed his face and head in frustration.

Conrad warned, "These times are like no other, people! We are livin' in the end times! This isn't your forefathers' America anymore! We have to keep hold of our God-given right to bear arms and remember that God gave us this country!"

Willie barked, "Yes!"

He swung around and started to pace again but came face to face with a fuming Catherine. They stared each other in the eye for several moments, in silence except for the radio noise.

"Don't let anybody stand in the way of what God meant to be! If we have to, we can kill them! God gave us that right too!"

Catherine glared at Willie. He glared back. His lips twisted, and his nostrils flared.

She demanded, "Turn it off."

His face relented. "Catherine, I'm listenin' to this. This is stuff we need to know."

Conrad interrupted, "There are many instances in the Bible where God ordained killin's in order to position his called-upon where they needed to be."

Catherine's stare intensified, and her brow lowered. "Turn it off, Willie."

Conrad cautioned, "And there were always these radicals who were tryin' to stop it from happenin', to change the Will of God, so to speak."

Willie moved away, exhaled loudly, walked over to the computer, and reluctantly turned off the volume. "This stuff is gonna happen, ya know. It's for real."

Catherine was annoyed. "And the end of the world has been coming for thousands of years!"

"This is real, Catherine. I know you don't believe—"

"Willie! Stop! I want you to stop this madness right now! You're scaring Colton, and you're making me have nightmares! I'm sick of this paranoia game you play with your family to see who's going to get it right about the details! For God's sake! You are all educated people!"

"And so are you, Cath! That's why none of us can understand how you can be so complacent at a time like this!"

"You are all eaten up with this conspiracy theory idiocy! It surpasses ridiculous!"

Willie's chest puffed up as he inhaled. "That's enough, Catherine. There is no need to insult my family."

"Then stop acting like the sky is falling every single day!"

They exchanged tense glances.

Catherine's voice returned to calm. "Let's stop talking about this now."

Willie bowed up. "Done."

Catherine spun around to leave. "Good."

"Yeah. Good."

As Catherine left the room, Willie rocked his head and beat his fists together in exasperation.

***

Along Mandolin Road, in rural Beebe, the heat of the rising sun pushed a cloud of drifting condensation across the rich green lawns of two neighboring stately homes: Fuzzy Rose's and Jim Barton's. Each sat on a multi-acre span with elegant swimming pools (the Bartons' being under construction), wide garages, work sheds, and exceptional fences and horse barns.

Horses and colts galloped and played with dogs as the sun's rays burned through the treetops and birds chirped.

***

Fuzzy was a 70-year-old Vietnam vet. He had a long scruffy beard, long hair, and extraordinarily hairy neck, chest, and arms. He donned an old, stained, flat-brimmed cowboy hat, baggy plaid shirt, and old, dirty jeans tucked inside his worn-out buckskin cowboy boots. His weathered skin and wrinkles of hard living were pronounced over his face and tall slender body.

His barn was a huge, beautiful structure that contended with most single-family homes in the area. This morning, the barn doors hung open.

The old man emerged with his German Shepherd, Smokey. He stood in the barn doorway with a Bible in one hand and several property marker flags in the other. On his hip, he wore a pearl-handled 1911 Colt 45 in a worn alligator-skin holster.

He tossed the markers into the barn. Then he took off his hat and beat it against his leg. He looked up toward the sky and took a long, deep breath of fresh air. After a moment, he opened his Bible to an earmarked page. With a shaky, gravelly voice, he read, "Pursue, for thou shalt surely overtake them, and without fail, recover all." He scratched his head, looked up at the sun, and smiled. "And for that, I thank you, Lord. For my property and my God-given right to bear arms."

Bible opened in one hand, he drew his gun from his hip with the other and fired once into the air, shattering the serene calm.

The shot startled the animals nearby and scattered flocks of birds into the sky. Even Smokey ran into the barn to hide.

As Fuzzy looked up at the flocks of birds fluttering away, he spotted a squadron of seven Air Force C-130s in a V formation, flying toward him. He muttered, "Goddamned trash-haulin' pigeons!"

***

Next door, in the Bartons' home, the oversized stone-tiled kitchen was exquisitely modern and clean. Equally upscale were the décor and china.

Jim's wife, Laura, was a middle-aged woman who was attractive in a practical and sensible way. Her bouncy, brunette, shoulder-length bob framed her diamond-shaped face; perfect, cute, freckled nose; and beautiful, glowing smile. Her eyes were gentle and kind. They emanated the shy, somewhat naïve, and somewhat insecure side of her personality. Her disguise, however, was being a book club president, expert gardener, and former PTA supermom. Most of all, she loved her family. Her dedication to her husband and kids always came first.

As Laura prepared breakfast at the counter, her college-aged daughter, Emily, wandered in behind her.

"Aw, Momma. You are absolutely too cute. Being away at college, I've missed all the mommy stuff you do." She sat at the breakfast table and took an apple from the fruit bowl.

Laura's tall athletically built biracial son, Kyle, trotted in, wearing a t-shirt and shorts. He winked at his mother. "Hey hey! What's up? Sounded like you and Dad were setting off fireworks early this morning."

Laura commented, "Fireworks? Oh, that was probably Fuzzy taking a shot at an imaginary coyote again. His eyes are failing him these days."

Kyle looked around the room. "Where's Dad?"

Laura put her hands up to signal for everyone to be quiet as the sound of the C-130 engines grew louder. "I think he's flying overhead again right now."

Emily moved next to the plate glass window in the dining room and looked up to the sky. "Yep. That's them. Second round."

Kyle said, "Wow. He must have gotten up early this morning."

Laura asserted, "Yes, Son. That's what he does—cleans it all up and takes it to work. I'm hoping someday it will rub off on you."

Emily sat back down and continued eating her apple.

Kyle mused, "Air Force? Nah. I kinda like college. I think I'll just stay there a few more years."

"Now, Kyle."

"Just kidding, Mom! Just kidding!"

He twirled around, sat beside Emily, and affectionately leaned into her shoulder to irritate her. Then he reached out and poured cereal and milk into a bowl.

Laura joined them at the table. "Kyle, you're going to have to graduate someday and get a job."

Emily boffed. "He won't. He'll still be in college after I get my doctorate, work my whole life, and then retire. I'll have great-grandkids, and he'll still be going to college in his HoverChair, hitting on all the cute chicks!"

She playfully punched Kyle in the arm as he tried to spoon cereal into his mouth, sloshing some on his arm.

He retorted, "Hey! Chicks like HoverChairs! Take note, Emily. My elderly professor has one, and he says his lap is always ready for—"

Laura lifted her arm and cautioned, "Enough, you guys!"

Kyle whined, "But—"

Laura reached out and put her hand on his arm. "Kyle, your father wants you to venture out to the shed when you're done eating. There's a great little riding lawnmower out there that's been waiting for some serious action."

"Awww," he moaned.

Emily gloated, "Hah!"

Laura continued, "Emily, I need you to help me out back, weeding the garden."

"What?" she whined.

Kyle gloated, "Hah!"

Laura shifted her stern look toward Kyle. "Or you can help us weed the garden."

Kyle rushed to finish his cereal and took his bowl to the kitchen sink. "I'm sorry, Mom. I'd love to, but I've got a date with a Jurassic lawnmower." He rushed toward the door and blew her a kiss. "I love ya!"

Laura yelled, "Make sure Fuzzy knows you're not a coyote!"

Kyle bolted through the door, closing it loudly behind him.

Laura yelled again, "Kyle!" She set her coffee down. "Good grief."

"They're all like that," Emily explained.

"Who?"

"Men. They think they know what they're doing, but watch. Kyle will have half the neighbor's lawn mowed before he realizes where the property line is."

"Now, what makes you think he can't figure that out? There are flags out there for the new fence."

Emily bit her apple. "Because I saw the old man taking down the markers."

***

Outside, Kyle picked up a stick and played with his shaggy dog as he walked toward the detached work shed some 30 yards from the main house. He jogged as he threw the stick. "Go get it, Elvis!"

Across the way, Fuzzy worked outside his open barn doors. He carefully focused on running a polishing cloth down the barrel of a realistic-looking cap gun. Then he heard Kyle playing with the dog and spotted him walking across the back lawn. He squinted his eyes and watched him suspiciously.

Kyle entered the work shed and looked around. He walked over to the lawnmower where he noticed some odd-looking fluid on the tarp. He ran his finger through it and sniffed. "I have no idea." He threw the tarp off the mower and checked it for fuel.

***

The interior of Fuzzy's home was a roomy open-concept design with expensive artwork hanging on buckskin-colored walls.

Bobby Joe, a middle-aged, younger version of his dad, walked over to the back sliding glass door and pulled it open. He stuck his head out and shouted, "Dad! Hey! Fuzzy!"

Outside the barn, Fuzzy stopped working, lifted his head, took a step, and shouted back. "What the hell do you want?!"

"We're leavin' Annabelle and Levi here while we go to Little Rock!"

"Annabelle?! She's goin' to Little Rock?!"

"No! She's stayin' here with Levi! She wants to swim in the pool!"

"Yeah! It's okay by me if she wants to go shoot pool!"

Fuzzy mumbled to himself, "Don't know why that boy has to ask me 'bout his own damned kid gonna shoot pool. He never did make no sense."

Bobby Joe yelled, "We're leavin' now! Levi's in the house! She's sittin' in the pool!"

"Good God, Son! I don't care if she's shittin' in the stool!"

Fuzzy mumbled again, "Damn boy. Stupid as a box of rocks. Takes after his momma. God rest her soul." He limped into the barn and over to the work table where he looked out the window. He took his hat off, put it over his chest, and looked up to the sky. "I don't mean nothin' by it, Anna. I swear. I do love ya, honey."

***

Kyle stepped out of the work shed with a big smile and began walking back toward the house, with Elvis at his heels. As he walked, he glanced across the back lawn toward Fuzzy's extravagantly landscaped swimming pool area.

Annabelle rose out of the pool in her skimpy bikini.

Kyle stopped in his tracks. He lost his breath; he became captivated by her beautiful, shapely body.

Meanwhile, Fuzzy saw Kyle emerge from the work shed. Out of curiosity, he pulled his binoculars from his pocket and aimed them right at the young man. In a close-up view, he saw Kyle stop, pause, and stare toward his house. He positioned the binoculars in that direction and saw Annabelle looking back at Kyle, smiling sexily and posing in a seductive manner.

"Oh, hells no!"

Fists clenched and cursing wildly, Fuzzy stomped out of the barn toward Kyle.

Kyle noticed him and took a step back.

Fuzzy, somewhat confused, strutted toward Kyle, then changed his route and stomped toward Annabelle, then shifted and changed his path again back toward Kyle. Still cursing, the anger on his face raged.

Kyle, somewhat unsettled, jogged toward his own home while looking over his shoulder from moment to moment.

At the same time, inside Fuzzy's house, 21-year-old Levi Rose sat at the dining table, working on his computer gaming code. His gaunt appearance; long brown hair; cleft lip; and geeky glasses made him a misfit compared to the rest of the Rose clan.

When Levi heard the commotion outside, he walked to the sliding glass doors next to the pool and looked out. There, he saw Annabelle flaunt her sexual prowess as she winked at Kyle, even with Fuzzy hot on his tail.

Fuzzy belted, "Yeah, that's it! You git on back in that house and keep your fuckin' eyes off my granddaughter!"

The old man then changed course and headed directly toward Annabelle. She slithered into the pool.

He angrily plodded right up to the pool's edge. "Annabelle!"

She looked up at him innocently and sweetly. "I love you, Grampa. What's the matter?"

"What do you think you're doin'?"

"Why Grampa, I'm just swimmin' in your pool. I love this pool. The water feels so good wrapped around my whole body."

"Stop talkin' like that, Annabelle. Your gramma would roll over in her grave."

"Aw, I don't mean nothin' by it. It does feel good, and you know it. After all that time away at school, I need a vacation like this."

"Well, you can thank Fuzzy Rose & Sons Gun Shows and the gun shop for that there fancy swimmin' pool. I ain't never been much into fancy things, but it does feel nice to sit in that water sometimes."

"Aw, get in here with me, Grampa! It's gonna be 90 degrees out there! Come on!"

"I cain't do it right now, Annabelle. I have important things to do," he said as he pointed his wicked forefinger at her. "You don't leave this property, and don't you go makin' friends with that Barton boy next door. I mean it, Annabelle! That boy's trouble with a capital 'troub!'"

"No, Grampa. That's just Kyle. Don't you remember him? They've lived next door for a couple of years now. He's just back from college. Like me."

"I say stay away from him! Them folks is California liberals and want the government to ban all our guns and wreck my business. You wouldn't have this fancy swimmin' pool no more! Not to mention that my guns ain't none of their damned business! Besides that, they're tryin' to steal my land!"

"Oh, Grampa."

He caught his breath and rubbed his head. "My stupid little brother, Asa, had to leave his property to that bitch wife of his, then she turned around and sold it to fuckin' liberals just to spite the family. But them Bartons just keep edgin' the line more and more on top of me! Stealin'!"

"Grampa, I love you so much, but I am 25 now. I'm not a little girl anymore. I can go anywhere I want. I'm just stayin' here to help you out through the summer. And the Bartons are not like you say. They're nice folks."

"Are you arguin' with me? I knew it. I should've shot that boy in the ass!"

Annabelle gasped, "What?! No! Grampa! You're not shootin' anybody!"

"Oh yes, I will! I protect me and mine! You stay away from him, and I mean it!" He strutted off with a slight limp toward the barn.

Levi stepped out of the house and stood beside the pool. Admiringly, he grinned at his sister. "You're causin' trouble, Annabelle."

Defiant, she slid her head under the water, came back up, and mockingly spewed water out of her mouth like a fountain.

From a window in the Barton house, Kyle watched Annabelle intently.

From another window in the Barton house, Emily watched the goings-on as she methodically toked a joint.

CHAPTER 2

The Air Force base in Jacksonville, Arkansas was a prominent facility with many high-ranking officers from all over the country stationed there. Its expanse was over 6,000 acres of what had once been lush fertile farmland.

Being about 20 miles north of Little Rock, it provided officers and military personnel with plenty of opportunities to absorb the local culture. Many of them chose to live near the base rather than on it or in Little Rock. One of those was the chiseled, handsome silver fox, Jim Barton.

The officers' club inside the base was a clean but sparsely decorated space. Its smell was of Pine-Sol and liquor.

Dressed in uniform, CMSAF Jim and other officers mingled, chatted, and drank. Everyone had a story to tell, and everyone felt safe telling it there. Jim, however, preferred to keep his stories to himself. Ironically, he had no problem with listening and laughing with others at their tall tales.

Eventually, Jim's older, dear friend, CMSAF Carl Smith, pulled him aside from the crowd. "Hey, Jim. How did training go this morning?"

"Just fine, as always." He sipped his glass of bourbon.

A voluptuous female server named Dorene Toller walked up to the men with a tray of drinks. She leered and exchanged glances with them. "Do you need another drink, Jim?"

He grinned and nodded. "No thank you, Dorene. Not just yet."

She winked. "Carl?"

"I'm good. Thank you."

Jim watched Dorene's sexy body as she sashayed away.

Carl noticed Jim ogling. "Anyway, how are you and Laura doing? Do you still like living the rural life out in Beebe?"

Jim faced him. "Yes, we do. The neighbors are sometimes a pain in the ass, but I suppose they think the same of us."

Carl advised, "From what I hear, you ought to be careful with those folks. Those pro-gun natives are on a warpath with touchy trigger fingers and a chip on their shoulders. They'll shoot anything that gets in their way."

"Oh come on, Carl."

"Seriously. It's not a laughing matter, Jim. I worry about you out there. The Roses are practically the poster family for the National Firearms Organization. They think they are going to win this thing and have no gun control laws at all in the end."

"I have to laugh at it to an extent, Carl. I can't change the situation, and I'm not going to sell my home to move again."

"Well, please tell me that your gun-toting, tea-partying neighbors don't know that you're a bleeding-heart liberal!"

"They might."

"Jesus Christ, Jim. You do know that an ATF agent went missing out that direction a couple of years ago? Never found him."

"Look, Carl. This is a momentary hysteria. It will pass. I grew up in Heber Springs. I know what these folks are about. I'm not going to put myself in harm's way, but I'm certainly not going to hide behind a veil of fear either. That's what got this all started. Fear turned to paranoia. I won't do it."

"Okay. But keep this in mind: Momentary hysteria can cause wars that last decades, sometimes centuries."

Jim patted his friend on the shoulder. "Advice well taken, my friend."

They turned to walk away.

Jim continued. "Now when are you and Joy coming out for an old-fashioned barbecue?"

"Oh, I don't know. Maybe next week?"

"How about Wednesday?"

"Wednesday sounds great."

***

A little later at Fuzzy's house, the old man and Annabelle sat together, watching TV, as Willie and Catherine walked in the front door with Colton.

Willie carried a basket of dirty laundry and set it down on the floor. He looked at Fuzzy. "Why aren't you ready to go, Dad?"

"Go where?"

"We've got a meetin' at the shop. I told ya I'd be pickin' you up."

"Then why are ya doin' laundry?"

Catherine explained, "Our washer broke today. I'm going to do clothes here while you guys go to the meeting if that's okay."

Fuzzy gave Annabelle a dirty look. "I reckon so, and you can keep an eye on Annabelle. She's under house arrest."

Willie slapped his dad's socked-foot off his knee. "Come on, Dad. Get your boots on. We're late."

***

A bit later, Catherine loaded clothes into the washer while Annabelle sat atop the dryer. Through the doorway, Colton could be seen as he watched cartoons in the living room.

Catherine shook out clothing piece by piece before putting it in the machine. "What was that house arrest thing all about earlier?"

Annabelle shifted her weight and crossed her legs. "Grampa doesn't want me to associate with Kyle next door."

"Oh, don't worry about your grampa's cantankerous attitude. I don't think he means half the things he says."

Annabelle twisted her hair. "Catherine? Are you prejudiced like the menfolk here are?"

"Um, no. I'm not, and I don't think the menfolk here mean to be either."

"If they don't mean to be, then why are they so mean to people with darker skin?"

"I haven't seen that happen, Annabelle."

"It did today."

"What do you mean?"

"Grampa was awfully mean to Kyle because he was lookin' at me."

Catherine rolled her eyes and snickered. "Well, Annabelle, that's probably because all young men look at you. I suppose they can't help it, but it's no wonder that your grampa wants to protect you."

"I'm not a virgin, ya know. I'm not a child."

Catherine shot a look at her. "Annabelle!"

"Grampa wanted to shoot Kyle today."

"Oh, he wouldn't really do that."

"Said he would."

"He was just saying that."

Annabelle vented, "See! That's what I don't get. Maybe it's goin' to college that makes you see things differently. I don't know, but these folks around here—" She shifted her butt again on the dryer and continued. "They swear they are Christians, they aren't prejudiced, and they love everybody, but they don't mean that they love everybody. It's a lie." She looked at Catherine, raised one brow, and flopped her arm in the air. "And why do they have to have so many guns? Guns and God. How in the world does that all fit together?"

Colton blurted out, "Hi, Dad!"

Catherine and Annabelle snapped their heads around and were startled to see Willie standing in the doorway to the laundry room.

He suspiciously cocked his head. "Am I interruptin' anything? What's goin' on in here? You both look like you just saw a ghost or somethin'." He warily glanced at each of them.

Catherine jarred herself to normal. "No, Willie. Nothing's wrong. We were just talking about private girl stuff. What are you doing back here?"

"Oh God. Girl stuff."

He peered around Catherine's feet. "We got a couple miles down the road, and Dad realized he didn't have his gun and started freakin' out. Said he must've left it on his dirty jeans he tossed in here."

Catherine looked to her right and saw Fuzzy's jeans on the floor. She picked them up and handed them to Willie.

He pulled the gun and holster off and dropped the jeans back onto the floor. "Thanks, honey. We're late!" He disappeared as quickly as he had appeared.

The two women looked at each other and sighed with relief.

Colton blurted out, "Bye, Dad!"

24.

At the Barton house, the professionally decorated living room was a considerable space with a mega-sectional surrounding two walls. A 75" HDTV hung in front of it while a voluminous, expensive flower arrangement adorned the coffee table.

Kyle sat peacefully, watching a college baseball game.

Laura and Emily walked through the front door with their arms full of shopping bags. They plopped them down in the foyer and walked into the living room.

Without taking his eyes off the TV, Kyle reacted, "Hey! Where have you guys been?"

Laura jeered back, "Hey, yeah! I thought you were supposed to be mowing the lawn."

"You were still here when I came back in to use the restroom. Besides, something's wrong with the mower. It won't start."

Emily teased, "Maybe it needs gas."

Kyle mocked, "I checked that, smarty pants. Besides, what happened to weeding the garden? Where did you guys go?"

"We couldn't find the gardening gloves so we went to get some," Laura said.

Emily stood behind her mother, leaned sideways, and winked at Kyle.

With a depressed attitude, Kyle grunted. "Must've bought a lot of gloves."

Emily threw her arms to her side. "What's the matter with you? Grumpy old man."

"I had a problem with the neighbor. That old man Rose doesn't like me."

Laura wagged her head. "Oh, that's not true. Why would you say that?"

"I think it's pretty obvious. He came after me today."

Emily piped up, "Well, yeah. You were ogling his granddaughter. Duh."

"What?! I was not! Where were you, Miss I-Saw-Everything creepy girl?!"

Emily shrugged. "Just looking out my bedroom window. Nice bikini, huh?"

"Yes. Yes, it was! Too bad you'll never fill one out like that!"

Emily punched him in the arm.

Laura yelled, "Okay, you two! Stop it! Deep breath!"

After a moment of quietness, Laura continued. "Now, Kyle. What makes you think that Fuzzy doesn't like you? Other than eyeballing his little Annabelle, exhibitionista?"

"Because I'm black."

Emily ribbed, "You're white too, dummy."

"Shut up, Emily," he said.

Laura assured him, "That's not true! I mean that you're a dummy."

"Come on, Mom. Look at me. I'm black. Not that I'm a bit ashamed of it. You and Jim taught me to be proud, and I am. It's just—"

"You are half me, Kyle. And your real dad was a good man. Don't let anyone tell you differently. We've gone over this so many times."

"I know, Mom. But that doesn't change the fact that there are people who still don't accept dark skin. Period."

Emily backed him up. "He is right, Mom."

"Oh, alright. You are both right. You're all grown up now, and I'm still talking to you like you're little kids. I'm sorry."

Kyle responded, "It's okay. Don't worry about it. I'm just saying that Fuzzy doesn't like me."

Laura sat beside him, smiled at him, and touched his face. "You are so very beautiful, my son. Your father would be so proud if he was alive today. You are so much like him."

***

An enormous, elaborate sign that read *Fuzzy Rose & Sons Gun Shop* towered over an expansive concrete-block-and-aluminum warehouse that sat on the side of a busy road just outside of Beebe.

In front of the building, fabulous foliage was carefully landscaped around a gigantic bronze statue of a tall muscular confederate soldier armed with an intimidating Gatling gun.

Willie's new black Dodge Laramie Limited 3500 4x4 pickup truck pulled into the parking area. It stopped by the back door at an empty parking space marked with a sign that said: *Reserved.*

Willie quickly got out of the truck while Fuzzy cautiously opened the passenger door, placed his left boot on the chrome running board, and slowly stepped down to the ground.

He grumbled, "Why ya gotta have these damned trucks so tall for? A fella could hurt hisself."

Willie waited patiently. Then they proceeded into the building together.

***

Once inside the gun shop, the two made their way along the counter where sales staff assisted several customers.

All around, hundreds of rifles and assault weapons lined the walls. Just as many handguns filled dozens of glass display cases.

In the center of the warehouse, elevated up high on a giant platform were a genuine antique Gatling gun and a canon. Lights danced around these centerpiece items in true altar form.

A mountain of a man named Jimmy "Toad" Walker wore a plastic name tag that proclaimed him *Store Manager*. He looked up from helping customers at one of the glass displays and signaled to the two owners as they walked past.

"Hey, Fuzzy! Hey, Willie! They're all in the back already!"

Willie sternly acknowledged, "Thanks, Toad."

Fuzzy and Willie walked behind the counter and through a door into a hallway leading to a back room.

With a sly grin, Toad dipped his head and continued waiting on his customers, father and son, Gene and Robert Collins. "So, I really think that this AR-15 over here would fit your needs nicely." Toad handed it to Robert.

Gene, a middle-aged, gruff-looking man, questioned his much younger son. "What in the hell do you need that for?"

"'Cause I want it. Come on, Dad. You know we need somethin' like this." He rubbed his hands up and down the gun like a hot date on a Saturday night.

Toad added, "This is one of the most popular items we have in the shop right now. They're sellin' like hotcakes, especially with the threat of Obama takin' all our guns. Better get 'em now while you can."

Gene argued, "We live in the woods. All we ever needed guns for was huntin' and shootin' wild animals that threaten our well-bein'. Goddamn animals don't shoot back. Besides, you hit a deer with one of those damned guns, and the meat ain't gonna be worth shit for eatin'."

His son defended his position. "But Dad, what about the meth heads out there cookin' up poison drugs, runnin' off our wildlife, and stealin' from our barns?"

Gene berated him. "You and me both been to war. You mean to tell me you're gonna blast 45 rounds of ammo into a human bein' without no goddamn conscience about it whatsoever?"

"It ain't just for shootin' humans."

"Then what the hell else was it made for?"

"Havin' fun."

Gene, disgusted, walked away from the counter. He mumbled, "Ain't how I raised that boy. God forgive me for whatever I done wrong."

Robert handed the gun back to Toad and chased after his father. "Dad. Hey Dad! Wait a minute."

Gene halted. "Son, I didn't raise you to be no murderer, and even if you don't plan to use that gun for killin' human beings, you're thinkin' about it. Don't tell me you're not. I'm no idiot and I'm no softie like both you and Toad over there are thinkin'. I see it in your eyes. You're wrongheaded. Your thinkin' is skewed. I didn't raise you to be so narrowminded and crazed in your thoughts."

"But Dad—"

"Son, I guess after all these years, I don't really know who you are." With that, he walked out of the shop.

Robert looked at Toad and shrugged. "I'm sorry. I'll come back another day."

Toad placed the gun on a rack behind him. "Don't make no difference to me. We're flooded with people comin' up from Little Rock. Someone else will be in here in 15 minutes and buy it. Your loss."

Robert walked after his father. "Dad!"

***

The back room was dimly lit as many male members of the Rose family huddled around. With looks of anticipation on their faces, they listened.

Handsome Rhett and his equally good-looking son, Luke, leaned against the bar and drank Jack Daniel's with Coca-Cola.

Meanwhile, John Mark, Cletus, Bobby Joe, and Levi sat around a broad, round table with a custom Smith & Wesson pool table light hanging over its center.

Searcy Rose was named after the town he was born in, as folks around those parts often did back in 1952. He was also Fuzzy's no-nonsense, younger brother whose balding head and shaven face made him appear the complete opposite from his older sibling.

As Searcy listened on the telephone, everyone waited patiently.

Willie and Fuzzy moved in from the darkened hallway to join the crowd.

Rhett commented to them in a serious tone, "Dad's on the phone with the State Capitol."

With his ear to the phone, Searcy beamed and shouted with excitement, "Fabulous!" He covered the receiver with his hand and faced the others in the room. "The Patriots Act 746 that the governor signed back in April is now in effect as law in the great State of Arkansas!"

All the men whooped and hollered in celebration, except for young Levi. He appeared bothered by their cheers.

Then Searcy spoke into the phone, "Good work. We'll see you at the lunch meetin' in a few days."

Fuzzy dropped his normally, grumpy tone, laughed, and exclaimed, "We need to have a get-together and celebrate at my place tonight!"

***

At Fuzzy's house, Catherine and Annabelle folded laundry. Catherine held up a grease-stained shirt. "Look at that! Ruined it first time he wore it!"

Her smartphone rang. As she looked at it, she saw Willie's photo on the screen and answered, "Hi, Willie. Are you done already?"

"No. We've got more to do here, but we're gonna have a big shindig there at Dad's tonight. Can you call up the other womenfolk and figure out the food?"

"For how many?"

"I don't know. A whole bunch."

Catherine glanced at Annabelle, scrunched her shoulders, and grinned. She asked, "Can I invite the neighbors over?"

He hesitated. "Sure. Why not."

***

A little later, the Bartons' front doorbell rang.

Laura opened the door. "Hi. You're Annabelle, aren't you?"

"Yes, ma'am. That's me."

"Come in. It's been a while since I've seen you. You're a beautiful young lady."

"Thank you, ma'am. I've been away at U of A Fayetteville. I'm just back for the summer. Me and my cousin Luke are here helpin' Grampa out with some things." She stepped inside the doorway as she shyly looked around for Kyle.

Laura insisted, "You don't have to call me 'ma'am,' sweetie."

"Yes, I do. It's respectful."

"Well, what can I do for you this afternoon?"

Emily cheerfully bounced onto the scene. "Hi, Annabelle."

"Hi, Emily! How was your year at school?"

Emily threw an exaggerated nod. "Good. It's really good."

Kyle came around the corner to see who was at the door. He appeared caught unaware at first, then embarrassed.

Annabelle waved faintly at him. "Hi, Kyle."

"Um. Hi, Annabelle. What's up?"

She quickly gathered herself and looked at Laura point-blank. "Oh yeah. My family is havin' a gatherin' at the house tonight. They sent me over to invite y'all to join in."

Laura gleamed. "Oh! That sounds wonderful! Tell them yes! We'd be honored. Should I fix something to bring?"

"Sure, if you'd like to. It's just dinner and pickin'."

"Okay. We'll be there. What time should we come over?"

"They'll start eatin' about seven."

"Seven it is!"

Annabelle's smile shined at Kyle. "Okay. See you all there, but…" she hesitated, "I was just wonderin' if you guys might like to go ridin' horses with me and my brother Levi before dinner. He's a computer nerd and doesn't get out too much. I thought it might be good for him."

Kyle pointed to himself. "Me? You want me to go?"

"Yeah, you and Emily, silly. I'll get Luke to join us too."

Laura was elated. "Hey! Great idea! You all go riding. I'll start cooking a couple of dishes for dinner."

Emily agreed, "Sure! Sounds like fun!"

"Great! Meet y'all at Looper's tree about five o'clock?"

Kyle added, "Sure. We'll saddle up Flight and Stealth. Meet you there."

Annabelle bobbed out the door. "Cool!" She raced away.

Laura reassured, "See, Kyle. I told you Fuzzy didn't hate you. Now, let me call your father and tell him we have a dinner to go to." She headed toward the kitchen.

Emily made a cocky smiley face at her brother.

"Oh, shut up!" he sneered.

She punched his shoulder and sped off. He gave chase as she squealed.

***

Across the hills and a couple of valleys, a smoky-grey cabin sat in the extreme rural outskirts of Beebe. It was obscured with overgrown trees, vines, and bushes. The backyard was decked out with shooting targets set at different ranges.

Bert Black and his wife, Joelle, hovered over their 6-year-old son, Buddy, as he aimed his child-sized 22-caliber rifle and shot a nearby target dead center.

Bert howled proudly, "Way to go, Son!"

Joelle praised him too. "Yay! You did it! You're gonna be the best target shooter ever in the whole wide world! Yay!"

Little Buddy radiated with excitement. "I am?"

Bert said, "Heck, yes, Son! You are!" He picked him up and lifted him high into the air as the boy giggled. "You cute little devil, you!"

The cell phone in Bert's pocket rang. He sat Buddy down, looked at the phone, and answered. "Hey, Willie. How's it goin'?"

Joelle looked at him, lurching her head sideways, curious about the call.

Bert yelled, "Oh hell yes. We'd love to come over to your party tonight! Right now, we're outside with little Buddy, target shootin'. Gotta teach 'em young, ya know."

He kissed Joelle's hand, hung up the phone, and shoved it back into his pocket. "We've been invited to the Roses' for dinner and pickin' tonight. I hope you don't mind, I said yes."

"I heard the call, goofy. Of course, it's okay."

Buddy pulled out his best dance moves. "Pickin', hooray!"

Joelle took him by the hand. "Yes, little man. We have to go in the house and clean up now."

"Clean up?" He soured his face. "Boo."

Bert agreed. "Yeah. Boo. Let's just go like we are."

His wife gave a harsh look. "No. We are gonna clean up. We are not gonna visit our friends smellin' like a herd of buffalo."

"Buffalo? That's not buffalo. That's survivalist, baby!"

Excited, Buddy clowned, "I want to smell like a sur-bible-ist!"

Joelle glared at Bert, so he corrected himself.

"Not tonight, Buddy. Let's go in and clean up so we make Momma happy, and we can get on the road."

Buddy complained, "Oh, darn. Okay."

The three entered the back door of the cabin, where several cork boards full of conspiracy theorist articles and survivalist materials covered the walls. They read: "President seeks to Abolish Second Amendment: Confiscating all Firearms;" "NFO Rallies Members for Civil War;" "Communism is alive in the U.S.;" and "Evidence Uncovered: Concentration Camps in Wyoming."

As they walked past the stockpile of articles and hoarded junk, Bert said, "If I have to clean up, I think I'm gonna debut my new uniform."

"We're not goin' anywhere with you dressed in that silly Halloween costume." She held her nose. "Good God in heaven! What is that awful smell?"

***

Looper's tree was a massive, 300-year-old oak tree that grew in a forked path in an open area several hundred yards behind the Roses' and Bartons' horse barns. Its majestic girth and height silently held dominion over the land. Its leaves, every single one, listened to the chirp of a single cricket as carefully as it did every word whispered from the mouths of humankind from at least a mile away. Today was no different from all the others.

While Emily and Kyle rode closer, they observed Annabelle, Levi, and their cousin Luke as they waited underneath the great tree. The dogs, Elvis and Smokey, trotted along behind the horses' heels.

Emily could not take her eyes off Luke. His muscular, tanned torso donned a button-down denim shirt with cutoff sleeves. His ruggedly chiseled jawline, perfectly shaped nose and eyes, crushingly handsome looks, longer hair, distressed Henschel leather hat, and saddle scabbard equipped with a rifle made her heart pound with excitement with every step she moved closer.

Annabelle shouted with glee. "Hey! Look who showed up!"

Kyle smiled at her with affection. "Good afternoon."

Emily asked, "Hi. How are you doing, Levi? Haven't seen you in a long time."

Levi seemed somewhat annoyed. "I'm doin' alright. I'd rather be workin' on my video game though."

With a baritone voice, Luke commented, "Don't be such a nerd, Levi. Enjoy the outdoors and fresh air, why don't ya." Then he leaned his head in, smiled, and winked at Emily.

She melted.

Levi quipped, "Ya mean the smell of horseshit, don't ya?"

Emily tried to hide her glow. "So, you must be their cousin Luke."

"Yes, ma'am, and you must be Emily. Nice to meet ya." With that, he grinned, guided his horse away, and began to ride down the trail.

Levi leaned toward Emily. "Never mind him. He was born like that. A natural Marlboro Man."

***

This area of wilderness in North Central Arkansas was blanketed with a plethora of species of trees, bushes, plants, and flowers. In places it was so thick, it was nearly impossible to navigate through. Then, without warning, it would open up to a grassy field, rocky bluff, or barren patch. The trail was ever-changing.

As the young people rode on a winding path along a hillside, each observed with wonder the beauty of the landscape and took it in. They also took in the fact that Levi was pointing, smiling, and laughing more and more as they rode on. His behavior was changing.

At one point, Emily halted her horse and dismounted. As she tightened the girth on her saddle, gunfire blasted out.

Elvis and Smokey barked and ran away. Emily's horse was startled, reared up, and tried to run until Luke grabbed the reins and brought it under control.

Emily—knocked to the ground—gave Luke a look of wild contempt as heat trailed from the end of his rifle. "What the hell did you do that for? If you thought that would be funny, it wasn't!"

Luke waved his rifle toward the ground beside her.

As she sat on her butt, reclined back on her arms, she turned to see the body of a copperhead with its head split by gunshot, uncontrollably jerking around near her. She scrambled to her feet and screamed.

Kyle was impressed. "Whoa! Good shot! Good thing you had that rifle!"

Emily, still stunned and recovering from fright, mounted her horse. "Yeah."

Annabelle sighed. "Whew! Damned snakes!"

Levi chuckled, "I have to program this into my game! I really think this is excitin' stuff!"

They all laughed with Levi and poked fun at Emily.

She caught up with her new hero and muttered in a muffled voice, "Thank you, Luke."

He tipped his hat. "Ain't nothin', sweetheart."

Kyle watched as the two exchanged glances. "Oh, boy."

CHAPTER 3

Fuzzy's house resounded with jovial chatter and laughter as visitors filled the spacious living room.

Whenever guests arrived, they promptly carried casserole dishes and other food items into the kitchen. Then they migrated back into the living room that was the hub of all the action.

The powerful aromas of homemade bread, homegrown fried okra, and potatoes with onions made everyone's mouths water. It was truly like Christmas in July.

The Bartons came in the front door and immediately began introducing themselves, creating their own chatter. Jim and Kyle blended in with a group of men as Laura and Emily carried food into the dining area.

Laura placed a casserole dish on the table and joined Catherine and other women who were lingering around the kitchen.

Annabelle and Levi surrounded Emily as she placed a bowl of salad on the table.

Levi said, "Hi, Emily! Glad you could make it!"

"Hey! Thank you for inviting us! This looks like fun. So many people here."

Annabelle forewarned, "Yeah, just wait 'til they start pickin'. Do you dance?"

Emily stammered, "No, probably not."

"Does your brother?"

Emily pondered the thought for a moment. "You know what, I believe he does! Yes! I'm quite sure of it!"

Annabelle gushed, "Good! Do ya mind if I ask him to dance with me?"

"Oh, not at all! Go for it, girl!"

Annabelle squealed, "Yay! Thank you!"

Levi and Emily moved into the living room while Annabelle pranced off like a young gazelle to look for Kyle. Then Emily spotted Luke across the room. She could not stop herself from staring at him.

Levi noticed her lack of attention and watched her love-smitten gawk. He bowed his head in disappointment.

From the center of the room, Fuzzy raised his arms and cleared his throat. He shouted, "Okay! You people! I mean, friends! Listen up, here! I want to thank y'all for comin' to this here shindig. This has been a pretty good year so far. In Washington, with the help of the NFO, we defeated the attempt by that illegitimate president to sneak a gun registry on us through more unnecessary background checks. But today..."

He suddenly appeared confused. "Today..."

Searcy patted his beloved brother on the shoulder and tipped his head in support. "What my brother is tryin' to say, is that last February, State Representative Henry Shoemaker snuck some unique language into 'The Right to Defensive Firearm Carry Act' and pushed it through the State Legislature. In April, the governor signed that bill into law, effectively creatin' 'Constitutional Carry' for the State of Arkansas. It's July now, and the law is in effect! That means that you and I can take our guns, open or concealed, anywhere we want to go in our great State!"

The crowd erupted in applause.

Emily was rousted out of her daydream as she saw Luke clap and whistle to the news. Next to her, Levi's face reddened with embarrassment. He sank into a nearby chair in an attempt to vanish.

The Bartons exchanged serious glances from across the room. They moved slowly through the crowd and gathered together, inconspicuously, by the back wall where Jim gave Laura a questioning look.

She pulled his arm and whispered into his ear, "I didn't know."

Searcy took a big swig of beer and held his stein high in the air. "And here's to the one true God that made it happen, in order to protect the rights that our infallible forefathers granted to us, their sons!"

The crowd applauded again, whistled loudly, and cheered.

Jim seemed intrigued. He whispered to Laura, "We need to stay. This could be important."

While Emily and Laura agreed with Jim, Kyle spotted Annabelle across the room. Their eyes locked. Her face was also wrought with embarrassment. She lowered her head.

Fuzzy glimpsed Annabelle's reaction then suspiciously squinted and looked around the room. Eventually, he thought he recognized Kyle as he stood with his family behind the crowd. The old man's face frowned. A fire within began to burn.

At that moment, Searcy interrupted his brother's inner rage. "Now Fuzzy here is gonna say Grace for everybody because, as we know, faith is an integral part of who we are!" He joked, "Separation of church and state doesn't work around here! Now, say Grace, Fuzzy!"

Fuzzy bowed his head and obeyed as told. "Thank you, Lord, for this day and this reason to celebrate. Thank you for the Christian ways that set up this here country, and the forefathers that fought to give us these rights, that You protected for us yet again today. Keep us safe, Lord, and never let them scroungy liberals make us change our traditions. Your traditions, Lord! Amen."

The crowd murmured in unison, "Amen."

Searcy shouted, "Let's eat!"

***

Outside, in the beautifully landscaped back patio and pool areas, visitors walked around with plates filled with food as they ate and mingled.

The evening was pleasant. The lighting from the tall pedestal gas lamps was simply magical. Nearby, visitors sprayed themselves for mosquitos and gathered around a flickering fire that burned in the fire pit.

The Bartons nervously attempted to blend in. They succeeded.

Family and visitors alike unpacked their guitars, banjos, harmonicas, and tambourines. They played country and bluegrass music.

Annabelle invited Kyle to dance. At first, he reluctantly accepted but was not so shy after she showed him a few easy steps.

Emily danced with Luke. Their joy was contagious. The elderly, the youth, and even the babies joined in and danced.

Jim and Laura laughed and tapped their feet to the flawless music as they looked on. At one point, they even rose to their feet to slow dance together.

Into the evening, visitors packed up their belongings, said their goodbyes, and left a few at a time. Emily waved to

Luke as she and her family exited. Shortly after, Annabelle, Levi, Luke, and others left as well.

***

Eventually, the crowd was mostly gone.

Fuzzy, Bobby Joe, and his wife, Mary, visited in the living room. Their young grandchildren, Mauser, Gunner, and the twins, Hope and Faith, sat on the floor and played video games on the TV.

Tired and irritable, Fuzzy snapped, "Where the hell is John Mark and Darcy? They done went and forgot their brats again! Confounded kids leave their toys layin' around everywhere! That's dangerous, ya know!"

Mary laughed, "Why? Because you cain't see and trip over them? Finally glad you're admittin' that. And I got a surprise for you."

Bobby Joe gazed intently at his dad. An ornery grin crept across his face.

Fuzzy yelled, "I don't need no goddamn surprise, Mary Carter Rose!"

Bobby Joe prodded him. "Nah! That ain't why he's bitchin'!" He slapped Fuzzy's leg. "You went and polished Mauser's cap gun again, didn't ya, Dad?"

Fuzzy squirmed as he shoved his arm away. "Shut up, boy."

Mary asked, "What? You cain't tell a cap gun from a real gun?"

"You shut the hell up too," Fuzzy advised as he walked toward his bedroom. "Y'all makin' me tired relivin' all this work I done today. Y'all and them god-danged ankle-biters."

Mary advised, "Better rest up, Fuzzy. I'm takin' you to the eye doctor tomorrow."

"Ain't neither," he mumbled.

Bobby Joe said, "She is."

Completely irritated, Fuzzy pointed out, "Don't need no eye doctor! I got Jesus leadin' me the way."

Mary insisted, "Jesus said eight o'clock."

"I'll be sleepin'."

Bobby Joe joked, "'Nite Daddy. Cross your fingers, they don't have to cut out your eyeballs tomorrow."

"Shut up, Son! Don't need to cross my fingers 'bout nothin'. Got my Bible where your momma used to sleep, God rest her soul, and got my gun in my hand to shoot any money-grubbin' quacks who wanna steal my body parts whilst I'm sleepin'. Now, good night!"

As Fuzzy left the room, Searcy followed.

Gunner asked, "Grampa. Who's Pawpaw gonna shoot?"

"Nobody, Gunner. Go back to playin' your game there."

Hope commented, "I heard him alright. He wants to shoot some doctors."

Then, Faith added, "No, Hope. He said money-grubbers. But it don't matter. They're all Obamabots."

Excited, Mauser yelled, "Cool! Whackin' some freeloadin' blisterheads!"

Mary took a deep breath then ordered, "That's enough talk about shootin' real people. Y'all just go on shootin' them cartoon people on that video game and stop all this talk about shootin' real ones."

Faith glared at Mary with confusion. "Gramma. That don't make no sense."

"Faith, go back to playin'. I'm not sayin' it again. You talk too much."

Bobby Joe laughed. "Takes after her gramma."

"Bobby Joe! Take that back. Take it back now, or you may be the one missin' two eyeballs come mornin'."

***

In the bedroom, Fuzzy flipped on a lamp, pulled his pajamas out of a dresser drawer, and tossed them on the bed. He noticed his aged Medal of Honor laying out where the kids had been looking at it. He sighed and pushed it back toward the mirror. Then he turned around to see Searcy standing behind him.

"Are you here to give me shit too?"

Searcy held a glass of water and a capsule in his hand. "They don't mean nothin' by it. Folks just worryin' about you, Brother."

"I know I'm losin' my edge, but I don't know why everybody's gotta be such a smartass about it."

Searcy handed the glass and the capsule to him. "Here. Take this. It'll help."

Fuzzy swallowed the medication and sat the glass on the dresser. "I don't know why ya keep makin' me take those damn things. They ain't helpin' nothin'."

Searcy gently placed his hand on Fuzzy's shoulder. "They are helpin'. It's okay. You needn't worry. I've got everything covered. You don't have to worry about a thing. Nothin' at all."

***

A bit later, Bobby Joe, Mary, and the kids were gone. Searcy joined his wife, Mabel, with Willie and Catherine at the dining table.

Willie appeared concerned. "How's he doin', Uncle? His health doesn't look so good. He won't tell me nothin'."

"You've gotta remember; your dad did three tours in 'Nam. That's a triple dose of Agent Orange, and that shit ain't good for nobody. His eyes are gettin' worse. His hearin' is gettin' worse. And his mood, forget it. Hell, Levi

44.

told me that he polished Mauser's cap gun today and had no idea it wasn't a real gun until he had it glistenin'."

Willie grinned. "They still make cap guns?"

Mabel answered, "Oh God yes."

Searcy explained, "Only they're makin' them fancier. Nowadays, they look almost just like a pure, unadulterated hunk of He-Man firearm."

Willie drooled. "Dang. I'm gonna have to do some shoppin' for one for Colton now that he turned 5."

Catherine was taken aback. "Wait just a minute. We didn't talk about this."

Willie said sweetly, "Darlin', it's a man thing."

"Don't darlin' me, Willie Rose! We are talking about it. Period."

As she shoved her chair to the table and angrily went out to the patio, Mabel followed.

Willie muttered under his breath, "Ain't neither."

Concerned, Searcy cautioned, "Boy, you gotta control that thing goin' on right there. You're the man. You got to lead."

"I gotta lead alright, but I've gotta do it nice and subtle-like. Catherine's a good woman. She understands how we think down here, but every once in a while, them liberal roots creep up."

"I told you not to marry her."

"Not again."

"Well, I mean it. People ought to marry with their own kind. God meant it to be that way."

"Oh, come on. It ain't like she's from some foreign country."

"Might as well be. It's all the same, boy. Them differences are gonna bite you both in the ass."

"We'll work through it. I'll talk to her. I'll get her to change her mind a little more to our way of thinkin'. Just takes some time."

"And what if it backfires?"

"Backfires?"

"What if she ends up changin' you?"

Willie laughed. "Ain't gonna happen, Uncle. Not in a million years. Nope. This good ol' boy is a Southern man through and through."

"That's what they all say."

***

Outside on the patio, the late evening brought with it sounds of crickets, katydids, and bullfrogs in the not-so-distant woods. The gas lamps still glowed. The smell of overgrown honeysuckle filled the cool night air as did the odor of chlorine from the pool water.

Infuriated, Catherine sat on the swing with her face in her hands.

Mabel sat beside her. "Catherine. They don't mean no harm by all that talk, really."

Catherine rubbed her face, wiped away a tear, and looked at Mabel. Somewhat confused, she asked, "What?"

"Aw, they talk all tough and what not, but they don't mean none of it like it sounds." Mabel pulled a tissue from her pocket and gently blotted Catherine's face. "You're so pretty."

"Thank you, Mabel." She accepted the tissue from Mabel's hand. "You are so nice to me. But I hate all this talk about guns and fighting. And now that Searcy told Willie about the cool cap guns, he will obsess over it until he finally goes out and buys one for my little boy. Why does he have to do that? He's just a little boy. He's my baby, and he's very content playing with his stuffed animals right now. Cap guns—that look real? Seriously?"

"Oh, I know Colton likes playin' with his stuffed animals, sweetie. He's such a precious thing. But he is a boy, and eventually he'll have to learn how to use a gun. Might as well get him used to the idea."

"But why can't he just be a little boy right now?"

"Honey, you're not from here, so I know it's hard for you to understand everything we do, but guns are a part of our culture, always have been. They're as much a part of our culture as our religion. As much as we love God, we love the land and sustainin' ourselves by huntin' and, well, we even kind of enjoy the pride and self-esteem that comes along with protectin' ourselves. So many people in the world can't say that."

"That's something else I don't understand, even though I really do try. How on earth can you mix guns and God? I'm not the only one in the family asking that question either."

"Well, sometimes it ain't easy, darlin'. Sometimes the lines are blurry. They're kind of like lines in the sand. Sometimes they shift and move a little bit this way or that way. Sometimes you have to re-draw the lines, move them around, ya know. But you have to lay them down somewhere."

Catherine was exhausted. "I am finally seeing what I am up against."

"No, Catherine, you don't want to go there with this. You really can't see what you're up against, dear. Things are not always what they appear to be. This thing, it's too big for you to see. It towers to the heavens and reaches far and wide into all the crooks and crannies of this whole nation. You can't fight it, sweetie. It will swallow you up."

"You tried?"

"Maybe for half a second, until I saw how huge and deep-runnin' the roots of this culture are. And I grew up in it. Still shocked me."

"Mabel. I have to try, for my son. He's my baby."

"Keep in mind that these folks around here, and many other parts of the country, consider themselves strong, God-fearin' people. And they do pride themselves on protectin' every ounce of their way of livin', whether it's right or wrong. And sometimes, it is wrong."

"And nobody wants to fix that wrong part? Just ignore it, huh?"

"I reckon they're scared, Catherine."

"Scared of what? What can possibly make them so scared that they hide behind guns but still declare God as their savior? What makes them so scared that they will resort to violence? What are they scared of?"

"Change." Mabel smiled lovingly at Catherine. A long, quiet moment passed. Then, she continued. "It's that simple."

Mabel sensed the overwhelming tension between them and waved her arm toward the house. "But these two in here, they ain't nothin' compared to Fuzzy. I swear, that man is scared to change his shart-filled underwear."

The two women broke out in laughter.

Mabel snorted, "He'll wear the damned things until they're so hard and crusty." She elbowed Catherine. "What? Tell me you didn't think that was pocket change rattlin' around!"

***

In the dining room, Searcy and Willie were chatting about things in general when a sharp knock rapped on the front door. When Searcy opened it, there, on the other side, stood Bert.

He pushed past Searcy and jogged into the living room area. "Now Searcy, what did I tell ya 'bout openin' that door without findin' out who's on the other side first? Damn. I could-a been a government man ready to haul your scrawny arse off to a concentration camp in Idaho! Dammit, man!"

Bert slapped Searcy on the back as Mabel and Catherine re-entered from the patio. The women looked on with curiosity.

Searcy reacted reluctantly. "Hi, Bert."

Willie happily stood by his friend to shake his hand. "Well, if it ain't Survivorman Bert Black in the flesh!"

Searcy said, "You're late. Dinner's over. Pickin's over. What brings you out here now?"

"I know I'm late. I'm sorry for that. Had a little trouble at home. Anyway, looky here!" He stuck his chest out, shoulders up, and chin high while he slowly rotated in a circle to show off his homemade outfit.

Searcy quipped, "What in the hell is that?"

"It's my uniform, Searcy! Put it together myself." He threw his head back and chest out again.

Searcy teased, "Are you gonna faint, Bert? Should I get the smellin' salts?"

Bert relaxed and cocked his head sideways. "Dammit, Searcy!" He turned to Willie and again threw his chest out. "Willie! What do you see?"

"Uhm. It looks like a really old confederate jacket."

Bert heehawed and slapped him on the shoulder. "Ding-ding-ding! We have a winner! This right here is an artillery man's jacket, the kind worn by General Lee's Army of Virginia! Check out these buttons! CSA! That's the Confederate States of America! Goddamn, I'm good!"

Willie put the backside of his hand to Bert's forehead as if to check for fever. "You do know the South didn't win that war?"

Bert answered, "Oh, but we will this time! Just look at this gun holster!" He showed off his Glock 27 40-caliber Smith & Wesson in a shiny, black-leather holster on his belt that also held four nine-round clips. "Ain't it a beaut?"

Agitated and out of patience, Searcy demanded, "Bert, go home."

"What? Searcy, this is important, buddy! Won't be long 'til they're sendin' more ATF men out here! Then what? There's gonna be war!"

Even more irritated than before, Searcy threatened, "Shut up, Bert. Go home. It's late."

Bert stared into Searcy's eyes as if to challenge him.

Willie moved close to Bert and carefully took him by the arm. He agreed with Searcy. "It is pretty late." He guided Bert toward the door. "We need to go on home too, but hey! I like the uniform!"

"Well, thank you, Willie. At least someone by the name Rose has a good head on his shoulders."

Searcy grumbled, "You're crossin' the line, Bert. Shut the hell up and go home. Now."

Bert snickered, "Oh, I'll leave. But I'll be back tomorrow to talk important business with you folks. Good night y'all. God bless." Bert shut the door behind himself.

Searcy sat in a recliner and shook his head. "Idaho."

***

The interior of the Barton home glowed with the dim luminescence of classy ceramic nightlights scattered throughout. The sweet smell of freshly-cut flowers wafted through the front rooms and down the hallway to the master bedroom where Jim patiently waited in bed.

Laura came out of the bathroom in her robe and kicked off her house shoes.

50.

Jim anticipated as he watched her. "You know, I actually kind of enjoyed myself tonight. I even liked the music."

Laura turned off her bedside lamp. The room became almost pitch-dark. She took off her robe, quickly slid underneath the sheets, and cuddled with her husband. "Well, I am sorry about it being a celebration for that gun law thing, though. I had no idea."

He growled sexily, "That's okay. You can make it up to me right now."

The sounds of passionate kissing and moaning and the rustle of the blankets went on for a few moments. Then there was an abrupt stop to everything.

Laura rolled out from under Jim and exclaimed, "Hey!"

"I just thought maybe we could try something new."

He glanced at her with disappointment and regret. She gawked back at him with astonishment and suspicion.

***

Monday, July 8, 2013. The renewal of morning ushered in an underlying, new curiosity and enthusiasm that filled the air. The Bartons sat at the dining table and enjoyed breakfast together.

Jim rubbed his chin. "That was some shindig last night, wasn't it?"

Laura shifted in her chair. "It was different. I'll say that."

Kyle added, "You know, after all that talk about the gun carry bill, things eased up, and it was actually kind of fun."

Jim mentioned, "Yes. Come to think of it, I did see you cuttin' a rug with a cute, little thing."

Emily burst out, "Funniest thing I saw all night! Did you see his arms flailing all over the place?"

Kyle defended, "Well, now wait a second! Miss Emily, you were doing a little boot-scootin' with Brad Pitt, yourself!"

Emily rolled her eyes. "Brad Pitt? That's original."

Laura popped a grape into her mouth. "The food was good, and the women seemed nice. Now, the music, that was just impressive."

Jim poked his fork in the air. He squinted his eyes as he recalled a fond memory. "My family used to jam like that when I was growing up."

Kyle asked, "Really?"

"Yes, sir."

Emily played with her scrambled eggs. "No kidding? Why don't we do that anymore?"

Jim leaned back in his chair. "Oh, everybody's scattered and busy. Carol's usually bogged down with work, and Scott's traveling around the country with Robyn. I'm glad they're doing what they like to do though. As long as we get to see them from time to time."

Emily played with her food. "That's sad."

Laura put on a big smile. "We're not going to let it be sad! We have each other, and we are going to stay busy! Let's see! What do we have going on today?"

Jim muttered, "Kyle."

"I know. I know. Mow the lawn."

Jim muttered again. "Emily."

"Yes, Dad. Weed the garden today. Promise."

Laura hopped up out of her chair with a somewhat nervous reaction. "Cool beans! See! We've got lots to do together! No time to be sad! No siree!"

Emily touched her mother's arm. "Mom."

"Got it. I'm dorky. I'll shut up now." She gathered up the dirty dishes from the table and carried them to the kitchen.

The others followed her and helped rinse the dishes off and put them into the dishwasher.

***

A little later in the morning, Kyle and Jim pushed the riding lawnmower away from the work shed and into the backyard near the Rose property line.

Jim said, "Someday there's going to be a fence built along here."

Several yards away, Emily and Laura donned wide-brimmed, floppy gardening hats and fabric gloves as they pulled weeds from the garden. Elvis watched over them. Then something caught Emily's attention. She stared into the distance.

Jim looked long and hard one direction and then the next where the invisible property line lay. He scratched his head. "Where in the world did all those markers go? Did Elvis pull them up? All of them?"

Kyle shrugged his shoulders and looked toward the Rose's barn.

There, Luke worked mending tack outside the barn doors. His distressed leather hat and muscular, sweat-shimmering, tanned torso were enough to catch anyone's attention, even at a distance.

Smokey raised his head from near Luke's feet. Something drew his attention as well.

Annabelle and Levi sat by Fuzzy's pool as they watched everyone hard at work.

Just inside Fuzzy's home, behind the sliding back doors near the pool, Fuzzy looked out across the landscape with his binoculars. "Busy mornin' out there."

Colton tugged on his pants legs. "Pawpaw. Let me go outside."

"Oh, okay, Colton." Fuzzy slid the door open.

The little boy careened outside and raced around the pool.

"Stop runnin' 'round that pool!"

Jim and Kyle worked on the lawnmower, struggling to see the inner workings and poking and prodding here and there.

Kyle backed away and pointed at it. "See, Dad. I told you it has plenty of gas."

"Yes. I see that, but I don't understand why..."

Kyle put his hands on his hips as Jim lightly kicked the back tire. Both men stepped back and studied the machine.

Colton tried to make Annabelle and Levi play with him. "Play dump truck with me! Come on! Scoop me up!"

Levi commented, "I'm goin' over there to see if I can help. Maybe it's something electrical."

Annabelle encouraged him. "Go on. It'll do you good to interact."

Colton whined, "I wanna go too."

"Okay, Colton. Come on." Levi took the boy's hand.

They walked toward the Bartons and their lawnmower.

Suddenly, Fuzzy stuck his head out from the sliding glass door. "Hey! Y'all don't need to go over there! Leave them be! They'll figure it out!"

Levi shouted, "We'll be right back, Grampa! Don't worry! I thought you went to the eye doctor!"

"I did! Glasses on order!" Fuzzy closed the door and observed with his binoculars.

A peculiar air, essence, an aura of something particularly dark or nefarious, seemed to settle upon the whole area of land. It was something hard to describe. It was invisible but thick enough to cut with a knife. It slightly singed the hairs in the nose when inhaled. It even seemed to pale the light of the sun to a dirty, yellowy bile tint.

Emily, being the sensitive she was, stopped weeding, stood upright, and looked toward the work shed. Something ominous was there, but she couldn't see it. She watched as Levi and Colton joined Jim and Kyle.

For no apparent reason, the dogs began to bark while the horses trotted in circles and kicked their legs.

Emily's brow furrowed. "Something doesn't feel right."

Luke stopped working, looked up, and took a step or two with a concerned expression on his face. He peered toward Jim and Kyle working on the mower.

The dogs kept barking, and the horses became edgier.

Kyle sat on the mower as Jim scratched his head.

"I can't figure out what's wrong with the darn thing."

Kyle bent over. "I'll try to start it up again."

The mower would not start.

Levi put his hand on the steering wheel. "Let me take a look at it. I think I can fix it." He pointed to a place far away in the yard. "Colton. You stand back over there. If it starts, it'll kick rocks everywhere."

Kyle got off the mower, took Colton's hand, and led him to the place where Levi directed.

Jim walked back toward the shed. "Let me look in here again. I must have an owner's manual somewhere around here." He went inside.

Colton twisted his hand loose from Kyle's, gave a carefree squeal, and ran toward the Bartons' garden to join the women. "Yummy, grapes!"

Kyle chased after him. "Colton!"

Levi sat on the mower and studied it closely.

Fuzzy stood outside by the pool with Annabelle as he looked through his binoculars. He moved them in time to see Levi sit on the mower. "Levi!"

Annabelle became concerned. "What's going on?"

Luke watched Levi closely, then turned, and locked eyes with Fuzzy from a distance.

Something, something dark was on the prowl.

Levi studied the wires on the mower. He spoke to himself as he adjusted them. "This wiring is all wrong. This one actually goes over here."

He then disconnected a wire and began to connect it to a different harness when the mower exploded into a fiery ball, blowing itself high into the air and throwing Levi several feet away.

His terrible screams were indescribably horrible as his burning body—engulfed in flames—stood and stumbled around. He waved his arms wildly.

The screams, those screams, were chilling.

Without hesitation, Jim ran out of the work shed with a tarp, tackled Levi, and rolled his body around on the ground to put out the flames.

Luke dropped the work tool in his hand and ran toward them as he yelled, "Levi!"

In the garden, Emily grabbed Colton in her arms and covered his face as they screamed in horror.

The dogs tucked their tails and ran into the nearby woods while the horses frantically raced in circles—heads held high and tails hoisted upward. Their screams also filled the air.

Colton shrieked, "Levi! Levi! He's burnin' to death!"

Kyle rushed to help Jim put out the flames.

Emily tried to bury Colton's face into her shoulder with one hand while she dug out her cell phone with the other. As she began to dial, Laura grabbed Colton from her and held him tight.

Meanwhile, Levi's blood-curdling screams pierced the veil of yellow bile, shattered the vibrations of the earth itself, penetrated even the bark of the trees, and melded into the inherent essence of every living being, each living thing, that heard that terrible sound. It shook them. It changed them, forevermore.

Every second, every moment, seemed to drag in slow motion. Each soul wondered what they could do or could have done differently to save Levi from the flames, to make that awful sound stopping ringing in their ears. Make it stop.

Fuzzy and Annabelle raced from the Rose house toward Levi.

Annabelle howled, "No!"

Fuzzy ordered, "Annabelle! You get Colton in the house! Now!"

Jim stopped rolling Levi's body on the ground. The flames were finally extinguished, as were Levi's cries.

Jim looked toward the garden and saw Emily talking on her phone. Kyle stood over the two men, riveted with horror.

Jim leaned over. "Levi? Buddy? You're okay. Hang in there, son. An ambulance is on the way." He slowly and painfully moved away from Levi's smoldering body and looked at his own slightly charred hands.

Kyle hovered over him. "Dad? Your hands!"

"Don't worry about my hands, Son. Get out to the street and guide the EMTs back here. Go on. Hurry," Jim demanded with a calmness that was almost annoying in light of the complete chaos.

As Kyle ran toward the street, Luke, Annabelle, and Fuzzy converged. Annabelle had a meltdown. She shrieked and cried with a touch of insanity.

Fuzzy repeated himself. "Get Colton back in the house! Now!"

Annabelle yanked her hair, clawed at her face, ran to Laura, snatched Colton, and ran madly back to Fuzzy's house.

Levi, barely alive, began to mutter lowly.

Jim noticed and leaned over toward him. "What, Levi? What did you say?" Jim placed his head near the young man's mouth to hear his faint whisper.

Levi muttered again into his ear.

After a moment, Jim lifted his head and looked up at Fuzzy.

Frustrated and worried, Fuzzy asked, "Well. What did he say?"

***

As the ambulance pulled away, turned onto the street, and sped off, Kyle, Luke, and Fuzzy stood with stunned looks on their faces.

Luke reassured Kyle, "Your dad will be alright. They just need to doctor his hands, and I'm sure he'll be back home tonight."

Fuzzy was greatly disturbed. "Not so well for poor Levi."

Luke angrily kicked a rock across the lawn. "I've heard of lawnmowers blowin' up but dear God! I've never heard of one blowin' a hole in the ground like that. I hope Levi's gonna be okay. We need to get on over to the hospital quick-like."

Luke and Fuzzy hastily walked toward the Rose house. Kyle, speechless, wandered around by the work shed, trying to stay out of the way of the police officers investigating the scene.

Deputy Barnes moved toward him. "Son, you should go on in the house now."

Kyle walked toward his own home but doubled back while dodging officers. Without being noticed, he bowed in to pick up tidbits of information.

Then Deputy Smith rushed up to Sheriff Thomas White, a serious-looking middle-aged Native American. "Sir! We found something!"

"Something besides a burnt lawnmower?"

"Yes, sir!"

Kyle listened intently, as Deputy Smith drew a long, deep breath and continued. "Sir. Over there where the machine exploded, it dug up a heap load of soil."

"And?"

"You'd best come over and take a look for yourself, sir."

Kyle's eyes widened as he crept quietly along behind them from a safe distance. He watched as the sheriff and Deputy Smith bent down on their knees to examine the burned area. Kyle's face contorted as he glimpsed a human skull half-buried in burnt soil.

HUNT & CONQUER

CHAPTER 4

The darkly tinted, curved windows of the White County
Medical Center in Searcy, Arkansas emitted a feeling of both
sterile welcome and hardened panic at the same time. From
the sympathetic, down-home hospitality of the staff to the
anxiety, fear, and grief of the visitors and patients, it was a
place not made for empaths whose souls absorb every grain
of energy that surrounds them. Even worse than all of that
was the awful dread of anticipation of what could be, yet to
come.

"Dammit!" Luke yelled.

The Rose family, Carter family, friends, and the Bartons
gathered in the lobby, waiting for word on Levi's condition.

Jim sat with a look of despair as he tapped his hands,
though bound with bandages.

Some chatted and wept while others paced the floor.
Some even crouched on their knees in prayer.

***

In the hospital room, Bobby Joe stood in tears as he
focused on his son whose body laid motionless and totally
incapacitated.

Mary stood on the other side of the bed and attempted to touch the top of her son's head, ever so slightly touching his hair but afraid to hurt him. Her eyes were blistery-red. Her face was soaked with tears. Her voice fluttered with grief. "Oh, Levi. Son, I love you so much. You can't leave me now, baby boy. I need you. You have to be strong." She took a deep breath. "Please. Wake up, Son." She wailed and stumbled backward.

Bobby Joe grasped her body and led her to a nearby chair. "Sit down for a bit, Mary. You have to breathe, or you'll pass out again."

She hopped back onto her feet. "I don't need a breather, Bobby Joe. I can't take time out right now." She resumed her place standing next to Levi's bed.

Bobby Joe nodded and resumed his place as well. "Son. I love you." He kissed Levi on the head. His body trembled, and his face distorted with grief. He sobbed. "It's okay to let go if you need to."

Mary moved around the bed. In a loud whisper, she scolded, "Bobby Joe! Don't say that!"

"Mary. Not here. Not now."

"Don't say that! He has to hold on! He has to try!" She pounded his chest with her fists.

He pulled her in and held her tight. "Mary."

She sobbed. "I'm not ready to give him up. I can't do this."

Within moments, Levi's heartbeat slowed. Then the bedside monitor flatlined. Alarms sounded.

Bobby Joe continued to hold his wife in his arms as she agonized in sorrow. With alarms blaring, medical staff flooded into the room.

As they exited, Bobby Joe held onto his weakened wife while she mourned in his arms. He struggled to guide her down the hallway toward the lobby. They passed Sheriff

White and Deputy Barnes as they walked in the other direction.

The sheriff recognized them. "Mr. and Mrs. Rose?"

Bobby Joe slowly looked up at him. "Yes, sir."

"I'm so sorry about your son."

"We just lost him."

Mary wailed in sorrow.

Deputy Barnes became somewhat emotional. "Oh no. I'm so very sorry."

Bobby Joe petted Mary's hair as he glanced back at the sheriff. "What do you need?"

The sheriff responded, "Sir. I'm so sorry. This timing is just awful. I need to speak to you for a moment if I may. I know things are really tough right now, but this is kind of important."

"I understand. Whatever you need. Let me help my wife to a seat. I'll meet you by the elevators in five minutes."

"Okay. Thank you, sir."

Bobby Joe and Mary continued toward the lobby. The sheriff and deputy walked toward the elevator area.

A bit later, Bobby Joe joined them. "What do you need? I only have a few minutes. I have to get back to my wife."

The sheriff said, "Yes, sir. We do apologize for takin' your time, especially right now."

Barnes added, "Before an announcement is made, we wanted to notify you first."

"Announcement? About what?"

Barnes faltered before continuing. "Mr. Rose, the lawnmower was tampered with."

The sheriff explained, "In fact, sir, 'tampered' is a mild description. Someone made it into a bomb."

Bobby Joe's face expressed shock. His body began to shake.

The sheriff continued, "Sir, your son was murdered."

62.

***

Tuesday, July 9, 2013. Fuzzy's home buzzed with family and friends. The air was filled with chatting, crying, and some light laughter with memories of Levi.

In one group, a middle-aged woman, Florence Hill, smiled at Luke and approached him. "Okay, now remind me who you belong to?"

"My momma and daddy is Rhett and Shelby Hook Rose. Searcy and Mabel are my grandparents."

She squealed, "Oh! Why, yes! I know you! You've grown up so big, and you're a looker just like your own daddy! Why, Georgia is one of my best friends! And I know that Hook family too. Fine upstandin' folks."

"Yes, ma'am. I suppose so."

She spoke with a hushed tone, "So, you knew your cousin Levi pretty well, I assume. Ya know he got that cleft lip from Fuzzy? That poison he got in Vietnam."

"Yes, ma'am. In fact—" Overcome with emotions, he took a deep breath and fought back tears. "He was a smart little guy. Just before all this happened, he told me that he always thought that he was the smart one. I was logically challenged 'cause I'd rather be workin' outside with the horses and my guns instead of learnin' how to work a computer. We took a horseback ride the other day, and I noticed him changin' right before my eyes. He was laughin' and havin' a real good time. Later on, he told me that he really wasn't all that smart 'cause he never learned how to work outside. He said I was the smart one, and my logic made more sense. He laughed and said that was the only part of me that he envied 'cause he never wanted to look like a Ken doll. I thought he meant it, for real. Then he said nah, he was just kiddin'."

The folks that listened in on the conversation laughed.

Luke continued with sincere emotion. "If you ask me, I'd given anything to be like Levi—just like him. I'm gonna miss that little guy."

In the dining room, a group of women monitored the dishes of food that people brought in and took away by checking the bottoms of casserole dishes to see that there was a name clearly written on each one. After all, each dish needed to find its way back home at the end of the day.

A few men stood nearby as they talked and ate from their plates filled with tender brisket, fire-grilled chicken, corn on the cob, turnip greens, and homemade sourdough bread slathered with homemade butter.

Kids played in and around everyone's feet.

That was until Mabel spoke up. "Mauser and Gunner! You boys stop chasin' Hope and Faith around that table! Y'all are gonna knock it over! Stop it!"

The boys laughed and chased the twin girls around the table, one more lap.

Finally, Gunner obeyed. "Aunt Mabel? Where's Uncle Levi? Ain't he comin' back?"

A hush gripped the room.

Mabel looked around at everyone then bent down to Gunner's height. At that exact moment, Colton quietly wandered into the room and eavesdropped.

Mabel explained to Gunner, "Oh, sweetie, no. He can't come back."

"Why not? He promised to teach me a new video game he made up all by hisself."

Hope added, "Yeah. He told me that too."

Mauser suddenly became angry. "He's dead. What don't y'all get about that?"

Gunner rolled his eyes. "He ain't really dead."

Colton also became angry. "Yes, he is! He burned to death! I saw him!"

Every soul in the room gasped. Some cried.

Catherine heard her son's angry voice and rushed across the house to grab him up. She carried him out of the room, but not before his quivering voice belted out, "But I did! I saw him on fire, Mommy! He was burnin' and screamin'! I saw him!"

Tremendous solemnity drifted through the house. People stopped eating and put their plates down. Many left the room altogether.

Faith whimpered, "He's not comin' back? Ever?"

Mabel tried to comfort her. "Faith, it's okay, honey. We'll get to see him again."

Gunner complained, "When?"

"When we get to heaven." Mabel brushed his hair gently.

Mauser's anger intensified. "Ain't no heaven! Ain't no God!"

Mabel raised her voice. "Mauser! Why are you sayin' that? Stop it! That's not true!"

Mauser snapped, "Is too! If there was a God, why'd He let that happen to Uncle Levi?!" He began to cry and wiped his face. He flew past people on his exit and bumped into Luke's leg with force. He looked up at Luke for a moment then raced out of the room.

Mabel said, "Luke. Go find that boy."

"Nah, Gramma. I think we ought to leave him be. He needs some time."

Gunner manned up. "I'll go get him. He's my brother." With that, he flew out of the room, leaving Mabel to comfort the twins.

Luke asked, "Anyone seen Annabelle?"

***

Annabelle and Emily rested on their backs on the bed as they stared at the ceiling.

Annabelle pondered, "Why do you suppose shit like this happens to good people?"

Emily grimaced. "I don't know. It happens to everyone though, good and bad. We all have to die at some point."

"Thanks for stayin' here with me."

"You're welcome, but that's what friends do."

Annabelle gently tapped her shoulder. "Sometimes a girl just needs another girl, ya know?"

"Yes, I do know."

Tears welled up in Annabelle's eyes. "I don't understand what is happenin' to me. I feel okay sometimes, strong sometimes. Then, all of a sudden, I just want to claw my heart out of my body and scream to the moon."

"It's grief, Annabelle. It's natural. I hear that it subsides after a while."

"Then I want 'a while' to hurry its ass up and get on past! It's like a donkey in a rodeo!"

A long moment passed as both girls stared past the ceiling and into the universe. Then, both broke out in laughter, giggling and snorting. "Hurry its ass up."

Annabelle kicked her legs, rolled over, and hugged her friend. Perplexed, Emily's eyes widened hugely.

Holding onto her friend, Annabelle paused. She realized how awkward her movement of affection was and rolled over on to her back. Embarrassed, she said, "I just wanted to hug you. That wasn't gay or nothin'."

***

Jim sat at the kitchen table, looking at his bandaged hands. Laura sat next to him while sipping her coffee.

"I still can't believe it."

"Jim, honey, you did everything you could. Not many people would have thought quick enough to do what you did."

"It wasn't enough. I can fly multi-million-dollar planes. I can train others to do the same. But I couldn't get that fire out quick enough. I failed. Goddamn mission failed."

"Honey, please don't do this to yourself. Please."

He looked her in the eye. "I'm just so sorry."

They shared a quiet moment. Then Laura softly put her fingers on his bandaged hand, trying not to hurt him.

"How are your hands today?"

"They're better. Where are the kids?"

"Emily went over to stay with Annabelle. You know, they're good for each other. I'm so glad they made friends."

"Where is Kyle? He was messed up pretty bad over this."

"He wanted to spend some time around the horses and Elvis to clear his head."

"Okay. Just so I know where they are. I worry about them. This was pretty tough on everybody."

Laura grabbed her purse. "Well, I have to go to the market and get a few things for dinner, and I want to make something to take over to the Roses." She bent down and kissed her husband on the neck. "I'll be back soon. Is there anything that you want me to pick up?"

"No. I'm good. My appetite is shot. Just don't be gone too long." He winked at her. "I may need to go pee."

Laura giggled as she headed for the door. "Okay. I'll be right back, sweetheart."

Jim sat alone at the table. He glared at his hands then sipped warm coffee from a straw standing tall from his coffee mug.

***

The woods surrounding Bert's cabin emitted a haunting, heavy, and dangerous energy. The sun burned through the trees like a sepia-colored furnace. Something was badly off. Even birds and wild animals sensed the danger and swerved away from the area.

Inside the home, Bert and Joelle stood eye to eye. Their faces boiled with anger. Little Buddy played with his toys at a table in the background, talking and humming to himself loudly while trying to ignore his parents' behavior.

Joelle seethed and glared harshly at Bert. "Why didn't you tell me?" She slapped his face.

Bert fumed with fury. Fists clenched, he punched her in the face with all his might. She slumped over in agony, moaned, and cried.

After a few moments, she rose up to face him again. Her busted lip quickly swelled. Her face twitched with pain. She looked him in the eye then slapped him again.

His stout body barely even moved, standing there and towering over her like a concrete column. He quickly reached out like a snake in the grass and viciously clocked her in the head.

Her body fell unconscious onto the floor—lifeless.

Little Buddy strained to focus on his toys. His humming grew louder in an attempt to block out the sounds. Then, unable to cope anymore, he violently threw his toy truck at the wall and ran out of the room.

Bert stood over his wife's crumpled body. He looked at her, rubbed his face, then walked over and sat in a nearby recliner. He took a swig of his beer and lit a cigarette. His face snarled as he puffed out billows of smoke while staring at her.

68.

After a few moments, Buddy—face red and wet with tears—returned to the room. He carefully studied his father, then cautiously sat beside his mother on the floor and patted her head. "Mommy?" He lifted her hair and made little twists with it. "Mommy. Wake up now." He touched her face and eyes. "Can I have some macaroni and cheese, please?"

Bert sulked in the recliner as he looked on. He drew in a prolonged toke off his cigarette and laggardly blew smoke toward his wife and son.

***

Meanwhile, on Mandolin Road, many people gathered throughout Fuzzy's home, chatting, eating, and mingling. The aroma of home-cooked food filled the air but the weighty anxiety of grief gave it a nauseating weirdness.

Searcy moved through the crowd and stepped up onto a short step ladder. He cleared his throat and, with a deep voice, yelled, "Everyone! Hey! Everybody! Can I have your attention for a moment, please?"

Visitors, family, and friends all quietened down and gave Searcy their undivided attention. Those who gathered in the dining area and the kitchen moved into the living room so they could hear what Searcy needed to say. Everyone knew the man demanded their respect. He got it from everyone—almost.

At that moment, Annabelle and Emily discretely exited the bedroom and stood behind the crowd. They observed with curiosity.

Searcy continued, "My nephew, Bobby Joe, Levi's daddy, has something that he wants to tell y'all." He stepped down from the ladder and motioned for Bobby Joe to step up on it.

Bobby Joe refused. Instead, with his body slumped and seemingly weak, he stood next to his uncle. His voice cracked as he tried to speak. "My wife would like to be here, but I hope y'all understand that she just can't face people right now." There was a grim lull. "And y'all probably want to take the kids out of here about now."

Adults quickly ushered all the younger kids out of the living area and into the side garage.

Bobby Joe waited patiently with his head bowed down. He felt his blood pulse through his body, up his throat, and around his face and head. His left arm stung with pins and needles. His chest throbbed with pain as if it would cave in at any second.

Finally, he lifted his head and continued. "So first, I want to thank my dad, Fuzzy, for allowin' us all to meet here to remember my son. He was such a joy." He choked up. His voice shattered. "Second, I want to thank each and every one of y'all for comin' by to support us and celebrate the life of Levi. But there's something else that I have to say before y'all hear it somewhere's else." He stammered. "This wasn't no accident."

The crowd was caught off guard.

His voice quivered, "The police say it wasn't no accident. Someone made a bomb out of that lawnmower. My son was murdered. That's all I gotta say."

Distraught, he collapsed into a chair. People rushed around him to help him and comfort him.

Across the room, Annabelle's demeanor bucked with indignation. She glanced at Emily, ducked back into the bedroom, slammed the door shut, and locked it.

The buzz of chatter throughout the room vibrated the air like a low, irritating roar. Emily—stunned, rejected, and confused—quietly crept out the back door.

Willie slid over to Searcy as he stood beside Bobby Joe. He whispered, "What about those bones we heard about?"

Searcy responded in a hushed tone. "Don't know nothin' yet. Police are testin' on 'em."

Luke walked over and joined their conversation. "I can't believe it. I'm angry as hell." He put his arm around Bobby Joe, patted his shoulder, and whispered in his ear. "I swear to God, Cousin, I will find whoever did this. I will kill the son of a bitch myself."

Fuzzy also ambled over to the men around Bobby Joe. Luke tried to remain expressionless as to the statement he had just made.

The old man was oblivious. He shoved his hands deep into his jeans pockets, scouted around the room, and leaned in toward the men. "Ya know, I think that Barton boy did it."

Searcy reacted negatively. "What the hell are you talkin' about, Fuzzy?"

He mockingly looked his brother in the eye. "I said I think he did it."

Sarcastically, Willie asked, "Because he's black?"

Fuzzy then mockingly looked Willie in the eye. "No, Son. I ain't prejudiced."

Luke pitched in, "Kyle didn't do this! What the hell do you mean? He was sittin' on the damned thing before it blew up! I saw him!"

Fuzzy stuck to his guns. "I still think he did it."

Searcy shrugged. "You're full of shit, old man."

One at a time, the men walked away to distance themselves from Fuzzy as he continued mumbling to himself.

"I think he did it 'cause, well, he just did. And I don't trust that boy." After a moment or two, he looked around to see that he was standing alone. "Where'd y'all go?"

***

Across the way, at the Barton home, Jim still sat alone at the kitchen table. He studied the crisscross pattern of his bandages, pondering the guilt he felt.

When the doorbell rang, he yelled, "What did you forget?! Besides the fact that I don't have hands right now?! What am I supposed to open the door with?! My dick?!"

He managed to pick up a loose coat hanger with his mouth and somehow figured out how to open the door. Then he froze in complete astonishment.

Dorene—sexily dressed with her breasts pushed up in a low-cut dress—stood on the other side. She held a beautiful bouquet of mixed field flowers in her hand.

Jim dropped the hanger to the floor. "Dorene? What are you doing here?"

"Well, I brought ya some flowers, silly. What does it look like?"

He stuttered nervously, "You. You can't be here right now!"

"Whatever do you mean?" she asked as she slipped into the doorway and nudged his neck with her nose.

Jim panicked. "I mean you can't be here. You have to go away. Now!"

"Well, that's not a very nice way to treat a girl who brought you flowers and just wants to console you in your injured state."

"Dorene! I asked nicely! My kids are here, and my wife will be back any minute! Now, go!"

"Okay. I'll go. But you have to promise to make it up to me later."

"Done. Now go."

Jim pushed Dorene and her flowers back through the doorway, shut the door, and blocked it with shoes, a backpack, and whatever else he could find to kick in front of it with his feet.

He rested his head against the door and listened to Dorene start her car and drive away. He closed his eyes, panted, and unblocked the door, carefully kicking everything back into place.

***

Florence and Searcy's daughter, Georgia Rose Tucker, stood outside the front door of Fuzzy's home and chatted. A summer breeze blew over them as birds sang. Hedges and shrubbery lined the sides of the home. Flowers grew near the doorway.

Florence opined, "I feel so sorry for the family. Losin' a child must be so hard. I can't even imagine how Mary feels right now."

Georgia sighed. "Mabel went over there to comfort her, see if she needs anything. And there's other family there too."

"But my God."

"I know. This is my family. I just can't believe it."

"And Georgia, now don't be mad at me for sayin' this, but there's folks all around this country that every day lose a child or family member to gun violence, and well, your family—"

Georgia put her hand up, looked around cautiously, and whispered. "I know, Florence. You've gotta be careful what you say around here. They might think you're disrespectin' the family and then, well, you're done. They'll out you for sure."

"They'd do that?"

"Without a second thought." Again, she looked around for eavesdroppers. She whispered, "To Daddy and my family, guns are the answer to everything. The forefathers gave them the right to own as many and whatever kind they want, and nobody can take that right away."

"But to disagree isn't disrespectful."

"To them, yes, it is." She pulled Florence closer. Her whisper grew softer. "Now, you don't tell. Searcy's my daddy, and he'd have my hide. But what they don't know is that me and William are raisin' Cutter differently."

"What do you mean?"

"We're Christians. Members of the Church of Christ in our town. We work hard, both of us. We send Cutter to school every day. We eat together. We pray together. We even play board games together. But we do not have one firearm in our home, not one."

She scouted around carefully before she continued in a subdued whisper. "We don't hunt. We don't live in the boonies. We don't need one. My daddy would have a conniption if he knew, but we don't believe guns is the answer. We believe love, patience, and tolerance is."

Florence held her hand. "Oh, darlin'. Nobody's gonna fall back on you for that. That's God's love right there."

Georgia became nervous. "It's breakin' long-held tradition is what it is, Flo. Ya see, they think that once one piece of the family falters—falls out of place—the entire empire will begin to crumble. The power structure weakens. It's bad."

"Oh my."

"And they see it as a betrayal. So there's that."

Florence muttered, "Oh good grief."

"Now Flo, don't you tell a soul. I trust you."

"Okay, Georgia. Whatever you say. I won't tell a soul."

Georgia grabbed her by the arm. "Let's get back inside."

The two women went in and closed the storm door behind them.

A second later, Mauser stepped out from underneath a bush on the side of the house. He put his hands on his hips and glared at the door.

CHAPTER 5

Wednesday, July 10, 2013. It was midday when Carl and Joy visited Jim and Laura. Plans for the barbecue could have easily been placed on hold, but Jim didn't want their lives turned upside down any more than they already had been. He longed for normalcy. So, the barbecue was on.

Carl examined Jim's hands. "Boy! That could have been worse. How are you feeling?"

"Doin' okay. How's everything at the base? Are they missin' me yet?"

Carl wisecracked, "Hell yes they are because now they've got me!"

Joy asked, "Laura, how are you? It's been so long. I'm sorry. And all this stuff is going on. I just feel so bad."

"Oh no. Don't feel bad. It's okay. We've all been pretty busy."

Jim walked toward the patio. "Let's all go out here. Laura's got some great stuff on the grill. We'll have some drinks!"

They watched Laura turn the food over on the grill.

Joy exclaimed, "This was very nice of you to go to all this trouble!"

Laura answered, "No trouble at all! Let's just try to have fun!"

Carl rolled his lips. "Well, I wish it could be all fun, but we do have to talk about a few things."

Jim asked, "Like what?"

"Well, we're all liberals here so I can speak freely, thank God. But you know the Democrats are having a rally in Little Rock week after next. I think we all need to go and be supportive. But I'm a little worried about how your neighbors would feel about that."

"How would they know if we went?"

"It's going to be televised. Reporters are going to interview attendees."

Laura replied, "Aw, you really think the neighbors would mind? They seem to be pretty nice. Although they do seem kinda solidified in their Republican ideas."

Carl continued. "They would mind, Laura. This event is going to address everything that repulses them: immigration reform, women's reproductive rights, voting rights, racial discrimination, and most of all, gun control."

Laura moaned, "Ugh. You're right."

Jim maintained, "I hate to cave in and give up going to an event that we believe in just because someone else disagrees. That's not how I operate, Carl."

"Maybe just this once. I mean, for safety's sake," Joy pleaded.

Jim snapped, "Dammit. Immigrants are people just like us, sacrificing everything—sometimes even their lives—so they can come here and make a life, just like our ancestors did. Women's choices about their own bodies belong to them, and not a bunch of angry old geezers sitting on a throne. Voting rights belong to all of us, no matter what color or religion we are! We fight so we all can have that right! As far as racial discrimination, not one American, not one human being, should have to deal with that garbage!"

"Jim," Laura pleaded.

He tromped around the patio. "It's insane how many people of color are tortured, shot, and killed every day in this country! And gun control! That shit's out of hand! There is not one citizen who should have the right to own or possess military-grade weapons that are meant to kill as many human beings as they can in the shortest amount of time! No one! So, please!"

Joy whimpered, "I'm so sorry. I need to go use your restroom." She tore into the house.

Laura gave Jim a sharp, cutting glance as she chased after her friend. "Joy!"

Carl tapped his fingers on the table. "Are you alright now?"

Jim sat down. "I'm sorry. I messed up." He looked at his friend. "But I cannot cower away from this. It's just too important."

"I understand that. But you need to think about your family too, and their safety. That's all Joy meant. There'll be other events down the road."

"Shit. I'm sorry. You may be right, but I don't know. I just can't tuck my tail and hide."

"Whatever you think, Jim. Do whatever you think." Carl went into the house.

Jim looked up at the sky. "Dammit."

***

As dusk came around, Fuzzy stepped outside through his patio doors and aimlessly walked around in the back yard. He walked over to the explosion site with squinted eyes and examined the dug-up burn spot. When he saw Kyle walking from the Bartons' house toward his, he called out to him. "Hey! Barton boy!"

Kyle was somewhat startled as he looked in Fuzzy's direction. "Yes, sir?"

"I know you killed my grandson!"

Confused, Kyle defended himself. "What? I certainly did not!" In his attempt to ignore the crazy old man, he changed direction and went into his dad's horse barn.

Fuzzy yelled, "You done it! I know!"

***

Kyle entered the barn where he discovered Emily hanging out on a pile of straw. The barn rested in pale darkness, lit only by a dim security light in the ceiling.

"Hey."

She muttered, "Hey."

"Sorry. Am I bothering you?"

"No. Come on in. I'm just thinking. What is the old man yelling about out there?"

"Aw, he's accusing me of killing Levi."

"No way."

"Yep."

"That's ridiculous."

"I know, but people listen to that shit. It plants a bad seed even if it's not true. I'm having a hard enough time coping with the fact that I didn't help Dad put the fire out quicker."

"Oh no. You couldn't. There's no way."

"Tell Fuzzy that."

***

Nighttime always made loneliness much worse. Even more so when you knew you'd done something terribly wrong. To this, Bert Black was not immune, no matter how tough he thought he was.

As he sat alone in his disheveled home, he wore his homemade uniform, drank whiskey, and read conspiracy newsletters. His unbathed body reeked with a rank odor. His face and neck were neglected and unshaven.

He flipped pages with hostility and fiercely vowed, "Fuck 'em. Fuck 'em all." He took a swig of straight whiskey. "Nobody wants to believe me, and all I do is try to help out." He spat a hawker onto the floor. "Wait 'til they come and get their asses. You watch. Take all their guns and haul their asses to those camps."

With a hard shove, he lifted himself out of his chair and heaved. "Well, not my ass! They can have my guns when they pry 'em from my cold, dead, red hands! Fuckers!"

He violently kicked furniture over and threw lamps and wall art to the floor. "I ain't got no reason to fuckin' care anymore! Thank you, Joelle, my love! Fuckin' bitch!"

In a wild roar of deep-seated anger, he continued destroying his home so loudly that a flock of birds flew from the trees outside.

The madman's shrieks continued into the night.

***

Searcy's six-car garage was an immaculate piece of work. One end of the room was occupied by three expensive automobiles and one beat-up pickup truck. The other end was reserved for a big table and a refrigerator.

Bobby Joe, Searcy, Willie, and Luke sat around the table as they drank beer and discussed serious issues.

Searcy ran his finger around the rim of his can of beer. "We've gotta figure out how to do this and not let Fuzzy find out about it."

Willie agreed, "He'd ruin it all for sure."

"He's my brother, and I love him. But he ain't got the ability to tackle this kind of mission no more."

Mabel opened the side door leading to the kitchen and popped her head in. "Y'all need any more beer or somethin' to eat?"

Willie smiled at her. "No thanks, Mabel. We've got everything we need right now."

"Okay, then. Holler if you need somethin'. I'll be in here watchin' TV." She ducked her head back in and closed the door until it clicked.

Searcy walked over and locked the door. "God bless my wife, but she don't need to hear none of this stuff, even if she is involved in some things."

Luke thumped the table. "First thing, we need to find out who done it."

Searcy paced the floor. "And that's where our connection with the Sheriff's Department comes in handy."

Luke stopped thumping. "We have a connection?"

The men clammed up and looked at one another as if in secret code. Luke submitted and bowed his head.

Poor Bobby Joe appeared ragged, exhausted, and frail as he sullenly studied the others' faces and movements.

Searcy determined, "So we find out who it was. Then we find out if he's armed and with what. That second part won't be too hard 'cause everyone in this neck of the woods buys their guns from us whether they know it or not."

Luke assessed, "Won't be hard then to match whatever the bastard has."

Willie walked to the refrigerator, pulled out another beer, and opened it. "Let one thing be said, and it rings truer than true: The only thing that beats a bad guy with a gun is a good guy with a gun."

Luke replied, "True."

Willie continued, "Bobby Joe, we can't blame ya if ya want to sit out this time. We love ya too much."

With dark circles around his eyes, Bobby Joe glared at Willie. "He murdered my boy. What the hell do you think? Of course, I'm in."

Searcy smiled. "Good."

Luke patted Bobby Joe on the shoulder.

The grieving father blasted deadly serious looks at each of the men. With a trembling voice, he warned, "I get the kill shot."

***

Thursday, July 11, 2013. At the church hall, women and children filled the enormous, rectangular room as they carried in shopping bags full of items. The long folding tables that lined the walls held separate piles of photos of Levi, letters, poems, and decorations.

Mary quietly sat behind one of the tables as the others, including Catherine, pampered her. It didn't matter. Eyes glazed over, she just stared at the women and the tables as if emotionally disconnected from it all.

Laura walked in, mingled, and made her way over to where they sat.

Catherine greeted her. "Hi, Laura. I'm so glad you could join us."

"Well, thank you for the invitation. I just wish it was for a different reason. I'm so sorry." Laura bent over to speak to Mary directly. "How are you doing, Mary?"

Mary coldly uttered, "Fine."

Laura asked, "Is there anything I can do for you?"

"No."

Catherine pulled Laura aside and whispered, "She's not herself. They've got her on sedatives so she can be here and

82.

make decisions on how the service should be. Don't take it
personally."

"Oh, I see."

"Would you like a drink? We have coffee, soda, water,
or Kool-Aid—the good kind, of course."

"Water is fine. Thank you."

Catherine reached into the cooler and handed Laura a
bottle of water.

Laura scanned the room with curiosity. "Wow. This is
really something."

"You've never seen this before? Maybe it's just this
family that does memorial planning like this. It makes it
easier on the family, and the whole community gets to
participate. So, that's kinda cool. My family doesn't do
anything like this, but then again, we're considered dirty
Yankees."

"Really? How long have you been, I mean..."

"It's okay. I know what you mean. Willie and I have
been married about ten years. We met at the University of
Arkansas, Fayetteville."

"Oh, you met in college?"

"Don't sound so surprised. A lot of these folks actually
have college degrees." She glanced at Laura, who appeared
stunned. "I know they seem to be ignorant, illiterate
rednecks, but they do have some redeeming qualities. They
are fiercely loyal to their families, even though men will be
men and have affairs. Sex is a whole different thing. They
have faith in God—even though it seems a little skewed—
and they can be the most romantic, loving people you've
ever met."

"Yes, I know. My husband is from here."

"Has he cheated on you yet?"

"Uh, no. No!"

"Oh, I didn't mean to sound so nosy. I'm sorry. It's just a fact of life for so many of us. Willie cheated on me once. Us womenfolk kind of bond around that issue."

Laura became frustrated. "Then why do you get married?"

"Security, and to procreate."

"What about true love?"

Catherine explained, "Honey, they'll tell you that you're their true love, but every woman in this room knows that it's a pipe dream. And that part, I'm told, is not just a Southern thing. All men lust after any female that shows a little tits and ass. Next step is to jump on it and hump it like a dog. Willie says that's just the way they're made—they can't help it—can't change it—don't want to if they could—so deal with it."

"But—"

"Ain't no 'buts' in the equation, Laura. I got my own lesson on that recently, from Mabel. I still don't get all this logic, but it is what it is; that is all that it is. True love is a fallacy, wishful thinking. It isn't real. No man will be true to you. But if yours is, well, honey, you've got yourself a rare diamond! Better hold on to him!"

Laura's mouth hung open as Mabel headed directly toward them.

Catherine made their introduction. "Hello, Mabel. This is Laura. She was at the party the other night. Have y'all met?"

Mabel extended her hand. "Hi, Laura. I'm Searcy's wife. I wear the pants, but he don't know that yet. I don't believe we did meet."

Laura gathered her composure. "Hi, Mabel. Nice to meet you."

Mabel kept moving. She waved her arm. "You two come on over to the refreshment table, would ya, and help serve?

If I can get your help servin', then I can go stay with Mary and help her through all of this."

Catherine and Laura followed in obedience.

***

Jim sat on the sofa, watching TV, when Emily popped into the room.

"Hey, Dad. I'm going over to check on Annabelle. She said she was staying next door for the summer. See you later, okay?"

"Okay, sweetie. I hope she's doing alright."

Emily asked, "Do you need me to do anything for you before I go?"

"No, honey. I'm alright. See you later."

"Okay, Dad."

As she left out the front door, Jim grunted, "Wait." It was too late.

He studied the situation in front of him. His hands were bandaged, so he figured out how to use an ink pen with his mouth to press the buttons on the remote.

Then the front door opened, and Kyle walked in.

Jim called out, "Hey, Kyle," as he put the pen down. "How are you feeling today? Better?"

"No." Kyle sat on the sofa and picked up the remote.

Jim stared at his son as he complained.

"I'm having visions. I can't sleep."

"I have them too."

Kyle seemed surprised. "Really? The kid burning?"

"Yep."

"How do you stop it?"

"Can't. Just think about other things, I guess. Watch a lot of TV."

"Well, it can't hurt that you're on pain meds either. At least you get to sleep."

"Okay. I'll give you that. I want to help you, Kyle. Would you like to get some counseling?"

"No. Counselors are full of bullshit."

"You only tried it once."

"And it was stupid. They treated me like I was a little kid. They just regurgitate what they read in a book. They've never lived it."

"You were a little kid."

"I was never a little kid. I was born old."

"Is that what's wrong with your mother?"

Confused, Kyle asked, "Huh?"

"Well, giving birth to an old man your size. I mean, you must have frightened the doctor when he saw your big ol' hairy head crowning. And your mother, poor woman."

The two broke out in laughter.

Jim continued, "I bet the nurses ran for cover, screaming 'It's *The Thing!* Run!'"

After a few moments, the laughter died down.

Kyle became serious. "I'm tired, Dad. I want to sleep without seeing all that in my head over and over."

Jim thought for a moment then shrugged his shoulders. "Kyle, I'll give you one pill, so you can sleep right now. But that's it. No more. Tomorrow, your mom can take you to the doctor for whatever he needs to give you. Deal?"

Kyle smiled. "Deal."

"And you cannot tell a living soul I did this."

"Thanks, Dad."

Jim signaled toward the kitchen. "It's in there on the countertop. You'll have to open the bottle, you creepy old man."

***

At Fuzzy's house, Emily pressed the front doorbell, waited nervously, and twisted her hands together.

A friendly young woman opened the door. "Hello. Can I help you?"

"Hi. I'm Emily from next door. I just wanted to check on Annabelle. Is she here?"

"Oh, Emily. Hi. Yes, she is here." She held her hand out. "I'm Darcy, John Mark's wife. I think Annabelle was hopin' that you'd stop by. Come on in."

Emily went inside.

Darcy pointed. "You know where her room is? Feel free. I'm cookin' something for Fuzzy. Picky eater, that man," she said as she walked back into the kitchen.

Emily made her way to Annabelle's room and softly knocked on the door. The door slightly opened, so Emily slid through it. Annabelle sat on the floor, legs crossed, still in her white teddy, playing with a bag of marbles.

"Annabelle?"

"Hi, Emily. I was hopin' you'd come over. How is Kyle?"

"You wanted me to come over to tell you about Kyle?"

"Oh, no. I didn't mean it that way. I just wondered how he's doin' with all of this."

"He's going to be okay."

Annabelle continued playing. "These are marbles that me and Levi used to play with."

"They're, uh, pretty."

"I know. It's weird." She put the marbles away. "Hey, listen. I know I got really mad last night, but it wasn't you, okay?"

"Good. I'm glad to hear that."

"I was mad because my dad didn't bother to talk to me and tell me about the whole thing bein' murder before he made that sweepin' announcement to God and everybody."

"I kind of thought that might have hurt a little bit."

"My dad never paid much attention to me. I don't think he even really loved me. Levi and John Mark are the boys. That's all he wanted was boys. I was a disappointment to him."

"Oh, Annabelle, I'm sure that's not true."

"Yes, it is. I'm no fool. Well, not since I grew up. Did you ever feel like that?"

"Um. Actually, yes."

"Tell me about it. It's your turn to share."

"Well, Kyle is older. He is the boy. He's good-looking and athletic. He works on stuff outside with Dad. I guess I just feel left out."

"Exclusion is a bitch, eh?"

"It is, yes, but you can't stay focused on it. That's not healthy. You just go find someone who does want to spend time with you instead."

"Who cares about 'healthy'? We're all gonna die, right? Aren't we supposed to be lookin' forward to dyin' so we can go to heaven and be with our deceased loved ones? Not to forget the Lord Almighty who saw fit to let them die in the first place. Aren't we supposed to be creamin' our pants to go see Him? You know, Jesus?"

"Wow. Annabelle, I wasn't expecting all of this."

Annabelle jumped on the bed. "I'm sorry, Emily. You don't deserve this. I'm just mixed up. I don't know if I believe in God anymore, and I know I'm not believin' in this whole 'more guns is better' bullshit. I'm seriously conflicted. And then there's this guilt thing. Ya know, I told Levi to go over and help with the lawnmower. I told him it would be good for him to interact."

"Oh no, Annabelle. Don't think like that. You couldn't have known. No way."

"Yeah, well."

"You're my friend. I love you. Nothing was your fault. And as far as all the other stuff, let it go."

They smiled at each other.

Emily continued, "Hey, I know what can fix your confliction. What do you say we go to town and get some ice cream?"

Annabelle leaped to her feet. "Double-double chocolate with pistachios, chocolate chip bits, and chocolate syrup! Now that's love, baby!"

***

Fuzzy's barn seemed especially quiet in the middle of the day. However, buried deep in a stall filled with loose straw, a movement began to stir.

After a bit of a struggle, Fuzzy's head burrowed through. His hair was a tangled mess. He looked really rough.

He pulled out a bottle of whiskey, took a big swig, struggled to get the lid back on, and then fell back into the straw, completely drunk.

***

Clouds rolled in, and a rare, cool breeze blew through. The back parking lot of Fuzzy Rose & Sons Gun Shop was half-filled with pickup trucks, cars, and minivans.

Searcy, Willie, Luke, and Bobby Joe—dressed in jeans, plaid shirts, belts, boots, and cowboy hats—exited the building carrying pistols and long guns. They strutted in angry badass-style across the asphalt. Then they loaded up into Searcy's Dodge Ram 2500 4x4 double-cab truck.

As they traveled down the road, each man grasped tightly to his rifle. Bobby Joe held his especially tight and rubbed it against his face as he peered out the window.

Searcy spoke. "My connection said the P.D.'s person of suspicion lives somewhere out on 367 toward Kensett."

Willie asked, "Any more detail than that?"

"Nah, but we'll poke around and see what we find. I've got a feelin' we're gonna make one murderin' son of a bitch a nervous bag of scum."

Luke added, "I hope so. I'm ready to do this thing."

Bobby Joe mumbled quietly, "Kill shot is mine."

***

The clouds were now thicker, and the breeze was still gusty. Outside the White County Sheriff's Department, a dark-grey SUV pulled into the parking lot near the building.

Joelle put her SUV into 'park,' turned off the motor, and sat quietly.

Eventually, she exited the vehicle and wavered in her steps. With nervous eyes covered with dark sunglasses, she carefully scouted the surroundings. She closed her eyes, licked her cracked, bloodied, swollen lip, and pulled a scarf around her head to help cover her swollen black eye. She put her hands over her face, took a deep breath, and walked timidly toward the front door.

Once inside, she reassessed what she was about to do. Then she walked up to the counter and waited for the clerk to acknowledge her.

"Hello. How can I help you?"

Joelle stuttered, "I need to speak with a deputy, please."

"Which one, ma'am?"

She put her head down and became more nervous. "I suppose it doesn't matter."

"Are you here to report a crime, ma'am?"

She swallowed hard. "Yes. I am."

***

Searcy's huge pickup truck sped down the narrow, two-lane highway. It zoomed by pasturelands filled with cattle, horses, decades-old homes, mobile homes, and a lot of woodlands.

The men were restrained until Willie shared a realization. "We should stop by and pick up Bert."

Searcy disagreed. "I don't think Bert should go with us on this hunt."

Luke asked, "Why not?"

"He's got a big mouth," Searcy quipped.

Bobby Joe stared out the window, still holding his rifle close to his face. In a raw voice, he said, "I want him with us. He's the best tracker."

Willie agreed. "I think he should go too."

Searcy kneaded his thumb on the steering wheel. "Alright, Bobby Joe. If that's what you really want." He scratched his scruffy two-day-old beard.

***

In Little Rock, Catherine and Laura laughed, shopped, and bonded as they strolled through a department store.

Catherine beamed. "This is a lot of fun."

"It sure is. Thank you for inviting me again."

"Oh, I'm glad you could come along. I had to come and pick up these things for Mary anyway. It's always more fun when you have a friend with you. Men don't get it."

"No, they don't. They just complain and want you to hurry up."

"Yeah, but we do the same thing when it's football season. 'When will this hurry up and be over?'"

They laughed.

"Anyway, I'm glad you could get out of the house."

"Me too. I needed a break."

"Are the kids with Jim today?"

"Kyle is. Emily texted me. Her and Annabelle went to get ice cream."

"Aw. I'm so glad those two girls are getting along. Annabelle sure needs her right now."

"I'm glad too. I think I misjudged Annabelle early on. She seems like a nice girl."

"She is. She's got some quirks alright, but don't we all. Anyway, yay! You're free! At least for a while! They're getting ice cream; let's me and you go get coffee!"

"Sounds wonderful!"

"Great. Let's go this way." Catherine paused to justified going shopping. "It is a sad thing, you know. Tomorrow is Levi's service. But we need to fuel up with a little happiness before we have to go deal with all of that."

Laura asked, "I'm just a little curious because I don't really know anybody all that well, but I'm not clear on how Mary and Mabel are related. Are they close?"

Catherine explained, "They are very close. They're first cousins in the Carter family from over at Tumbling Shoals and Heber Springs."

"Tumbling Shoals. That's an interesting name for a town."

"Oh, it is. We should drive over there sometime. It is gorgeous. It's over by Greers Ferry Lake." She waved her arm. "But anyway, the family is super wealthy. They make their money by owning outdoor sporting goods stores around the country, and they have an outdoor TV show too. That's not to mention their investments in real estate and oil."

Laura stepped backward. "Oh, my word."

"Yeah. No kidding. They're pretty powerful too. You know, rubbing elbows with high-level politicians, foreign land investors, stuff like that. Some folks think that's the reason Searcy married her, but heck, who knows."

"I had no idea. Wow."

Catherine whispered, "I'll tell you a secret if you swear never to tell another soul."

"I promise."

"Annabelle's not Mary's biological child. Mary adopted her, but I don't think Annabelle has a clue, so shhhhhhhhhh."

"Oh my gosh."

Catherine straightened her sweater and readjusted her hair. "I feel a little uncomfortable. I shouldn't have told you that. Let's just forget it, can we?"

Laura shrugged her shoulders. "Sure. It was getting a bit uncomfortable. Let's go back to laughing and fun stuff."

The two women trotted down the store aisles pointing at items and trying things on for size.

***

Jim was sitting on the sofa, watching TV, when the doorbell rang. He opened the door with a strap that Kyle rigged up for him.

Dorene quickly slithered underneath his arm. He closed the door behind her. Then he turned around and kissed her neck and shoulders. She panted heavily as she enjoyed the affection.

"Where are the little lady and pesky kiddos today, Jimbo Bear?"

She returned his kisses as he pulled her body to his.

"Laura is out shopping in Little Rock. Emily is out with a friend."

"Isn't there one more you're forgettin' about?"

"He's unconscious in bed, on a painkiller I gave him to help him sleep. Hasn't slept in days, so he'll be out for several hours."

They passionately kissed and molested each other.

Jim rubbed her breast with his bandaged hand. "God, you drive me crazy!"

"Let's take it to the bedroom before we run out of time. Sounds like we need to hurry." She grabbed his arm. "Here. Let me show you the way." She hurriedly led him directly to the master bedroom.

He groaned with a deep-burning lust.

Once in the bedroom, she squeezed his crotch and kissed his hands. "Too bad your hands are bandaged, baby. How are you gonna feel these tits?"

He kissed her neck down to her breastbone. "With my whole face, darlin'."

***

At the ice cream shop, Emily and Annabelle sat on a picnic table with a jumbo umbrella that gave them shade. They ate their ice cream and chatted.

A tired homeless man covered his head and sheltered on the side of the building.

Soon, a random woman took a coat out of the trunk of her car and took it to the man. She handed it to him, gave him a $10 bill, patted him on the shoulder, then got into her car and drove away.

Annabelle watched the lady's kind act and caught the fever. She bought an extra ice cream and gave it to the man. He graciously accepted it and thanked her.

She returned to where Emily sat. "Feels good to be kind to someone who needs it."

Then, a car with two young, handsome local guys pulled up. They whistled and called out to the girls. Annabelle

94.

twerked her butt at them, but Emily—embarrassed—pulled her to sit back down.

The guys drove off after they got their orders. The girls giggled and cheered.

***

Searcy's truck pulled up to Bert's cabin.

Willie went to the front door and knocked. "Bert! Hey, Bert!" He waited patiently then peeked into a side window. "Bert? It's Willie Rose." He knocked on the door again. "Open the door, Bert! It's me, Willie!"

The door opened.

Bert stepped out, unexpectedly clean, shaven, and dressed. "Hey, Willie. Is that the boys out there in the truck?"

"Yeah. Bert, we want ya to come with us."

"What are y'all doin'? What's up?"

"We're on a hunt, and you're the best tracker around. We need ya."

"Who are ya huntin' down?"

"Oh, come on, Bert. Like that ever mattered to ya before."

"Just askin'. I like to know who I'm chasin' down."

"Why are ya so depressed? Your face looks awful."

"Thanks, Willie. I work hard at it."

Willie walked away, throwing his arms up in the air. "That's it. I give up."

"Wait."

Annoyed, Willie stopped and turned around. He put his hands on his hips.

Bert continued, "I'm sorry, Willie. Joelle left me and took little Buddy. I'm not handlin' it too well."

"I'm sorry, Bert. I'm sure she'll come back, though. Women do that shit all the time. Leave and come back. Leave and come back again."

"I don't think so this time. Anyway, I'll go help ya out, but let's keep this thing about Joelle to ourselves, okay?"

"Promise. But ya need to do one thing before ya crawl your ass in that truck with me."

"What's that?"

"Get your ass in there and gargle with some Listerine or even better, a little Clorox. That goddamn hangover breath could kill us all."

As Willie walked back to the truck, he muttered to himself. "Especially if Searcy goes to light one of them damned cigars." He threw his arms in the air. "Blow us all to hell."

Bert grinned and went back into the house.

***

Kyle began to wake up, although, disoriented with blurry vision. He sat up, slowly scooted to the side of the bed, and tried to steady himself. He tried to stand on his feet but teetered and fell back onto his bed.

He tried again and got to his feet. Rubbing his eyes, he slowly stumbled toward the upstairs bathroom door. It was locked. So, he cautiously opened his bedroom door and stepped out. As if in a surreal dream, he walked carefully toward the downstairs bathroom.

Something caught his attention and distracted him. He heard strange noises coming from the master bedroom, so he turned and stumbled in that direction instead.

When he reached the doorway, he gently pushed the door open and leaned against the door jamb. He tilted his head, trying to understand what he was seeing. He wiped his eyes in an attempt to clear the blurriness. Again, he stared at the strange vision of the comforter on the bed bulging, buckling, swirling, and heaving. He heard laughter.

Then, like a shot, Dorene scuttled out from under the blankets. She stood completely naked while looking at the bed. She laughed, "You crazy beast!" Then she noticed Kyle staring at her. Concern swept over her face. "Uh, Jim."

Jim playfully bucked the comforter up and down. "What's the matter, my little Jenna Jameson? Come back here, baby." He threw the comforter off himself and saw Kyle standing in the doorway. He stopped solid.

Confused, Kyle rubbed his face and looked again. "Dad?"

Dorene grabbed her clothes, ran into the master bathroom, and shut the door.

Jim put on his robe, guided Kyle to the guest bathroom to pee, and then guided him back to his bed.

***

Searcy's truck traveled down the highway at a good clip of speed. The radio blared country music.

The men seemed somber as they were cramped in pretty tight.

Bert, a little on the anxious side, noticed Bobby Joe— sullen and withdrawn—hugging his rifle like an obsession.

***

Back at Bert's cabin, marked cars from the White County Sheriff's Department pulled onto the dirt driveway. With bullet-proof vests and guns holstered to their hips, Deputies Halp and Collier got out and knocked on the front door.

An unmarked car pulled up behind them. Two plainclothes investigators named Lage and Wilk got out and looked around the cabin.

Lage pulled out a cellphone and began dialing. As he spoke on the phone, Collier motioned that he was going to the back of the cabin.

Meanwhile, Halp broke down the front door, and the men rushed inside.

Once inside, they searched for any living thing then browsed through all the conspiracy and survivalist articles and materials scattered all around. Headlines read: "It's Raining Dead Birds in Arkansas;" "Thousands of Dead Fish Floating in Lakes and Streams;" and "Chemtrails, Conspiracy, and How to Survive the End Times."

Halp and Collier carried dozens of firearms and boxes of ammo from the cabin and secured them in the trunks of their cars. Investigator Wilk scratched his head in disbelief.

***

Later that night, several of the Rose men sat in Fuzzy's living room, watching TV and chatting.

Fuzzy asked, "Where did y'all go today? I couldn't find none of y'all."

Searcy answered, "We had something to go check on."

"Well, next time, you could tell me as much."

"Didn't even think about it."

Willie assured, "Ain't nothin' to worry about."

Luke tactfully changed the subject. "Did you get your glasses today, Uncle Fuzzy?"

"Yeah, I did. Nice way to change the subject. Mabel took me to get 'em."

Searcy prodded, "You can see now?"

"Yes, I can see now. Don't you go start that up again."

Bert nodded his head in agreement, although he was half asleep.

Fuzzy sneered at him and snarled. "Would somebody take that crazy hunk of putrid roadkill out of my house and dump it over in the lake for the gators to feed on? It's stinkin' up my house, and gators gotta eat."

Bert opened his eyes and looked at Fuzzy.

Fuzzy yelled, "Searcy!"

"I ain't takin' him nowhere. He done stunk up my pickup once today."

Bert mumbled, "I don't stink."

Fuzzy argued, "The hell you don't. Willie!"

"Catherine would kill me. Cain't do it."

Fuzzy looked at Luke. "I'm a-lookin' at you 'cause you're the only one left. Bobby Joe done had his fill of troubles."

Luke shrugged. "I won't drive him all the way back to that cabin tonight, but I guess he can stay in Dad's garage. There's an old sofa out there."

Fuzzy shouted, "Done! Take his ass out of here. He's makin' me nauseous."

Bert pleaded, "Y'all take it easy on me. Ya don't know what I'm goin' through."

Searcy snickered, "Better yet, what Jo's goin' through."

Bert glared at him as he stood up and grabbed his backpack. "Not funny. Not funny at all."

Bert and Luke walked toward the door.

Searcy yelled, "Bert!" He then motioned for him to zip his lips.

Bert rolled his eyes. "Y'all act like little kids sometimes."

Fuzzy snorted. "Nope. Little kids is smarter."

"Whatever."

Luke pushed Bert's arm toward the door as he turned to the other men in the room. "Good night, y'all. See you at the service tomorrow."

After they exited the home, Fuzzy looked at the rest of the men. "Now when are y'all goin' home? Stink ain't all gone yet."

***

Over at the Barton house, Jim, Laura, and Emily sat watching TV together. Kyle stumbled in and sat on the sofa to join them.

Laura helped him get seated. "Are you alright?"

"Fine. I think."

Emily studied his face. "You don't look too good."

"I think I need some pills. I'm not sleeping too well. Having some really strange dreams."

Jim squirmed in his seat as Laura sat back down. Whether an attempt at sympathy or distraction, Jim said, "Boy, sometimes those dreams can be pretty weird. I have them too."

Laura added, "It has certainly been traumatic for a lot of people but my God, imagine the parents."

Emily said, "True."

Laura continued, "I guess it can make us all say and do strange things, even in our sleep."

Emily stood up. "I'm going to bed. It's been a long day. What time are we leaving for the service tomorrow?"

Laura looked at her watch. "Oh, we probably need to leave by nine in the morning."

"Okay. I get the shower first. Dibs."

Kyle threw his hand at her. "You can have it. I'm not going."

Jim concurred. "That's probably a good idea if you're not feeling well. Does Mom need to take you to the doctor?"

Emily waved as she left the room. "Good night."

Kyle slurred his words. "No. You all go on without me. I just need to get better sleep."

Laura watched his movements. "I think you're depressed."

Jim scoffed, "He's not depressed. He just needs to sleep."

"And you're always right, aren't you? I'm going to bed too. Kyle, let me know if you need anything." Miffed, Laura left the room.

"Okay, Mom. Thanks." Kyle looked at Jim. "Just one more. Please?"

"I don't think I should."

"Oh, come on. Just one. Please."

"Okay. But then, no more."

"Great."

"You know where the bottle is. Just take one. I mean it."

Kyle walked into the kitchen and picked up the bottle.

Distant thunder rattled the night sky as a storm brewed on the horizon.

CHAPTER 6

Friday, July 12, 2013. The church parking lot was full. Side streets were packed with cars. Yet people parked wherever they could find a tight space to squeeze into.

Mourners—dressed in Sunday clothes—emerged from their vehicles and walked toward the church entrance.

The sky darkened as ominous, heavy clouds churned. Distant thunder gave an eerie vibe to the already grievous ambiance. Despite the foreboding calls of the birds and the barking dogs, carefree children played cheerfully nearby.

Just inside the church entrance, visitors, family, and friends signed the guest book. Next, they walked past blown-up photos of Levi and small tables that displayed some of his personal items, poems, artwork, and, of course, a computer.

Hundreds of flowers were displayed in every nook and cranny. Their sweet fragrance drifted softly throughout the building.

In the sanctuary, pews filled up fast as people mingled with one another. At the front of the room stood a closed coffin atop an expensive-looking silver bier surrounded by countless beautiful standing sprays and arrangements on pedestals.

On the pulpit behind the coffin stood a display decorated with more photos, flowers, and Levi's personal items. Towering above the choir loft was an enormous stained-glass image of Jesus releasing a dove from his hand.

Soft ambient music played in the background.

The front two rows of pews were reserved. They remained empty as visitors filled the pews beyond. Among the guests, Joelle and Buddy sat solemnly.

Jim, Laura, and Emily drifted in and took their places among the attendees.

Then Searcy and Mabel slowly assisted Bobby Joe and Mary to the first pew nearest the coffin.

Soon, the entire Rose family piled into the front of the sanctuary. Those that couldn't fit in the first two rows meandered further back to be seated, small children included.

Catherine and Willie sat a row behind Jim, Laura, and Emily. Catherine placed her bulky handbag in the spot next to her to save it for someone. She patted Laura on the shoulder and whispered, "Hi Laura."

Jim and Laura both looked back at her, smiled, and nodded. Jim made a double-take on the empty place Catherine was reserving. He thought it was a bit odd considering the church was packed with folks looking for seating, but he made no comment about it.

Emily spotted Luke and ogled at him with admiration and lust.

Distant and solemn, Annabelle sat in the front row by her parents.

Finally, Pastor Riley—dressed in a fine suit and tie—walked up to the podium. "Good mornin', folks. I'm sure Levi would like to thank y'all for comin' to pay your respects and say farewell, but the Lord wants you to know that this is just a body up here—an empty shell. Levi isn't here anymore. He has moved on to a more beautiful place."

The pastor cleared his throat and took a sip of water from a glass tucked under the podium.

A rash of shuffling was heard in the back of the crowd.

Pastor Riley looked on. "Yes, come on in! You're not too late! Go ahead and take a seat anywhere you can! Otherwise, it's standing room only. Levi was a popular young man."

The shuffling moved behind Jim and Laura. As they turned to see what was going on, Dorene scooted past people's knees to take the empty spot next to Catherine.

Startled, Jim's eyes bulged, and his jaw dropped. Dorene smiled sweetly and gave a tiny finger wave to him. Quickly, he faced the front of the sanctuary and directed his full attention to the pastor.

He tried to act cool as Laura leaned her head to his shoulder and whispered, "Do you know her?"

Jim stared straight ahead. He became as motionless as the sun over Avalon.

Laura studied his strange response. "Jim?"

He mouthed, "I'm trying to be respectful. Be quiet."

Laura whispered again. "I asked you a simple question."

After a moment, he mouthed, "No."

Laura appeared content with his answer, momentarily. She refocused her attention to the preacher's speech.

"Levi was a young man to remember for so many things. Oh, how many of us have called upon him for help when we had problems with our computers! Am I right?"

The crowd quietly laughed.

"And there's no tellin' how many secrets he could tell about what he found on some of our computers."

The crowd laughed again.

"Now, Levi wasn't into guns and all the things that other young men here are, but he was into kindness. He would help someone else no matter what it was. Even if it was just a smile." He held for a long pause. "Well, I'm gonna stop talkin' now and let some of y'all come up and speak about your memories about this wonderful young man, but first, Miss Tammy wants to sing a song."

A young woman walked to the podium as the preacher sat down nearby. She sang a popular Christian song called "I Will Rise."

Toward the end of the song, loud shuffling once again interrupted the service from the back of the sanctuary.

It was Bert. Dressed in his confederate uniform, he struggled his way through the standing crowd. He bobbed his head around as if searching for someone. Shortly, he reached a spot in the side aisle where there was a clearing. He stood there, still searching.

Then he spotted Joelle and Buddy many pews away on the other side of the sanctuary.

As Tammy sang, Bert's body roiled. His eyes rolled back into his head as it swayed backward. He whispered, "Dear God, I love her. Please forgive me."

Without another second's notice, Bert pulled out a gun from his holster. He fired toward Joelle and Buddy. Then, purposely, he fired toward Jim.

The crowd panicked, screamed, ran, and ducked behind pews. Many shoved their way toward the exit doors. The screams were deafening. It was pandemonium.

Within seconds, several men tackled Bert to the floor. They wrestled the gun from his hand.

One man yelled, "Bert! What the fuck is wrong with you?!"

The men held him down tightly.

One punched him in the face so hard, it knocked him unconscious. "Rise from that, motherfucker!"

The crowd shrieked, screamed, squalled, and trampled one another as they tried to get out of the building. The screams of the children were most heartbreaking, as some were separated from their parents and lost amid the chaos.

Joelle laid steadfast on the floor, as if dead. Her blood pooled between the tongue-and-groove wooden slats.

Little Buddy clung to her side, cried, and wiped her blood on his face. He screamed, "Mommy! Mommy wake up! Please, Mommy, wake up again!"

***

An hour had passed. Outside the church, the storm continued to build in the distance. A gusty breeze blew.

Nearly everyone had already left the area. Although, a few remained gathered in different small groups on the church lawn. Pastor Riley made his rounds to comfort them.

While Searcy and Mabel walked toward the parking lot, the church secretary, Pamela O'Brien, ran up behind them. She grabbed Searcy's arm. He spun around with a nervous twist.

She seemed panicked. "Searcy. I have to talk to you."

He acknowledged her and turned to his wife. "Mabel. You go on. Ride with Willie. I'll pick you up at Fuzzy's after while."

Mabel gave him a staunch look then walked on.

He returned his attention to Pamela. "Ya know, you shouldn't do that."

Pamela whined, "My nerves are shot. I really need to talk to you, in private."

Searcy and Pamela walked toward the church office while, on the other side of the lawn, police and reporters interviewed people. Others still hung around trying to make sense of the incident.

Jim held Laura and Emily in his arms as they spoke with Sheriff White.

"Jim, any idea why he took aim at you specifically?" the sheriff asked respectfully.

"I have no idea at all."

"Well, maybe it will come out in the wash. The man in front of you was hit, ya know."

"Yes, I heard that."

"Okay, well, give me a call if you think of anything else and thank you, sir, for serving."

"Yes, sir, I will. And you're welcome."

The sheriff walked away.

Jim squeezed Laura and Emily as tight as he could. He closed his eyes, "Thank you, God."

When he opened his eyes and looked up, Willie, Catherine, and Dorene stood in front of him.

Willie kicked his boot on the ground. "Are y'all alright? Damn that Bert! I could kill him!"

Catherine added, "I hope you all are okay."

Laura responded, "We are. Thank you."

"I know this isn't the best timing, but I just wanted to see if you were okay and introduce you to Willie's cousin. This is Dorene Toller. She's a good friend of mine."

Dorene extended her hand to her and smiled. "Laura, right?"

Laura nodded.

Dorene continued, "Well, hi, Laura. I've heard so many wonderful things about your family. I also hear that you're quite the interior decorator."

Jim glared at her with deep hatred.

To the contrary, Laura lifted her head with pride. "Well, thank you. You must come over sometime, and we'll have tea or coffee. Any friend of Catherine's is a friend of mine."

Dorene stood poised with exhilaration. "Oh, we must!" She extended her hand again. "Jim."

He lightly and quickly shook her hand.

Laura noticed the tension between them. "You two know each other?"

Dorene rationalized, "Oh, I work at the base. We see each other from time to time. He probably doesn't remember me."

Laura looked at him with suspicion. "But Jim, I asked you—"

Jim nervously interrupted, "Oh, yes! I remember now! You served us drinks! Yes."

Willie lofted his head into the air. "I just can't get over all this shit. I really think I'm gonna kill ol' Bert."

Catherine frowned. "You have to stop saying that, Willie. Someone's going to take that seriously."

Emily shyly asked, "He doesn't mean it?"

Catherine replied, "Oh no, of course not. Well, listen we have to go. We have to catch up with family and see that they're alright. I'll call you later, Laura."

Dorene pointed her finger. "I'll have to get your number. Cell phone. I'd love to chat sometime."

Laura agreed. "Sounds good. But right now, I think we need to go too."

Willie pulled Catherine and Dorene away. "You women can talk all day long. We've gotta go."

As Willie walked away with the two women, Laura and Emily took another look at Jim.

His response was classic. "I love you both, and I'm glad we're all okay. Let's go home and check in on Kyle."

Laura was obviously bothered. "Kyle. Yes, let's go."

As the family got into their SUV and drove away, the storm clouds towered higher and darker. Thunder drew nearer.

***

Pastor Riley's office had the most upscale décor with bookcases and a huge ornate executive desk. Religious paintings of Jesus, the Cross, and the Lord's Supper hung from the walls in grandiose splendor within their grand, wide, golden inlaid frames that displayed them.

Pamela urged, "I'm really struggling for money to pay my bills, Searcy. I need to know when the next shipment is coming in." She pressed, "I got kids, ya know."

"It'll cost ya."

Pamela reluctantly undressed as Searcy pulled his pants down. There was no affectionate foreplay. Instead, they got right down to business.

In a few minutes, their sexual encounter was over. As Searcy's chest heaved for air, he kicked back in the preacher's pricey leather high-back chair.

Pamela lit two cigarettes. She handed one to him. "The shipment?"

He winked at her. "The church secretary ought to have more respect, ya know."

"You never worried about that before, big guy. Besides, my nerves were all shook up after this shooting. What was I supposed to do? You said if I ever needed you—"

"You didn't need me, honey. You just needed my dick and my money." He tossed a $100 bill on the floor.

She smarted off, "Oh, don't go actin' like you own the place or nothin'."

He looked at her with squinted eyes as he blew smoke at her. "I do."

She scoffed.

He pulled his pants up and walked toward the door. "Now clean this mess up, and for God's sake, wipe your face. You look like a whore."

Deputy Halp stood watch outside the pastor's office. As Searcy opened the door, Pamela attempted to hurry and put her clothes back on, but not before Halp caught a glimpse of her.

He and Searcy exchanged glances as the old man walked out of the office.

Searcy slapped him in the chest. "Maybe one day, when you're old enough to shave, you'll get your ugly ass laid by a dime-store slut too."

Halp sneered at him. Then he leaned around the doorway, peered in at Pamela, raised an eyebrow, and grinned. She burned a 'go-to-hell' look at him.

Searcy continued through the outer doorway by the preacher's office, down the steps, and onto the lawn where several worshippers were still being comforted by Pastor Riley.

A smiling, young boy stopped playing with the other children and ran up to Searcy. The old man patted the boy on the head then casually strutted toward his truck.

***

At Fuzzy's house, much of the family sat stunned.

Mabel rubbed the baked enamel on the rim of her coffee cup with her thumb. "Fuzzy, where are your new glasses you just got?"

"They broke."

"How did they break?"

"Somebody landed on top of me."

"What did you do with 'em? Maybe we can fix 'em."

Fuzzy pulled the broken, twisted mess out of his pocket and handed it to her.

Mabel took it. She held it up to look at it closer. "Oh my." She carried it to the kitchen.

Hope and Faith crawled into Fuzzy's lap. "Grampa. Will you teach us how to shoot a gun?" Hope asked.

"What for?"

Faith spelled it out clearly. "So we can shoot bad guys like Bert before they hurt someone else."

Fuzzy admitted, "That just might be a real good idea, ladies."

Catherine scolded, "Don't tell them that, Dad!"

"Why not? Takes a good shooter with a gun to stop a bad one, don't it?"

"Well nobody had to shoot Bert down today, did they?"

Willie cautioned, "Catherine."

Faith pulled Fuzzy's beard. "Forget it. I'm takin' karate."

Catherine gave Willie a hostile look and left the room. Annabelle followed her.

Fuzzy guaranteed, "Tell you what, girls, I'll teach you as soon as I get my glasses fixed, and we know Aunt Catherine ain't lookin'. Okay?"

Hope and Faith giggled. "Okay! Yay!"

The twins leaped off Fuzzy's lap and raced outside to play.

Fuzzy yelled, "Ouch!"

Bobby Joe sat on the couch with his face buried in his hands. Out of nowhere, he began to weep loudly.

Willie put his arm around his brother. "It's okay. It'll be okay."

When the doorbell rang, Mabel answered it. Sheriff White and Deputy Smith walked inside. Searcy and the menfolk shook their hands and greeted them.

The sheriff asked, "Bobby Joe. Are ya doin' alright?"

He slightly swayed his head.

"I know the timing is really bad, once again, but can you come down to the station with us?"

Speechless, Bobby Joe indicated 'yes.'

"Bert says he'll talk, but only to you."

Bobby Joe, with swollen, red eyes and face, finally looked up at the sheriff with curiosity.

Together, they walked out the door—Searcy in tow.

***

Beebe, Arkansas. The thunderstorm rolled overhead, but the rain held its breath. Strong gusts of wind blew intermittently, bending trees and foliage back and forth while others nearby stood still. The Mandolin Road sign flipped crazily in the wind.

***

Jim, Laura, and Emily entered the front door of their home to find Kyle collapsed on the floor. Laura and Jim tried frantically to wake him while Emily dialed her cell phone.

Within minutes, paramedics worked feverishly on Kyle.

One medic asked, "Has he been takin' any medications, legal or illegal?"

Laura answered, "No."

Jim flinched. "Wait. Yes. He took one of my painkillers."

Emily shouted, "Only one?!"

"I don't know if he took more. We weren't here."

The paramedic advised, "You know it's illegal to give someone else your prescription meds? Has he been depressed lately?"

Laura sniveled, "Yes. He went through a very traumatic thing recently."

The medic asked, "The lawnmower explosion?"

"Yes."

Then the paramedic ordered, "Sir. Will you bring me the bottle of pain meds you've been takin'?"

"Sure. I'll go get it."

As Jim rushed away, the paramedic pointed out, "Looks like an overdose. We need to get him to the E.R. immediately. Does he have insurance?"

Laura sobbed. "Whatever he has through his college."

Frustrated and worried, Emily added, "That means none."

Jim returned with his bottle and gave it to the paramedic. The EMTs loaded Kyle onto a stretcher and wheeled him outside.

Laura was distressed. Her body quaked. "I don't think I can take all of this."

Emily held her mother in her arms. "He'll be okay, Mom."

"He can't die on me. He can't."

***

The interrogation room at the White County Sheriff's Department was muted, cold, and dark but for the recessed lights in the ceiling. The concrete-block walls—painted gunmetal-grey—only agitated the mysterious churn of insidious ectoplasm left behind by each criminal and their bad act, whether done by mistake, bad judgment, or pure evil.

Bert, in an orange jail suit, was cuffed at the hands and feet. He donned a swollen black eye as he sat alone at a portable folding table. His head hung low.

The door clicked. Deputy Barnes entered with Bobby Joe and then waited quietly by the door.

Bobby Joe ambled over to the table. He stalled and stared daggers through Bert before he sat down.

Bert slowly lifted his head. "I'm real sorry, Bobby Joe."

"Ya hurt a lot of people today, Bert. I never thought you were capable of doin' all that." He drew a deep breath. "What made ya do it?"

"They're recordin' everything, ya know."

Bobby Joe kicked the table hard with his boot. "You shot innocent people today, and you're worried about bein' recorded right now!"

"With Joelle? I don't know. Lost my mind. Couldn't take her leavin' me, I reckon."

"What about Jim Barton and the others you took aim at?"

"I honestly didn't mean to hit them others. They just got in the way."

"And Jim? Folks saw you take direct aim at him."

"Jim is Air Force."

"What's that got to do with anything?"

"Jesus Christ, Bobby Joe! You're in the loop! You know he's responsible for fillin' our air with chemtrails. Chemicals that affect our health and what we think. He's poisonin' us all. He's one of them."

"One of who?"

"He's a government man, Bobby Joe! He's a scout. He's tellin' the government who-all's got guns and where they are, so they can come and get us and haul us off to concentration camps! Just like Hitler did!"

Bobby Joe gawked at Bert with disbelief. "The whole goddamn State of Arkansas has guns. You are a very sick man, Bert." He walked toward the door.

"Bobby Joe."

The grieving father paused and turned around to listen.

"I'm sorry about the lawnmower. That was supposed to get the government man."

The ghastly realization hit Bobby Joe like a knife in the heart. Brewing anger flooded over him. His face turned red. He barreled toward Bert, knocked him out of the chair onto the floor, choked him, and beat him until Deputy Barnes raced over and pulled him away, leaving Bert bleeding on the floor.

Bert screamed, "Levi was just a casualty of war! Don't you understand?! God, man! This is war!"

Bobby Joe struggled to get loose from the deputy's grip as he pulled him through the doorway. Once they were through, the door clicked and locked.

Bert sobbed, "It's fuckin' war, man. Why don't you understand?"

***

In Sheriff White's office, Bobby Joe paced the floor, shuddered uncontrollably, and slammed the wooden windowsill with his hands. Deputy Barnes handed him a cup of coffee.

Bobby Joe grumbled, "No thanks."

The sheriff asked, "Can I get you anything?"

"My gun! I want to shoot that son of a bitch!"

"Can't do that, Bobby Joe. You do realize that he is a very sick man?"

"Fuck that! Sick or not, I want his ass! He killed my son! He sat beside me in the truck and acted like he was helpin' us hunt the culprit! And he did it all along!"

"Settle down, my friend."

Bobby Joe sat down, took the coffee, and with shaking hands, tried to drink it.

At this moment, Sheriff White asked Searcy to step outside and wait in the lobby. Reluctantly, the old man complied.

The sheriff continued, "Bert ain't right mentally, Bobby Joe. Now, I'm not gonna talk politics with you, but someone sold guns to this man when they shouldn't have. That part, I can't argue because we don't have no background checks. Ya already know how that all turned out. And all of his guns were illegal or undocumented, as you might say. From what we can tell, he paid cash for all of them, and none of them were registered. I can't argue that either because the law doesn't require them to be registered."

Bobby Joe stared into his black coffee.

The sheriff took a deep breath and continued, "What happened today at the church, that's a whole other mess because, as you know, Arkansas passed a bill in February sayin' it is okay to carry guns in church. The only thing I can do something about is that it was supposed to be with a concealed weapons permit, which he does not have. But tell me, who is gonna stop him and ask him if he's got a permit before he starts shootin'? Hell. Any gun-totin' man is gonna get offended real fast-like."

Bobby Joe trembled. Tears welled up in his swollen, red eyes. "What do ya want me to do? I can't change the law or the NFO. I can't change my family or the world. What do ya want me to do?"

"Tell me who sold him the guns."

Bobby Joe peered sorrowfully into the sheriff's eyes.

***

Just outside the door to the Sheriff's office, Searcy stood leaning against the door jamb, eavesdropping.

***

Later, in Joelle's hospital room at the White County Medical Center, she laid still as family and friends sat around her. Then her eyes opened slightly.

Betty noticed and moved to her side. "Joelle, sweetie. It's Mom."

Others in the room observed. One raced out of the room to get a doctor or nurse.

Betty continued, "You're okay, honey. I love you."

A nurse and Deputy Smith entered the room.

The deputy whispered to the family, "Can I ask y'all to kindly step outside for a minute? Please?"

Everyone exited except for the nurse, Smith, and Betty.

Joelle looked around the room. She weakly asked, "Buddy?"

Betty assured her, "Little Buddy's okay, sweetie. He's just fine. He can't wait for you to come home."

Barnes bent over to speak quietly to her. "Joelle, I'm glad you're alright."

With a fragile voice, she asked, "Did you find the bunker?"

Smith was perplexed. "Bunker?"

Joelle muttered, "Hidden in the woods." She wheezed, "Behind the cabin."

***

Thinking about her brother resting in the hospital, Emily quietly sat on her bed and paged through the book *Speeches of President Obama*. She pondered the words and ideas written there.

She read aloud, "We know this is a complex issue that stirs deeply held passions and political divides. And as I said on Sunday night, there's no law or set of laws that can prevent every senseless act of violence in our society. We're going to need to work on making access to mental health care at least as easy as access to a gun. We're going to need to look more closely at a culture that all too often glorifies guns and violence. And any actions we must take must begin inside the home and inside our hearts."

Sprinkles of rain tapped on Emily's window. She walked over and peered outside. She ran her finger down the pane of glass, following a raindrop as it descended.

The dark clouds that loomed overhead seemed like a welcome secure canopy; one that enhanced her solitude and emotion.

She walked into her closet and returned with a shoebox. She locked the door and sat on the bed. She opened the box and meticulously removed a bag of marijuana, a pipe, and other paraphernalia. She prepared the pipe, cracked her bedroom window open, turned on the ceiling fan, and lit the pipe.

As she inhaled and held her breath, she closed her eyes. Then she slowly exhaled, blowing the smoke toward the window. After a couple of tokes, she cleaned the pipe in the bathroom sink, replaced everything back in the shoebox, and returned it to its hiding place in her closet.

She stood at her bedroom window and watched the dark clouds roll in. "Interesting storm."

***

The thunderstorm rolled in with fury across the night sky, as lightning flashed and thunder boomed near and far.

Masses of deputies and investigators descended upon Bert's property and scattered throughout the woods behind the cabin.

One investigator yelled out, "Here! Over here!"

The authorities worked desperately to pull bushes and tree limbs off the opening to the bunker. Finally, it was cleared.

Deep thunder roared.

Once inside the bunker, investigators and deputies documented and cataloged everything from massive stockpiles of explosives, assault weapons, and bomb-making materials to DIY books.

Then one deputy opened a trapdoor in a side wall. He surged backward, wilted onto his knees, and called out, "Y'all need to come see this!"

An investigator asked, "What is it?" He rushed over, looked inside, and backed away, coughing and choking.

The deputy kicked the floor. "A dead body."

The storm outside raged on.

NECESSARY TARGETS

CHAPTER 7

Thunder rolled. Lightning flashed in the night sky. Swift gusts of wind rattled the busted hinges that hung from where the outer door used to be on Bert's bunker. An inside door quickly slammed shut with great force.

Investigator Lage yelled, "Jesus Christ!"

Gloved deputies and investigators—some who were stooped over the corpse—nervously recoiled and aimed their flashlights toward the door.

Deputy Halp laughed. "Get your boxers in a fright, don't it? Funny, the power got knocked out too."

Lage scowled, "Shut the fuck up."

Halp reluctantly joined the others at a nearby countertop.

Lage walked over to examine the corpse. He kneeled. "Photographs all done?"

Investigator Wilk assured, "Yep. All done. Waiting on the coroner."

Lage started to walk away. "Good. Let me know."

Wilk replied, "There he is now."

The coroner stepped in, nodded at the others, and made his way directly toward the corpse.

Lage approached the countertop where Halp and others gathered, cataloged, and photographed documents. He glanced down at an article titled "Necessary Targets and the Collateral Damages of War." As he stared at the document, he asked, "Sheriff on his way yet?"

Deputy Collier answered, "He just called. Said an uprooted tree was blockin' the road, but he was goin' around and he'd be here in about five minutes. Said the storms are pretty bad out there."

Lage said, "Doesn't surprise me. We are in Tornado Alley." He returned his focus to the articles. "Lots of folks around here have these kinds of underground bunkers. A bit worrisome, don't you think? Considering most of these rednecks are hyping themselves up for a war?"

As the photographer continued snapping shots, thunder clapped loudly.

Deputy Halp laughed. "Well, you know what they say! Give everybody guns and the good guys will win out automatically!"

The others glared at him with anger and annoyance.

He stepped back while nervously laughing. "They say that's a given fact right there. I don't mean that I believe it or nothin'. It's just what they say around here." He put his hands in his pockets and walked away.

Lage muttered, "Idiot. They all seem to think that the government is out to come and get them. And this big dumbass hasn't figured out yet that it's the government that gave his lame brain a job to pay his rent and feed his family. It just makes me—"

Across the room, Wilk sprang to his feet and shouted, "You will not believe what we just found!"

Lage walked over to the corpse. "Don't tell me he's ATF?"

The coroner stood up. "Ah, no. That guy's been missing a couple of years. This body isn't that deteriorated."

Sheriff White stumbled in. He walked directly toward the corpse. "Who is it?"

Still wearing plastic gloves, the coroner handed a card to the sheriff. The others looked on.

The coroner said, "Nah. That there is an Air Force I.D." He pointed. "This man's name is Matthew Toller."

***

Saturday, July 13, 2013. In the interrogation room at the Sheriff's Department, Dorene, wearing a tight, short dress with a low-cut front that exposed her pushed-up cleavage, sat in a chair on one side of the long table.

Sheriff White sat in a chair on the other side as he tried to not let Dorene's seductive movements distract him.

Other deputies and investigators stood quietly against the wall, observing. Some took notes. Some lustily stared at Dorene.

One deputy tried to attach a camera—aimed at her and the sheriff—to a tripod in order to record the session. He looked at the small screen on the camera to check the picture angle. Dorene's wink and movements clearly made him nervous.

Sheriff White looked into the camera. "Are we good to go yet?" He paused. "Good." He leaned on the table with his elbow and purposely and directly looked at Dorene's face, only. "Now, Dorene. We've got the camera up and goin' this time like you agreed to do. So let's go over this one more time, to make sure I've got it right. Ready?"

"Always ready, sweetie."

"Your name is Dorene Toller?"

"Yes."

"And before that, your name was Dorene Rose?"

"Yes. It was."

"And which Rose are you descended from?"

"Searcy is my daddy. Mabel is my momma. I have a brother named Cletus, a brother named Rhett, and one sister named Georgia. They all live around these parts." She looked around the room. "All of y'all know them."

"We just want to get it clear for the record, Dorene. So how did Matthew come into the picture?"

"He was an Air Force man. I work over there on the base, and that's where we met."

"And when did y'all get married?"

"Um. Year before last."

"Y'all have kids together?"

"Nope. Rose family's got enough screamin' kids for the whole county; don't ya think?"

"This isn't about my personal opinion, Dorene. This is to get the facts and your side of the story."

"What story? Matthew left some months ago. Left me alone and disappeared. Now y'all find him dead in some crazy man's bunker. I ain't got no side of the story. That's it."

"You don't know Bert Black? Never had any dealings with him?"

"Nope."

"Never had any knowledge of interactions between him and Matthew?"

"Nope."

"Do ya know Jim Barton?"

Dorene was caught off guard. Her seductive grin morphed into a nervous twitch. "Barton?"

"Yes. Jim Barton. He and his family live next door to your Uncle Luke, Fuzzy Rose."

"I seen him a time or two, I reckon."

"He is also an Air Force man. Sure ya don't know him more than you're sayin' here, Dorene?"

"Are you callin' me a liar?"

"Not at all. Just sometimes folks get nervous and confused."

"I told you, I seen him a time or two. Why are ya askin' me that? It ain't got nothin' to do with Matthew."

"Well, it might. Seems like ol' Bert had it out for Jim too. A little coincidental, wouldn't ya think?"

Dorene rose up. "I'll tell ya what I think! Bert is a crazy fuckin' nutbag! Why does a guy like that need a reason to go after anybody? Ya think I can read a crazy man's mind?!"

"Please sit back down, Dorene. There's no reason to get your feathers all ruffled. We're just talkin'."

Dorene gathered herself together and sat down.

The sheriff continued. "Is there anything else that you'd like to say, for the record?"

Dorene peered square into the camera. "Fuck you all."

***

Later the same day, in the same interrogation room, the same deputies and investigators lined the wall as, this time, Sheriff White interviewed Jim Barton.

The sheriff assumed the same position at the table as before. Jim sat upright—his face devoid of emotion.

Sheriff White sympathized, "First of all, I'm sorry to hear about your son. How is he doin'?"

"Got his stomach pumped but he'll be okay. He'll be home today. We'll get him some therapy."

"Good deal. Real good. Now, down to business." The sheriff took a breath. "Do you know Matthew Toller?"

"No, sir."

"He was Air Force."

"Sir, there are many, many service people on the base. You cannot possibly remember everyone."

The sheriff was skeptical. "I see. So, it's not like a tight-knit community? And what about Dorene Toller? Do ya know her?"

"She served us drinks at the base a few times."

"Did ya know that she's Fuzzy Rose's niece?"

"Not until lately, sir. She was at the church."

"Oh, yes. Her and her entire family." He closely observed Jim's expressions. "Any idea why Bert wanted you dead?"

"No, sir. I've been wondering that myself."

The sheriff tapped the table. He looked at the deputy manning the camera. "That's it. Turn the camera off."

As the deputy turned off the camera and dismantled the set-up, everyone exited the room.

The sheriff extended his hand. "Thank you, Jim. I hope things turn out alright for you and your family." He looked closer at Jim's hand. "Oops. We'll pass on the handshake for now. How are those hands healin' up?"

"Very good, thank you."

"Good deal."

As the two men walked toward the front door, the sheriff continued talking. "By the way, I need to let ya know what we found out about those bones that turned up when the explosion happened."

"Please, do tell me."

"Old Indian bones."

"What?"

"Not surprising, really. The Trail of Tears cut through just north of here up by Batesville back in the 1830s. Many Indians died on the trip to Oklahoma. Some got away and hid. Those old bones belong to some poor old soul that someone didn't have time to bury very deep. Over the years, it appears the soil eroded away enough so that the explosion brought them right on up out of the ground."

"Oh my God."

"You don't have to worry about it. Not that I agree with it. I'm Native American myself. But we've got people who took the remains to a local cemetery and buried them properly, so the poor thing can finally have peace. Maybe."

The sheriff waved his arm toward the front door, then turned to walk away. "I'd love to spend more time chattin' with ya, Jim, but as you can imagine, I'm pretty busy around here right now. Call me if ya need anything or have questions."

Jim looked off into the distance, thinking about his own Native American heritage. For a second, he wondered if it might have any deeper meaning.

***

Willie walked up to the counter in the office at the shooting range while Fuzzy waited outside with the kids.

The manager sat behind the register, glanced out the glass door, and smiled. "Hey, there, Willie. I see ya brought the whole gang in today!"

"Yeah. The kids wanna shoot. I can't argue with 'em."

"Well, ya picked a good day to come in. It's slow for a little bit. Since the shootin', business has been nutso. We've been slammed, but hey! It's good business for us! We're makin' a killin'. I suppose it ain't hurt y'all none either."

"Nah. Business is good. It is."

"Hey. You've helped us grow our business, so today is on the house! Just grab your targets over there and you're good to go! Have fun! And keep sellin' those guns and referrin' 'em to us!"

Willie picked up several paper targets. "Hey! Thank you! Next time ya come into the shop, tell Toad I owe ya some free ammo."

"Why thank ya, sir! Y'all have fun out there!"

Outside, Fuzzy and Willie carried firearms and ammo toward the firing platform. The kids stumbled along behind, popping each other with their protective eye goggles and earmuffs. Mauser appeared irritated.

Willie attached the targets to the frames and walked back to the platform. Then Fuzzy and Willie sat the children up to shoot at the measured targets.

Without notice, Mauser quickly grabbed his gun and began firing. He hit the bulls-eye five times in a row.

The girls and Colton held their ears and cringed.

Gunner was fascinated. "Cool."

Fuzzy yelled, "Dammit, Mauser! You're supposed to wait 'til we're all set up! Ya done blowed out my goddamned eardrums! Crazy kid!"

Faith agreed. "Yeah, you stupid kid! You blowed mine out too!"

Willie added, "Mauser, I know ya love to shoot, but ya have to show some patience. You don't even have your goggles or earmuffs on."

Mauser slammed his gun down on the bench. "Don't need 'em."

Fuzzy continued setting up the other kids with their guns. Clearly frustrated, he mumbled, "Huh. Don't need 'em. Damned cocky kid."

Mauser became angered. "Y'all think when we go to war, they're gonna wait around for us to get our goggles and 'muffs on?! You're the idiots!"

Hope furrowed her brows. "What are you so mad for?"

Mauser shouted, "I'm mad 'cause y'all are all stupid! Y'all are all stupid, and that's why Uncle Levi is dead! 'Cause of all y'all!"

As Mauser ran off toward a nearby tree, Fuzzy quipped, "Why y'all gotta have all these damned moody kids?"

Fuzzy then grabbed Colton by the arm and stood him in front of the wooden firing platform. The young boy began to cry as his grandfather wrestled gear onto his head.

"Stop your cryin' and man up! Pick up that gun and start shootin' at that target out there! See if you can do what Mauser did! Now shoot!"

Next, Fuzzy grabbed Hope's arm with force. He began manhandling her.

Willie quickly stepped up. He held Fuzzy's arm and looked him in the eye. "Dad. Stop."

They focused intently on each other for a moment.

The old man was confused. "Well, now, Son. I was just... uh..."

"It's okay, Dad. I know ya thought you were doin' a good thing, but you're scarin' these kids. Let's just calm things down here a bit."

Fuzzy's head quivered, as did his voice. "I didn't mean to scare nobody."

Faith cried, "You're scarin' me."

Colton bawled, "Me too."

Hope's faced puckered. "And me."

Willie patted each of the kids on the head. "It's okay. Everybody's okay."

Gunner defended the old man. "Me and Mauser ain't skeered of nothin'! Y'all are all pansies!"

Colton's cry faded to a whimper as he gently put his gun down on the platform. Then, unnoticed, he removed the headgear and set it aside.

Fuzzy got teary-eyed as he looked around at the children. His face twisted with emotion. He patted and hugged each of them. "I'm sorry. I didn't mean to scare nobody. Guess I was just agitated at Mauser."

Willie finished setting up the girls to shoot. "Well, let's change the tone here. Let's get to shootin' and have some fun! Gunner, you all set up?"

"I am!"

Willie looked down the platform. "Colton?!"

The little boy demanded, "No. I don't want to shoot a gun. And I don't want nobody to catch on fire."

As Colton stepped away from the platform, Hope, Faith, and Gunner began shooting. Colton covered his ears and cringed.

The shots and vibrations immediately frightened Hope, so she quickly put her gun down and stepped away too.

After a few moments, the shooting stopped.

Willie asked, "What's the matter, Hope?"

"I don't like it."

"Why not?"

"I just don't like it. Guns scare me."

Faith noticed her sister, then put her gun down too. She stepped over to comfort her. "It's okay, Hope. You don't have to if ya don't want to."

Fuzzy became upset again. "What did we bring little girls here for?"

Faith snapped back, "Hey! I'm good at shootin'! But Hope doesn't have to like it if she doesn't want to!"

Gunner rolled his eyes. "Girls."

Willie searched around for Colton. He finally found him sitting behind the platform, playing in the dirt. "Colton? What are ya doin', Son?"

"I don't wanna shoot guns, Daddy. I wanna play in the dirt and build things."

"Okay, you can do that too, but ya have to come up here right now and learn how to shoot a gun. Ya might need to do this someday. This is important."

"Why?"

Hope interrupted, "'Cause they say a war is comin'."

Colton rebutted, "Momma said we ain't havin' no war."

Willie explained, "Well, Momma don't know everything, Colton. Now, come on up here and shoot this thing a couple of times. Come on, now! Just a couple of times, and then you can do whatever ya want."

Colton dragged himself up onto the platform grudgingly. "Okay."

As Willie propped him up to shoot, Hope sat down on a bench. She played with her shoe. "If there's gonna be a war, I don't want to be shootin' at nobody. I'd rather be a nurse mendin' them back up and gettin' them well again."

Gunner got up in her face. "Dumb girls."

Hope snapped, "Ain't dumb!"

"Too!"

Faith lunged into action and wedged herself between the two. "You gonna face me down, boy, if you don't get your ugly mug out of my sister's pretty face, even if you are my brother!"

Willie pulled them apart. "Good God! What is goin' on with all of you kids?"

Hope begged, "I don't want to shoot."

Colton echoed, "I don't want to shoot."

Gunner shouted, "Well, I do!"

Faith quipped, "And I will if I have to! But ya need to respect everybody's feelin's here!"

Fuzzy rolled his eyes, stepped back, and mumbled. "Damned kids. Respect everybody's feelin's, and when the war comes, we walk up to the enemy, poke a daisy in their muzzle, and say—" His mocking voice leaped to a high-pitch, "I respect your feelings today. The sun is shinin'. Here's some chocolate-chip cookies and milk. Have a nice day now, ya hear?!"

Stunned, Willie watched his father wandering around, fantasizing and muttering.

The children laughed at him.

Fuzzy walked toward the truck, muttering to himself. "Y'all go on and laugh at me. I'm just an old fucker with a bad attitude. Ain't fittin' to be around no kids. Not even if I love 'em to death. Sometimes, a man just gets hisself ruined. Completely ruined."

***

Fuzzy sat in Willie's truck watching his son interact with the children. He turned the ignition key over and turned on the radio. The song "Hurt" by Johnny Cash was playing.

Fuzzy listened to the words as he looked out upon Willie and the kids. His eyes glazed over with conflict, and his face trembled.

***

Searcy's house sat on a hillside not far from Fuzzy's property. Mandolin Road separated the hillside from the lower land.

On this day, a nice summer breeze blew across the valley.

Searcy wore bifocals, reading, as he sat on the front porch in a rocking chair.

Mabel sat in the porch swing, knitting. She kinked her head as she looked over the top of her glasses. "Have ya heard from Dorene today? She was supposed to have a meetin' with those investigators that found Matthew. God rest his soul."

Searcy continued reading. "Nope."

"I can't help but wonder how that all went."

"She's a big girl."

Mabel defended Dorene. "And she's still your daughter, Searcy Rose. You've gotta get over all that mess ya keep hangin' over her head. You wouldn't like it done to you."

He ignored her and kept reading.

Mabel went on, "Sometimes you're as hardheaded as an old mule! I wonder why I ever married you!" Frustrated, she tossed her knitting into a basket, went into the house, and slammed the screen door.

Unfazed, Searcy leered over his glasses and his book, titled *The Republic of Plato*, as he stared at Jim's truck driving down the road. Then he returned to reading. "The heaviest penalty for declining to rule is to be ruled by someone inferior to yourself."

He put his book in his lap, removed his glasses, and suspiciously eyed Jim's truck.

***

As Jim drove his truck down Mandolin Road toward his house, classic rock music played on the radio. He tapped his fingers on the wheel. He admired the beautiful landscape. Then the expression on his face shifted to gloomy. He turned the radio off.

A flashback ensued.

Jim looked down at Levi's badly burned face.

The injured young man looked back up at him with horror. He lowly muttered something.

"What, Levi? What did you say?" Jim bent down and placed his head near Levi's mouth to listen more closely.

Levi whispered faintly, "Gum shot mac, year of meteors."

Jim struggled to make sense of the words as he pulled away. He then looked up at Fuzzy, who hovered over them both.

Fuzzy scowled, "Well? What did he say?"

Jim snapped himself out of his vision and back to driving. He grimaced as he continued looking outside the vehicle at the landscape swooshing by.

For no reason at all, he looked up the hill toward Searcy's front porch. He noticed the old man giving him a menacing frown over the book he held in his hands. Slightly rattled, he continued driving toward his home.

***

Without glasses on, Fuzzy sat on a stool in his barn and polished a gun. Next to him, guns lined along a workbench awaited his careful attention.

He glanced out the window and, slowly and methodically, rubbed his polish cloth up and down the barrel of the gun. As he moved his hand up and down, he skimmed over at a photo of himself and his wife, Anna, taken when they were young and in love. He smiled as he savored the moment.

He placed the gun on the workbench directly in the path of the sun rays burning through the window.

While he masturbated, his face showed the psychological intensity, love, and passion of a lonely old man reminiscing.

Then the intense heat of the sun burning through the window seared the metal on the pop gun. Without warning, it loudly popped off a shot that startled the horny old man and sent him flying backward off the stool with a loud crash.

***

As Laura worked in her garden, she faintly heard the shot and dull crash in Fuzzy's barn. She stood up, looked around, waited for a moment, shrugged, and continued pulling weeds. "Fireworks."

At that moment, Jim drove up, parked his truck and got out. He walked over to the garden.

At first, Laura ignored him.

Nevertheless, he attempted conversation. "Hi, honey. How is your day?"

She blinked at him. "Probably not as interesting as yours. But I did bring our son home while you were gone." She fumbled, "If you want to know, he's alive. Thank God."

"Good. I'll go in and see him in a minute. I can't say that mine was all that interesting. They just asked if I knew Mr. Toller, which I didn't."

"And did you say 'hi' to the cute little clerk down there? Isn't that what you do?"

Jim pleaded, "Laura. Please. Can you just stop this already? This is all hard enough. Let's get along. Please."

Laura bowed up, gnashed her teeth, and then forced a little smile. "Alright. I'm sorry. Things have been very stressful lately."

"Yes, they have. More reason to get along and be happy." He smiled at her lovingly. "Kyle's in the house. Where is Emily? I thought we might all go do something together today if Kyle feels better. Maybe horseback riding?"

"Kyle and Annabelle already took Flight and Stealth out for a ride. Nice day for it. He needed to peace out. And Emily went somewhere with Luke. He is an awfully good-looking young man. Don't you think?"

She stood upright in her apron and gardening gloves, flinging soil around. She jerked her wrists excitedly and giggled nervously. "He reminds me of a young Robert Redford, or Brad Pitt, or maybe a rugged, young Matthew McConaughey. Something like that." She nervously continued weeding.

"That's what worries me. If he can make you giggle like that, what does he do to Emily?"

"Oh, Jim. Don't be such a prude. With the sexual appetite you have, you shouldn't be surprised about these kids. Besides, they're adults now. What are you going to do? Spank their little hands and say, 'no-no?'"

He walked toward the house. "And he has to be a damned redneck."

Laura yelled, "Let them be, Jim! Let them have a little fun while they are here for the summer! They need a little happiness!" She continued weeding and muttered to herself. "Wish I was young enough to hang out with them. I could certainly use some fun too."

***

Fuzzy walked into his house from the sliding glass door by the pool, rubbing his head. His shirt was in shambles and his pants were unzipped. As he stumbled in with a limp, he continued rubbing his head.

Rhett came around the corner with a beer in hand. "What in the heck happened to you?"

"I fell in the barn."

"Are ya okay? Here. Let me help ya." He guided Fuzzy to a living room chair.

Fuzzy ordered, "I can do it myself. Let go of me." He jerked his elbow away. "I gotta go piss."

***

Fuzzy wobbled into his bedroom toward the master bathroom. He walked past his dresser and patted it. He continued into his bathroom and relieved himself.

Then, as he walked back through past the dresser, he noticed that his Medal of Honor was not there. He checked

the whole top of the dresser, moving things around. He
looked in the top drawer. It was not there. He looked all
around. It was gone. He groaned and rubbed his head as he
left the room.

***

As Fuzzy returned to the living room, Rhett tried to
assist him again since he was still wobbling.

"I said let go of me!"

Rhett let go and sat in a chair next to his. He took a drink
of his beer. "Okay, well, how are ya doin' otherwise?"

"I know y'all are plannin' to plant my ass in a nursin'
home purty soon."

"Where in the world did ya get that idea?"

"I can tell. Y'all run off and leave me here all the time.
Talkin' quiet behind my back. I can hear the whisperin'."

"I have no idea what you're talkin' about, Fuzzy. You
must've hit your head on somethin'."

"I thought I could trust my family, but now I see I can
trust y'all 'bout as much as I can trust the damned
government. Scammin' lazy politicians don't listen to us,
never have, don't care about us. So many folks is poor and
still payin' taxes, but where the hell does it all go? I'll tell
ya. It goes to minorities and immigrants, every goddamn
penny. Nobody thinks 'bout us no more. They just let us
sink, and they'll keep it up 'til we cain't make it no more."

"Where is all this crap comin' from? Have you been
watchin' the news again?"

Fuzzy continued, "Let me tell you a story. I came back
from 'Nam, needed a job, couldn't find nothin'. People
treated us horrible. Met us on the streets screamin' we was
baby killers and murderers. Nobody would give us jobs.
What was we supposed to do? Gotta eat. I even tried to get a
job harvestin' crops, as bad and ugly as it was. Landowner

said no, couldn't use me. He hired goddamned Mexicans that worked for $1 an hour. Why would he want to hire me for minimum wage? I had nothin'. Nothin'. Nowhere to go. No way to make money. From that day on, I vowed to do everything I could to get those fuckers out of this country. And government, fuck it."

"Jesus Christ. What bit your ass and got you chatterin'?"

"Hell. He didn't help us none either. I done seen too much. I used to watch my mama, poor, white, broke, strugglin' to put food on the table, drinkin' out of fruit jars, patchin' up old clothes to have somethin' to wear. She never complained. And I saw her sit in her rockin' chair, knittin', singin', prayin' to God to help us. And I saw her sittin' in church and puttin' her last $5 bill in the offering plate, 'cause the preacher told her to give whatever she had as her duty to spread God's Word. She never had nothin'. Was broke her whole life. Damned church milked her dry. Jesus, I guess it weren't His fault directly, but He sure never seemed to help. We was always poor and forgot about."

Rhett rubbed his face. "I really don't understand where all this is comin' from, but—"

"I'm tellin' ya all this 'cause you can only be tossed away and forgotten for so long. Then ya have to stand up and fight, goddamnit! Ain't nobody gonna come and save your ass!"

"Okay. I can get that."

"When I got my ass kicked, I understood that the government wasn't gonna help us 'cause we weren't black, brown, yeller, or green. All our taxes were never gonna help us out, 'cause we weren't included in any groups that got the help, even when we fought for our country and got treated like shit. Couldn't find any jobs 'cause people hated us for fightin'. The Mexicans took the only jobs we could maybe get, I got mad! Fightin' mad! Made it worse that the churches weren't gonna help us either, 'cause all they seemed to care about was takin' what little of our money we still had. I got mad! Fightin' mad!"

"Why are ya tellin' me all this now?"

"Hell, Rhett. You ain't listenin'. It was all of that, what caused me to find my callin'. I finally found a military man, ol' friend of mine. He told me he would sell me some guns cheap, and I could resell them and make money. I took him up on it! And we are all here today 'cause I did it. I didn't have a choice back then, but you all ought to be glad I did it."

Rhett took a swig off his longneck. "I didn't know that."

"Now, I listen to them bleeding-heart liberals cry 'bout rights for minorities, give money to help 'em, give money to help immigrants. I get so fuckin' mad, I'd do anything just to piss 'em off. What 'bout takin' care of us? They don't want to do that, 'cause we're white, 'cause if you say anything 'bout helpin' whites, you're instantly a racist, and they think ya hate everybody else. So what the fuck? Let's just hate everybody else and be done with it. And here's somethin' I never told nobody: Anna went to beauty school back in the day. One day she got cornered by a bunch of black girls screamin' at her that she musta thought her shit didn't stink 'cause she was white! They were about to beat her black and blue when someone stopped it. She come home all messed up. She never was the same again. That sweet woman never did a bad thing to nobody! I couldn't even get her to kill a bug! But nobody wants to hear those kinda stories!"

"Fuzzy, I don't think—"

"Look boy, ya cain't win the game. It's rigged against us. In liberals' eyes, we cain't do nothin', say nothin', ask for help, or whatever, without them sayin' we're racist. I gave up tryin' to take care of everybody else a long time ago. Ya gotta take care of your own, and fight for your own."

"I'm not sure what to say."

"I'm not goin' to no goddamned nursin' home! And I'm not givin' all my hard-earned money away! I will fight you all, my own goddamned family, if I have to. Trust nobody. But boy, if you listen to anything I say, hear me on this: I fought too long and hard to take care of this family and get us where we are today, every one of us makin' good money and livin' alright. Listen to me now. You promise me you'll help me. I'm not goin' down."

Rhett was stunned. He stuttered, "Okay. I promise. Whatever I can do."

"Everybody else in this goddamned country got rights. Now I want mine too. I'm too old. I ain't goin' out like that."

"Okay. I think I understand."

"Good."

Rhett finished his beer, leaned back in his chair, and took a deep breath.

Fuzzy slumped in his recliner and rested his head on the back. "I'm tired now."

"Me too."

Fuzzy squirmed a little, grimaced, and readjusted himself in his jeans. "I think I cut my dick on my zipper. Shit hurts."

CHAPTER 8

Cletus, Toad, and a couple of other shop employees, wearing black t-shirts bearing the gun shop logo, raised guns and ammo into a hulky, black unmarked van.

Cletus remarked, "This gun show is gonna rock!"

Toad replied, "Ya know, you don't have to go Cletus if ya wanna stay here with the family. I mean, damn. It is a bit of a long trip in case someone back here needs ya."

"I'm goin' so no one else has to leave right now. Besides, it'll help get my mind off everything. Maybe some Memphis barbecue will make me feel better."

"Okay. It's up to you. Just sayin'."

***

As Elvis pounced through the tall grass of a wide-open field, Kyle and Annabelle rode their horses while they laughed and talked.

Annabelle asked, "Sure you're okay to be riding?"

"Oh yeah. I'm okay. Thanks."

"Well, just let me know if we need to go back, okay?"

He smiled at her thoughtfulness. "Okay."

"So, what's Emily's major?"

"Psychology."

"Seriously?"

"Yeah. She's always had a niche for figuring people out. Don't laugh. Says she feels it in her spirit."

"Oh, well, studyin' psychology will take that oomph right out of her. Anything spiritual will become some sort of mental disorder to those guys."

"I think that's why she wants to do it. She wants to prove that the two can be combined to help people."

"Wow. Ambitious."

"What about you? What's your major?"

"Aw, I've changed a couple of times, but I think I'll stay with Secondary Ed."

Kyle looked astonished. "No kidding."

"Why is that surprising?"

"Well, I mean, I don't know. You're so beautiful and sexy, I thought you might be going for something different. That's all."

She laughed. "I love kids. I love to be wild sometimes and sexy sometimes, but I really do love kids. I think they need people in their lives who truly care about them. Encourage them to succeed. Too many kids around here don't have any idea of the possibilities for their own futures. They all get sucked into this frickin' gun culture bullshit. I want to help change that."

"Wow. That is great! You are amazing!"

"Thank you, Mr. Barton. And, tell me, what is your major?"

He gloated loudly. "Hah! I'm going to be a professional lifetime student!"

"No way. Why would ya want to do that?"

"I love learning. I thought I wanted to major in history, then social work, then geology. But I think I'm going to settle down and marry the idea of being an English major."

"English? Ew. Why? All ya can do with that is teach, right?"

They halted the horses, dismounted, and walked. Elvis ran up to Kyle to be petted. He scratched the dog's neck and ears.

"Oh hell no. That's the misperception. You can do anything with an English major. But I want to be a writer." He waved his arms toward the sky. "I want to document all the stories of people I meet. I want to talk intelligently about all the great literature that people have written over the ages! Stories we should never forget! It is absolutely fascinating to me!"

Annabelle rolled her head. "You're so weird!"

The horses stopped to feed on the dense green grass. Kyle stepped closer to her. They fixated on each other for a moment.

Then, Kyle softly touched her face with admiration. He moved her long hair. They kissed tenderly.

He admitted, "I have to say, though, you're going to make one very sexy teacher."

She giggled. "And you're gonna make one very sexy English nerd."

They laughed at one another. Their hands grasped together and squeezed gently.

She continued, "Guess you're out of your funk now, huh? Life is too short to be sad, down, depressed, and upset."

He interrupted, "Look who's sounding like a nerd." He playfully placed his hand on the back of her neck and pulled her close. "Shut up and kiss me, teach."

She giggled and kissed him passionately.

***

As Luke and Emily rode their horses on a grassy two-lane path through a wooded area, Luke held his rifle in hand.

Emily said shyly, "This is my first time. I've never been hunting before."

"Why not?"

"Um. We're not pro-gun supporters, you know."

"I don't understand that, but I reckon you're entitled to your own thinkin'."

"My dad is in the military, but he doesn't believe that guns are something that contributes to the overall well-being of society."

"Why not?"

"Yeah. I don't know. I don't think... I mean, everybody doesn't need to have a gun or many guns. What's the purpose?"

Luke waved his arm. "People have a right, first of all. It's in the Constitution. We don't need government tellin' us what we can and cannot have or need. Besides, if the government turns on us, how are we gonna fight back? With our nail clippers?"

"But if the government comes after you with what it has, you won't have a chance anyway. How are you going to fight a Stealth bomber or a Bunker-buster?"

"That's not the point. The point is, we have a constitutional right to fight back, at all. Now, if it ever came to be, the government would rather it be easier to whip our asses, right?"

"But, I don't—"

He pointed with his rifle. "Ya see that tree there?"

She pointed. "That big one over there?"

"That tree was growin' in this soil for hundreds of years before any human bein' ever laid eyes on it. It started out as a seed, then soaked up the soil and minerals and grew into a seedlin'. As those hundreds of years passed by, it continued soakin' up its surroundin's, its foundation. It never knew nothin' else. In essence, it became what it soaked up."

"Makes sense."

"By lookin' at it now, it's still flourishin' and perfectly happy right where it is."

"True. I think."

"Many folks around here are like that tree. Generation after generation has flourished in soakin' up its surroundin's, its beliefs, its culture. For us, that includes guns, but most of all, God."

"Oh..."

"Ya see, we're rural folks. All we've known is takin' care of ourselves, huntin' our own meat, growin' our own gardens, raisin' our own animals, and protectin' our own. That's the way it's always been."

"I have never heard it put that way. You have a great way with words, Luke."

"We're thinkers too. We're not all stupid and uneducated like a lot of outsiders think. Just about everyone in my family has a college degree."

"Really? I didn't realize that."

He gave her a sarcastic glare. "And why not?"

"Oh. I'm sorry. I didn't mean it the way it sounded. I don't know, why I said that. I'm sorry."

"'Cause you've been conditioned to think we're all stupid people."

Emily conceded. "You know, that just may be the case. I have never thought about it."

"Look. I think you're a smart woman, Emily. You'll get this. America's gun culture is somethin' that is deeply ingrained in our traditions and tied in with our religion. Oh, there are some crazies out there who take it over the edge, but ya got those in every facet of life. I'm here to tell ya though, that until people can talk calmly about those deep threads of cultural traditions, the idea of any compromise with gun control is null and void. It's like forcin' that tree

144.

over there to bend and bend 'til it snaps in half. It can't change what it is."

"Wow."

They continued riding in calm for several moments until Luke finally changed the topic.

"What are you studyin'?"

"Psychology."

"You're kiddin'."

"Yeah. I get that a lot. Actually though, I'm very spiritual. I want to merge the workings of the mind with those of the spirit."

"Well, I'll be damned." He pointed his rifle again. "I got somethin' to show ya. You'll like this. Come on."

They rode the horses up to the edge of a swampy lake heavily surrounded by cypress trees and foliage. Luke pointed to a particularly colossal cypress tree with carved markings on it.

"See that tree over there?"

"Yes."

"They say an old Indian marked that tree back when the whites started invadin' this land." He gazed at her eyes. "Ya think I'm kiddin'."

She rubbed her nose with doubt. "Um. No."

"Well, it's true, they say. He marked the tree with knife cuts to ward off the evil that whites were bringin' with 'em."

They pondered the stories the landscape had to tell. As they studied the area, birds clamored and bullfrogs croaked nearby.

Luke continued, "Ya say ya have a spiritual side. Do ya feel anything here?"

"Not really. Not yet. There's nothing striking me so far, except that atrocious smell."

He searched closely. "Well, if ya got a spiritual side, ya ought-a be feelin' it here." He hung back. "That odor, that's just how the backwater smells, like a wild beast soaked in methane, pig slop, and horseshit." He turned his horse around to leave.

Suddenly, both horses became jittery.

Emily noticed a glowing ball of light as it formed by the marked cypress tree. "Wait a second, Luke."

The light became brighter and began to move. They watched as it floated across the surface of the water and stopped under a canopy of dense foliage.

Luke asked, "You see that?"

"Yes, I do. What do you think is over there under that brush?"

"Good question."

Emily pinched her nose to close off the stench. "Can we go see?"

The ball of light dissipated.

Luke demanded, "Emily, we are not takin' these horses into that water. There's gators big enough to eat you in one gulp or take down a whole horse. We ain't goin' in that water."

Emily gave him a sarcastic look. "Alligators? Really? In Arkansas?"

"How long have you lived here, sweetie?"

"A couple of years, except for goin' to college."

"Figures."

She announced, "I'm goin' in then. I'll walk or swim across."

"Like hell, you will!"

She dismounted her horse and waded into the water.

Luke leaped off his horse but not fast enough to pull her back. "Hey! You git back here! Goddamnit, you're crazy!"

He grabbed both horses' reins and held them with one hand. Panicked, he stepped into the water, grabbed her arm with his other hand, and jerked her back onto the bank.

At that same moment, a giant alligator snapped at her feet. She screamed with fright.

Luke quickly struggled to pull her and himself to a safe place, away from the water's edge. He yelled, "Git back on that horse right now before that thing comes runnin' up on land to bite your ass for lunch! Now! Move it!"

Luke, dripping wet, mounted his edgy horse, grabbed his rifle with one hand, readied it, and aimed at the water.

Emily took her reins and flung her wet, shivering body up onto her frightened horse. But, in one quick earth-shaking move, the gator exploded out of the water and lunged toward her.

Luke fired his rifle, hitting the gator in the head and killing it.

The horses bucked, whinnied, and panicked. Emily's horse ran away with her.

Luke gave chase. The two raced across a tall thick meadow. Nearing a beaten ATV path, Luke pulled up beside Emily's horse, grabbed the reins, and slowed it.

"Calm down, Trigger. Calm, boy."

The horse settled down at hearing his voice.

Emily clung tightly to the saddle. "I... I could have done that myself."

He scoffed, "Don't think so, She-Ra. He knows my voice. He trusts me."

"Yeah. Well." She mockingly wagged her head. "Me too."

"Alright." After a moment, he asked, "Are ya okay?"

Still shaken, she answered, "Always. I'm always okay."

"Of course, you are."

She smiled at him and chuckled. "Fuckin' gators. What the hell are they doing here?!"

"I told ya."

"Hey. Thanks for calming the horse down."

"No problem." He dismounted. "Let's walk and let them rest for a bit." He held his hand out to help her down.

"Okay. Good idea. You often have good ideas."

"Oh yeah?"

He watched her swing her leg over the saddle and slide to the ground. When she turned around to face him, he focused on her wet blouse clinging to her breasts. He tapped her chin with his fist, lured her with his chiseled grin and blue eyes, and walked away, leading his horse behind him.

She gulped, caught her breath, and wiped her forehead. "Breathe, Emily." She walked after him, leading her horse along. "Thank you for saving me! Hey, you up there!"

He continued walking. "Nah. You know how to ride a horse."

She tried to catch up to him. "I meant from the alligator!"

"Oh. That."

"That's twice you've saved me with your gun."

He grinned. "Is it?"

She struggled to breathe, catch up with him, and talk at the same time. "Yes. Remember the snake?"

"Oh, yeah. I reckon so."

"I think I'm beginning to understand why guns are so important to you and your family."

"They are useful."

"Yes. I can see that now. I'd be dead twice if you didn't have a gun with you." She took a deep breath. "Thank you, Luke. I mean it."

He stopped, turned, took her horse's reins, and turned on that charming smile. Startled, she nervously grinned back at him.

He hung his leather hat on his saddle horn, released the horses' reins, and turned back to her. He gently touched her waist, kissed her cheek, and then ever so lightly tickled his lips against hers.

Cautiously, she put her arms around his neck.

He faintly touched her breast and ran his finger around her nipple as her wet blouse still clung to it. He kissed her neck. Her body shivered.

They embraced in a passionate kiss and disappeared beneath the tall grass.

***

The Harps Food Store in Cabot was a clean and orderly store of only 11 perfectly-defined aisles. The staff was exceptionally friendly and helpful.

Patrons shopped, visited, laughed, and chatted while blocking pathways but were nonetheless amicable.

Georgia pushed her cart up one aisle and down another as she filled it with all the staples and items her family loved. Cutter followed her while performing karate moves, dancing, and pretending to be fighting an unseen assailant. Other regular customers lingered, watched him, and laughed.

One woman gushed, "Aw, Georgia. He's so cute. You should get him on TV. He'd make y'all some money cuttin' up like that. Funny kid."

"I don't think so. I hear Hollywood's a crazy place."

As they continued closer to the checkout stand, Georgia halted her son. "Okay now, Cutter. You need to stop before ya knock someone over. I mean it. Stop."

She pushed her cart into position and unloaded her groceries onto the conveyor belt. Cutter continued acting a fool as boys do.

Georgia stood at the counter and watched as the checker ran each item over the scanner.

The bagger boy—a young man in his teens—looked closely at her face, furrowed his brow, shook a bag open, and roughly threw her items in. At one point, he picked up her carton of eggs, held it momentarily, and then slammed it into a bag. The eggs crushed.

The bagger boy casually said, "Oops."

Georgia looked at the checker. "I'm not payin' for those eggs. Did you see what he just did? Are you gonna let him get away with that?"

Cutter stopped goofing off and became subdued as he watched what was happening in front of him. The bagger boy cocked his head back and gave an evil grin.

The checker continued scanning. "Ain't nothin' I can do about it, Miss Georgia. If ya want more eggs, ya have to go back and get 'em, but I cain't guarantee—"

Georgia was appalled. "What? What is goin' on here? Why is he throwin' my things? Where is your manager?"

The checker pointed to the customer service desk. Georgia glanced over and saw the store manager staring at her. His arms were crossed as he subtly cranked his head from side to side in a negative manner.

Georgia became unnerved. She grabbed her purse and her son by the arm. "Y'all can just keep your busted eggs and everything else. I don't want it." She dragged Cutter out of the store.

When she got inside her SUV, the tears poured out.

Cutter sat in the back seat, concerned. "Momma? Are you okay?"

She heaved and caught her breath. "Yes, I'm fine. Are you okay?"

"Yes, Momma. But why was he throwin' our stuff around? That was mean."

"I don't know, Cutter."

She started her vehicle and quickly drove away. As she sped down the highway, she racked her brain in thought.

Finally, her face showed disgust, her eyes squinted, and her nostrils flared. She muttered, "Florence."

***

Later in the day, Searcy and Mabel quietly ate a meal together. Afterward, Mabel cleared the table.

Then, as they drank coffee, she stared at the table's centerpiece. "Faith made that centerpiece for us. Precious little girl."

"I know what you're aimin' at, Mabel."

"Then you already know that Georgia called. I suppose you also already know what happened to her today at the grocery store."

"Yep."

"Searcy, do not start in on that girl like ya did with Dorene. I realize that whore you got pregnant dumped Dorene off on ya and left, but Georgia is yours and mine and I won't stand for it."

He explained, "If ya don't give them a lesson, they'll never learn."

"Learn my ass, Searcy Winston Rose." She slammed her hand on the table. "No more. I mean it. Georgia is a good girl, always has been. Kept her nose clean and her legs closed 'til she got married. She's got a good heart, and you're not gonna ruin her like ya did Dorene."

"Dorene is an agent and she's good at what she does. I'm not forcin' her to do anything she don't already wanna do."

"Bullshit. She does it to please you, her daddy. She never was accepted by you, and she thinks it will win her your affection. Don't try to pull the blinds over my eyes. I see it."

Searcy crossed his arms and scowled.

Mabel continued, "And ya know, one of these days, Annabelle's gonna find out that Dorene's her real momma, and then what? Huh? How are ya gonna handle that one?"

"Handle it if it ever happens."

"Oh really? Well, I want to be there. I want to see it all go down, 'cause let me tell ya, that young woman ain't playin'. She's for real, and she's gonna be a force to reckon with. Sound like anybody you know?"

She moved closer to his face and whispered, "I want to see it when you have to man up and tell her that you're her father."

Searcy rose to his feet, violently kicked the table, and broke the centerpiece. "Shit!"

Mabel walked toward the living room. "By the way, you and Pamela are makin' too much noise. Better keep it down or folks are gonna talk."

As he watched her walk away, his mouth hung open.

Mabel turned to him. She pointed at him. "Call the dogs off. Leave my Georgia alone. I mean it."

***

Rhett and Shelby's home was a modest three-bedroom house with a two-car garage and a typical American Dream white picket fence, well-manicured lawn, and lots of trees. Their neighborhood was lined with similarly constructed homes.

As Rhett and Shelby ate dinner, they were joined by their children: Luke, Magnum, Violet, and Charity.

Rhett took a swig of beer and asked, "How did y'all's day go?"

Magnum answered, "Good. Spent most of it fishin'."

Charity swallowed her food and answered, "I studied. Did a lot of readin'."

Still chewing, Violet answered, "I babysat for Darcy and John Mark."

Shelby replied, "Baby, you saw me here. I had a great time gardenin' 'til you sent me out for more beer."

Rhett asked, "What about you, Luke? How was your day?"

Luke grinned sweetly and hesitated. "My day was good. Real good."

Charity said, "I tried to call Grampa Searcy today to ask him a question about Tolstoy but he didn't answer the phone. Guess I have to just go over there."

Rhett added, "Well, that's typical. He never answers his phone. He hates talkin' on it. He'd rather be in your face."

Shelby was taken aback. "Rhett."

"That's how the man is."

Luke added, "He's reserved. Doesn't like to waste his time."

Violet piped up. "He longs for the old times when folks actually showed up and interacted. Nothin' so wrong with that."

Magnum said, "Yep. He's a true Republican Conservative Christian. Values the things that were real, not fabricated, like they are nowadays."

Rhett took a swig of beer. He jeered, "Well, then, I guess y'all can throw your cellphones out the window, and let's go sell those damn fine cars you're all drivin'."

Magnum defended himself. "Wait. I didn't say that."

Shelby begged, "Rhett. Stop."

Rhett looked around at the startled faces looking back at him. "I'm sorry. I didn't mean that."

One at a time, the children left the room. Rhett put his head down in shame.

Once all the kids were gone, Shelby put her hand on his arm. "Rhett. It's okay. I understand."

His face flushed red as he drank his beer. "Thank you, Shelby. I appreciate ya standin' beside me. But I don't know how long I can keep up this charade."

"We can. We'll do it together. I'm with you, Rhett. I love ya so much."

"You really do? Will ya stay with me even when we are shunned, stalked, bullied, and ostracized?"

"Yes, baby. I'm in this for the long haul. I'm with you."

Rhett's face showed great sadness. "How in the hell did our kids fall into this trap?"

"They live here, in this community your family built. They're around other kids at school and work. It rubs off."

"I love my kids so much. God, I do."

"I know, baby. I do too."

"Do ya think they will still love me if they ever find out that I'm a closet liberal?"

Shelby smiled, ran her fingers through his thick hair, and kissed him. "Baby, I know they will." She pulled his arm. "Let's go to the bedroom and turn on some MSNBC. Whad-ya say?"

He pulled himself to his feet and hugged her. Then they meandered into the master bedroom and closed the door.

CHAPTER 9

It was dusk as Jim worked at his workbench in his shed, arranging tools and equipment by the light of the hanging fluorescent fixture above him. Then, he heard a loud noise. When he walked to the door, he heard clatter and bangs coming from Fuzzy's barn. He stood in the doorway and waited.

Within moments, Bobby Joe stepped out of the barn. His appearance was thin and haggard. He emerged holding a tractor-sized bolt-cutting tool. When he noticed Jim looking at him, he balked.

The two men stared curiously at each other for a moment.

Bobby Joe shrugged. "Well, shit."

Jim called out to him. "Hi, Bobby Joe. Need some help?"

Bobby Joe kept staring at him.

Jim asked, "Are you alright? I've got some time. I can help you."

Reluctantly, Bobby Joe caved. "Come on, then." He walked toward his truck that was parked by Fuzzy's house.

Jim rushed to walk beside him. When he caught up with him, he asked, "So, what kind of project have you got going here?"

Bobby Joe turned and threw a hard glare.

Jim stepped back. "Personal. Got it."

Bobby Joe surged onward. Then, he had a thought. He stopped in his tracks. "I got somethin' important to do. I need your help, but you cannot say one goddamned word to anybody. Swear it."

Jim's eyes blinked rapidly. "Sure thing, Bobby Joe."

As the two men continued walking toward the truck, Bobby Joe asked, "You got time to go with me somewhere?"

"Sure. Laura will never miss me. She's mad at me anyway." He teased, "Women. Can't live with them. Can't live without them."

Jim noticed the serious expression on Bobby Joe's face and his lack of response. He cleared his throat and quickly tried to adopt the same demeanor, out of sympathy.

When they reached the truck, Bobby Joe put the tool in the bed. They both climbed in. The truck took off down the road.

Jim asked, "Where are we going?"

"Cain't tell a soul."

"Got it."

It was a long, quiet, bumpy drive.

***

Eventually, the truck pulled up and parked in the empty lot behind Fuzzy Rose & Sons Gun Shop where the two men got out of the truck.

Bobby Joe removed the tool from the bed. Jim followed him to the back door where his friend pulled out a key, unlocked the door, and turned off the security alarm.

Once inside, they walked into the side-room that served as a work/repair area. Bobby Joe put the tool on a workbench, walked over to the refrigerator, and took out two beers. He handed one to Jim, opened the other, and began to drink.

"They got this place loaded with cameras. Don't worry. I'll delete everything. They'll never know you were here with me."

Jim drank his beer as he gawked at all the guns and ammo all around. "I think I can understand why."

Bobby Joe sat his beer down. "Gotta piss. Be right back. Make yourself at home." He went into the restroom.

Jim wandered around, passing by guns of all kinds, guns disassembled, gun parts, tools, papers, computers, and an iMac—still up and running.

He mumbled to himself, "A Mac." He shied away and continued walking around the room.

Then, it dawned on him. 'Gum shot mac. Year of meteors.'

He walked back over to the iMac and peered at the screen. He saw a folder on the desktop named *Year of Meteors*. He whispered, "Gun shop Mac."

As he peered closer, Bobby Joe came back into the room.

"What are ya doin'?"

Startled, Jim answered, "Oh, nothing. Just wandering around. Saw the light from the screen on. You've got a lot of cool stuff here."

Bobby Joe sat at the workbench, drank his beer, and unfolded a piece of paper that he stared at intently.

Jim asked, "Just wondering. What does 'Year of Meteors' mean?"

Bobby Joe kept staring at his paper as he explained. "Stephen Douglas. He wrote it in 1860 after Whitman wrote about it in '59. Basically, it's about political conspiracies and such. Why? You interested in that stuff?"

"Ah. I noticed it on the computer screen over there. It sounds interesting."

"Pay that no mind. It's not important. What is important is that I get this plan figured out." He focused on the paper in his hand.

"Can I help? What do you have there?" Jim moved closer to him to get a glance at the paper.

Bobby Joe jerked it behind his back. He looked into Jim's eyes. "Are you my friend? Really? I need a friend right now. Cain't trust nobody else."

Jim assured him, "I'm your friend. Anything you need."

"Good. I may need anything you got."

Bobby Joe brought the paper back around in front of himself so Jim could see it too.

Jim pored over it closely. "So, what's the plan?"

"I'm gonna break into the jail and kill Bert Black."

Jim stood upright. "I'll pretend I didn't hear that, Bobby Joe. I know you didn't really mean it."

***

The evening hours were tranquil. A soft breeze wafted the smell of honeysuckle, lavender, and freshly-cut grass around the neighborhood. In the moonlight, a fawn and a raccoon frolicked and played, chasing each other in circles over carefully manicured lawns.

Inside, Willie and Catherine watched TV in the living room. Colton lazily traipsed into the room with a stuffed animal and his G.I. Joe in his arms. He climbed into his mother's lap. She kissed him and ran her fingers through his hair.

"Momma. Do I have to go shoot a gun again tomorrow?"

Catherine was confused. "Shoot a gun? Again? When did you shoot a gun, baby boy?"

Willie purposely ignored the conversation and focused on the TV. He knew this wasn't going to go over well.

"Today. Daddy made me go do it with Grampa Fuzzy and the twins and Mauser and Gunner. I didn't like it though."

She patted his head. "What?" She glared at Willie with sullen fury.

"Grampa made me cry. He made everybody cry."

She picked him up and carried him out of the room. "Let's go to bed now, Colton. You don't have to go do that again, I promise. But you do have to go to bed and get some sleep."

"But Momma..."

As she carried him out of the room, Willie put his head down with a wry face. "Shit."

Within a few minutes, she returned to the living room. "Willie Rose."

He cringed, then slowly stood to his feet and cocked his head up proudly. "That is my name, Catherine Nelson Rose."

"Why the hell would you take him out to the shooting range without talking to me first?"

"Because it wouldn't be a discussion. You'd say 'no' then dig your feet in and demand that I didn't take him. That's not a discussion. That's not a compromise."

"Oh, but your method is? Just override me completely?"

"Look. He shot the gun and he didn't like it. So now we know."

"Are you saying you won't take him out there again?"

"Hell no. Boy needs to learn how to use a gun. It's his heritage."

"And I suppose you think that statement is a compromise?"

"No. It's a demand just like your statements are."

"Then how do we ever work this out? All I'm asking is that you wait until he gets a little older."

"And tomorrow, he'll be a little older."

Catherine picked up a ceramic vase and threw it at Willie's head. He ducked as it crashed against the wall.

Her face boiled with anger. "I'm going to leave you, Willie! And I'm taking Colton with me! How do you like that compromise?"

"You knew what you were gettin' into before you married me, Cath! I never hid nothin'!"

"The hell you didn't!"

"Like what?!"

"You said you loved me, and there would never be anything that we couldn't work out together! You lied! I hate you for that!" She sprinted out of the room.

Willie collapsed onto the sofa, rubbed his face, and moaned. "Goddamnit!"

***

In the interrogation room, Bert and the sheriff sat alone at the rectangular table. The sheriff flipped an unopened pack of cigarettes between his fingers as Bert watched with anticipation.

"Want these real bad, don't ya?"

"Yep."

"Answer my questions and they're all yours. All of them."

"I answered all your questions, Sheriff."

"Nope. You didn't, Bert."

"What didn't I answer?"

"Why do ya want Jim Barton dead?"

"Answered it already."

"Not good enough. Try again."

Bert floundered. "He's a government man. He puts chemicals in our air. He contaminates our brains. And he's a spy, tellin' the Feds where we all live so they can come and get us, haul us off to concentration camps." His head jerked from side to side. "It's real! It is not a lie! Now give me those smokes!" He tried to calm himself, but his contempt was more than obvious. "Please."

"That's the answer you already gave me, Bert. I know there's something else. What is it?"

Bert bucked with frustration and bellowed, "Alright!" In an insidious rumble, he said, "He's fuckin' Dorene. Now ya happy? Let me have those smokes!" Bert reached out for the cigarettes.

The sheriff pulled them away. "In a minute. Just tell me why it bothers you that he's fuckin' Dorene. She's of no interest to you." He paused. "Or is she?"

Bert seethed with hatred. He huffed loudly as sweat beaded across his forehead.

The sheriff noticed. "Go on. I know ya wanna say it."

"She's mine. He shouldn't be messin' with her."

"But you're a married man, Bert. What about Joelle?"

"Joelle's a baby maker. That's all. Dorene, she's mine."

"Is that why you killed Matthew Toller? Is that also why Searcy don't like ya too much?"

"Don't know. Don't care. Searcy's a sicko. He does things no real man ought-a do. He's a perv. He dresses like a … Never mind. He should-a never had no kids."

The sheriff worked hard to show no emotion, no reaction, to the information Bert was telling him. He continued. "And Matthew?"

"He didn't treat her right. Another fuckin' government man. Another spy. Another conspirator. He deserved to die." He held his cuffed hands out. "Smokes please."

"Just a minute. Why isn't it botherin' you to speak up now, Bert? You've kept silent all this time about these things. You really want these smokes that bad?"

"Yep. And I'm a dead man anyways. What's the point of holdin' out? At least let me have a little joy. Give me those smokes."

"One more question."

Bert howled in frustration. He growled like a wild animal. He clenched his teeth, then leaned back in his chair and threw his arms and cuffed hands up behind his head. "Fuckin' cop."

"Okay then. Two."

Bert leaned forward and slapped the table in heated exasperation.

The sheriff was unimpressed. "Who sold ya all those weapons?"

"Roses."

"Why did the Rose family invite you into their homes and put up with ya, knowin' ya as well as they did?"

"'Cause I could put 'em under, that's why!" He stared at the cigarettes. "And 'cause they needed me on their side when this war goes down."

The sheriff stood and threw the pack of cigarettes to Bert's chest.

Bert grabbed them desperately with his cuffed hands, opened them up, pulled one out, and put it in his mouth.

The sheriff walked toward the door.

Bert asked, "Got a light?"

"Wasn't in the deal. That'll cost you 15 more questions."

The sheriff exited as Bert stood, threw the cigarettes on
the floor, and stomped them. He turned over the table and
chairs and raged around the room, screaming and cursing.

***

It was late when Jim returned home. He walked up the
driveway, reached the front door, and wavered. An eerie,
intuitive feeling made him survey his lawn suspiciously.

Guardedly, he unlocked the door and went inside.
"Honey, I'm home! I love you!" He heard people talking and
cautiously peered into the living room.

There, Laura and Dorene sat, talking over the coffee
table. His face flushed pasty white.

Laura beamed. "Hi, honey. I love you too. Look who
dropped by!"

Dorene winked at him. "Hi, Jim."

Laura pointed. "Come on in and sit down with us. I was
just telling Dorene about the interior design work I did in
here."

Jim could not move or speak. Shut down in disbelief and
horror, he couldn't take his eyes off their visitor.

Dorene asked, "Jim?"

Laura walked up to him. "Jim? Is something wrong?
What happened?"

He slowly emerged from his trance. "I'm okay." He
shifted. "Dorene. I didn't know you were here. There is no
car in the driveway but mine, so—"

Dorene cackled innocently. "Oh yeah. I parked at
Daddy's and walked over." She patted her tummy. "Gotta
keep this girlish figure, ya know! Little exercise don't hurt."

The women laughed together.

Laura belted, "Isn't that the god-awful truth! Jim, come
on and sit down! Dorene is a lot of fun!"

Jim mumbled, "I'll just bet she is." He sat beside Laura.

The front door opened in the foyer. Emily entered. She looked a mess but smiled from ear to ear as if she was high as a kite.

Concerned, Laura immediately rushed to her daughter. "You're all wet! Are you alright? What happened to you?"

Jim also seemed concerned. "Emily?"

Finally, she answered dreamily. "I'm okay, Momma. I just fell in some water, but I'm okay. We had a great time, but I need a shower and I'm going to bed. See you in the morning." She broke away from Laura's grip and walked away.

Meanwhile, Jim and Dorene exchanged bitter glances.

Laura called after Emily. "We're going to talk about this more in the morning, young lady!"

Emily calmly said, "Okay, Momma. Whatever you want. Good night."

Laura rejoined her husband and fun-loving company in the living room. "Now, what were we talking about?"

Dorene refocused. "The scheme. I mean, the color scheme, and how you came to make these colors work together so well."

Jim still could not take his eyes off Dorene. He stared at her with suspicion. She glanced back at him with a smile and winked.

Laura appeared oblivious. She totally focused on her interior design work.

Jim rubbed his forehead as if a headache was setting in.

Laura chattered, "Well now, I'll tell you what, these colors are nearest on the color wheel. And when you use these cooler colors—"

Again, the front door opened in the foyer.

Kyle entered, smiling and happy. "Hi. How's everybody doing this evening?"

Laura looked skeptically at her son. "What the heck is going on with you kids? I swear, you both act like you've seen aliens or something tonight." She walked over, took Kyle's arm, and led him over to the sofa. "Kyle, honey. This is my new friend, Dorene."

Kyle shook her hand.

Dorene tried to hide her nervousness while Jim sat still—completely washed out—white as a ghost.

Kyle crooked his head. He looked closely at her. "I've seen you somewhere before."

"Nope. Not me. I've never seen you before in my life, sweetie."

Eyes wide open, Jim was still in shock—blood drained from his face.

Laura added, "I'm sure you've never met before. Kyle, you didn't go to the church with us. You couldn't have met her."

Kyle seemed confused. "But—"

Jim finally broke loose from his fear, stood, and patted his son on the shoulder. He led him away. "Come on, Son. Let's go in the kitchen and have a drink. Tell me all about your day. Let these women talk."

As they walked toward the kitchen, Kyle lingered. He peered back over his shoulder at Dorene. "But I'm sure I know her from somewhere."

Jim urged, "Aw, forget it. Come on in here with me." He pulled Kyle into the kitchen.

Laura and Dorene sat together, talked, and laughed.

Abruptly, Kyle dodged back around the corner into the living room. Jim was on his heels in desperation.

Kyle nodded to their guest. "Isn't your name Jenna?"

***

Sunday, July 14, 2013. Local Christian churches across White County welcomed people from all around the area to gather, mingle, socialize, gossip, bond, pray, and worship God.

It was no different at Pastor Riley's church, except that there were two armed men at the front entrance and one at the side entrance. Even though one might think that this would deter people from going to church, it didn't. Instead, it gave a peculiar sense of security.

As the congregation filed into the sanctuary, piano music played. Some folks seemed nervous and, with their morbid sense of curiosity, searched for any remaining scars, bullet holes, or bloodstains that might have lingered. Some pointed and whispered, curious about how the authorities had cleaned up the mess so quickly.

When Pastor Riley walked out and stepped up to the podium, the music stopped.

He looked around at the crowd. "I know y'all must be a little nervous today. After all, there was a horrendous shootin' in this church, just two days ago. I'm very thankful for you showin' up here today, and I know God is proud of you too. It's important that we don't let the devil win. It's important that we show up to serve our one true God! And it's important that we support one another and our church, so we can keep the lights on and continue spreadin' God's infallible Word."

A man in the crowd yelled, "Amen!"

Pastor Riley continued. "So now, the ushers are gonna pass around the offerin' plates to give you an opportunity to give and be blessed. God sees you, and He will bless you accordin' to how much you give back. Do not hold back

from the Lord thy God or the blessin's He wants to give you.
He wants to bless you today."

Another person in the crowd yelled, "Amen, Pastor!"

Pastor Riley motioned to the pianist. "Please continue
playin' for the grace of God."

The music began. The ushers got busy passing the
offering plates up and down the rows of believers.

***

At the gun shop, Fuzzy and Searcy sat at a countertop,
drinking coffee.

Searcy tapped the woodgrain laminate with his fingers.
"It's almost time for 'em to get here. Nice day outside. Was
a good day to close the shop and let the employees have a
day off." He pulled the window shades down.

Soon, there was a knock on the back door. Fuzzy
answered it. Two men ambled inside.

Silver-haired, long-toothed Earl Burns stood with his left
hand in his jeans pocket. He extended the other hand to
Fuzzy for a handshake. "Hello, Fuzzy. How are ya doin'?
Good to see ya again."

Fuzzy accepted the handshake and squinted his eyes.
"Do I know you?"

Searcy shook Earl's hand. "Yes, ya do, Brother. This is
Earl, the NFO lobbyist friend of ours." Then he turned to the
other man—dressed in jeans and a Hawaiian shirt—and
shook his hand.

"I'm State Representative Henry Shoemaker," he
laughed. "Good to see ya again, Searcy Rose."

"Good to see you too. Shall we get started?"

Fuzzy asked, "Are they gonna buy some guns or what?"

Searcy guided his brother onto a bar stool. "Sit down
here, Fuzzy. Just sit here and listen. You don't have to do a
thing. We just need ya to sign a paper here in a little bit."

"Okay."

Searcy then poured the men some coffee and pushed the sugar and creamer in front of them. "So what is the legislative status on things these days?"

Earl answered, "Well, Henry and I have been workin' closely together on this thing, and we've accomplished a great deal."

Henry added, "In fact, we have! As ya know, we got the constitutional carry through! And now we're workin' on makin' 'em prove 'intent' to use a firearm!"

Earl shouted, "They never even saw that comin'! Bit them right in the ass!"

As they laughed loudly, Henry continued, "As for what's ahead, let the prosecutors have the burden of proof to say what a gun-carryin' citizen's 'intent' is!"

Earl slapped his hand on the countertop. "Better yet, let them wallow in tryin' to explain what exactly a 'journey' is!"

Searcy pulled a paper and pen from a desk drawer while Fuzzy's head rotated from side to side, trying to keep up with the conversation.

"I think this is just great, but would ya please explain all this to me? My memory, it ain't what it used to be."

Earl faced him. "I'm sorry, Fuzzy. I forget about that."

They all laughed at the pun.

Earl continued. "Ya see, we wrote this bill and tagged on this part about constitutional carry, which pretty much means that anyone can carry anywhere in the State. That bill got passed, and the governor signed it! Now we've gotta get a court to agree that we can open carry without a permit, as long as we don't have the intent to harm another person. Also, that we can carry whenever we are on a journey. So, ya see, it leaves the interpretation wide open! A journey can be damned near anything! And intent, well, ya can't climb up into a person's mind now, can ya?"

Henry added, "But we'll see how the courts handle it all. We have no idea right now, but at least we got the door open."

Earl continued, "We're hopin' that the prosecutors will be stumblin' all over themselves tryin' to prove what a person's intent is in carryin' a gun wherever, whenever they want. That is our constitutional right, after all!"

Fuzzy hollered, "Amen!"

Searcy grinned with his head cocked high and proud. "I am pleased, fellas. We already had one celebration for this thing but I'm sure we can rustle up another one. Maybe next week."

Earl declared, "Well, ya surely should! We're now movin' to the next phase! We thought you'd be happy about it, but we wanted to tell you ourselves. This law will get more guns into the hands of the good, law-abidin' citizens so they can arm up against the bad guys. 'Cause we all know, that you're never gonna get the guns away from the bad guys. Obviously, they don't give a rat's ass about any laws. Now, this next step, this will take a little more maneuverin'."

Searcy agreed. "Exactly." He placed the paper and pen in front of Fuzzy. "Now if you'll just sign right here on this line."

"What for?"

"It's just a power of attorney in case ya get sick at any time, sayin' I can help ya out whilst you're sick. Then these two guys are gonna witness it, so it's all legit."

Fuzzy took the pen in hand. "Okay. I trust ya." His shaky hand scrawled his name across the paper.

Earl elbowed Searcy with glee. "Somebody's gonna be makin' a little extra beer money." He stammered, "I mean off of these gun laws we're workin' on."

***

The sun sizzled down in 94-degree heat.

After the Sunday service at the church concluded, the congregation gathered outside.

Several men set up barbecue grills and folding tables underneath centuries-old oak trees while women spread tablecloths and brought casseroles and food out from the fellowship hall.

Some children played chase and soccer. Others got slathered with sunscreen lotion by their mothers.

Older male teens and young men stripped off their shirts and played basketball on the asphalt court by the parking lot while teen girls giggled and fawned over them.

Some of the youngest children had the luxury of playing in wading-pools and staying cool.

A couple of nearby residents allowed their young children to ride their small ponies over to the church lawn. Needless to say, that was a hit. All the younger children wanted to have a turn at taking a ride.

The sounds of laughter, chatter, and communal bonding was incredibly therapeutic, not just for the church members but also for the surrounding community whose nerves had been rattled by the shooting. This village, it appeared, would eventually heal and go on.

***

A sheriff's deputy knocked on Jim Barton's front door.

Jim answered it, conversed for a moment, and walked outside with the officer.

Then, Jim got into the officer's
car and waved to Laura as it
drove away.

***

A sheriff's deputy knocked on
Dorene Toller's front door.

She answered, appearing caught
off guard.

They spoke for a moment.

Then, she grabbed a colorful
pashmina from behind the door
and wrapped it around her
shoulders. She locked her front
door and then got into the car.

They drove away.

***

In the interrogation room, the
sheriff sat across the table from
Jim.

"Some discrepancies have come
up."

"Such as..."

"Do ya know Dorene Toller?"

***

In the same interrogation room a
while later, the sheriff sat across
the table from Dorene.

"Do ya know Jim Barton?"

***

Jim answered, "Not real well."

***

Dorene answered, "I just know of
him. I served him drinks."

***

Sheriff White asked, "You
swear under oath?"

Jim responded, "Of course."

***

Dorene responded, "Of course."

***

"Okay. I'll ask again, then, now
that you understand that you're
under oath. How well do ya
know Dorene Toller?"

Jim reeled. "I know her. That's
all I'm prepared to say at this
time, Sheriff."

***

Dorene became frustrated. "I told
you. I know of him."

***

The sheriff cast a wary eye and
held off before he continued.
"We know that you two have
been sleepin' together."

Jim grew straight-faced. "I
would like to speak to my
attorney."

***

Dorene was appalled. "I need to
make a phone call."

***

The sheriff stood. "Also, we
know you gave your son your
prescription pain killers. That's
against the law."

He left Jim alone in the room.

Jim vigorously rubbed his
reddened face in anguish. The

intensity grew moment by
moment until tears flowed. He
violently kicked the table.
"Fuck!"

**

The sheriff left Dorene alone in
the room.

She pondered what had just
happened. She raised one eyebrow
and laughed.

**

Laura sat alone on the patio, sipping coffee and enjoying
the morning air.

Kyle came onto the patio with a glass of orange juice.
He sat with his mother. "Mom. You okay?"

With melancholy, she answered, "Yes. I guess so."

"What's the matter?"

"A deputy came this morning and took your dad in for
more questioning." She sipped her coffee. "I just wish this
was all over."

"I didn't hear anything. I must've been in the shower."

"Probably."

He glanced lovingly at his mother. He put his head
down. "Mom. I have to tell you something."

"Go ahead. It can't be anything harder to deal with, I
suppose."

"It is."

"It's okay, honey. Just say it."

Kyle was reluctant. "I thought I dreamed it. But I
didn't." In front of her, he placed a tube of lipstick that had

Dorene's name printed on the side. "This rolled out from under your bed when I was helping you put laundry away."

After a moment, he further explained, "I really thought I dreamed what I saw the other day, but no. It was real." He took a deep breath. "Dad is having an affair."

Laura, somewhat stunned, set her cup on the patio table and restlessly tapped her quivering chin. Her eyes watered. Her stomach grew nauseous.

Kyle continued, "That woman, Dorene..."

"I know, Kyle. I know." She burst into tears.

He held her tight. Then, he, too, became teary-eyed. "Oh, Mom. I'm so sorry. I didn't want to tell you. I knew it would crush you."

She struggled to catch her breath. "I already knew it. I just didn't want to face what was right in front of me. I'm so stupid."

"I'm so sorry, Mom. And no, you're not stupid."

As he held her, Emily walked out onto the patio, dragging herself along sleepily. "Hey, what's wrong?" Emily patted her mother's shoulder. "Mom? What's wrong?"

Laura wailed, "You might as well know it too!"

Kyle began, "Dad—"

Emily panicked. "No! Dad's okay, isn't he? What happened?"

"He's having an affair," Kyle said.

Shocked, Emily stepped backward. "What the hell? With who?"

"That woman who calls herself Dorene."

"No way!"

Laura affirmed, "It's all true."

Emily paced the patio floor as her anger grew. "I can't believe it! I'll kill them both! Fuckers!"

Laura wiped her face and demanded, "No! You won't do any such thing! Don't even say that! This cannot tear this family apart! I've spent far too many years making this all work! It has to work!" She shifted in her seat with an uncomfortable wiggle. "Besides, it's probably all my fault anyway. I never could satisfy your father's fantasies. Dorene, she's fun. She's lively. She's sexy. She's everything I'm not." She slumped down in her patio chair.

Kyle flinched. "Stop it, Mom!"

Emily stomped across the patio. "That's it! I'm getting dressed, and I'm going to find his sorry ass! Where is he? At the base?"

Kyle answered as he comforted his mother. "The Sheriff's Office."

Emily grumbled. "Oh! How fucking appropriate!" She marched back into the house and waved her arms wildly. "Damn it!"

***

Catherine raced throughout her home, picking up things to cram into an open suitcase. Colton quietly clung to his mother's side everywhere she went.

Willie sat in the living room, listening to Conrad on the radio, as he tried to ignore Catherine's busy activity.

Conrad raged on. "And here we go, folks! I told ya this day was comin'! We got UFOs! We got chemtrails! We got birds fallin' from the skies! We got tar sands oil spills right in our back yards! We've got a police state! We've got the government agencies targetin' us because we're Tea Party! We've got manmade tornadoes rippin' apart our red states! What's next, folks?! Take a stab at it! I've already told you what it was! War! All-out war!"

Catherine became more desperate, and her movements sped up rapidly.

Willie put his head in his hands. He began to tremble.

Conrad continued. "It's time! We've got to do it right now! Time cannot be wasted! We've got to focus on those necessary targets, take aim, and fire!"

Willie walked around the living room. Tears flooded his face as the blood veins protruded from it.

Conrad continued, "What? Ya say ya don't know what those targets are? Bullshit. You do know! And you'd better take aim right now before it's too late!"

Terrified, Catherine closed the suitcase, grabbed her purse, threw it over her shoulder, and snatched her car keys. Quickly, she clutched the suitcase in one hand and Colton in the other while running for the front door.

Willie slammed the radio off and ran to block her off at the entryway, using his whole body.

They stared at each other eye to eye. Colton shivered with fear but didn't make a sound. Even the child knew it was too dangerous to speak.

Catherine's nostrils flared as she sternly demanded, "Let me go, Willie."

"No. You're not leavin'."

She threatened, "Let me go, Willie."

"No." He calmly took the suitcase from her hand and set it aside. He patted Colton on the head softly and kissed him.

Colton was confused. "Daddy?"

Catherine was confused too. She couldn't decide which emotion she should use at that moment. The expression on her face said it all.

Willie—red face wet with tears—smiled at her lovingly. He kissed her softly and touched her hair. "No more."

"No more?"

"No more radio. No more fighting." He kissed her again. "I love you. I'm not gonna lose you and Colton over some stupid conspiracy theorists. No more."

Catherine was still confused, stunned, and somewhat frightened but tried to smile anyway. Her face fluttered with nervousness.

He explained, "It all comes down to this: You're all that matters to me, and if the world is gonna end, if the government is gonna come get us, then it's gonna be. But whatever happens, I don't want to live without you and Colton. Nothing else really matters."

Catherine finally broke through with a gentle smile. "You mean it?"

"I do."

As they hugged, Colton laughed, squeezed their legs, and danced around the room. "No more fightin'! Yay!"

Willie closed his eyes. He breathed in the sweet, herbal smell of her hair in his hand. When he opened his eyes, he stared at a photo eye-level with him on a nearby bookcase.

The photo of a straight-faced Searcy judgmentally observed him. The old man's frown served as a warning— one of intense emotional power and conflict.

Willie held Catherine even tighter.

***

It was later that evening when Emily rang the doorbell at Fuzzy's house. Annabelle opened the door.

Emily angrily blurted, "Is Luke here right now?"

"Um. He might be out back. What do ya need? What's wrong?"

"I need a gun."

Annabelle was dumbfounded. "What?"

"I need a gun, right now."

"Emily, you do not need a gun. Ever."

Emily charged around the exterior of the house toward Fuzzy's barn. "You said he's out back?"

Annabelle chased behind her. Then Kyle appeared from the direction of the Barton property and followed both of them.

Finally, Emily stood outside the barn door. She called out, "Luke?! Are you in there?"

The barn door opened.

Luke stepped outside. "Hey there, good lookin'. What are ya up to?" He looked past Emily and saw the concerned faces of Annabelle and Kyle. "What are y'all out here for?"

Emily boiled. "I've been thinking about it, and I need a gun."

Luke laughed half-heartedly. "You need a gun? What do ya need a gun for? Gonna go target shootin' at night?"

"Protection."

"Protection from what?"

Emily kicked the ground. "I don't want to shoot anyone. I just want to feel safe. I've never felt safer than when I was with you. You saved my life twice with your gun."

"Huh?"

Annabelle rushed forward and grabbed her shoulders. "Jesus Christ, Emily!"

She whipped around and threw Annabelle's hands off her. "Shut up, Annabelle! You've lived in a safe house all your life! You don't know what it feels like to be naked and vulnerable!"

Annabelle was insulted. "Excuse me?"

Kyle moved forward. "What the fuck are you talking about, Emily?"

Luke said calmly, "I'm assumin' she wants a gun."

Emily agreed. "Right!"

Kyle yelled, "Wrong!"

Annabelle's head began spinning. She excitedly agreed with Kyle. "Wrong! I mean wrong with you, Kyle, not wrong that you're wrong." She mumbled, "I mean, no!

Nothin's wrong with you. I'm with you!" She looked around at everyone. "Shit! I'm so confused!"

Luke added, "Guns have a place in our lives. It's a God-given right."

Emily threw her hand up. "I believe that now! I didn't before, but I do now!"

Kyle scoffed, "That's ridiculous, Emily."

Luke asked, "Why is it ridiculous, Kyle? God is on our side, and He wants us to rule the nation. Simple."

Annabelle looked at him with disbelief. "Ridiculous."

Luke chastised her. "Shut up, Annabelle. Just 'cause you're porkin' the boy—"

"Luke Rose!"

Kyle tried to keep a calm composure. "Then tell me this, redneck boy, if God is in control, if He is on your side, if it's God's Will that your side should rule the nation, then why do you need your guns? Why do you need to conjure up a war that will kill thousands of people? If it's God's Will, He certainly doesn't need your help, and He doesn't need your fucking guns."

Angered, Luke lunged toward Kyle. "You don't even know what you're talkin' about, you pill-poppin', hippie, liberal asshole!"

Luke and Kyle threw punches until they were rolling around on the ground. The fight intensified as the girls tried to pull them apart.

Then, out of nowhere, Luke grabbed a sharpened tool blade and, with Kyle underneath him, raised it high in the air.

The girls screamed.

Luke froze.

Terror showed on Kyle's face.

***

On the other end of the enormous barn, Fuzzy was fast asleep. His gun and holster were on the workbench near the window. Lying next to his body on the hay was an empty bottle of whiskey and a long wooden walking stick.

One of the horses near Fuzzy moved around and knocked something off onto the floor. That noise, combined with the commotion of the fighting at the other end of the barn, awakened him.

His slovenly head bobbled as he rubbed his eyes and forehead and rolled over. Reluctantly, he opened his eyes and saw the bottle and walking stick near him.

As his vision zoomed in and out, the blurriness and movement of the items were confusing and frightening. He studied them for a moment then scurried to his feet. He opened the door and ran sock-footed out of the barn. As he ran, he yelled, "Snake! Big-ass snake! Big-ass tarantula!"

Panicked, he ran around the barn past the fighting young people. He twisted his head back to look at them. He screamed with arms flailing and knees wavering. Just as he turned forward to see where he was going, he slammed into a sizeable oak tree. It knocked him out cold.

Shocked, Luke threw down the blade, let go of Kyle, and ran to check on Fuzzy. The others followed.

As Emily and Kyle looked on, Annabelle fell to her knees.

"Grampa. Are you okay?"

Luke examined his bloody forehead and nose. "He's out like a rock. Better call the ambulance."

SECOND CHANCES

CHAPTER 10

At nighttime, the sterile, white concrete walls of the White County Detention Center were haunting. An air of choking stress permeated the trees, the grass, the concrete, and everything within proximity.

One hefty pine tree nearest the building was clearly dying. Its needles were scorched and fallen. Its balding limbs and shorn trunk seemed to cry out for help.

A dark, male figure faded in and out of the shadows as he stealthily crept toward the building with a big black box and rifle in his hands. The figure moved closer until he reached the side of the building where he crouched low.

He meddled with the box for a minute or two then ran away from the building. His shadow disappeared toward a side road with a sign that read: *Queensway Street.*

Within a few minutes, a huge explosion rocked the detention center. The side wall, where the dark figure had placed the box, crumbled to the ground.

Moments later, wounded victims that included inmates and a security guard wandered aimlessly across the grounds. They wiped dust and debris from their eyes and burning skin. They coughed and gasped to breathe.

Soon, nearby residents of the community raced to the area to assist.

An older resident, George Flynn, stooped down to help inmate Travis Lorre stand to his feet. "What in the hell happened here?"

Dazed and confused, Travis answered, "A bomb went off."

George was flabbergasted. "Who would do such a thing like that?"

Travis coughed. "I seen him runnin' down the street over there. He was watchin' us run out."

"You saw him? Who was it?"

"It was Barley Pop." He continued coughing. "That's what we always called him."

***

The phone at the Sheriff's Department rang off the hook. The dispatcher couldn't keep up with the incoming calls so she cleared one line and called Sheriff White.

"Sir. There's been an explosion at the detention center. Several inmates have escaped, includin' Bert Black."

She paused. "Yes, sir. The phone is ringin' like crazy. We need to get officers over there asap."

Again, she paused. "Sir. Just one more thing. Y'all don't pay me enough money."

***

Later, at the detention center, the sheriff, deputies, and investigators scoured the scene, the debris, and the surrounding area with flashlights. Patrol cars slowly idled back and forth, shining searchlights up and down the streets and into residents' yards.

The late-night air was getting cooler as a gentle fog set in. A lone coyote wandered across the landscape nearby. Then a barn owl hooted. The eeriness was dialed to nine.

As the authorities interviewed witnesses, inmates, and nearby residents, George approached the sheriff. The frantic pace of trying to get interviews and take notes was frustrating, so it took a while for the sheriff to notice that he was standing there.

Finally, the old man announced, "Sheriff. My name is George Flynn. I'm a resident. I live right over yonder." He pointed to his home. "I'm also a witness."

"Okay. Okay. We'll get to you in just a minute. Don't leave. Just hold on." He turned his back to the old man and continued talking to a deputy.

George kicked the ground as he waited patiently. Then, his patience ran out. He blurted, "I helped an inmate that saw the guy that did it!"

Sheriff White swiveled around. "You know who did this?"

"Yes, sir. The inmate I helped was named Travis Lorre. He said he saw a man hidin' out over yonder watchin' as it happened. He said he knew the man. Name is Barley Pop."

"Travis Lorre. Where is he now?"

"Oh, they took him to the hospital. Got a pretty bad gash on his head and started vomitin'."

The sheriff patted George on the back. "Give me your info and phone number, please. I want to talk to you some more tomorrow. But right now, I need to get to the hospital real quick-like and see this Travis Lorre."

"Okay. That's fine with me."

The sheriff wrote down George's information. Then, he climbed into his SUV and sped off toward the hospital.

George walked back toward his house. He put his hands in his jacket pockets as he looked around at the chaos. "I think it's time to move back to Dallas. Jesus, the racket 'round here."

***

Monday, July 15, 2013. Jim woke up with a light throw over him as he rested on the sofa in his own living room. His appearance was rough. His beard was gruff and covered not only his face but also down his neck. His silvery, salt-and-pepper hair was oily and matted. His face was stressed. His vivid blue eyes had dark circles underneath them. His body smelled horrible.

Emily and Kyle walked into the foyer. They glanced at him with disgust then left through the front door and slammed it.

Laura—ridden with grief and sorrow—strolled into the living room with a cup of hot coffee and a chunky-knit blanket wrapped around her shoulders. She sat in a chair beside the sofa but refused to look at her husband.

He slowly sat upright and rubbed his face in shame. "Laura. I am so very sorry. I fucked this up so bad."

"Yes. You did. I know about Dorene."

"Is there anything that I can do to make this up to you? My God. I don't want to lose you."

Laura's face was swollen. She wore no makeup. Her nose was shiny and red from all the crying. "I don't think there is anything you can do to fix it, Jim. You broke my trust. You broke our marriage."

Jim wept, and his body heaved. "I don't think I can take this, Laura."

"Honey, you did it to yourself. You did it to me. You did it to the kids."

Angrily, he shouted, "I did! I did!" He shrugged mockingly. "I fucking did!"

Laura became nervous and stood up. "I think I'm going to go to another room until you calm down."

"Wait!" He yelled. "Please. I'm sorry." He used a softer tone. "Please sit down. I would like to talk to you."

She reluctantly sat down but still avoided looking directly at him.

He stammered, then said, "I would like to explain something to you. It's not an excuse. But you need to know the whole story."

She ridiculed him. "You didn't think that a few short hours ago."

"Laura. Please. Stop. Let me say this." He faltered at whether or not to continue. Then he took a breath. "Dorene is a spy."

"Oh my God, Jim. You're really going to do this?"

"I'm not lying. She is. She works as an agent for the Rose family. It is her sole mission to seduce 'government men' and bring them down, destroy them."

"Why? What's the reason for doing that? They've got all the guns in the world. Why not just shoot them and get rid of the bodies?"

"Well, they've done that too. They found the body of her husband in Bert's bunker. And there's an ATF agent still missing from a couple years back."

"Oh my God."

"But it's Dorene's mission to destroy, not only the men but also their families, rip them apart."

"So, you're not owning any responsibility for cheating on me? Is that what you're saying?"

He became emotional. "No! That is not what I'm saying, Laura! Didn't you hear what I said?!"

"Jim, if you don't calm down, I'm leaving."

He put his hands out to her, lowered his voice, and
begged. "Okay. I'm calm. See? I'm calm. Just listen to me,
please."

"I'm listening."

"I was set up. And yes, I took the bait. I'm sorry. Our
sex had become stale and boring, and I took the fucking bait.
Goddamn me. I'm a fool."

Laura agonized. "You think I'm boring in bed."

"Oh Laura, honey. We've been married so long, and I
think we just forgot how to have fun. It's all my fault. I
should have said something to you, but I was afraid of
hurting your feelings like I am right now." He strained for
words. "Then, when Dorene started coming on to me, it was
exciting. I wanted that with you! But how was I supposed to
tell you that? Huh?"

Laura couldn't talk. She couldn't even breathe. She felt
the crushing weight of a three-ton elephant on her chest. Her
throat closed up. Blood veins protruded from her face and
neck. Tears rushed over her cheeks, down her neck, and into
her shirt.

Jim tried to touch her hand, but she jerked away. He
mourned, "Oh honey. I'm so sorry. I've crushed your heart. I
swear, I never meant to. I love you so very much."

There was a long, deafening sullenness that vibrated the
ninth circle of hell with shattered dreams, fear, insecurity,
confusion, and early seeds of hatred.

Husband and wife sat there, not knowing what to say,
not knowing how to feel or how to act. Their heavy tears, so
full of the burden of shattered lives, trailed down their faces
and onto their chests where their hearts skipped beats from
the choking pressure of grief.

Infidelity, broken hearts, sadness, and loneliness have
killed many good people through the ages. It was the most

hopeless place a person might go. It was the lowest place a marriage could go. And here, sat Jim and Laura.

Through lumbering tears, he asked, "Laura. Can you give me one more chance? Please?"

After a long while of staring back and forth at each other, refilling coffee mugs, and formidable, wordless waves of weeping, she finally answered.

"I will. I want this marriage to work out too, mostly for financial reasons and for the kids, but only if you go by my rules."

Jim prayed, "Please. Tell me what I have to do."

"To start, we sleep in separate rooms until I'm ready. You do not get the master bedroom."

"Deal."

"We go to counseling two or three times a week."

"I'll make it work."

"You get tested for STDs and HIV."

"I will."

"We're throwing out our bed and getting a new one. I'll sleep on the daybed until it arrives."

"We can go shopping as soon as you're ready."

"I can go alone, thanks. But you're on your own about hauling that old one out of here. Do it asap. I'm not helping you." She took a deep breath. "Also, you don't even touch me until I'm ready to let you, if ever."

"Okay."

She added, "Oh. One other thing. You have to make this right with our two children. And you're on your own there too."

He complied, "Okay. I will try."

She stood. "Good luck on that one." She began to walk out of the room. "Please take a damn shower. You smell like a rotted sack of horse shit." She left the room.

He slouched his head. "Okay."

***

It was a cloudy, foggy morning in Rose Bud, Arkansas, yet the sun tried to burn through.

The rush hour traffic was low, even for a small rural town while on Reid Road, Bert sat underneath a tree. Filthy, mud-covered, hungry, and exhausted, he fixated on the rusted, paint-peeled Ferrellgas tanks lined in rows.

Then he walked across the dirt road to where several salvaged vehicles were parked. He scavenged through them thoroughly and found a decent pocket knife, some loose coins, and an old forest-green hunting jacket.

Knowing he couldn't be seen with the jumpsuit he had on, and as dirty as he was, he crouched as he carefully worked his way across Highway 5, behind the Conoco station, and behind the Sherwood Hometown Grocery.

There, he found crates of milk, bread, lettuce, ginger root, and Little Debbie's snacks sitting near the back door, waiting to be taken inside. Cunningly, he crept through, grabbed a knapsack from the ground, and filled it with food. Then he ran, trying to stay inconspicuous, and hid behind a semi-truck parked close by.

The low-lying clouds and fog concealed Bert as he continued moving west. Then he stumbled upon a church where he hid his knapsack under a bush and, carefully watching ahead and timing his movements, made his way to the back-door area where a few boxes of old clothes were discarded.

Bert hit the jackpot. He made off with a complete outfit almost just his size, a ballcap, and a strapping backpack. He ran behind an old metal building, jerked off his jumpsuit, and gleefully put on his new duds.

"Damn! Couldn't be more perfect."

He hid the jumpsuit underneath the metal building and shoved rocks around it. Then he recovered his knapsack and continued onward.

Even though he no longer wore a bright orange target over his body, he still had to be careful and unnoticed along his journey. One mistake could mean he would be caught and sent back to the detention center. So, he avoided traveling along the main highway as often as possible, instead using side roads. To further throw off suspicion, he pretended he was a resident or a tourist.

At the intersection of Highways 124 and 36, he hung back. He watched carefully for any traffic, but there was none. As the heavy fog drifted in waves across the highways, Bert dodged across the road and headed up Highway 124, going west.

He walked carefully along the shoulder, watching for speeding cars taking the curves too fast for conditions. He didn't want to get hit.

Without warning, a pickup truck—loaded with toolboxes and equipment dangling from it—whipped past him. It swerved, knocked off Bert's ballcap, made him buckle to his knees, and sent a fishing rod flying out of the back of the truck into the ditch.

Bert gathered himself, slapped the grass and dirt off his legs and chest, and took a long, deep breath. He picked up his cap, put it back on, and set his backpack aside. He then wobbled into the ditch to fetch the fishing rod. He shook it loose from the tall grass to carry it back up by the road.

As he walked up the embankment, he noticed that the pickup truck was parked there, waiting for him.

A rough-looking bearded fellow with his hands on his hips, wearing a dirty ballcap and overalls tucked into oversized work boots, stood at the back of the truck. "Hello there, fella."

Bert pulled his cap lower to hide his face. He rambled nervously, "Good mornin'."

The man whooped, "Sorry about that! Almost hit ya!"

Bert responded. "Yeah. 'Bout did."

The man extended his hand. "Name's James."

Bert firmly shook his hand. "Nice to meet ya." He dallied in thought for a second. "My name's Roy."

"Well, dammit Roy. Where ya headed? Maybe I can give ya a lift."

Bert hesitated. "Well, I reckon that'd be real nice. I'm goin' west."

"Okay then. Jump in the truck. I can git ya up the road a-ways. I'm goin' to Mountain View to do a job. I was plannin' to do some fishin' afterwards. Glad you found my rod." He laughed boisterously. "Damn, boy. If I'd-a hit ya, it'd-a been KAPOW! And you don't want to go out like that!"

The two chuckled as they got into the truck and buckled their seat belts. The truck engine roared to life and propelled the vehicle off into the fog.

***

At the detention center, the crime scene was cordoned off. Officers and investigators loaded inmates into vans to take them to another detention center until the building could be examined and deemed safe and functional again.

Helicopters flew back and forth overhead while canine units searched the local neighborhoods.

Where the vans were being loaded, Sheriff White stood to the side and spoke with FBI agents Crowley and Lage and ATF agents Shook and Wilk.

Sheriff White was baffled. "For the life of me, I don't know why anyone would want to blow up the detention center. Just why?"

Crowley clarified, "Most often, it's revenge, either on an individual who works at the targeted place or an individual who is incarcerated there."

Shook concurred, "That's right. Maybe a deal went bad. Could even be over a love relationship. I've seen it all."

Crowley asked, "Have any idea who Barley Pop is?"

The sheriff conveyed, "No. I have no idea, but I'm gonna interview the inmate who identified him as soon as doctors allow me to. Right now, he's out of it."

As the cuffed inmates continued piling into the vans, the sheriff eyed each one of them. "Wait. Did we recapture all the inmates that escaped after the explosion?"

Crowley said, "Sheriff, I know you've been busy, and you've got a lot on your plate. But you've got to focus."

He patted the sheriff on the back and tugged his arm to pull him away from the other men. He continued, "We told you earlier that there are two that have not yet been apprehended. We also told you that we put out statements and photos for those two. I'm confident we'll catch them soon."

The sheriff looked confused. "You already told me this? When? Was I sleepin'?"

"You might've been. I think you said you haven't slept in two or three days. Must be hard on the missus too," Crowley chuckled.

"Nah. I haven't. And I don't have a wife. So who are the two still missin'?"

"Conner Thompson and Bert Black."

The sheriff stood up straight with a look of grave concern. "Bert Black?"

"Don't worry. They'll surface. They can't hide forever."

The sheriff looked Crowley square in the eye. "You don't know Survivorman Bert."

Crowley started to respond but instead pointed behind the sheriff. "Um. You've got company."

Sheriff White turned around.

Bobby Joe tipped his hat. With chewing tobacco tucked in his lower lip, he uttered, "Hello, Sheriff." He stuttered, "I heard... I heard what happened. I wan... wanna help."

The sheriff strained a smile to be as polite as possible. "Thanks, Bobby Joe, but ya need to go on home."

"I heard Bert's loose."

"He is, but there's nothin' you can do so please go on back home."

"But I really want to help."

"Bobby Joe! I don't want to sound mean because I know what you've been through but please, just go home!"

Bobby Joe angrily kicked a rock with his boot, turned slowly, spat on the ground, and walked toward his truck.

The sheriff rubbed his face in exasperation and regret. He thought for a moment. Then he walked after the old cowboy and called out, "Hey, Bobby Joe!"

The grief-stricken father was highly disgruntled. "What?"

As the sheriff caught up to him, Bobby Joe held up, hoping he had changed his mind.

The sheriff asked, "Do you know anyone who goes by the name Barley Pop?"

Bobby Joe frowned at him for a long, drawn-out moment. Then, in a low, rumbling voice, he answered definitively, "No."

The sheriff looked on as Bobby Joe got into his truck and drove away. He rubbed his face hard and yawned. "I've gotta sleep, or I'm bound to fuck this up."

***

Early morning in West Memphis seemed mystical as the fog lifted from the Mississippi River. The river bridge finally peeked through. Its metal construction began to glitter in the dim sunlight.

Inside an expansive metal building, Cletus, Toad, and a few other gun shop employees worked diligently to prepare folding chairs, tables, displays, and gun racks for the show.

Toad rolled out a rectangular banner that read: *Fuzzy Rose & Sons Gun Shows, The Best Firearms in the U.S.A.* Cletus helped him hang it from the metal rafters. Then they stepped back and admired it.

Toad bellowed, "Oh yeah!"

Cletus smiled. "We're gonna make a killin' here today."

***

James' work truck pulled into the parking lot at Archey Fork Park off Highway 65 at Clinton.

He put the truck into park. "Well, Roy! I guess this is a good 'nuff spot to part ways since you're goin' west."

Bert was pleased. "Yes, this'll be just fine. Thank ya." He opened the door, pulled out his knapsack and backpack, and turned to James. "Thanks a lot for the ride. Saved a lot of wear and tear on my ol' feet."

James handed Bert the fishing rod, a handful of plastic worms, a small utility flashlight, and a cigarette lighter. "Here. You take this. You found the rod. Besides, I doubt I get a chance to use it today anyway."

Bert's mood perked up. "Are ya sure?"

"Oh hell yeah." He leaned across the seat. "One more thing, Roy. If'n you're in trouble and headin' over by Jasper to hide out in the forest, look for my little brother Curtis.

He's at Sand Gap. He'll help ya out." With that, James slapped the console. "See ya!"

"Thank ya." Bert slammed the door shut.

Off the truck went again, barreling northward.

Bert walked down by the fork and cast a line. Before long, he caught a nice-sized bluegill.

At the barbecue grills, he found some used tinfoil and cold, leftover charcoal bricks. He shoved the foil and several of the bricks into his backpack. Next, he started a small fire in one of the grills and cooked his fish. He ate, savoring every bite and choking it down with lukewarm milk.

He wasted no time. Re-energized, he walked with a bounce in his step, going west on Highway 16.

***

At the White County Medical Center, it was a busy day. On top of the regular patients coming and going, there were several injured inmates cuffed to beds in the emergency room. Off-duty staff was called in to handle the flow.

Upstairs, in a private room, rested Fuzzy. His nose was black and blue as were both of his eyes. Searcy, Mabel, Luke, and Annabelle waited for a sign of life beyond the beeping monitors.

Soon, Dr. Tate arrived, checked the machines and his chart, shook the family's hands, and perched himself against the wall. The family studied his face and waited for him to speak.

"So Luke, you told me this all arose out of a sudden, frantic hallucination where he ran out of the barn screaming about a giant snake and a giant tarantula. Then he ran into a tree. Is that correct?"

"He didn't say 'giant.' He said 'big-ass.'"

"Oh, yes. My apologies."

Annabelle asked, "Is he gonna be okay?"

Dr. Tate continued, "Yes. Physically, I think he's alright. But mentally, he seems to be slipping fast." He looked around the room. "Have you all considered a nursing home facility, where they can watch him better?"

Searcy added, "Well, Doc, we were gonna ask you what ya thought."

Mabel argued, "He ain't gonna like that one bit."

Dr. Tate spelled it out. "So you have two choices. If you put him in a nursing home, he'll have excellent care 24/7, and you won't have to worry about this happening again. Or you can take him back home and next time, he might really hurt himself much worse. Or even someone else."

Luke debated, "But what if he's not happy in a nursin' home?"

"You can always take him out and bring him home," the doctor added. "If I may ask, who has his power of attorney?"

Searcy lifted his hand. "That'd be me."

"Okay, so when you decide what you want to do, just let me know. We'll take care of the paperwork for you, Mr. Rose."

"No problem. Thank you."

Dr. Tate left the room.

Searcy turned to the others. "Y'all wanna leave us be for a minute?"

Mabel, Luke, and Annabelle solemnly filed out of the room.

Searcy peered admiringly at his older brother lying helplessly in the hospital bed. Fuzzy's aging crow's feet and wrinkles wedged deep into his leathery, tanned skin. His beard was long and matted. His face was a canvas to a myriad of bruising colors.

Searcy whispered, "Brother, I am sorry."

Engulfed with swelling, Fuzzy's hazel eyes twitched and then opened slightly, crinkling the tape that held white gauze over his nose.

He softly muttered, "What for?"

Searcy patted his brother's chest and smiled. "You never cease to amaze me."

Fuzzy lifted his head. "Where am I?"

"You're in the hospital. You had a bad bout last night. A tree ran into your face."

Fuzzy groaned, "No shit? Don't surprise me none these days."

They chuckled together.

Fuzzy tried to sit up. "Well, that was a hoot. Now I'm ready to go on home."

Searcy pulled him back onto the bed. "Brother, ya can't go home just yet." He moved over to the nightstand, picked up the pitcher, and carefully poured water into a glass. "Ya need some more medical care."

"What do ya mean? I cain't go to my own damned home?"

Searcy pulled a capsule out of his pocket. "You're not well enough yet." He put the capsule to his brother's lips, and then the glass of water. "Take this, and you'll be up and around in no time."

Fuzzy let the capsule dangle from the side of his mouth. "Ya promise?"

"Yep. I promise."

Fuzzy appeared to swallow the capsule then bent his head back onto his pillow. "Alright! All better. Let's go home."

"Brother. Listen to me now." Searcy bent over to whisper to his brother's face. "They're gonna put you in a nursin' home where ya can get better medical care."

Fuzzy's eyes widened in horror as he stared blankly at his little brother. His face twitched, and his chin quivered. He tried to blink the tears away. His voice cracked, "Searcy, no. I beg you."

"There's nothin' I can do."

Fuzzy's heart was shattered. Tears flowed down his trembling face. "Searcy, please. No."

Searcy whispered, "I love ya, Brother." He stood upright and patted Fuzzy's legs on his way out. "It'll be alright."

Searcy's brand-new, sterling alligator boots seemed to shake the walls like an earthquake as he walked out of the room. He pulled the door closed behind him as if to seal the deal.

Traumatized and rattled, Fuzzy wheezed and focused on the white ceiling tiles hovering above him. He spat out the capsule that he had hidden between his cheek and gums. In a broken, gravelly voice, he whispered, "Anna?"

***

It was a beautiful, calm morning at Betty's house. The aroma of home-cooked food filled the air. The atmosphere was jovial and full of gratitude. After all, Joelle was alive, recovering, and at home.

As Betty hummed and cooked up a meal in the kitchen, Joelle rested on the sofa while wrapped in a soft hand-quilted blanket.

She played with little Buddy as he rolled his toy truck over her hips and belly and made funny engine sounds. They laughed as Joelle walked a toy dinosaur over, growled, and dove it on top of the truck.

The doorbell rang.

Betty tapped the wooden spoon on the side of the pot and laid it down. "Are you expecting any visitors?"

Joelle shook her head. "No. Not me."

Betty answered the door. She allowed Deputy Barnes to enter.

He took his hat off. "Hi, Joelle. How are ya doin'?"

"I'm doin' alright, I suppose." She prodded her son. "Buddy. Go to your room."

"Aw, Momma. Do I have to?"

"Buddy. Go. Now."

The little boy grabbed his toys and reluctantly walked toward his room. "Alright."

When Deputy Barnes heard the bedroom door click shut, he sat in a chair next to Joelle and spoke in a low, soft voice. "I'm very sorry to bother ya. I know you're still on the mend."

Betty listened carefully, nosing in. Then, she remembered her food cooking. "Oh my goodness! Our food is burnin'! I'll be right back!" She ran into the kitchen.

Joelle asked, "What's goin' on now?"

Barnes kept his voice to a whisper. "There was an explosion at the detention center last night. Everybody's okay. But Joelle, Bert escaped."

She pushed her body against the sofa. Her haunting eyes grew bleak and frightened. "You mean—"

"He's on the loose. We're searchin', but we haven't found any clues yet. We don't know where he is."

"Oh my God."

"We're gonna post an undercover person here, outside, just in case. You'll never know it, so it won't scare your son or your mother."

Betty ran back into the living room. "Okay. What did I miss?"

Joelle's vexed voice replied, "Nothin', Mom. They're just checkin' on us."

"Oh, isn't that sweet. I'm so glad we live in the South. You cain't beat Southern hospitality." She hopped up and ran back to the kitchen.

Barnes walked to the door. He winked at Joelle. "Everything's gonna be okay."

Joelle gave a nervous smile. "Thanks."

Betty darted back into the room and handed Deputy Barnes a plate wrapped with tinfoil. "Those are my famous chocolate-chip-walnut cookies! I hope you enjoy 'em!"

"I'm sure we will, Miss Betty. Thank you." With that, Barnes left.

Betty locked the door behind him. Buddy ran back into the living room where he pounced on top of his mother.

She groaned. "Buddy! You can't jump on me like that, sweetie. Momma's not all well yet."

He rolled his truck on her shoulder. "Oops. I'm sorry, Momma. I forgot. BRRRRRRUUUMMMMM brrrrrummmmmmmm!"

***

Showered and clean-shaven, Jim worked diligently alone in the kitchen, putting a whopping breakfast together. He struggled somewhat with his still-healing hands but he was accomplishing the task pretty well.

Laura sat on the patio, reading a book and drinking coffee. Kyle and Emily passed through the kitchen to join their mother.

Jim smiled and cheerfully said, "Good morning, kids!"

They gave him the cold shoulder and kept going.

Once on the patio, Emily asked, "Why is he still here?"

Kyle agreed, "Good question."

Laura looked at each of them and said, "Because I'm fighting to not let a stupid mistake break this family apart. I expect the same from both of you."

Emily flared up, "Seriously?"

Laura sipped her coffee. "Seriously. My own ignorance and prudishness played a small part in it. I own that. We will all own our own shit and try to do better. I expect that of you too. If, at some point, things cannot be healed, then we'll move on. But I am not ready to throw away all these years of hard work, marriage, kids, everything, as a knee-jerk reaction. Do you understand?"

Kyle and Emily both answered respectfully. "Understood."

The doorbell rang.

Jim raced around the kitchen, trying to keep up. "Can someone get that, please? I'm really trying not to burn all this food!"

Kyle, Emily, and Laura went to the front door, where Kyle answered it.

Deputy Smith nodded. "Hello, folks."

At first, Laura seemed concerned. "Um." Then she tipped her head and became annoyed. "Jim! I think this is probably for you!"

Emily was repulsed. "Again!" She dashed from the foyer.

Kyle jabbed, "The man really cannot stay out of trouble, can he?" Then he stomped off too.

Laura stepped back as Jim walked into the foyer.

He accepted his kids' rebuff and sighed. "Hello, Officer. What can we do for you today?" He forced a fake smile. "I just made a huge breakfast. It's still hot if you want some. I doubt that my family is going to eat any of it now."

Deputy Smith commented apologetically, "I'm very sorry, Mr. Barton. I had no idea."

"It's okay. You couldn't have known. What do you need this morning?"

Laura stood behind Jim, listening.

Deputy Smith continued, "I didn't come here to take you in again. I'm here to let you know that there was an explosion at the detention center last night. Bert Black escaped. He has not been located at this time."

Laura covered her mouth with her hands. "Oh, Jim!"

Compassionately and softly, Jim turned and instinctively put his arm around his wife to comfort her. She did not snub him.

Quietly, behind the wall to the foyer, Kyle and Emily lurked and eavesdropped. Their arrogant, judgmental faces morphed into horror as they quietly embraced one another.

Jim turned back to the officer. "So the man who tried to kill me twice is on the loose." He pondered with a tinge of sarcasm. "Okay. What do you need me to do?"

Deputy Smith directed, "Nothin', Jim. Just keep an eye out. Probably best to stay indoors 'til we find him. Keep your doors locked and window blinds closed. It shouldn't take long to locate him. Meanwhile, we'll have a couple of undercover guys positioned outside your home."

Jim shook the deputy's hand. "Thank you for letting us know. We appreciate the work you do."

"Thank you, Jim. And thank you for serving. Our country needs you. Despite all that has happened, we all make mistakes, we're all human, and we will heal and move forward. I'm sorry about your breakfast."

Jim closed the door and locked the deadbolt. He held his wife tight. Around the corner, Kyle and Emily hugged as well.

***

Dorene's home was lavish with exquisite works of art and décor. The smell of freshly-brewed espresso and oven-crisped toast filled the air. The light in the living room was grey-washed but for the fire in the fireplace and a floor lamp in the corner.

As the morning fog swept through in waves, she opened the curtains to watch it pass. Then, in her pristine, red silk robe, she cuddled up on the sofa with a blanket, her little Chihuahua named Dolly, her generously buttered toast, and a cup of espresso.

On the coffee table was a metal box full of old family photos.

Dorene thumbed through them one by one. She smiled at a photo of her and Bobby Joe as kids, climbing trees down by the creek. She blissfully reminisced at another of her and Rhett chasing each other around the old rock mill. Then she came to an image of herself in a hospital bed, holding a newborn baby.

Her chin quivered. Tears filled her eyes as she ran her finger over the image.

She walked into the kitchen, finished her breakfast, and refilled her coffee cup. Then she sat down at the kitchen table where her Colt 1911 Combat Elite Defender semi-automatic pistol and cleaning materials were already set out.

She wiped her hands on a dishcloth. Carefully and methodically, she removed the magazine, released the safety, and disassembled the slide, frame, spring, bushing, and barrel. She cleaned the barrel and parts and put it all back together.

A loud knock at the door startled her. Dolly barked. Dorene hid her gun and cleaning materials in a kitchen cabinet. Then she answered the door.

Deputy Halp stood on the other side. "Dorene."

Dolly continued barking.

"What do you want?"

"Wanna shut that little mutt up so we can talk?"

She lashed back, "That little mutt's name is Dolly, so address him as such."

"Him? You named a boy dog Dolly?"

"He was born my little doll."

Halp hee-hawed loudly. "Sounds like he's trans."

Dorene continued angrily. "You're disgusting. There's nothing wrong with bein' trans. This comin' from a man who named his dog Jerkoff. Now get out of here. I've already told the sheriff everything I'm goin' to."

"Okay then. I will." He turned to walk away. "And I won't tell ya that Bert got loose." He resumed walking.

"Wait!"

He turned around. "Oh. Now you want to talk to me."

CHAPTER 11

Fog burned off around the Christian church. The sun came out, and the morning proved to be simply gorgeous as a banner hung from a brick casing next to the street. It read: *Vacation Bible School!*

Vehicles pulled into the parking lot and formed a long line into the street. As each vehicle pulled up to the front door, it released children into the waiting grasp of volunteer workers. The organized chaos was filled with the sounds of laughter and happiness.

Georgia's SUV was next in line to stop at the front door.

Cutter clambered to gather his small Bible as he held the door handle with excitement. "Momma, can I go now? Can I?"

"Not yet, Cutter. We're next. Let me pull up a little further. I'll tell ya when ya can dive out. Okay?"

"Okay, Momma."

The car ahead of them drove off slowly. Georgia moved her SUV forward.

"Let me stop the car. Not yet."

Cutter squealed.

When she put the vehicle into park, she smiled. "Okay, little man. You can go now."

The young boy let his seat belt fly off. It dinged the passenger window with a "clink!" He shoved the door open and started to bail out when a loving pair of arms caught him on the outside.

"Whoa there, young man! You're gonna hurt yourself! Be careful!"

It was Florence. She released Cutter, who then ran into the church. Then she leaned into the passenger side of Georgia's vehicle. "Hi there, gorgeous!"

Georgia glared back at her with a seething look. "Get out of my car."

Florence was disconcerted. "Who in the world put rat poison in your midnight chocolate bar, Miss Georgia? Why, you're actin' mean as an ol' snake."

"I know you told what I said the other night. You promised not to. You're a liar."

Florence defended, "What? Well, I'll tell you, Missy. I didn't tell a soul, and I am not a liar!"

"Daddy found out! You're the only one I told."

At that moment, Mauser, Gunner, Faith, and Hope walked toward the front door of the church. Mauser saw Georgia and doubled back to taunt her. He stood behind Florence, like a soldier with his legs parted and arms crossed, staring at her.

Florence noticed him from her peripheral vision. She waved her hand. "Shoo. Go on now."

Mauser mocked her. "'Shoo. Go on now.' Said the coward to the treasonous betrayer." He laughed loudly and ran inside the building.

The two women were mortified.

Florence asked, "Did he say what I think he just said?"

Georgia shot daggers straight ahead. "He did."

"Where in the world did he learn such big words?"

Georgia gripped the steering wheel. "From his grandfather."

A little slow to the punch, Florence gulped. "Georgia! He must've been in the bushes!"

Georgia lowered her head. She kindly put her hand on Florence's. "I am so very sorry, Flo. Please forgive me."

Florence was confused but responded, "Okay." She thought for a moment, then brushed Georgia's hand off hers and pointed her finger. "But listen here, lady! This is your second chance! You've only got 999 left in your bucket!"

They chatted together lightheartedly until the car behind them began to honk.

Florence said, "I've gotta run! Let's catch up after Bible School."

Georgia agreed. "Good idea. Let's do. See ya later."

Florence shut the door. As Georgia drove away, she turned up the radio and clenched her teeth.

***

In the darkened back room at the gun shop, Bobby Joe, Searcy, Rhett, Luke, Willie, and John Mark huddled together around the center table. An oscillating fan close to the table whirred and clicked as it slowly rotated left to right and back again.

Willie tossed seven brown paper bags on the table, one in front of each man. "Brought lunch so we don't waste time. There's an extra, just in case."

Searcy asked, "Y'all lock all the doors since Toad's not here?"

Luke answered, "Yes, sir. They're locked. Closed sign is up."

Searcy looked to Bobby Joe. "Find anything out at the detention center this mornin'?"

Bobby Joe shoved his bag to the side. "Wouldn't tell me nothin'. Wouldn't let me help. Nothin'." A more serious draw pulled down his face. "There was one thing though. Sheriff asked me if I knew who Barley Pop was."

Searcy slammed the table with his fist. "Dammit!" He leaned back in his chair. "In what goddamned context did that come up?"

Bobby Joe answered, "They wouldn't tell me that either. Just asked if I knew. I said no, of course."

Searcy grumbled, "I knew he was gonna get sloppy at some point. Well, shit. We'll have to deal with that later." He continued as he paced the floor. "The bigshots are all gonna be here for a meetin' tomorrow after we're done huntin'. I'll call them in when I know what time exactly. Then we'll deal with this shit all at once."

Most of the men opened their bags and began devouring their sandwiches. John Mark got drinks from the refrigerator and handed them out.

Willie asked, "So he's gonna be here too?"

Searcy snarled, "Yep. He sure damn better be."

Luke asked, "So what's next? Are we goin' out to hunt Bert down?"

Bobby Joe demanded, "Yes!"

Searcy touched his arm. "Let's stay calm."

He threw Searcy's hand off and yelled, "Fuck it! Stay calm! My son is dead! His murderer is on the loose, and you fuckin' tell me to stay calm! Fuck you!"

Searcy looked him in the eye. "I understand, Bobby Joe. I'm pissed off too. But we're gonna have a better chance at catchin' him, if we're smarter. And calmer."

Bobby Joe blinked hard. He sat down in submission. Willie tossed him a pack of cigarettes and a lighter. He accepted and lit up.

208.

Searcy folded his hands together. "We've gotta start somewhere. Let's get this posse goin'. We'll go out to Greer's Ferry and work our way back. See what we come up with."

He looked around at the men as they ate. "Did anyone happen to say Grace?"

Except for Bobby Joe, they quickly put their food down and bowed their heads in prayer.

***

Sunrise Hill Nursing Home in downtown Searcy, Arkansas was a simple red-brick building with an extended wing on each side of the main entryway.

A white transportation van was parked underneath the front awning. Even though many local businesses were within walking distance, the facility often took residents on outings for shopping, field trips, and activities. On this day, the van was being loaded up for such an excursion.

Inside the facility, a reception area and nurses' station greeted all who entered the front door and, of course, Big Brother-style cameras aimed in every direction.

Down one of the long hallways, lined with hotel-like doorways, was door number 45. Like the gust of a hurricane wind, the door flung open, and Fuzzy—battered face and all—struggled to pull himself out of the room against the counterweight of the nurses trying to pull him back inside.

"Y'all better let me go! Or else!"

The male nurse yelled, "Or what?"

"Ain't got nothin' but this gown on, and my backside's showin', an' I ate eggs and cheese! I'm fixin' to fart!"

The female nurse reached for a needle and shoved it into Fuzzy's ass. "Goodnight, sweetheart!"

Fuzzy immediately faded and wilted to the floor. "What the hell?"

The male nurse lifted his limp body. Together, the nurses moved him back into his bed.

The male nurse asked, "Why do you have to be so cantankerous, Mr. Rose?"

Fuzzy's words were heavily slurred and unintelligible as he lay mostly paralyzed. The nurses pulled blankets up over his body.

Within moments, Annabelle showed up with a bouquet of wildflowers in her hand. She tapped on the door then entered. "Grampa?"

The nurses abruptly looked up.

The male nurse suggested, "He's just gonna take a nap for a little while. You might wanna come back a little later."

Annabelle looked suspiciously at them. "No... I think I'll stay. Thank you anyway." She found a glass vase by the sink, put the flowers in it, and placed it on a table by the window.

The nurses quickly exited the room but left the door wide open.

Annabelle closed it and returned to Fuzzy's bedside. "Grampa? Are you okay?"

Fuzzy's teary but lucid eyes gazed upon his granddaughter. He could not move. He whispered something, but she could not make it out.

She held his hand. "I'm so worried about you, Grampa. I just don't know what to do."

His fingers moved slightly and grasped hers.

She smiled. "You better get well soon. I want ya back home." She kissed his forehead then rested her head on his chest.

He closed his eyes. His lips quaked as he tried to speak. "I love you."

210.

***

At the gun show, hundreds of buyers wandered down the aisles, shopping for all types of guns. Handguns, rifles, shotguns, AK-47s, and every other kind of military-grade weapon were on display along with bump stocks and ammo.

Cletus and Toad were busy showing and selling guns to whoever stopped at their tables.

Over the roar of the industrial-sized fans blowing through the space, Cletus announced loudly, "Come on over, folks! We've got any kind of firearm to fit your needs! No background checks! Get your guns right here! Take 'em home today!"

Customers and admirers alike moved toward their decked-out tables to view their products.

Cletus continued shouting, "Better come and get 'em now before Obama tries to take 'em all away! Protect your family! Come on now!"

One young woman came to the table. She pondered over the handguns.

Toad winked at her to make her smile. "So, young lady, what's your medicine today?"

Shyly, she explained, "I'm lookin' for somethin' for protection. I think my ex-boyfriend is stalkin' me."

Toad grabbed a small handgun and gently put it into her hand. "Feel this little beauty right here, darlin'. It's small but it fits your pretty little hand. Now don't be fooled; it would do some damage if that nutbag tried to hurt you."

"You think it's right for me?"

"Oh, absolutely. And the price is right too. Tell you what, I'll even knock off another 10 percent just for you if you buy it here and now."

She beamed, "Okay. I'll do it." She pulled out a wad of cash. "So how much will that be?"

At another table, Cletus was engaged in a political conversation with a man who wore a priest's collar.

Cletus proclaimed, "Well, ya know it's true. Him and them dirty liberals want to take away all our guns, take away all our rights, and then open up the southern border. Can ya imagine what that's gonna look like?"

The priest answered, "I do believe some of that is true, but I mainly want to buy something small to protect my congregation. Now that it's legal for anyone to carry into a church, I feel I have the obligation. You know there was a church shooting over west recently?"

"Oh yes. I do know. I live there."

"You do! Well, then you know what I mean!"

"Yes, sir, I do. But one question. Do ya think you're really up for shootin' anybody, especially in a church?"

The priest contemplated the question for a long moment. "Yes. If they were threatening my flock, yes indeed. I believe God would understand and forgive me if I had to do that."

"Great answer! Let me show ya this handy-dandy, little firearm right here," Cletus said as he showed the priest a pearl-handled handgun.

Back at the other table, Toad was now working a deal with an odd, little man with crazy eyes and thick glasses. The man's eyes darted left to right and back again as he asked Toad which firearm would do the most damage in the quickest manner.

Toad answered, "Sir, I will sell to anybody 'cause there's no law sayin' I cain't, but you really shouldn't be askin' questions like that in a place like this. It could get us both in a lot of trouble."

"Oh. I'm sorry. I was just curious."

"That's okay. Maybe just slow up a little there."

"My apologies."

Toad smiled. "No problem. Let me show you this new AK-47 over here," he said as he handed the man the firearm.

"I can take this home today?"

"If you've got the cash, yes, sir."

The little man chuckled. "Yes. I do."

Back at the other table, a middle-aged man caught up with Cletus.

"I just need a new huntin' rifle so I can put food on the table."

**

Just north of Crabtree, Bert came across a pond. He cast a line and soon caught a small sun perch. Without any more luck fishing, he built a small fire from kindling. While he waited for the tiny meal to cook, he gathered worms and beetles from underneath rocks and snacked on them for nourishment.

After he ate his main course, he put out the blaze, rubbed out any signs of having been there, and found a place to nest in the tall grass. He drank from a bottle of water he had stolen from the grocery store, laid his head on his backpack, and napped for about a half-hour.

When he awoke, he cautiously scouted about the area until he decided it was safe to move on. He roughed up his nesting spot, covering his tracks as he went along.

The fog was lifting more rapidly as he got further away from the big lake. This, he knew, would make his journey more difficult and more dangerous as he would have less cover to hide behind. Nevertheless, he knew he had to keep moving west as quickly as possible in order to put as much distance as he could between himself and the detention center.

***

Inmate Travis Lorre sat at the table in the interrogation room at the Sheriff's Department. His head and left wrist were bandaged.

He turned his head nervously with jerking movements as he muttered to himself. "What if I can't? I don't know. Stop whinin', you little bitch."

Sheriff White entered. He sat down across from the ill man. "How are ya feelin', Travis?"

"I dunno. Fine, I reckon."

"I heard ya got a nasty burn on your head from the explosion."

"No shit. I'm sorry. I didn't say that."

"Are ya sure you're feelin' alright? I don't want to stress ya out or anything."

Travis began to sway back and forth. "I'm sorry. Yes, I'm stressed out, but I'm always stressed out. Ya see, they sold me some bad shit up there in the hills. I thought it was good stuff. They said it was good stuff, but it wasn't good stuff. It was cut with rat poison, or bleach, or some kinda shit. Done fucked my head up real bad."

"I'm sorry to hear that. I wish ya hadn't gotten into that crap."

Travis yelled, "You wish I hadn't! Hell, I wish I hadn't! My poor ol' momma wishes I hadn't! I'm her only son, and I let her down! I made her cry!"

After a drawn-out time of watching a blubbering grown man cry, the sheriff said, "I feel for ya, Travis. I really do, but I need to ask ya something really important. Is that okay?"

Travis wiped his tears on his arm. "Yeah, I reckon. I'm sorry for cryin'. It just bubbles out of me sometimes. Cain't stop it."

"I need to ask you who Barley Pop is and how ya know him."

Travis laughed with a shaky tenor. "The one and only Barley Pop! That's how I know him. They call him that 'cause he's somebody's pop, he's an old fuck, and barley 'cause he makes the best barleycorn moonshine west of the Mississip'." He leaned over the table and whispered, "Dude also sells the finest damned firearms anywhere around, dirt cheap." He put his finger to his lips. "Shhhhh."

The sheriff sat erect, taking careful mental notes. "What's his real name?"

"Fuck if I know! He don't never tell nobody his real name! He ain't stupid!"

"And you saw him at the detention center last night?"

"Yep." He bawled again. "I didn't never think he'd do such a thing to me. I'm his friend, buy all my shit from him, and he damned near kilt me."

The sheriff asked with a calm, stable voice, "Where did you see him last night?"

Travis got a serene look on his face. "After the bomb went off, the wall came down, and a bunch of us fellas crawled out. And there he was, off yonder, all dressed in black, watchin' it all happen. I seen him. That's who it was alright. And then he took off down the street."

"On foot?"

"Yep. What I seen."

"Thank you, Travis. You've been a big help. I hope you're feelin' better soon."

Suddenly, Travis began to panic. "Oh my God, what have I done! I narked! I broke to the fuzz! They're gonna kill me for real now! Oh shit!" He kicked the table repeatedly.

The sheriff lifted his hands. "No. Nobody's gonna hurt you. I promise. You didn't do anything wrong. It's okay."

"Oh yes, I did!"

"No, you didn't. See, I already knew all this stuff, so ya didn't tell me anything I didn't already know. You didn't do anything wrong."

Travis calmed down and thought about it. He then agreed. "Okay. Yeah. You're right. I didn't do anything wrong. Ya already knew it all." He cracked his neck. "I'm good. I'm good."

The sheriff winked at him. "Take care, my friend. See ya later."

Travis giggled like a child. "See ya later, alligator."

***

Searcy's big truck traveled north on Highway 16. It pulled over occasionally to let traffic pass or to allow the men to scout the landscape.

The heat of the sun cleared the fog while, overhead, helicopters canvassed the area.

Inside the truck, country music played on the radio. Each man tightly held a long gun while a handgun rested on their belts.

Out of the blue, John Mark shouted, "Pull over! I saw somethin' in the brush!"

Luke asked, "Where?"

The truck quickly pulled onto the shoulder of the road.

John Mark leaped out and pointed toward a thick patch of underbrush and trees. "I saw it right back in there!"

Bobby Joe pounced out in front of John Mark and aimed his rifle. "I'm gonna kill that motherfucker."

Searcy walked up behind him. "Be careful what you're shootin' at now."

Instantaneously, a rabbit hopped high into the air. A shot rang out. The animal was dead before it hit the ground.

John Mark exclaimed, "A rabbit?! No. I saw somethin' much bigger than that back in there!"

Rhett teased, "Yeah, right."

Bobby Joe appeared disappointed as he lowered his gun.

Searcy ordered John Mark, "Go down there in the brush and git it. We don't waste nothin'."

John Mark carefully crawled down the embankment to recover the carcass. He picked it up and heard a loud rustling in the underbrush.

"Hey! Guys!"

Before he could utter another word, an ear-piercing squeal sounded as a wild pig ran out of the underbrush and charged John Mark. Rabbit in hand, the young man vaulted over a fallen tree and scrambled toward the embankment. The pig ran the other direction.

Except for Bobby Joe, the men taunted John Mark and made jokes.

As he climbed up the incline, he heard a hiss. At the same time, a snake leaped out of the tall grass toward the rabbit carcass. Needless to say, John Mark found a renewed energy and ran up to the truck like a shot.

The men continued laughing and slapped him on the back.

Out of breath, he said, "Yeah. Y'all go on and laugh it up. But what now? Cain't skin it right here."

Searcy ordered, "Throw it in the back. It'll do."

John Mark tossed the dead rabbit into the bed of the truck. The men piled back in. The engine roared to life and thrust the massive machine northbound.

***

Inside the truck, Luke sniffed around. "I think I smell piss."

Willie asked, "Are ya sure that's not shit?"

The men kept ragging John Mark, except for Bobby Joe who stared intently out the side window.

John Mark sneered, "Ha-ha. Very funny. Y'all go on and laugh. Don't bother me none."

The truck continued up the highway, occasionally pulling over and stopping. When it reached Pangburn, the fog was heavy. It pulled into the Citgo station where Searcy got out and filled it up with fuel.

On the side of the building, Willie noticed an old man huddled low beneath an old, torn Native American blanket, with a scuffed-up rifle and a red gas can at his feet.

Willie moved slowly toward him. The others looked on.

The scruffy, old man held his head up. "You can come on over if ya ain't gonna hurt me."

Willie promised, "I ain't gonna hurt ya. Where are ya from?"

"Between here and Dewey, along the Little Red River. Bought a small piece of land years ago when I was workin' and saved a little money."

"What 'cha doin' out here? I hate to sound nosy, but ya look kinda down and out."

"Just lost my wife 'cause I ain't got no health insurance. I couldn't tell if it was cancer, or her heart just gave out from all the stress. Then they made me bury her and charged me more than $10,000 I ain't got. I'll never pay that off. They want me to sell my little parcel of land, but if I do that, then I ain't got nowhere to go."

The old man shifted his weight. His voice splintered, "I couldn't do nothin' for her, and I cain't do nothin' for myself. Cain't work 'cause I hurt my back years ago workin' for the railroad. Kids won't have nothin' to do with me 'cause I ain't got nothin' to give 'em. People thank I'm a sack of shit. The State don't wanna help me none, so I reckon I'm 'bout to die too. Social Security denied me four times, and I went and paid into it all those years. Go figure."

Willie was speechless.

The man cast down his head in embarrassment. "I ain't no panhandler. But I was kinda hopin' somebody might throw me a little somethin' so I could fill up my gas can and go back home."

"Aw, I'm real sorry about your wife. But don't say that you're gonna die. There's plenty of good reasons to live. Do ya believe in God?"

"Nope. If there is one, He ain't up to no good that I done seen."

"Listen. Do you have a way to cook at your place?"

"Yep. It's a small cabin, but I like it. I got a wood stove in there and a fireplace. It works, I reckon."

"Wait right here."

Willie walked to the truck, pulled out the rabbit and some ammo, and returned to the old man.

"We just shot this a little while ago. It's still good to eat if ya get on home with it soon. And here's a little ammo so you can hunt."

The old man accepted the gifts. "Thank you, young man. I'd say God bless, but ya know..."

Willie smiled. "I understand." He pulled his wallet out of his back pocket and thumbed through the contents. He pulled out a $100 bill and handed it to the old man. "Here. Take this."

The old man took a step backward. "Are ya sure?"

"I am. It's not much, but I hope it can help get ya along for a little while."

The old man blinked at the money. "I ain't got words."

"No words needed. Here. Let me help ya get that gas."

Willie grabbed the gas can and filled it up. Then he handed it back to the old man. "Here ya go. And I'm gonna say God bless you if ya don't mind."

The old man nodded. "Thank you, son." He gathered his things. With a serious limp, he slowly wandered off down the road with his dirty, old, torn blanket wrapped over his shoulders.

Willie paid for the gas and got back into Searcy's truck where the others were waiting. There was a lingering stillness.

Eventually, the truck started up again.

The next stop was the Pangburn Café where the men unloaded and hurried inside.

Luke said, "I'm so hungry."

Willie prodded him. "You just ate! We're only stoppin' for coffee and to take a dump!"

"I'm still hungry, okay?"

Bobby Joe warned, "You better get it to-go 'cause we gotta get back on the road."

***

The afternoon sun blazed through Kyle's bedroom window as he rested on his bed, reading Ralph Ellison's *Invisible Man*. The flickering shadows of tree leaves blowing in front of the sun's rays interrupted the stillness of the moment.

Kyle turned on a box fan, walked to the window, and peered out at the undercover cop guarding the house. "I can see you," he quipped. "Some undercover protection."

He closed his bedroom door then walked into his closet. He came back out with an old, worn-out shoebox that had been taped back together many times over. He sat on his bed and took the top off. Inside were dozens of old photographs, notes, and memorabilia.

The bed creaked as he kicked back against the headboard. "Why not?"

As he looked through the items that included old swim medals, newspaper articles, and other keepsakes, he noticed a small figurine of an African woman wearing traditional clothing. Her gentle smile was mesmerizing as were her dark eyes. He held her up, observed her, and felt a great peace come over him from head to toe. He basked in the moment.

Then he noticed an old photograph of his mother and father holding him as a newborn infant. They looked so happy and proud. He was transfixed on the photo for several seconds until he turned it over. On the backside, it read: "Laura and Walter Kingsman, with baby Kyle, 9-24-86 in Los Angeles."

He laid the photo next to the figurine on his bed and looked at them side by side.

"Why did you go and die on me, Daddy?" He lamented, "I needed you."

The front doorbell rang. It jolted Kyle back to reality. He scrambled to put the box back together and place it back in the closet.

***

Downstairs, Jim peeked through the peephole. Laura and Emily stood behind him, curious to see who was there.

He opened the door to Catherine, Georgia, and Shelby standing there with casserole dishes of hot food and shopping bags filled with junk food and staples.

Catherine said, "Hello, you guys!"

Laura's face brightened with joy. "Hello. Come on in! What a surprise!"

The women shuffled inside and went straight to the kitchen.

Shelby said, "We heard what was goin' on and decided that we weren't gonna let y'all go through this alone. You just say what ya'll need, and it's done!"

Georgia set her dish on the countertop. "I don't know y'all too well, but I'm fixin' to."

She held her hand out to Jim. "I'm Georgia. I met y'all at the party, but you might not remember. I'm one of Searcy's kids."

Jim nervously responded. "Oh."

Georgia continued. "Oh, don't be afraid of me! I'm one of the brood alright, but I'm a black sheep. I'm a Republican, but I'm not a believer in guns." She jested, "Daddy hates that shit."

The laughter lingered while Shelby gently took Laura's hand. "Remember me? I'm Shelby Hook Rose. I'm married to Rhett. Luke's our son."

Emily gushed over her as Kyle dashed into the room.

Shelby continued, "We're kinda black sheep too, but they'll get over it." She playfully pinched Emily's cheek. "One way or another, dead or alive!"

Laura looked at all the food. "I don't even know what to say, but thank you."

Catherine said, "That's all you need to say, honey. Now is there anything you need? We'll go get it."

Jim was overcome with gratitude. "Wow. Thank you. I don't think we need anything now."

Georgia picked up from there. She pointed. "Well, this over here is cheesy scalloped potatoes. That one is green bean casserole. We weren't quite sure what y'all like, but Rhett smoked y'all a brisket right here. And that one over there is Shelby's famous baked beans!"

Shelby added, "I hope y'all like it."

Kyle groaned, "I'm sure we will. Yum."

Catherine laughed. "That sounds like one hungry boy to me!"

Kyle and Emily grabbed plates and filled them up. Then they went to the dining room to eat.

Once the kids were out of hearing distance, Shelby whispered to Jim and Laura. "I know you don't have any guns. The three of us normally don't believe in them either, but there might be exceptions. This is one of them. Would you like to have a gun, just to hold onto until Bert is caught?"

Husband and wife looked at each other, unsure how to respond.

Laura seemed confused. "Jim, should we?"

Georgia interrupted. "Actually, I'd give a staunch 'no'!" She dug in her pocket, pulled out a pink pepper spray, and held it up. "Honey, this stuff right here will flat put their eyes out! No guns needed! You can have this one if ya want to, but I bought ten of them! They're in that bag right over there! I even got black ones for the boys 'cause sometimes they don't like to hold pink things!"

Shelby shoved Georgia in the shoulder. "Shut up already! Let them make up their own minds!"

Georgia threatened, "Watch it, Shelby! You're just an in-law!"

The women refocused and watched the couple's faces as they struggled to find an answer.

Catherine said, "You don't have to make up your minds right now. We just thought, that since Bert is on the loose, and since he's tried to kill Jim a time or two already, this might be a slight exception. But it's up to you."

Shelby chirped, "And ya don't even have to use it! It would just be a precaution."

Georgia joggled her head. "I'm tellin' y'all, pepper spray. Ghost peppers. Hell, I'll go buy you grizzly bear spray if ya want me to."

Jim asked, "Why are you ladies doing this?"

Catherine explained, "Because we're a community. A community of all kinds, and we stick up for each other."

Shelby added, "And we've seen that some folks around here haven't been too friendly to y'all. They're bein' too protective of their own. We want to welcome you into the fold and be part of who we are."

Jim confessed, "You do realize, we're liberals."

Georgia covered her mouth and squawked, "Oh my God! They're goin' to hell!"

Everyone laughed loudly until Shelby assured, "Some of us are too." She scrunched her nose. "Don't you think that just makes us all a little bit richer? More interestin'?"

They all hugged each other.

Georgia pointed at Jim's legs and shrieked, "Don't hug that boy! His pants are already on fire!"

Laura laughed so hard she had to balance herself against the countertop.

Jim mocked her. "Ha-ha."

When the excitement died down, Jim said, "Thank you for everything, ladies, including the laughs, but that other thing you mentioned, we'll pass on it for now."

Georgia shouted, "I won!"

Emily and Kyle returned to get second helpings. The laughter was contagious, and they joined in.

Kyle loaded up his plate. "These beans! Wow!"

Emily joked, "Until an hour from now! Wow!"

CHAPTER 12

It was late afternoon when Jim's cell phone rang. He answered and paused.

The voice on the other end spoke calmly. "Jim. Sheriff White. Can you come down to the office for just a bit?"

"Yes, Sheriff. I can come down there. Just promise me you've got my family covered. I want them to be safe."

"I've already sent an extra officer out there. They'll be safe."

"Okay then. I'm on my way." He hung up and gathered his wallet and car keys.

Laura asked, "What now?"

"Oh, nothin' too important. The sheriff just wants to chat again. It won't take too long. I'll be back soon."

He blew her a kiss, but she didn't reciprocate. He left without another word.

***

The sheriff folded his arms on the top of his desk. He snuggled his head inside them and yawned. Then he napped for several minutes.

Ultimately, a tapping knock on his door awakened him.

He lifted his head. "Hello, Jim?"

Jim entered and closed the door behind him. "Hello, Sheriff. Did I interrupt?"

"Oh, no. Come on in. Please. Sit down."

Jim took a seat. "What can I help you with?"

"We need to clean up a few things. I hope this is a good time."

"Well, other than wanting to be with my family so I can protect them—"

"Okay. I know. Let's get to it. I'm anxious to get to my bed too."

"I can imagine."

"First of all, I know it pissed you off and busted up your family, or damn near it, whichever the case may be, but you were caught lyin' to us about your involvement with Dorene."

Jim lowered his head. "I'm truly very sorry about that. I'm struggling to keep my family together. We'll see."

"I can't bring charges on you for sleepin' around and cheatin' on your wife. That's not against the law. However, lyin' to us to cover up somethin' or obstruct an investigation might be."

Jim reflected, "I believe so, yes, but I'm telling the truth when I say, I did not know Matthew Toller or Bert Black, nor did I know Dorene's role. I only knew her from working at the base. She hit on me, and I took it like a horny idiot."

The sheriff turned on a box fan and kicked back in his chair. "I believe ya, Jim. You're too smart to get involved like that. However, if I do find out that you did know somethin' about it and you didn't disclose it, I will seek to prosecute you and throw away the key."

"I understand."

"Now, there's also the issue of givin' your adult son pain pills that were prescribed for you."

226.

"I had no idea how many he would take."

"Somehow, I believe that too. I don't see any reason why you'd let him have enough to harm himself. I do believe he knew where your bottle was and took them himself. I could go after him for stealin' your meds, but I don't see any benefit in doin' that, especially if ya have him in therapy now."

"Yes. He is." Jim pleaded, "Please don't go after him. He's having a hard enough time coping with Levi's death and our marital issues."

"I believe that too. So I'm lettin' it go, but it best not happen again."

Jim assured, "It won't, sir. I have them locked up."

"Okay. Good. I hope you can mend your family, Jim. It would be a shame to see y'all go down that road. Divorce is a sad and horrible thing."

"I will fight for them. I will not leave them."

The sheriff leaned forward on his desk, stretched his arms toward Jim, and looked him dead in the eye. "I have one more question. Then I'll let ya go back home."

"Let's hear it."

"Have ya ever heard the name Barley Pop?"

Jim pondered for a moment, then answered, "That is a very unique name but I swear to God, I have never heard it before in my life."

The sheriff walked Jim to the door. "I believe ya. Now go home and hold that beautiful family together."

Jim headed for the front door. "I will. Thank you, sir. I hope you get some sleep soon."

"Me too."

***

It was now dusk at the gun shop. Fog was slowly rolling in over the treetops. The red-orange sunset was fading fast.

The earthy smell of soil and damp foliage swept across the property.

In the distance, a barn owl hooted, and a whippoorwill sang. A coyote trotted across the parking lot under the eerie glow of the security lights mounted high on utility poles.

As Searcy's truck engine broke the natural, peaceful ambiance and pulled into the back lot, the coyote quickly disappeared into the dense woodlands that surrounded the property. A small Mexican free-tailed bat swooped past one of the security lights.

The truck parked in the reserved spot next to the back door. As the men piled out onto the black asphalt, their cowboy boots stomped and clicked on the hard surface.

Searcy demanded, "Y'all get all your shit out of my truck. I don't want anything left in here."

Willie jabbed back. "Done. I'm goin' home. I've got a wife and kid waitin' for me. See y'all tomorrow." He hurried off to his own truck.

Rhett agreed. "Yep. Me too. I'm wiped out." He too rushed off to his own truck.

John Mark and Luke followed suit.

As Bobby Joe unlocked the back door to the gun shop, Searcy stood by the driver's side of his beast.

"Bobby Joe! You goin' home?"

"Nah. I'm workin' on somethin' for Levi's headstone. You go on home. I'll be packin' it up soon."

"Alright. Don't stay up late. We're goin' out again tomorrow to find that son of a bitch. We pushed that big meetin' tomorrow out a bit. We'll still fit it in. All I gotta do is make a phone call."

"I'll be ready."

Searcy ducked into his truck and drove away. Bobby Joe entered the shop. The door closed and locked behind him.

At the far edge of the parking lot, a giant female opossum, with babies clinging to her back, waddled across the pavement to get to the woods on the other side. The bat swooped past the security light again, feeding on bugs that swarmed there.

**

Inside the shop, Bobby Joe turned on a lamp over the workbench. His demeanor was dire as he picked up his cellphone and dialed. He listened as the phone rang four times.

Finally, Jim picked up. "Hello, Bobby Joe. How are you doing?"

"Can ya come to the shop? Right now?"

Jim hesitated, then withdrew. "I wish I could, but I can't do it tonight."

Bobby Joe was disappointed. "Okay. No problem."

"Are you going to be okay?"

"Yep. Fine."

Jim clarified, "Listen. Bobby Joe, I would love to come over and help you. I'm your friend, and I mean that. But there are undercover cops everywhere out here. We still don't know where Bert is. My family is scared out of their minds. I hope you understand. I'm sorry."

"Oh yeah. I forgot you were bein' watched. Maybe next time."

"For sure!"

Bobby Joe breathed heavily. "'Nite." He hung up the phone without waiting for a response.

**

At the nursing home, Searcy entered the front door where he was quickly summoned to the front desk by a staff person. The worker who sat there had a nurse come to the desk.

Looking at a chart and taking notes, the nurse said, "Mr. Rose. I just need to get a little background on your older brother. He is older, right?"

"Yes. Older brother."

"Are you his only sibling?"

"No. We had a middle brother."

"Can you please tell me a little about him? It's just for our records."

"His name was Asa Rivers Rose. Born 1950. Died in '70 at 20-years-old. Killed in Vietnam. He was married to Isabella Bleue in '67. No idea where she is now. Anything else?"

"Oh, sorry. I apologize. I just needed to know if he had any health issues that might be genetic between siblings. I'm so sorry about your brother."

"You should-a said that. Answer is 'no.' I don't think none of us had any genetic shit goin' on. However, Fuzzy did do several tours in 'Nam and got exposed to Agent Orange, explosives, and no tellin' what else while he was over there. That's why his head ain't all right."

"Okay. Thank you. I'll put that in his chart. I'm sorry to hold you up."

"Welcome," Searcy muttered as he turned and continued toward door number 45.

***

Fuzzy was fully and meticulously dressed in his pressed blue jeans, ironed western shirt, polished old cowboy boots, and his worn-out cowboy hat. Both eyes were black-and-blue, and a bandage covered the bridge of his nose.

He sat in a rocking chair in one corner of the room, staring at his TV that was not turned on. His dinner tray sat untouched on a side table. The floor lamp next to his window flickered which did not seem to bother him.

Searcy tapped on the door, then entered. "Fuzzy?"

The old man didn't answer but continued staring at the blank TV screen.

Searcy sat at the end of the bed. "What 'cha watchin' there?"

No response.

"Can ya hear me?"

Fuzzy cast a look that could have seared holes through him. "I can hear you just fine."

Searcy pulled back. "Are ya mad at me for somethin'?"

"You know why I'm mad at you, Searcy Rose. You let them put my ass in this hell hole."

"Brother, the doctors did that! Not me!"

"You're full of shit!"

Searcy pulled a capsule out of his pocket. "I am not. You can be as mad as ya want, but it won't change the fact that your health ain't what it used to be. Hell. You're polishin' cap guns, cussin' out the young'uns, and slammin' your face into trees. That ain't me! That's you!"

Fuzzy started to tremble as he tried to find words to defend himself. "I—"

Searcy interrupted by handing him the capsule with a glass of water. "Here. The nurse asked me to give this to ya."

Fuzzy inspected it. "Nurses already been around with our pills."

"They forgot this one."

Fuzzy took the capsule in his hand. "I'll take it in a bit."

Searcy pushed the glass of water toward him. "I think you're supposed to take it now."

At that moment, Annabelle, Luke, and Darcy barged into the room, carrying flowers, balloons, and candy.

Annabelle giggled, "Hi Grampa! How are ya doin'? We brought ya some stuff to cheer ya up!"

Fuzzy put the capsule into his shirt pocket. Searcy withdrew the glass of water and retreated to the other side of the room.

As everyone greeted one another, Annabelle looked at her uncle. "Hey, Uncle Searcy! How are you?"

Searcy muttered in a shrewd voice, "Hi, Annabelle."

"Maybe it's me but, I swear, you always seem so uptight around me. Is it somethin' I done?"

He avoided making eye contact with her. "I'm sorry. I never meant to seem uptight. There's just a lot goin' on, I guess."

Fuzzy snapped, "I reckon so."

Luke asked, "How are ya doin', Fuzzy?"

"I wanna go home. How are you doin'?"

Darcy patted Fuzzy's leg. "Look at you! All cleaned up! Clothes all pressed and ironed! Oh, it's not all that bad now, is it?"

Fuzzy glared at her. "It's hell. I hate it."

Searcy walked toward the door. "I can see that you've got a lot of company right now, Brother, so I'll catch up with ya tomorrow."

Fuzzy grunted, "Bite me."

Searcy walked out the door.

Annabelle responded, "Hey now. What's goin' on between you two?"

Fuzzy raised his eyebrows and warned, "He's the devil."

They laughed.

Darcy added, "Well, that's one way of puttin' it." She broke open the box of candy. "Here let's have some sweets to liven up this party."

Annabelle noticed the untouched tray of food. "Grampa. You didn't eat a bite of your dinner."

232.

Fuzzy rocked the chair slowly. "You eat it."

"Grampa, I don't want to eat your dinner."

"Then give it to the dog."

"I don't understand what is wrong with you. Did they do something to ya earlier today?"

He reasoned, "Dog's gotta eat too." Then he pulled the capsule out of his pocket and handed it to Annabelle. "Here. Take that away too. Don't want it."

"Grampa! You're hidin' your pills! Good grief!"

"I ain't hidin' nothin'. I don't want it. Searcy brung it in. I already had my pills today, so take that one away from me."

Annabelle put the capsule into her jacket pocket. "Okay, but you've gotta eat."

Darcy and Luke also agreed. However, no amount of coaxing in the world would change the old man's mind.

As he rocked in the rocking chair, his visitors laughed, joked, sang songs, and turned the TV on. They pampered the old man until he fell asleep where he sat. Then, they helped him change his clothes and put him into bed.

When he was fast asleep again, they dimmed the lights, held his hand, kissed him, and said goodnight.

They left the room on their tiptoes.

***

The evening was peaceful and loving at Catherine and Willie's home. Although the living room was dark, the TV flickered with an old episode of *The Dick Van Dyke Show*. The couple held each other as they snuggled underneath a thick fleece blanket.

Willie beamed proudly, "I love you so much."

Catherine melted in his arms. But before she could respond, a terrible scream split the air and shattered the calm. Both parents sprang to their feet and hustled down the hallway.

In Colton's room, they discovered their son banging his head against the bed railing.

He screamed, "Stop it! Levi's burnin'! He's burnin' to death! Stop it!"

Willie snatched his son up into his arms. He held him tight. "It's okay, Son. No one's burnin'. Everyone's okay."

Catherine patted him and kissed his face. "It's okay, Colton."

The young boy whined, "I want to sleep with you, Mommy!"

Willie carried him to their bedroom. Catherine yanked the covers down. She crawled into bed.

Willie tucked the boy in with his mother. "I'll shut everything down and be right back."

As he walked out of the room, Catherine cradled her son. "It's all okay, baby. We're all okay."

***

The play between darkness and dimmed light gave a mysterious tone to the living room where Jim battled his pillows and blankets, trying to get comfortable on the sofa. He forced his eyes to close and sighed.

After a few minutes, he gave up, sat up, and grabbed his iPad from the coffee table. He put his reading glasses on and leaned back in a more comfortable position.

He typed *Year of Meteors* into the search browser. He read in a whisper, "Year of Meteors: Stephen Douglas, Abraham Lincoln, and The Election that Brought on the Civil War." He mulled over it. "The bizarre and explosive election of 1860. Set the North and South on the road to disunion." He stared intently at his iPad. "Wow."

Unbeknownst to him, Laura—wrapped in a warm blanket—had entered the room and was now standing near him. She asked, "Wow what?"

Jim was startled. "Oh. Hi, honey. I couldn't sleep, so I thought I'd read a little."

She sat beside him. "Oh yeah. What are you reading?"

He tilted the iPad so she could see too. "See there. *The Year of Meteors.*"

"What prompted you to search on that?"

"I've always been a history buff. You know that."

"But what made you get interested in that, in particular?"

He smiled. "Honey. I just heard it somewhere and wondered about it. That's all. I couldn't sleep."

He closed the iPad case and placed it back on the coffee table. "But that can wait. Right now, I want to focus on you. How are you doing?"

Laura stretched her legs out and rubbed her upper arms. "I can't sleep either." She admitted, "I'm scared."

He asked respectfully, "May I touch you?"

Reluctantly, she whispered, "Yes, please."

He gently put his arm around her shoulders. She rested her head on his neck.

"Jim, do you think we'll ever get through this?"

"Oh yeah, if we work at it. As long as it takes, I'm not leaving you. I'm not giving up."

***

Upstairs, Emily was reading a book by a dim light when she heard whimpering sounds. She put the book on the side table, tossed her blankets aside, and wandered into the hallway. She followed the sounds to Kyle's room where she pushed open the door.

"Kyle?" She rushed to his bedside. "Hey, what's wrong?"

"Levi."

She put her hand on his arm and whispered, "Oh my God. You're shaking. Are you on any pills?"

He whispered, "No. I promised. Besides, Dad has them all locked up."

Emily patted his shoulder. "Stay here. I'll be right back."

A minute later, she returned with her secret shoebox in hand and quietly closed the door. She flipped on a lamp. Then she opened up the box.

Kyle sat up in bed. Stunned, he asked, "You smoke weed?"

She giggled. "You didn't know?"

"I thought maybe, but I didn't want to assume."

She pulled out a pre-rolled joint and lit it up. "Watch me. It's easy. Just inhale, hold it in, and slowly blow it out. I can't believe you've never done this."

He rationalized, "I'm an athlete. I couldn't do this stuff, or I'd get kicked off the team."

She took a toke then passed it to her brother. "Stupid rule."

He followed her example. Then he immediately started to do it again when she grabbed it from his hand.

"Slow down there, big boy. You've got to wait a minute and see how it affects you. It happens to everyone differently."

"Oh yeah. I heard that somewhere."

After she took another drag, she handed it back to him. "Okay. Now, you can go again."

He did it again, as instructed.

They chatted then sat quietly—just being.

He asked, "So, are we gonna sneak down and clean out all those leftovers like right now?"

She chuckled, "I think they would notice that." Then she asked, "How do you feel?"

He popped his neck and laid back on his pillow. "Calmer. That shit works pretty fast."

Emily put out the joint, packed everything back up in the shoebox, and turned off the lamp. "Okay. Now, you get some rest. No more nightmares."

As she headed for the door, he whispered loudly, "Thank you."

***

Tuesday, July 16, 2013. Morning brought much better weather. The fog burned off much quicker, revealing overgrown tropical-like surroundings. The trees and foliage were intense with every shade of green imaginable.

At a little pond west of Dabney, Bert crouched low with his fishing line in the water. Next to him, he burned two bricks of charcoal.

In a short while, he reeled in a small fish, gutted it, and put the innards aside. He wrapped the fish in a tiny piece of tinfoil and buried it in the ground with a charcoal brick on each side.

While he waited, he took out another cold charcoal brick and a piece of cloth. He smashed the brick in half with a rock and put one half back in his backpack. Then he cut off the top part of his water bottle and placed the cloth loosely over it. He smashed the half-briquette with a rock, placing it on top of the cloth. He then ran pond water over it in an attempt to purify it for drinking.

After carefully filling his water bottle and drinking some, he checked on his fish. It was done enough. Being in a hurry, he quickly picked off the foil and pieces of charcoal and dirt that stuck to the meat. He ate eagerly.

When he was finished, he buried the innards, the charcoal, and the burnt tinfoil in the ground and covered the area with loose sand and fallen leaves. He carefully poured his filtered pond water into an empty plastic bottle that had a lid, closed it tight, and put it in his backpack. He ran a tree branch over the pond bank and anywhere he had left tracks. Then he gathered his pole, backpack, and knapsack and hit the trail.

Within minutes, a police cruiser raced by, and a helicopter flew overhead.

He hid. At this point, he was only steps from entering the national forest.

***

Once again, the posse was on the road, tracking Bert down. This time, they headed southeast toward Des Arc.

As they scanned miles and miles of farmland being worked by hundreds of migrant workers, George Strait blared on the radio. Each man held his firearm close.

Luke looked out the window and yelled, "What if he ain't headed this way at all?!"

Searcy turned down the music. "Say what?"

Luke repeated himself.

Willie agreed. "Luke might be right. How do we know which way he could-a gone?"

Rhett stayed silent, as the others fidgeted in their seats. Instead, he rolled his lips and nodded. After all, his heart wasn't in this one bit.

Willie explained, "It's our thinkin' that he might be headed to Des Arc so he can catch drift on the White River and float right on out of here. He could be in New Orleans in a week and jump a freighter overseas."

John Mark added, "Or he could be thinkin' a hundred different ways. I'm bettin' he couldn't float to N'Orleans in a week. More like a month. By then, somebody would see that scumbag."

Luke remarked, "I don't mean to sound disrespectful, but what if we're just wastin' our time? Wouldn't it be smarter to wait for word from the sheriff on any leads, rather than drivin' all over the State, not knowin'?"

Willie agreed, sort of. "We are kinda wearin' ourselves thin, cramped up in this truck and gettin' road-weary. I don't know about you guys, but it's wipin' me out. And I ain't gettin' nothin' else done in the meantime."

Rhett finally gave his nickel's worth. "Me too."

Bobby Joe was in the front passenger seat. He looked at Searcy. "They're right. We're wastin' precious time."

Searcy pulled the truck over on the shoulder of the road. He looked at Bobby Joe. "Are ya sure?"

Bobby Joe nodded. "I'm sure. Let's go home."

Searcy then announced, "Alright, boys! We're goin' back to Beebe! That big meetin' we pushed back is back on! Regular time! Y'all be quiet! I'm fixin' to make a phone call!"

John Mark put his travel mug of hot coffee to his lips just as Searcy punched the gas and swung the truck around. Hot coffee went up into his nose and down his shirt.

"Goddamnit, Searcy!"

Every man in that truck sat still—paralyzed with shock and fear. No one could say a word.

Quick with his wit, John Mark corrected himself. "I meant God an' Mother Mercy."

The men erupted with hysterical laughter.

***

Well within the forest, Bert walked along while cautiously watching and listening for any threatening adversary. Still, he knew that he was already better off now that he was away from the roadways and moving underneath a heavy canopy of trees. The biggest concern at this time was either running into random folks who were squatting on forest lands or getting snakebit.

At that moment, he came to a grinding halt. He heard a deep rumble. The vibrations churned his body.

Within seconds, a horrible violent pain struck. He grasped his abdomen, threw his things to the ground, and jerked his pants down as quickly as he could. He almost didn't make it. As soon as he squatted, a disgusting bout of diarrhea blew out of his ass so fast and hard, he lost his footing and fell backward.

"No!"

He rolled over, holding his abdomen. Then, he vomited a time or two.

After a while, when he felt his body was done purging, he gathered himself together. He found some safe-looking, tender, green leaves to wipe himself off.

Once he was ready to move on, he poured out every drop of pond water he had carried with him. He threw the bottle down. "Wasted fuckin' weight I been carryin'."

He dug around in his backpack, pulled out the ginger root, and took a small bite. "Damn lucky I got that." He marched ahead. "Onward."

***

It was late morning and a stunningly beautiful day. The sun was out, and the breeze was warm.

Kyle and Emily had gotten permission from the sheriff to visit Luke and Annabelle next door. So off they went, walking hurriedly just in case, you know. Bert.

While Kyle held a gift bag, Emily rang the doorbell.

Annabelle answered. Her defenses were definitely on high alert. Her voice was curt. "Hi. What can I do for y'all?"

Emily smiled. "We were hoping to make amends and apologize for the other night."

"Really?"

Kyle smiled and lifted the bag. "We even brought a peace offering."

Annabelle shyly strutted like an innocent cheerleader peddling her wares as if that made any sense. "Okay. Come on in."

They shuffled inside.

She quickly closed the door behind them. "I heard Bert is still loose. You guys shouldn't be walkin' outside. How did ya get out to go buy a gift?"

Emily blurted, "Amazon. Overnight delivery."

Kyle added, "And we asked permission to walk over here. I mean, not 'permission' like that, but they said it was okay. Those undercover guys are hard at work, by golly!"

Emily looked at him sideways. "Gawd, you sound like Mom."

Annabelle darted to the sliding back door. Giddy, she opened it and stuck her head out. "Hey, Luke! We've got company!"

She closed the door and returned to the living room. "Y'all sit down and relax. I'm glad you came over here. It's been too quiet and lonely since Grampa's been gone."

Emily put her hand to her face. "Oh no! Did he hit the tree that hard?"

Kyle added, "Oh, crap!"

Annabelle explained, "Oh, he's not dead, just very, very pissed off. They put him in a nursin' home ever since he knocked his lights out that night."

Kyle asked, "How long are they going to keep him there?"

Emily asked, "Is he okay?"

Annabelle pointed at Kyle. "I hope not long." Then she pointed at Emily. "His face is black-and-blue, and he's upset, but he'll get better. I know it."

The back sliding glass door opened.

Luke walked inside. As soon as he saw Kyle, he stepped back and puffed up. "What are y'all doin' here?"

Kyle walked toward him. "Listen, Luke. I'm sorry about what I said."

Luke checked him over for sincerity.

Kyle reached over and pulled a board game out of the gift bag. "Look! It's a peace offering!"

Luke smiled. "*Euphoria*. I've been wantin' to play that game. I can play for a while but then I have a meetin' I have to go to."

Emily clapped with childlike excitement. "Yay! We're all friends again!" She mulled, "Oh my God. I'm becoming my mother!"

They laughed and teased Emily about her cuteness.

Annabelle retrieved canned drinks from the refrigerator and bags of chips to snack on while Emily, Kyle, and Luke set up the board game.

Kyle asked, "You weren't really going to hit me with that thing the other night, were you?"

Luke smirked. "Best to keep you wonderin'."

EGOS & EXCESS

CHAPTER 13

By noon, the heat index in Beebe had reached well over 100 degrees.

Fuzzy Rose & Sons Gun Shop was abuzz with activity even though the signs in the window and out by the road clearly said *Closed.* One shop employee changed the marquee to read: *It may look like we're open but we're not. Closed today. Open tomorrow.*

The front door was locked; the shades were pulled low. The back door was monitored by J.D., a brawny, muscular, 6-foot-7 bouncer with a shaven head and long beard. Intimidation was obviously paramount.

The back parking lot was filled with 17 or 18 vehicles of all makes and models.

A catering truck was unloaded of foil food trays at the back entrance. The driver consulted with J.D. "Where do ya want me to park this truck during your event?"

The bouncer pointed. His baritone voice rumbled, "It'll have to be way out yonder. And y'all have to stay with the truck. Cain't none of y'all be in the building. It's a private meetin'."

The driver explained, "But we have ongoing nondisclosure agreements with y'all."

"Don't matter none. I said you cain't be in the buildin'. Just drop off the food and leave."

The driver obeyed. "Okay. No problem. Let me check that everything is inside and my people are coming out."

"Just do it. Ya got ten minutes. And just so ya know, those NDAs still count. Ya don't say one word about what or who any of you see here today."

The driver shuddered. "Yes, sir. Absolutely."

***

Sometime later, all the invitees were finally inside the gun shop, and the door was locked. J.D. stood watch outside.

Some display cases were pushed aside to make room for long folding tables. One entire countertop that ran the length of the shop was converted to a makeshift serving table. On top of it were trays and aluminum serving containers filled with fried catfish, frog legs, shrimp, hushpuppies, salad, beans, potato salad, turnip greens, cornbread, and many other Southern dishes. The aromas were incredible.

Other tables were set up with folding chairs for people to sit in during the meeting. Small signs were placed every 2 or 3 feet on the tables that read: *Absolutely NO note taking, NO photos, NO videos, nothing! Punishment is a bitch!*

Attendees sniffed the smells. They waited patiently to line up and dig into the food.

Eventually, Searcy came out from the back room. "Hello, everyone! I want to welcome y'all to this very important meetin'!"

The chatter died down.

He continued. "I'm gonna go ahead and let y'all get your plates and sit down while the food is hot. But first, we need to give thanks. For that, I'm gonna turn it over to Pastor Riley."

The pastor stood in front of the food line. "Everyone, please bow your heads. Thank you."

He speculated for a moment, then continued. "Dear Lord, we thank You for bringin' us together here today to discuss Your Will and purpose for our lives, and how You want us to go about protectin' our own while also spreadin' Your love and grace."

Some fidgeted and shuffled their feet.

One man said, "Amen, Lord."

The pastor continued. "Dear Lord, we know that, to some outsiders, it appears that we harbor hate in our hearts but You, oh God, know that's just not true. We love all people, all races, all genders. But God, we also know that accordin' to Your Word, we must also protect what You Yourself have established here for us and handed down to us from our forefathers and many generations of strong, hardworking, God-fearin' ancestors who came to this land before us. And accordin' to Your Word, the law of the land followed suit, in the Second Amendment of the United States of America. So, dear Lord, we are here today to receive Your blessin's and Your Will for us to protect those laws and advance new ones, that will modernize where we need to go from here. Thank You, Jesus. And now, we also thank You for this food. Please bless it to fill us and nourish our bodies to give us strength for what lies ahead. Amen."

The crowd murmured, "Amen." Then they lined up, took plates and utensils, and filled their plates.

Once everyone was seated, Searcy took the helm again. "Somebody take J.D. a plate and a sweet tea." He stood tall and spoke loudly. "Okay, everybody. Let's get started. I need y'all to pipe down and listen up. We can't be here all day."

He looked around the room and, with an annoyed smirk on his face, waited for silence and respect.

When the room was finally quiet, he continued. "Housekeepin'. First of all, I'm sure everyone has seen the signs on the tables and will abide by those rules. Any questions about it?"

No hands went up as people enjoyed their food.

Searcy went on. "Good. Next, my older brother, Fuzzy, whom y'all know, had a self-inflicted accident and is now in a nursin' home. He sends his best to all of you."

One voice rang out, "He didn't shoot himself, did he?"

Another voice joked, "With a cap gun?"

The crowd laughed.

Searcy answered, "No. It wasn't nothin' like that. But his health has been declinin' for some time. It was overdue that he had solid 24/7 medical care. So for now, I'll be handlin' his duties as president of the company."

Another voice from the crowd rose up. "Give him our love, Searcy!"

"I will. Thank ya for your wishes. Next, I'm gonna go around and introduce everyone out loud. Let's make this our roll call."

Searcy authoritatively pointed to each person as he called out their names. In response, each person promptly waved their hand.

"Pastor Riley, of course."

"Duvall Richards, NFO president."

"Earl Burns, NFO lobbyist."

"Charlie Burns, entrepreneur and NFO supporter."

"Henry Shoemaker, state representative and lawmaker."

"Lisa Turner, his intern."

"Conrad Davis, radio host, NFO supporter, and a voice we all know and love."

"Pamela O'Brien, church secretary and secretary for these meetings. She's officially the only person allowed to take notes."

"Deputy Halp, White County Sheriff's Department, out of uniform for this meeting, NFO supporter, and our friend."

Searcy took a deep breath and continued. "There's Fuzzy's two boys over there, Willie and Bobby Joe, and Bobby Joe's son, John Mark. Then there's my boy Rhett and his son, Luke. My other son, Cletus, is out at a gun show with Toad today. Finally, behind the displays servin' y'all food today, is my wife, Mabel."

Searcy fumbled with a paper in his hand until he saw Mabel give him a stern glare. He looked around the room, stewed, then continued. "Oh yes. And lastly, there's Dorene Toller back over there. Didn't see ya."

He took a drink of tea and continued. "I think y'all know why we are here today, but let's address a few issues that all kinda led up to it."

Mabel loudly banged a metal spoon on the side of an aluminum pan, making it sound like the pop of a gun.

Searcy was momentarily distracted. He looked out over the crowd. "First issue. I think we've all been noticin' the sudden appearance of foreigners movin' in locally. You see them at the store, at the colleges, at the base, and out in public, generally. Now, some of these folks are our friends. Some are not. Anyone want to address this?" He took this chance to fix himself a plate of food.

Deputy Halp recounted, "I think we should be concerned 'cause like you said, they're not all our friends. And if the influx keeps comin' in, where does it ever stop? I mean there's only so much the Sheriff's Department can do. We can hassle them, give them tickets at every turn, but then what?"

John Mark added, "Yeah. And what if that doesn't work? Are we just gonna let them infiltrate our whole community and take over completely? Their values may not be like ours."

Pastor Riley threw in his two cents. "My biggest concern is that we, ourselves, get lost in who we are. What am I supposed to do when they come to me wantin' to intermarry? I don't believe races should mix. The Bible says they should stay with their own kind. I think the reason God wants it that way, is so that we don't lose our heritage, our culture, and who we are as a people. So, am I gonna have to marry them or what?"

Duvall nudged his pricey Stetson 100X El Presidente cowboy hat with the tip of his finger as his deep, gravelly voice piped up. "Excuse me, Pastor, but you're the one that has the ear of God. Why are you askin' us?"

Pastor Riley reacted. "With all due respects, Mr. Richards, sometimes the ear of God responds back through the thoughts and ideas of those in solidarity with one another."

"Well taken."

Henry commented, "Being a political expert, my concern, of course, is that they take jobs away from local residents and deplete our resources. In effect, they could cost us all millions each year. That's not to mention how they could change our politics when they start votin'. What do we do when their numbers are substantial enough and they start votin' liberal? If that happens, that could cost you your guns and your business."

Halp questioned, "And what about all the crime they bring with them? We don't know who they are. How are you gonna feel if one of them rapes your little girl and then hops a flight back to wherever they came from?"

Searcy stopped picking at his food. "I think you all bring up valid concerns. Since I don't personally have any answers to any of these things, what do y'all suggest we do to control the flow?"

248.

Conrad's voice reverberated throughout the building. "Every single one of you knows what you have to do! You have to run 'em out! Now! Before they take root and ya never get rid of 'em! Now I'm not a full-time local here, but I've seen this scenario goin' down all over the country! You'll be sorry if you don't take action immediately!"

Searcy continued eating. "And how do you propose we do that without drawin' too much attention?"

Conrad continued, "By God, run 'em out! Whatever it takes! Give 'em speedin' tickets 'til they turn blue! The Mexicans don't belong here! The blacks don't belong here! The Asians don't belong here! Get your preachers to put out a warnin' from the pulpit! That's where folks are really gonna perk up and listen 'cause they don't want their souls to go to hell!"

He stood and pointed his finger around the room. "Every single one of you has to use whatever platform you have— influence, manipulate, gouge if ya have to—to make this happen! I'm tellin' ya, if you wait too late, you'll be sorry! If you're a preacher, your platform is religion, and on and on. The other thing is guns! Use 'em while ya have the right to use 'em! That's what this is all about after all, isn't it? Guns and God!"

At this, Conrad received a standing ovation. The crowd clapped, whistled, whooped, and yelled.

Jazzed, he continued, "Our forefathers founded this country on Christian principles and expected that we would fight for it as hard as they did! That's why they wrote the Second Amendment! That's not rocket science! I mean, come on! We know why we're all here! We're preparin' for civil war!"

Straightaway, Duvall's voice rattled the rafters. "Sit down, Conrad. You're grandstanding."

Conrad shouted, "You want grandstandin'?!" He flung his chair high into the air. It crashed down on one of the display cases with food on it. Then, without flinching, he barged toward the bathroom, fist-punched a hole in the door before he entered it, and slammed it shut.

Duvall proceeded in a calm collected manner. "Cooler heads will prevail."

He then stood and looked around the room at the crowd. "I know it's hard to not react based on emotions, but folks, you're not even trying to put your thinking caps on right now. What's the one thing that I haven't heard anyone elaborate on here today? Oh, Henry brought it up but, he didn't elaborate on it in a positive light." He peered into their eyes and commanded their attention. "Gun sales."

Someone in the crowd said, "Ohhhhh."

Duvall put his hand to his chin and paced to the end of the table. "Think on this. These foreigners, people of color, whatever you want to call them, they are going to need guns, especially if they are going to try to live here in the South. Right? And who's going to profit from that? You are. Each and every one of you."

Charlie spoke up. "But what if they start shootin' us?"

Duvall twirled around and answered, "Then we get what we want just that much quicker: all-out civil war."

Henry snorted, "And guns sales soar!"

"Right. Now, you all keep telling me that you're bringing me here to discuss your preparations for this war, but none of you are talking like the thinkers and leaders that you're going to need to be to get it done correctly. All I hear is bitching and whining and more questions that are all just superficial crap." He sat back in his chair and gave up the floor.

A small applaud erupted for Duvall as Conrad reentered the room. He stayed by the back wall.

Searcy stood before the crowd. "We have a couple of other issues to discuss, and then it belongs to you all. Next, is the little problem we have named Bert Black."

Bobby Joe shouted, "Kill him!"

Charlie yelled, "Agreed!"

Duvall commented, "You all don't learn nothin'."

Searcy added, "Okay. That's an option but, as Duvall said, you're thinkin' with your emotions. Is there a better way to use this situation to our benefit? Maybe a calmer, more level-headed option that would serve us better?"

Henry asked, "Maybe use him as bait or leverage with our vendors?"

Duvall smiled. "Excellent idea."

Searcy continued, "Great. Let's parse out those details outside of this meeting, mull it over, and get back in touch with the best way to do it. We need a great plan put together pretty quickly."

He took a drink of tea, wiped his mouth, and moved on. "Next. The sheriff has been inquirin' about the identity of one known as Barley Pop."

The entire room looked at Charlie.

He squirmed and sunk down in his chair. "Shit."

Searcy admonished him. "What the hell, Charlie?! Number one, ya can't just go flyin' off the handle and takin' shit on your own way! Number two, as far as I know, ya didn't ask what we thought about ya blowin' up the detention center! Number three, ya didn't kill Bert, ya let him escape!"

Earl winced.

Searcy strutted over and stood next to Charlie. "Number four, ya sure as fuck don't hang around to see what happened so someone can spot you!"

Charlie broke out in a cold sweat. "I'm sorry. I won't do it again. I won't."

Searcy assured, "You sure the hell won't!" With that, he jerked a handgun out of his pocket, shot Charlie in the head point blank, and quickly walked away.

Charlie fell onto the hard floor.

A deafening silence flooded over the room, except for the sounds of the dying man's throat gurgling loudly. His hands twitched erratically, and his legs contorted with spasms.

Earl began to cry and mourn as he hovered over his brother's dying body. "Charlie? Oh, Charlie. What am I gonna do with you now? I can't fix it this time."

J.D. poked his head inside the door momentarily. He asked Searcy, "Everything alright, sir?"

"When this place clears out, take his body down to Palarm Creek. Throw it to the gators."

"Sure thing," J.D. promised as he closed the door. Once outside, he then walked out across the parking lot and sent the catering truck away.

Most of the attendees expeditiously and nervously dispersed, got into their vehicles, and drove off.

Inside, as Mabel and Dorene cleaned off the tables and put the food away, the Rose boys put the tables and chairs back into the storage room.

Willie went into the restroom, closed the door, and locked it. He then proceeded to throw up in the toilet as quietly as he could. He almost choked in doing so.

Meanwhile, the pastor prayed over Charlie's dead body. Duvall and Henry dragged Earl away from his brother. They took him into the back meeting room to settle him down.

J.D. came inside the building with plastic gloves on, put the body into a body bag, and carried it out to a van that was backed up to the door. He mumbled, "Not my favorite part of this job."

***

Searcy soon joined the men in the back meeting room. He locked the door and shook his head. "I'm sorry I had to do that, Earl."

The grief-stricken man struggled to sit upright and rein in his emotions. He could not speak but nodded his trembling head.

Henry commented, "I hope to God I never piss you off."

Searcy contested, "Had nothin' to do with pissin' me off. He went rogue and got sloppy. If he got caught, we all got caught. Our mission would fail."

Henry asked, "But did you have to do it like that, in front of everyone?"

Searcy answered, "Optics. Sorry again, Earl. Ya see, now there's not a person in that room that won't perform flawlessly. And if ya keep 'em scared, they'll respect ya."

Earl stared off into space with tears rolling down his face.

Henry replied, "My God, you sound like a lawyer."

Duvall walked to the refrigerator and got a soda. He popped the top and paced back. "So Mr. Rose, are you king of the empire now that you got your older brother put into a nursing home? Let me guess, you've got his power of attorney too."

"I do have the POA and no, I'm not king yet. His son Bobby Joe is next in line. However, he's strugglin' with the loss of his son right now, so he can't function in that capacity at this time."

"Then who's next? I'm asking so I know who I'm dealing with."

"Willie's next after Bobby Joe. Those two sons, then John Mark."

"And what's wrong with Willie and John Mark?"

"Nothin' is wrong with them."

Duvall chuckled. "Yet."

"Willie went off and married a liberal. I think she's changin' him or, he may be doin' it to himself. Either way, he may have no interest in the family business before too long."

Henry asked, "That's what you're hopin' for?"

Searcy stated adamantly, "Let me assure you men, I hold all the cards. I am the one you will be dealin' with from here on out."

***

Kyle and Emily shuffled in the front door of their home as Jim slept on the sofa. Laura was reading a book in her recliner. Emily closed the door gently.

Laura whispered, "Hi kids. Have fun?"

Emily beamed, "Oh yeah. A lot of fun. I'm going upstairs to rest for a while."

Kyle said, "Hey, you know, I have to go to therapy. How is that going to work?"

Laura whispered, "I don't know. Why don't you call the sheriff and see if maybe an officer can take you this time?"

Kyle pointed to her. "Great idea. I'll go call."

"Shhhh. Your dad's sleeping."

Jim fake-snored loudly and smiled. "No, I'm not."

Laura threw an accent pillow that hit him in the head.

***

The late-afternoon traffic in the town of Searcy was backed up for several blocks on a double-yellow-line in the business district. Drivers were frustrated and honked for it to start moving. Everyone wanted to get where they were going. It wasn't normal for a small rural town to have such a backup.

Needless to say, most could not see around the vehicles in front of them or that there was something in the middle of their lane just ahead. One old, fragile obstacle prevented them from a normal weekday drive.

It was Fuzzy, dressed in his signature blue jeans, western shirt, leather hat, and cowboy boots. He still donned two black eyes and a band-aid across his nose as he sat in a golf cart that had broken down in the street.

One middle-aged man tried to help him push it out of the road, but Fuzzy refused.

"Sir, just let me push it to the side so the cars can get on by."

Fuzzy yelled, "Hell no! Help me get it runnin' so I can drive it! If you push it over there, I'll never get goin' again!"

A young male commuter rolled down his window and shouted, "Hey! Fred Flintstone! Yabba dabba doo that hunk of shit off the road, would ya!"

Fuzzy curled his fist and waved it high in the air. "I'll yabba dabba doo your ass, you skinny little fart! Your daddy must've suffered small-squirt syndrome when he laid your momma! You little wannabe shit!"

The man trying to help him said, "Sir. If ya don't let me help you get this thing off the street, we're both liable to get hit and killed!"

"Don't give a damn! I'm goin' home!"

"Where do ya live?"

"Beebe!"

"Do ya want me to give you a ride?"

Fuzzy stopped briefly. His demeanor changed. "I'd like that very much!"

"Okay, sir, but we have to get this thing off the road! All these cars want to go home too!"

Fuzzy decided to help push the golf cart to the side of the road. Once there, the traffic began to flow.

The kind helper asked, "Where did ya get this thing anyway? Is it yours?"

"Nah! I borrowed it!"

"From who?"

"The golf course back yonder."

"You stole it?"

Fuzzy scrunched his face. "Nah. More like, just borrowed it for a bit."

The man suddenly became nervous. "Hey, listen. I'm real sorry, but I've gotta go!" He ran back to his truck.

Fuzzy walked after him. "Wait! You said you'd give me a ride!"

"I'm sorry, sir! I can't have anything to do with aiding and abetting!"

"Aidin' and abettin' what? You don't think I can pay for it if I want to? Listen here, kiddo, I got more money than Gawwd!" Fuzzy bellowed.

The man drove off, leaving Fuzzy on the side of the road. The old man stomped the ground in rage. In fact, he threw an extremely public temper tantrum.

"Well, I'll be goddamn! You lyin' sack of shit! I just want to go home!" He punched his fists in the air. "Come back here, you whiny little son of a whore dog! I'll kick your ass!"

Fuzzy swung, punched, and kicked into the air. He spun around, slammed into something like a ton of bricks, and landed on his ass on the ground. He looked up and saw a tall broad silhouette standing in front of him. He squinted his eyes to see.

"Feelin' spry today, Mr. Rose?" the police officer said.

"Ohhhh shit."

"Sir, I'm gonna take you back to the nursin' home now. And we're gonna return that borrowed property back to its owner."

As the officer helped Fuzzy to his feet, he pleaded, "Can I at least get my whiskey out of it first?"

***

Jim was still resting on the sofa when his cellphone rang. He looked at it and appeared pleased.

"Hey, Scott. How are you doing?"

Laura stopped reading for a moment. "Tell him I said hi."

Jim nodded. "Hey, Laura says hi." He paused briefly. "Um, this isn't really a good time right now, Scott. I mean, we've just got a lot going on. Why don't you try me back in a couple of days, and let's make a plan for later in the summer?"

Laura whispered, "They want to visit?"

"Oh, we'd love to see you, Robyn, Carol, and Ed! It's just the timing."

Laura complained, "Oh my God."

"Oh, you're all going to share an RV on a road trip here. I get it. But really, give us a few days, okay? We just need a little bit more notice."

Laura leaned her head back on the chair. "Jesus."

"I will." He drew a long breath. "Okay. Chat later. 'Bye."

He disconnected the call, waved his phone in the air, and smiled at Laura. "They want to come visit." He put the phone down. "Yeah."

"What are we going to do? We're on lockdown. They can't come here now."

"I know," he said. "I've got a few days to think of something. Jesus. What next?"

Laura warned, "Never, ever ask what's next."

***

A couple of hours later, Fuzzy sat in his rocking chair at the nursing home. He was despondent. Out of sheer boredom and a stroke of luck, he looked out of his window. There, he saw Searcy's truck pull into the parking lot.

Instantly, Fuzzy had a rush of blood go to his head. His throat began to close up tight. He panicked and pulled the curtains closed. He closed the door to his room so he could hear it click when it opened. Then he undressed, put his pajamas on, turned off the light, and wriggled into bed.

Shortly, the door clicked and opened. In walked Searcy. "Fuzzy? You awake?"

The old man lay still in his bed.

Searcy turned on a lamp and touched his brother's arm. "Fuzzy. I need ya to wake up for a minute. The nurse told me to give ya this pill. They told me what you did today."

Fuzzy played opossum for a few seconds. Then he mumbled, "They gave me a shot."

Searcy put the capsule to his mouth. "I know, but you're supposed to take this too."

Fuzzy mumbled again, "Okay." He took the capsule into his mouth with a sip of water from the glass Searcy held up to him.

"Okay. I'm gonna let you rest now. See you tomorrow."

Fuzzy remained quiet until his brother turned out the light and left the room. He listened for the door to click shut. Then he spat out the capsule and put it underneath his pillow.

Cautiously, he waited until he heard Searcy's big truck engine drive away. He sat up in his bed. "That fucker."

***

A little later, Kyle had finished his therapy session and was at the Harp's Food Store in Cabot. He paced the aisles with his police escort. Some people stared at the two; others simply didn't seem to care at all.

Kyle apologized to the officer. "Hey, listen. I'm really sorry. My mom wanted me to pick up a few things since we were out and about."

"Not a problem."

"Thanks, man."

As they proceeded up and down the aisles, Kyle tossed several things into a shopping basket. He checked his list a couple of times. Then, as he picked up a bottle of ketchup and placed it in the basket, he noticed a man beside him going for the same brand name.

Out of friendliness, Kyle said, "That's the best brand right there. Best-tasting—" He stalled when he looked the man in the face.

It was Walter Kingsman, aged about 30 years, with a salt-and-pepper beard.

Kyle stumbled backward into the police officer.

Walter was gracious as he walked away. "Thanks for the tip."

The officer asked, "Do ya know him?"

Kyle was confused. "I thought... No. I don't know."

"Forget the groceries. Let's get ya home now. I don't feel good about this."

Kyle and the officer hurriedly left the store.

Once outside, the officer said, "I'll have another deputy pick up those items for ya. Please, get into the cruiser quickly."

Kyle was confused and speechless.

CHAPTER 14

Wednesday, July 17, 2013. During the early morning
hours, near Pedestal Rocks and Kings Bluff Trailhead in the
Ozark National Forest, a young couple parked their SUV,
grabbed their backpacks, and scurried off.

In the excitement of getting their hike started, they
forgot to lock up their vehicle. It was not a smart move,
although understandable considering the immense beauty of
the area with its incredible bluffs and waterfalls. It was
exciting to see nature at its finest.

As soon as the couple hightailed it down the trail, Bert
sneaked up to the vehicle and raided it for anything that
might benefit him, including the young man's wallet.

In all, he made away with $336.36, one paper map of the
State of Arkansas, two small granola bars, and two bottles of
water. He tossed it all into his backpack and rushed off into
the woods.

***

Willie and Catherine woke up in a tent by the side of a
small shallow lake. They yawned, had passionate sex,
laughed, and cooked breakfast together over a fire pit.

After they ate and had coffee, they stripped naked and went for a swim. They teased one another and made love again in the lake.

A little later, they huddled by the fire with blankets wrapped around themselves.

Willie whispered, "I love you so much."

"I love you too, sweetheart."

He peered into the fire. "I think Searcy is gonna do somethin' to try to pull us apart."

"Oh silly. Why do you think that?"

"Because he never wanted me to marry you. He said you and your family were too liberal. He said it would change me."

"Did he really say that?"

"Yep. And I think that he will do somethin'. I don't trust him."

"Willie. You're scaring me. Don't talk like that."

"I don't want to scare ya, hon, but I don't want to hide it from ya either. Ya need to know. What if I just disappear one day?"

"Oh, shut up. Don't say that."

"Ya never know."

"Mabel would. I'll ask her."

Willie panicked. "No! Don't ask her! Are you nuts? She'll tell him everything, and then we're really in trouble."

Catherine was bewildered. "Willie. Calm down. Mabel is my friend. I can talk to her."

"Cath, you don't understand. Mabel is not your friend. Only on the surface. Please. Don't say a word to her. Promise me."

"Okay. I promise."

"Good. Now let's not talk about it anymore. I want to get back to lovin'."

He kissed her on the neck. Then he gently leaned her back on the blanket where they made love again.

***

At the Barton home, the family went about their different tasks while snacking on breakfast munchies. Between the boredom and cabin fever, their attitudes and personalities were beginning to rub badly on each other.

Kyle and Emily snapped back and forth as Laura and Jim found ways to keep their distance for the sake of sanity.

The kids eventually retreated to their bedrooms and closed their doors. Laura camped out on her daybed to read another book. By this time, she was on, oh say, book number five since their lockdown.

Jim stayed in the living room, sitting on his bed—the sofa—and read a newspaper. When his cellphone rang, he reacted with utter delight. "Hello!"

On the other end, Sheriff White replied, "Hello. You sound chipper."

"You know, it's just nice to hear another human voice. This house-lockdown stuff is beginning to make us all batty."

"Well, I'm callin' to let ya know that I think you guys can all go out safely now. We found tracks and traces of Bert's movements as well as a witness who places him far away from Beebe."

"Oh, that's great news! I mean, not great that you didn't catch him yet, but great that he's far from here."

"You all still need to be careful though. This isn't over."

"Okay. So can I get any details? Where do you think he is?"

The sheriff hesitated. "We think he may have gone into the Ozark National Forest. Nothin' is absolutely certain, of course, until we locate him for sure, but we have found some evidence. In the meantime, I think it is safe for you and your family to go on with your lives as long as ya don't travel too far right now. Do not go out alone, always lock your doors and windows, and make sure to let others know when you're goin' out and how long you'll be gone. If ya do that, you should be good to go."

Jim sighed with relief. "Oh, that sounds great! Thank you!"

"One more thing, Jim. Stay in touch with me if you see or hear anything I should know about."

"Guaranteed, sir. Thanks again."

Jim took great joy in notifying his family of the good news: They were no longer prisoners in their own home. They were ecstatic and shouted with joy.

However, within moments, Jim's phone rang again. He moved out to the patio to take the call.

"Hello, Bobby Joe. How are you doing?"

"Good mornin', Jim. I guess ya got some good news this mornin'?"

"Actually, we did. Thank God. Hey, listen, I'm sorry I couldn't help you out when you called before."

"It's okay. I understand. There aren't too many folks that I trust. My own damned family cain't even be trusted. I know ya won't repeat this."

"Oh God, I won't repeat anything, Bobby Joe."

"I don't think ya will. And I need a friend like that right now."

Jim smiled. "And me too."

Bobby Joe continued, "I'd rather go find Bert, but this is more pressing at the moment. I need to ask ya for a favor if I can."

Jim poised, "Sure. Go for it. I'll do whatever I can."

"I can't even get in and out of the shop anymore without Searcy watchin' me. I need ya to go there for me. Levi set us up with a system, so I can unlock the doors and turn off the cameras and security system from my cellphone. So you're all good there. It'll be easy. There's a file on the iMac that I need ya to put on a flash drive for me while no one else is there."

Jim hesitated with uncertainty. "Um... Okay."

Bobby Joe continued, "It won't be hard and it won't take ya five to ten minutes, in all. No one will ever know you were there."

"Let me think about this."

"Ya said you'd help me, Jim, whatever I needed."

"Alright. I did say that."

"Now, the shop is closed 'til noon. All the staff is in a meetin' in Little Rock this mornin'. All my family is gonna be with me at the shootin' range 'til then too. I'll keep them busy and make sure they are. Do ya have an extra flash drive on you?"

Jim thought for a moment. "Sure. Yes, I do."

"Good. So, you'll need to park down the road by the liquor store. There's always a lot of cars there so ya won't be out of place. Just make sure you do go in and buy something to throw off any suspicion. Then walk down to the shop. At precisely 9:15 a.m., I will shut off the outside cameras so you can walk in through the parking lot, without being seen. You'll have two minutes to get to the door when I will unlock it. Understand?"

Jim answered nervously, "Yes."

"Once you get inside, manually lock the door behind you, just in case. Then, don't mess around. Get over to the computer and download the file called *Bobby Joe*. It's nested in the folder on the desktop called *BJs home files*. The password to the folder is *746mindyourownshit**. Once ya have it downloaded, delete the folder. Any questions?"

Jim groaned with anxiety. "Can I ask what this is for?"

"Didn't I tell ya, I don't trust my family?"

"Yes, I guess you did."

Bobby Joe continued, "I'll explain it to ya later when I get the flash drive from ya. Aw, hell. I'll tell you a short version now since ya deserve some kind of answer."

"That'd be nice. Thank you."

"My wife, Mary, is Mabel's first cousin. There's ten years difference between 'em, but they both belong to the Carter family. Do ya know that name?"

Jim ruminated. "I think I remember them from growing up around Heber Springs."

"Yes. That'd be them. Well, they're a powerful family with a lot of pull in places I cain't talk about. That's why my Uncle Searcy married Mabel. He saw my daddy buildin' a great business off of gun sales when he got back from the war, and he wanted some kind of power too. See, my daddy is a decorated war hero. Searcy, he got out of the draft 'cause of bone spurs. Can ya believe that?"

Jim muttered. "Oh wow."

"Yeah. Bullshit right there. And if he's the one that got my son Levi killed just to blame it on Bert, I'm gonna kill the bastard myself."

"Why would he do that?"

"Maybe, to get Bert out of the picture. Maybe, to make the Carters be afraid of him. More and more, that's what I think. He wants power. Always has. And, by the way, I'm next to inherit the Rose empire after my daddy is gone. So there's good reason for Searcy to try to take me out too. That's why this is so urgent."

"Okay, but what does that have to do with the computer exactly?"

"That, I won't tell ya other than I've got files that I need off of there asap."

Jim conceded. "Alright. I want to try to help you as much as I can."

"Thank ya for doin' this. I will pay ya back later on."

"No worries." Jim repeated, "So, 9:15 this morning and *746mindyourownshit**?"

"Yes. Good memory."

They synchronized the time on their phones and said goodbye.

After Jim hung up, he mused, "What the hell have I gotten myself into?"

***

At the nursing home, Fuzzy sat alone at a table in the dining room with a plate of over-easy eggs, bacon, and toast sitting in front of him. He eyed the food and poked the eggs until all the runny yolk bled out.

A nursing assistant walked by and noticed what he was doing. "Now, Fuzzy! That's no way to treat your food! There are starvin' kids in China who'd love to have what you do!"

Fuzzy grumbled, "Then ship this shit to China! Hell, that's where it came from anyway! Send it back!"

A gruff, worn-out-looking elderly man of about 75 overheard the conversation, struggled to push himself out of his chair, and sauntered across the room with a cane. When he reached Fuzzy's table, he bent over, and carefully studied his face.

Fuzzy bellowed, "What in the hell are you lookin' at, you old fart? Get your shit-ugly mug out of my face!"

Another resident warned, "Uh-oh. Here we go."

The crippled, old fellow let out a loud, baritone, belly laugh that rippled the airwaves throughout the dining room. Even the cooks in the kitchen poked their heads out to see what was happening.

One nursing assistant exclaimed, "I have never seen him laugh like that. Who knew?"

Fuzzy almost flipped backward in his chair. Annoyed, he yelled, "What the hell?!"

As the old man continued laughing, Fuzzy got a suspicious look on his face and stood to his feet. He took a closer glance at the old man and appeared amused.

"Well, I'll be damned!" Fuzzy roared. "If it ain't Hugh Tapper! Gawwd damn!"

Hugh calmed his laughter. "What the hell is right! Why the hell are you here, Fuzzy Rose?"

Fuzzy wisecracked, "I'm an old fucker just like you are, that's why! Sit down here with me! Tell me where ya been all these years!"

Two elderly women rose from their table and bustled down the hallway. One of them said, "Well, I never!"

Hugh slowly and carefully sat down. "Oh, after 'Nam, I moved with my wife to California where her family was. Eventually, they all died off one by one. We figured we'd move back to Northwest Arkansas since Cali was gettin' too expensive for our kind of livin'. Years later, I lost her too. Then my health went south, and the kids put me up in here so they could keep a check on me from time to time."

"I had no idea whatever happened to you. I tried lookin' for ya several times, but no luck."

"What about you? What've you been up to since the war?"

Fuzzy explained, "Aw, I started a business. Then Anna popped out a couple of boys. Got them all growed up, and they had kids. Too many damned kids."

They laughed together.

Fuzzy continued, "Don't you ever tell them I said it, but I do love 'em to pieces. Cain't let 'em know it though, or they'll bleed ya dry!"

Laughter erupted again.

One of the nursing assistants came over. "I ain't never heard either one of you laugh like this. You two know each other?"

Fuzzy said, "Know each other? Hell, we was in 'Nam together!"

"Yep. Boy, did we go through some shit."

The assistant took a place at the table. "Really? I'd love to hear some stories."

Fuzzy declined, "Nah."

However, Hugh decided to oblige. "Ya know, this man right here, he's a war hero."

The assistant gaped at Fuzzy. "You are?"

Fuzzy fidgeted in his seat. "Hugh. Ya shouldn't do that."

Nevertheless, his old friend went on. "Well, hell. Ya didn't think they called him Fuzzy just because he's a hairy bastard."

The assistant muttered, "Um. Yeah, we kinda did."

"Yep. He is hairy! But he's also known for blurrin' the lines. Let me tell you a story."

Fuzzy's face lit up bright red as he drew up a hawker and spat it into his plate. "Hugh!"

"I can still see it to this day, as vivid as ever. It's a ghostly memory, and often visits me when I'm tryin' to sleep at night."

"Dammit, Hugh."

"This man right here went into enemy lines knowin' damn well he would probably die. He went in there to save a friend, a black fella named Theo. Yep. Ol' Fuzzy came back out with that bloody mess of a man draped over his shoulders, runnin' like a bat out of hell. Bombs were droppin' all over the place. Debris was fallin' all around him, but he didn't stop, didn't even give it a second thought.

268.

He just kept runnin'. Me and the rest of our battalion waited for 'em behind the tree line."

Enchanted, the assistant listened with wide eyes. "What happened then?"

"This damned bomb dropped and threw soil and shit all into the air. We lost sight of 'em completely. Thought we lost 'em. Then, in a minute, we saw this fuzzy image comin' through it all. That fucker wasn't dead. Ya couldn't kill him. He was still runnin' like a wild animal that got its ass bit, 'til he got to us. It was a damned sight to see. Luke Porter Rose. Fuzzy. Blurrin' lines and cheatin' death. He ain't just hairy! He really earned that name!" Hugh laughed.

When they looked at Fuzzy, he had folded his arms on the table. His face was buried within them.

Hugh poked his arm. "I'll bet you're still cheatin' death, ain't ya?"

Eventually, Fuzzy lifted his head. He rolled his eyes and looked straight at the assistant. "Now it's my turn."

Hugh begged, "Wait now, Fuzzy."

"There was this cute little Vietnamese girl that used to sneak into Hugh's bed at night, oh, maybe two to three nights a week."

"Fuzzy!"

The assistant laughed. "This doesn't sound like a hero story."

Fuzzy exclaimed, "The hell it's not! He saved us all from gettin' the crabs!"

***

The Rose men set up their targets and lined up at the shooting range. They didn't wait for turns but fired at will until everyone was done. Then, they went at it again and again, in between bouts of slapping mosquitos.

Bobby Joe encouraged them to do better each time, declaring that no one could afford to miss the shot when they finally located Bert.

At 9:12 a.m., he stepped away from the platform and pulled out his cellphone. He monitored the security cameras at the shop and saw nothing. At precisely 9:15 a.m., he shut it all down and unlocked the door.

***

Jim quickly entered the shop, locked the door, rushed over to the iMac, logged in the password, popped in the flash drive, and began Bobby Joe's download.

As it processed, he saw the folder named *Year of Meteors*. He distinctly remembered Levi's words and decided to peek in the folder.

Surprisingly, it accepted the same password.

Once in there, he found files, letters, correspondence, maps, election secrets, and other incriminating information regarding the Rose family as well as politicians, foreign gun smugglers, other higher-up people, and the conspiracy to overthrow the government and begin a new civil war.

Jim's eyes were glued to the information so much so that he ignored the download when it was completed.

Then, he decided that he would quickly download the *Year of Meteors* folder as well. He thought he would sort it out later from Bobby Joe's file.

As the rainbow wheel spun round and round, he anxiously shook his legs.

"Come on. Hurry up."

***

At the shooting range, Bobby Joe waited for the time to be right to turn everything back on at the shop. He wanted to give Jim plenty of extra time to be out of the way just in case something tripped him up a little longer. After all, he didn't want to bring it all back online for Searcy to get the ping on his phone that someone was there.

Bobby Joe paced around, watched the guys shoot, and cheered them on. Then suddenly, he noticed that Searcy was no longer there. "Where did Searcy go?"

Luke said, "He forgot somethin' at the shop. He'll be back in a little bit."

Bobby Joe broke out in a cold sweat. His nervous pace grew long and hard.

***

At the gun shop, the downloads finally finished. Jim deleted Bobby Joe's folder, as instructed. He then ejected the flash drive, quickly jerked it out of the port, and closed the open windows on the computer.

Like an earthquake slamming the building, a loud truck engine pulled up quickly. Jim hurried and hid behind a display case that had a huge black cloth over it.

A vehicle door slammed shut, and the back door unlocked with a powerful jolt.

Sweat beaded across Jim's face and head as he held his breath. He did not move one muscle.

From behind the counter, Searcy grabbed an AK-47 and ammo to go with it. Just as he started to go back out the door, he noticed the light on the iMac shining brightly.

Jim froze stiff as Searcy's heavy boots plodded closer to him. His face turned heavy shades of red. He noticed dark blood pooled just underneath a display case next to him. He squinted his eyes closed and prayed.

Searcy griped, "Goddamned kids. Can't do nothin' right." He shut the computer off and charged out the back door.

Jim heard the door lock. He waited patiently and then breathed. He whispered, "I've got to get out of here."

As soon as he heard the truck drive away, he sped out the back door and into the woods at the closest point possible.

***

At the shooting range, Bobby Joe decided he could wait no longer and turned the security cameras back on. When he could not see Jim for a few seconds, he locked the doors and reset the admin settings.

In an attempt to cover his distraction from shooting, he rushed right back up to the platform, grabbed his gun, and fired. Considering his grief and strange behavior of late, no one suspected anything out of the ordinary.

Within a short while, Searcy returned. He walked up to Bobby Joe with his AK-47 in hand. "Those damned kids forgot to turn the computer off at the shop again. Talk to them, or I will."

"Don't press me, Searcy. My fuse is short."

"I'm sorry, Bobby Joe. But shit has to get done right. Talk to them, or I will have to."

Bobby Joe scoffed, "I will."

Searcy started to walk off but turned back again. "Oh. One other thing. I don't know what Levi did with the security system, but it's not workin' right on my phone. Can ya figure out what that's all about?"

"Are you sayin' Levi did somethin'?"

"I didn't say that, Bobby Joe. I said it isn't workin' right on my phone. Jesus. Can ya not take everything so damned personal?"

Bobby Joe glared at him with contempt.

Searcy removed his sunglasses. "I'm sorry. I didn't mean it to sound that way."

Not another word was spoken.

The men went back to firing. All were taken aback and covered their ears when Searcy let loose his AK-47 on a target in the distance.

The sound sent Bobby Joe to his knees.

***

Near Sand Gap was a little mercantile called Indian Creek Country Store that served hot sandwiches, hot dogs, and nachos at the deli counter.

The owner and staff were used to rugged-looking folks coming in from the area. After all, they were situated in the Ozark National Forest, just south of Jasper and west of Ben Hur. There weren't many places to get hot food or staples in between.

It was no shock or surprise when nasty, old Bert Black—aka Roy—walked in to order a foot-long hot dog with extra mustard and steaming hot nachos loaded with jalapeños.

He paid with stolen cash and took the food to an outdoor metal patio table. He grabbed a chair, scarfed down every bite of food within a few minutes, and then let out a belch that startled the birds in the trees. He pulled out his map and checked it twice. He then went back to the food counter.

"Excuse me."

The owner acknowledged him. "Yeah, whad-ya need?"

"This here's Sand Gap, right?"

"Correct."

"Do ya know a man named Curtis?"

The owner studied Bert with suspicion. "I do. Whad-ya need him for?"

"I'm a friend of his brother James. He told me to come find him here."

"Oh, I see. You're in trouble, are ya?"

Bert stuttered, "No. I'm not in trouble. I brung him somethin'. From his brother."

"Right."

Bert headed for the door. "Okay then, I'll just go on."

"Ain't ya gonna wait a minute so I can tell ya where to go?"

Bert wheeled around. "I'm listenin'."

The owner cocked his head over. "Hey, buddy. If you're wantin' help around these parts, you'd best get that chip off your shoulder, 'cause ain't nobody around here owes you nothin'. Ya hear? Guys like you come in here all the time lookin' for a place to hide 'cause they done got stupid and did somethin' they shouldn't-a done. So if you plan to hang out around here long, you'd best be a bit friendlier and stop actin' like we all owe your ass somethin'."

Bert choked on his own spit. He swallowed hard. "I'm sorry."

"Good. I seen you got a map. That's good. Ya gotta go west on this here road 'til ya get to Indian Creek Road. Once ya get there, go south. There'll be a cave off to the left. Ya gotta look for it. Nothin' comes easy. He'll find you before ya get near his place."

Bert humbly said, "Thank ya, sir."

The owner smiled. "That's much better. Ya keep learnin' that quick, and you'll fit in here real nice with the folks around here. Anything else I can do for ya?"

Bert asked, "Do ya have a cellphone I can borrow?"

"Sure thing. Let me go get it."

"Thank ya."

The owner went behind the counter. He soon returned with an old Motorola flip phone.

He handed it to Bert. "It's old, but it works."

"Thank ya. I'll step outside and be right back."

The owner nodded and went back to work.

Bert went outside and stepped several feet away from the door of the store so no one could hear him. He opened the phone, dialed a number, and paced slowly, kicking gravel as he went.

Finally, there was an answer. "Yep."

"Searcy. It's Bert."

There was a long, stiff numbness on both ends.

Bert continued, "Call 'em off. Now. Or else I'm talkin'." Then he quickly disconnected the call.

He took the phone back into the store and handed it to the owner. "Thank ya."

"Welcome."

Bert started to leave but turned around with a look of concern. "Can they track that number?"

The owner smiled. "I suppose they could, but it'll be disconnected and destroyed within the next five minutes, so I wouldn't worry too much about it." He shrugged. "Whad-ya think I keep hundred-year-old flip phones layin' around for?"

***

At home, Jim sat at his desk, downloading the contents of the flash drive to his computer. He leaned back in his office chair, rubbed his face, and yawned. He massaged his eyes in an attempt to alleviate the stress that drew them tight.

Meanwhile, Laura walked in without his knowledge and frightened him out of his mind. "Hello there. What 'cha doin'?"

"Oh my God! You scared me."

"I'm sorry. I didn't mean to. What are you doing?"

She tried to peek at the computer, but Jim turned it away from her.

"Honey, it's about work. I can't show you."

"Oh, I see. I'll just leave then."

"Honey, don't be like that. It really is about work. You know I can't show that stuff to you."

Waving her hand, she left the room with a slight attitude of feeling rebuffed. "It's fine. I get it."

Jim saw the download finish. He muttered, "Shit. No matter what I do, which way I turn." He hit his head with his hand. "Almost got my ass killed today, and what do I get for it?" He mimicked his wife. "It's fine. I get it."

He deleted the *Year of Meteors* file off the flash drive so that only Bobby Joe's file remained on it, with the date and time it had been retrieved at the gun shop. He quickly made an extra copy. He mumbled to himself again. "Is this what Levi wanted me to do all along? God, I hope so. Because it's been done."

The front doorbell rang.

Jim hustled to hide the flash drive in an interior pocket of his jacket and zipped it up. Then he shut down the computer. "God, don't let it be a Rose at the door."

***

Jim walked into the foyer just as Laura closed the door behind Carl and Joy. He said, "Hey! Look who it is!"

After they exchanged greetings, they proceeded into the living room where everyone sat down around the coffee table.

Jim continued, "You know, I was really rude to you last time, Joy, and I'm truly very sorry."

"Thank you, Jim. I'm sorry too. I didn't mean anything bad by what I said."

"Oh, I know that. It was just a tense time, and I was in a bad mood. Please forgive me."

"Already done. We actually came to check on Laura though, to see how she is doing—you know, coping with things."

Jim's eyes darted back and forth at them as he deciphered the meaning of what was happening between him and his friends. He stuttered, "Oh. My apologies. I'll just go back to what I was doing in the other room."

Carl admonished him. "Jim, we were just very disappointed to hear, I mean, you and Dorene..."

Jim rose up to leave the room. He held his hands out, palms to their faces. "Oh no. I understand. You don't need to bother getting up. I deserved that. I'm guessing it was a mistake I will be paying for the rest of my life, but you all sit right there and check on Laura. I'm good. Nice talking to you."

As Jim left the room, Emily eavesdropped from the kitchen. She watched her father sluggishly retreat down the hallway then followed him.

***

Jim sat in his office chair, staring at the dark, blank computer monitor. He was hammered with guilt, grief, and depression.

Emily entered. "Dad?"

He uttered, "Hi, kiddo."

"You know, what they said back in there, that was mean and uncalled-for."

"Nah. I deserved it. I guess I deserve nothing but hell for the rest of my life."

"Dad, it's a hard thing to understand. I mean, how could you do it? Why weren't we good enough for you? How can we trust you? That's hard stuff. And Mom, you have always been her whole world. You've got to understand that."

"Oh, sweetie, I do. I get it. I just can't see what I can ever do to make it alright again, no matter what I do."

"Hey, I'm just a young person, but I'm betting it's going to take time. Like, a lot of it."

Jim's head hung low. "I said I would never leave, I would never give up on the family, but right now, I'm not so sure that's the best choice anymore. I don't think I can live like this forever, and God knows, I don't want you or your mother to have to either. There's been enough unhappiness. Why put ourselves through more of the same? Unhappiness on my part is what pushed me there in the first place."

Emily gave him the side-eye. "Is that an excuse?"

"Oh come on, Emily. That's what I mean. Whenever I try to explain anything about it, no matter what I say, I get 'Oh, is that an excuse?' If you're going to ever have a productive discussion, you have to decide before you start, what you are going to call an explanation and what you are going to call an excuse. Because explanations are acceptable, excuses are not. You can't ask me for an explanation if you're always going to call it an excuse."

"Hey, Dad. I'm just a kid."

"No, wait. About 10 minutes ago, you were a twentysomething, young adult, psychology major, who smokes pot."

"You know about that?"

He laughed. "Jesus, Emily. Smoke billows out of your bedroom window like Cheech and Chong's love machine."

"What? Who?"

"You've never seen *Up in Smoke*?"

"I don't know what you're talking about, Dad."

Jim held out his hand.

She hesitated then reluctantly put her hand in his.

He smiled. "Thank you for letting me hold your hand again."

She fought back a smile. "You're weird."

"You think I'm weird, when your mother goes to bed tonight, you ought to watch that movie with me. Would you?"

.

"The love machine? Dad, that sounds like porn. Don't ask me that."

He laughed. "No! It's called *Up in Smoke*. You'll love it. Trust me. We can even sit on separate ends of the sofa if you want."

She asked, "Deal?"

He was delighted. "Deal."

CHAPTER 15

The noontime sun shimmered down like a torch in the night. It was an eerie glow that seemed to cast a surreal light, pervading through everything it touched. Nothing looked real. Nothing smelled real. Even the air stood still as if the earth itself had stopped breathing.

Rhett and Shelby's home sat in the center of this clabber-green vortex. It just sat there with complete indifference, even to its own existence. It did not glisten or greet passersby. Neither did the birds nor butterflies draw close to its semi-transparent dome.

Inside the home, the dark aura grew thicker as if one could cut it with a knife, sliver by sliver. An awful stench filled the air so intensely that it could sear the strongest of nasal membranes.

In the bedroom, Rhett was naked and passed out on the floor. He was covered with his own urine and feces that he had obviously rolled around in. Next to him was an empty bottle of whiskey and a nearly empty liter bottle of cola, the rest of which was all over the torn-up bed and floor.

Shelby and Georgia entered through the kitchen from the garage with shopping bags in hand. They were both immediately alarmed as they looked around.

Shelby furrowed her brows. She sat her bags on the dining table. "What in the holy hell?"

Georgia sat hers down too. "Oh my God, that smell! What is that?"

Concerned, Shelby rushed into the master bedroom. She shrieked, "Rhett! Oh, not again!" She bent down to wipe his face.

Georgia followed her. She fell to her knees next to her brother's head. "Rhett! Wake up! Are you okay?"

Rhett's eyes rolled from side to side. He slurred, "Hey, I'm over here. Help me."

Georgia hustled to her feet. "I'll go get a cold rag."

Shelby pulled a sheet off the bed and covered his lower body. "Why in the world did you do this again, Rhett? You promised you'd stop getting' drunk."

He rolled over and struggled to focus on her face. His words were garbled. "Shelby? Is that you, sweetie?"

"Yes. It's me."

Georgia ran back in, wrinkled her nose, and placed the cool cloth on his head.

He sobbed, "Thank you so much, Momma."

Georgia retorted, "I'm not your momma, Rhett. I'm your sister."

"Ohhhhh, thank you, Sister. What are y'all doin' here?"

Shelby answered, "I'm your wife. I live here. Now, why did you go get drunk again? You were doin' so good."

Georgia added, "Yes. He was doin' good! I was so proud!"

He moaned, "I'm so sorry I let you down, Wife and... I forget your name."

Shelby tried to roll him over to get her arms underneath him. "Georgia, if you can help me lift him from that side, let's get him to his feet, and throw him in the shower. Then I can clean this mess up."

As they lifted him, Shelby yelled, "Dammit, Rhett! Try to stand on your feet! Right now!"

He struggled to stand as they hoisted him up. They held onto him, putting his arms around their necks.

"I am tryin', Shelby. Give me a break, okay?"

Once on his feet, the two women steadied him.

Shelby advised, "We're gonna go one step at a time and get you to the shower."

He whined, "Okay. If you have to do that, I get it. I'm a dirty coward, I am."

Shelby insisted, "We're not havin' that conversation right now."

He lamented, "Well, why not? Dammit. He's dead."

Georgia asked, "Who's dead?"

Rhett cried, "I can't tell you that, Momma. Then he'll kill you too."

Shelby looked at Georgia. "Ignore him. He doesn't talk sense when he's like this."

He wailed, "Go ahead! You think I'm makin' shit up 'cause I had a teeny-weeny little drink."

They continued to the bathroom where Shelby turned on the shower. She let it warm up while Georgia held him steady against the wall. Then they wrangled him around and sat him inside.

Shelby closed the door. "We did it."

Rhett cried, "Shelby. I love you. Are ya gonna ever let me out of here?"

"No, Rhett. You're in jail, so just sit there and think about what you did."

He whimpered, "But I really did see a man die yesterday. Blowed his brains right out. Pssshhewww... And he made this... god-awful noise in his throat... and his hands and legs jerked all over the place. And I didn't do anything

282.

about it but throw up. 'Cause I'm a goddamned coward." He
moaned loudly.

Shelby and Georgia pondered the possibility. Chills ran
over their bodies.

Georgia whispered, "Shelby, I don't think he's lyin'."

***

Emily sat in her bedroom, reading a psychology
magazine when she came across an ad for a psychic analysis
session. A spark gleamed from her eyes.

"That gives me an idea."

She looked the ad over carefully, then picked up her
iPad and ran a Google search for local psychics.

She continued talking to herself. "I have wondered if
something else is going on with all the stuff that's happened
the past several days. Maybe, just maybe, I can find out.
Hmmm."

It didn't take long before she located a psychic in Eureka
Springs named Wilma Crow. Her website stated that she was
not only a true psychic but also of Native American heritage.

Within moments, Emily dialed the number and
scheduled a time for Wilma to drive down to Beebe for a
visit. She hung up and leaned back on her headboard.

"That was a good idea."

***

At the gun shop, Searcy sat alone in the back room,
tapping his fingers on the table. He sprang up, angrily
shoved his chair, and paced the floor. He punched his fist
through the bathroom door and ran his bloodied fingers
through his hair. He stomped, cursed, and threw things
across the room, sending them smashing into the walls.

Before long, he picked up the landline phone and dialed a number. He continued pacing the floor as the phone rang.

A man on the other end answered. "Yes, sir."

Searcy thought twice. Then he spoke. "Call off the search."

"You sure you wanna do that?"

"Yep."

"Consider it done."

Searcy hung up, slamming the phone into its cradle. A strong tap knocked on the door.

Searcy bellowed, "What do you want?!"

Toad opened the door. "May I come in?"

"Yep."

Toad's towering presence seemed to calm Searcy somehow, enough that he sat down and rubbed his eyes.

Toad tipped his head over to one side as he handed his boss an iPad. "I think you need to see what we caught on the security camera this mornin'."

Searcy directed, "I'm not good with these things. Get it rollin' for me."

Toad set it up so he could see it clearly. Then he started the video. There on the screen, as clear as day, was Jim's face as he turned to look back before he scurried out of the shop.

Searcy spoke in a low guttural growl. "Bert got the little shit out of the way, but he failed to get this fuck. Now it is imperative. Did he take anything?"

Toad answered, "It appears he did. He downloaded files off the iMac, sir."

"Fuckin' government man. First the ATF idiot and now this guy. Which files did he get?"

"He got the *Year of Meteors* folder that Levi told us was nothin' to look at. Turns out, it was full of our war plans, maps, correspondence, and other stuff."

"What else?"

"He also downloaded Bobby Joe's folder."

Searcy sat up straight. "Bobby Joe." He cupped his forehead with his hand and squeezed it like a vice.

Toad squirmed then continued. "That's not all, sir." He paused. "It appears that someone disengaged the cameras and security system and unlocked the door for him."

Searcy slammed the table with both fists. "Goddamnit!" He stood and scuffed his boots across the floor.

After a while, he tried to calm himself. "This means everything has to be bumped up asap. Call the nerve center and ground zero. Tell them to beef up security; there's been an information breach."

Toad saluted, "Yes, sir. Anything else?"

"Get Dorene on the phone. Tell her to get her ass over here now."

***

John Mark and Darcy's home was a simple ranch-style layout with traditional landscaping on a half-acre that was cut short for the kids to play on. Out back was a huge sandbox with a slide and swing. Off to the side was a set of elaborate custom-made monkey bars.

Mauser and Gunner played outside, chasing each other with cap guns. Hope and Faith sat on the swings, rocking their dolls to sleep.

Inside the home, Darcy chased behind John Mark as he darted from room to room.

"Ya need to tell those kids to get in the house and stay in the house."

Darcy asked, "Why? What are ya doin'? Have you lost your mind?"

He raced through the house, gathered all his guns together, carried them to the master bedroom, and lined them up—all 25—one by one across the bed.

"No. I have not lost my mind. I love you, Darcy. But please don't question me. Not now."

"Well, I'm gonna keep askin' ya 'til ya give me some answers. I'm your wife. I birthed four kids for you. I deserve answers."

"Pull that window shade down."

"John Mark! I'm not doin' another thing you ask 'til you answer me!"

He stopped moving and confronted her. "Darcy, someone is after me. And they might be after you and the kids too."

She was confused. "Why? Who would want to harm us?"

"I can't tell ya that 'cause I don't know."

She threw her arms down. "I swear to God, you're losin' your mind. I'm not doin' this."

He tilted his head back and exhaled loudly. "Someone was followin' me home from the gun shop today. I didn't recognize 'em. I thought I lost 'em, but if someone really wants to find me, they will. Now, will you please call the kids in the house?"

"You have no idea who it was?"

His voice raised. "I told you, no! It could be a pissed-off customer, a politician, a gun dealer. Anybody!"

She smarted off, "Not a pissed-off husband or boyfriend?"

He grabbed her by the shoulders and looked her in the eye. "No. I have not cheated on you. Now please get the kids in the house. Now."

Unexpectedly, one of the kids screamed loudly.

It jolted the parents to their souls. They sped through the house and out into the back yard where Faith had fallen from the ladder on the slide and skinned her shin.

John Mark demanded, "Kids! Get in the house right now!"

Mauser whined, "But I didn't do anything. Let me stay out here."

"No. In the house, now. I have reasons."

The kids knew better than to argue with their parents so they reluctantly dragged themselves inside.

Gunner turned on the TV, and the kids all sat down to watch. Darcy pulled the window shades down while John Mark made sure the garage, storage building, and all the vehicles were locked down.

The kids carefully watched their parents' strange behavior. When the phone rang, the entire family was taken by surprise.

Darcy answered, "Hello." She put the phone down. "John Mark! It's for you! It's Searcy!"

Out of breath, he answered the call. "Hey. What 'cha need?"

Searcy politely said, "Hey. I really need to get out and relax a bit. You wanna go huntin' with me in the mornin'? Time for squirrel."

"Sure. That sounds good."

"You sound kind of stressed out. Everything okay?"

"Yeah, I think we'll be okay. I can't talk about it now. The kids are all here."

"Oh, that's alright. We'll catch up tomorrow, before dawn."

"Sure thing."

***

The landscape along highway AR 1808 was incredibly stunning with tall overgrown canopies of trees and foliage. The creeks and waterfalls of jasper green were as striking as any in the world. The rocky bluffs and outcrops gave views to jaw-dropping photographic scenes. The air, the atmosphere, was akin to breathing in a piece of heaven with its hints of wildflowers, wild grasses, and earthen tones.

Bert paid no mind to the scenery other than what he was searching for because, after all, he had spent days traveling through it. He would, however, duck in and out of the woods from time to time, checking for any caves that might be nearby. Just a short distance of a few feet and he could completely pass it by.

Ultimately, his meticulous hunting and tracking skills paid off. He located a cave like the one the store owner had described.

As he began to crawl through the brush to reach the entrance, he heard a flock of birds flutter off into the distance. He crouched low, stayed buttoned up, and waited to see what had startled them.

There was no sound except for a few birds, crickets, and frogs. There was no smell except for Bert's own foul body odor. There was nothing to be seen except for the natural landscape and the entrance to the cave that Bert itched to get up close to. Yet his instincts told him to stay still and wait.

Like a lightning strike, a sharp knife slid in front of Bert's throat. He held perfectly still against the blade.

A surly voice whispered from behind, "Who the fuck are you?"

Bert stuttered, "Name's Roy. James sent me out here to find his brother Curtis."

The knife pulled back without cutting Bert's skin.

A feral-looking man quickly slithered around in front of him. "I'm Curtis." He looked Bert up and down. "I suppose ya went and got yourself in trouble."

Bert tried to remain cool and calm. "Not much. I lost my home. Just need a quiet place to hang out for a while 'til I get my bearin's."

Curtis examined Bert for sincerity. "Ya know, there's a whole network of us livin' out here. Don't nobody bother us too much. Maybe an occasional lost hiker or illegal hunter. Even the forestry folks don't pay much mind to us 'cause we help 'em keep the poachers and graffiti vandals outta here. They're all scared of us."

Bert refused to break eye contact with the man. "I'm sincere." He nodded, "I just need a place to stay for a while."

Curtis walked around him, sizing him up. "Nah. I believe ya. James don't send me no flakes, usually. However, there has been a time or two."

After a deliberate minute of staring at Bert and looking him over, Curtis smiled. He waved his arm. "Come on in my cave. I'll get ya somethin' to eat."

***

Searcy sat in the back room of the gun shop, looking over maps and papers. When Toad rapped on the door, he was ready.

"Come on in."

Toad escorted Dorene inside.

Searcy signaled with his head. "Thank ya, Toad. You can wait outside now."

When the door closed, Dorene stood there, silently inspecting her father.

He glanced back at her for a moment. He pursed his lips, placed his forefinger over them, then pointed. "Sit down."

She obeyed, as ordered.

He ogled her breasts, then her waist, then her hips. "I have an important assignment for you."

"Why do ya hate Jim so much?"

"Jim? I didn't say it was Jim. But yes, I do hate him. I really don't owe you any reason. But since you asked, the man is on my land. Asa should have never let it go to his wife. And, he's Air Force. And, he's a whinin', fuckin', liberal jackass. And, he's got an impure son. Any other questions?"

"No."

"Good. Now, are ya ready to shut the hell up and listen to your assignment?"

She did not speak but looked straight ahead.

He walked behind her as an intimidation tactic. "You will start immediately, like tomorrow. The target must be taken down and destroyed, killed."

Without moving her head, her eyes searched for him in her peripheral line of sight. She argued, "I don't kill. That's your specialty."

He arrogantly strutted closer to her so that his voice would resound more strongly. "You will do what you are assigned to do, Dorene."

She felt him breathing down the back of her neck. She nervously took a deep breath. "Then who?"

He stood upright and paused, anticipating a crazed reaction. "Willie."

Her blood ran ice cold. Her brow furrowed. "Our Willie?"

"Yes. Any problem with that?"

She scorned, "Yes. A big problem with that. I won't do it."

"Oh but you will," he demanded.

She belted, "No. I won't. Do it yourself."

He ambled around behind her with his hands in his pockets. The clap of his boots on the concrete floor was unnerving. "Dorene, if you don't do it, she will die." He warned, "Very horribly, I might add."

Dorene's skin rose with goosebumps. Her nostrils flared with rage. Her breathing became erratic as her face twitched and trembled.

He continued, "Do ya wanna reconsider?"

She remained still in her chair. A single teardrop rolled down her cheek. She squeamishly answered, "I'll do it."

"Good girl."

He bent down, fingered her hair, and whispered in her ear. "And Dorene, if you ever come onto my land again, or walk into this shop uninvited by me, I will shoot your ass dead. Do you understand me?"

She nodded 'yes.'

"Now get the fuck out of my sight."

Visibly shaken, she walked to the door, opened it, and hesitated. With her back to him, she held the door for only a moment as if to say something, then walked out and let it shut behind her.

Searcy smiled with pride at his artful manipulation. He sat back in his chair and thumbed through papers and maps. He chuckled out loud.

***

Dusk was fast approaching, yet the heat of the day was still scorching. Kyle and Annabelle decided to make the best of it by hanging out by the pool where they chatted and laughed at one another. It was a nice break from the recent stressful events.

Kyle said, "Thank you for spending time with me. I know I messed up a couple of times. You didn't have to talk to me ever again."

"Oh, you silly guy. I'm no hardass like some of the family. Besides, Luke owns most of that responsibility."

"Can we go do something tomorrow? I'd really like that."

"Sure! Hey! I know! There's a little lake just north of here goin' toward Searcy. You know where that is. Want to go take a walk up there?"

"Yes! That sounds like fun! Honestly, anything sounds like fun. I like spending time with you."

"Damn, you handsome athletes with English majors! You know how to wrap a girl around your little finger."

"I do not!"

They ribbed each other until the sun went down. Then they kissed and, like a true gentleman, Kyle walked home alone.

***

The sun had just gone down when Searcy arrived at the nursing home. His truck engine and signature boot-stomp alerted Fuzzy moments ahead of time, so he was prepared when his brother barged in.

"Hey, Fuzzy. How are you doin', Brother?"

Fuzzy laid in bed, pretending to be half-asleep. "Searcy? Is that you?"

Searcy sat in the rocker. "Yes, it's me. Can I get ya anything?"

"Oh noooo. I'm fine. They're takin' real good care of me here."

"Well, how are ya doin' otherwise? Anybody givin' ya any shit?"

"No. Nobody does that better than a brother."

Searcy chortled. "Yeah, I know that. I had two older brothers. Both pains in the ass."

"Say, how come you always had a grudge on me and Asa? Just 'cause we was older?"

"Pretty much. Older brothers are always first in line. Got everything first. Money, power, girls. Only left me their hand-me-downs."

"Oh, but little brothers got Momma's attention better. Pretty, little baby boy."

Irritated, Searcy quickly got up, poured water in a glass, and moved to the bedside. "Alright. I think that's enough. We don't want to start a battle right here and now, do we?"

Fuzzy became humbled. "Oh no. We don't. I'm sorry if I rubbed your feathers the wrong way."

"Nah, it's all okay. No worries." Searcy pulled a capsule from his pocket. "Now ya need to take this pill. Open up." He put it to Fuzzy's mouth and smiled.

Fuzzy took the capsule into his mouth. He feigned swallowing it down and burped. "Garlic and probiotics. Annabelle doubled my dose lately."

Searcy praised him. "That's a good boy. Now you go on to sleep. I'll catch ya tomorrow."

In an attempt to dig on his younger brother's self-esteem, Fuzzy gloated, "Yep. Goin' fishin' tomorrow with my friend. Goin' down to float my boat on Schroeder Lake."

"Who's takin' ya down there?"

"My friend, Hugh. We're gonna catch some big 'uns. Got us a hankerin' for some bass."

Searcy waved. "Okay, ya better go to sleep then. G'nite." He closed the door as he left. Then he hesitated, rubbed his mouth and chin in deep thought, and grinned.

In his room, Fuzzy spat the capsule out. He carefully listened for the boots to walk away. It seemed like forever, but then it finally happened. Energetically, he wiggled out of bed and hid the capsule in a small box he kept in his private closet.

When Searcy got home, he walked into the house with a slight limp. Mabel had a roast and potatoes on the table.

Searcy sat down to eat. "I'm exhausted. Long-ass day."

"As was mine."

"Oh please. All you do is sit here all day and go shopping or meet with your friends. You don't do any real work."

"If you don't shut up, you'll be fixin' your own damned meals for the next month."

"Okay. I'm sorry."

"Besides that, I spent all yesterday cleanin' up after your meetin', remember?"

"Okay. I'm sorry."

They began to eat. He scarfed down his food.

Mabel picked at hers. "Charlie's wife has called me seven times today wantin' to know where he is. She will likely call again."

Searcy spoke with his mouth full of food. "Tell her ya don't know. You're not his keeper."

Mabel glared at him. "My God! You're brilliant! I don't even know where ya get these fabulous ideas!"

He whined, "Mabel."

"Searcy, this woman is scared out of her mind. She thinks her husband is comin' home. He's not! You don't have one compassionate bone in your body, do ya?" She stopped to consider. "Never mind, I know the answer to that already."

He begged, "Please Mabel. It's been a very tough day."

She rose from the table and threw her plate in the sink. Then she headed out of the room. "You had a tough day? Eat by yourself. I can't even stomach bein' near you anymore.

And when the phone rings again, it's Charlie's wife. Just go on and tell her he's dead, and you killed him."

Mabel was gone in a blink.

Searcy stabbed his roast and shoved it into his mouth, chewing like a rabid dog.

The landline phone rang. He yanked the base from the wall and shattered the handset to pieces. Then he sat back down and resumed eating.

***

In a small classroom in a wing off the side of the church, the evening AA group for men was in session. Men of all ages, religions, ethnicities, and professions sat around a long rectangular table.

As men continued to file into the room and grab folding chairs, they greeted one another, laughed, and chatted. Some went for a cup of coffee while others poured a glass of water before settling down in their seats.

After the meeting began and introductions and announcements were made, the leader started off the sharing portion of the session. Each man paid close attention, focusing on whoever was speaking at that moment. It was a fine display of total acceptance and respect for one another.

Then, it was Gene Collins' turn to share. He sipped his hot coffee, lowered his head, and paused. When he lifted his head back up, he smiled at each man around him.

The leader asked, "Gene, are ya okay?"

"I thank God I am okay. And I'm sober. Fourteen years now. I'm a Christian man, and I'm lucky. I probably should be dead already, but God wanted me to live on for some reason. Maybe that reason is to say what I'm about to say to you fellas tonight."

He looked around at the men. "I've known most of you since we was kids. Some of you are new here. And we hope you'll stay in the group and stay sober."

Gene folded his hands together and continued. "I hope what I'm about to say isn't taken as strictly political. I personally think it's just a human thing, but y'all have the right to think what you want. So I'm just gonna put it out there and y'all can think about it."

He took a deep breath. "Me and my son, Robert, was at the gun shop last week. I saved up my hard-earned money and wanted to buy a new huntin' rifle so I could feed my family, but just have a better rifle and scope to do it with. On the other hand, my son was immediately drawn to those military-grade weapons they have down there. Of course, they were more than happy to show 'em to him and tried real hard to sell him one. But it made me mad, and I left without buyin' anything."

Gene took a drink of his coffee. "I was greatly disturbed by it. And now, I've had time to think 'bout why it messed with me so much. In this group, we talk a lot about egos and excess, humility, compassion, and love for all people. I think I was overwhelmed on all of those levels. Ya see, we don't need the excess that those kinds of weapons bring. We're supposed to keep our ego in check, remember? We're powerless, whether it's alcohol or ego. And to gain our power back, we have to get rid of ego."

One man agreed. "You're right, Gene."

"I know I'm rattlin' on, but please let me finish. I believe in the Second Amendment. And I used to believe that the government had no right to tell me what I could or could not have." He glanced around the room.

Half of the men had their heads bowed. The other half were either playing with their fingers or looking right at Gene, listening.

"I think y'all know where I'm headed with this, but I'll say it anyway. We all need structure. We need rules. We all want to wield the Second Amendment around like a dagger to defend our rights to own guns. But we despise it when that same rule of government tries to explain that military-grade weapons do not belong on our streets or in the hands of the public. So, I reckon what I'm tryin' to say, is that this passion that we defend to own those types of guns is excess, folks! Pure and simple. Ya don't need it. I been to war. It's only made for one reason, to kill as many people as quickly as possible. And ya don't need that! It's your damned ego talkin'."

He pondered in a hushed room. "So here we are talkin' 'bout our struggles with alcohol addiction and ego and all those other things. But my opinion is, if you're dead set on goin' all excess in other parts of your life, you're failin' at the mission that this very group is here to address. We're failin'. And that frickin' messes with my head and my own ability to cope with my own recovery process." He reflected. "I'm done now."

The room was so quiet you could hear a rafter creak. Then, one by one, the men began to applaud.

Gene put his hand up. "Please. Stop. I'm uncomfortable with that kind of attention. And my ego can't cope with it either. I didn't do anything outstandin'. I just spoke my mind."

The leader praised him. "Thank you, Gene. You have attended these meetings for many, many years. You're a great mentor. We appreciate the wisdom you bring to these meetings. Maybe you can look at the applause, not as praise for your ego, but accept it as an expression of gratitude from these men. You have just given us a new way to look at an important topic in our lives. Ego truly is the biggest thing we battle every single day."

Another man spoke up. "Thank ya for remindin' us, Gene. I appreciate you."

Without hesitation, the man sitting next to Gene began sharing.

Meanwhile, a robust farmer sitting behind Gene patted him on the shoulder.

The meeting went on.

***

In the corridor just outside the AA meeting room, Pastor Riley smashed his ear to the door, eavesdropping.

***

A second landline phone rang at Searcy's house. Searcy sat on his ass in his recliner, reading a book.

Mabel finally left her knitting, got up, and answered it. "Hello?"

A tearful woman on the other end sniffled. "Mabel, I'm sorry. I have to ask again. Have you or Searcy seen my Charlie?"

LIVE BY THE SWORD

CHAPTER 16

Thursday, July 18, 2013. The crisp, cool early-morning air in the woods made it an enchanting moment, especially in the summertime. Wildlife moved around freely as the soft dew dripped quietly from the trees onto the forest floor below.

As the fog lifted, John Mark and Searcy carried rifles to be ready at a moment's notice. They stepped gently, stalking, trying not to make a sound.

The animals instinctively sensed the hunters' approach and scattered into the dense overgrowth and high up into the trees.

The men continued on their path, moving slowly until they reached a clearing before the edge of a soaring granite bluff. The view was spectacular.

John Mark expressed gratitude. He lowered his rifle and walked out onto the rocky surface. He breathed in the fresh air as he looked out across the beautiful landscape. Through the lifting fog, he could see miles of green forests that covered hills and valleys with creeks that snaked in between.

On the horizon, the sun rose with the radiance of ten million angels.

He took a deep breath. "I can only imagine that this is what heaven looks like."

As he pivoted around to speak to his uncle, he got slammed as if a wild bull hit him full force. His body went flying over the edge of the bluff. With his fingers, he was able to catch on to a rocky outcrop right at the edge.

He cried out, "Searcy! Help me! I can't hold on!"

Searcy stood back away from the bluff, put his cowboy hat back on, and waited.

The blood-curdling screams continued. "Searcy! Help me! I know you're there! Help me, goddamnit! Searcy!"

The old man lit a cigar and propped himself against a tree. He pulled his cell phone out of his pocket and winced at it.

John Mark's screams became more desperate. "Help me! I'm slippin'! Searcy!" The young man shrieked. He screamed with frenzy as his body plummeted into the forest below.

Then there was silence.

A flock of birds took flight across the bluff and into the horizon.

Searcy dialed 911 on his phone. When a dispatcher answered, he said with a panicked tone, "We were huntin' and my nephew fell off a bluff! Can ya get someone out here immediately?"

The dispatcher urged, "Yes. Please stay calm, sir. Can you give me your location, please?"

***

Sheriff White was in his office drinking coffee and flipping through paperwork when the phone rang.

"Sheriff's Office."

"Good mornin', Sheriff. This is Crowley. How are you this mornin'?"

The sheriff chuckled. "Hi, Crowley. I'm doin' much better since I got some decent sleep. Thank ya. What's up?"

"Well, I'm not sure how to break this to you, but my superiors have directed me to call and notify you that you and your department have been taken off the Bert Black case."

The sheriff appeared puzzled. He leaned forward on his desk. "Did they say why?"

"That's all I have been directed to tell you, sir. I'm sorry."

"Nah. That's okay. Ya have to do your job. I'm just surprised. We've been workin' so hard on this case."

"I understand, Sheriff. I wish I could tell you more."

"It's okay. Thanks for callin'."

Crowley added, "Hey. Take care of yourself."

"Will do."

The sheriff hung up the phone. He looked around at his desk and walls strung with maps, photos, and paperwork regarding Bert. "I'll be damned."

***

Emily stood outside on the back lawn, looking at her cell phone. When a gold 2005 Toyota Corolla pulled up in the driveway, she rushed toward it with excitement.

A middle-aged, Cherokee woman stepped out of the driver's side. "Emily?"

"Yes! That's me! You're Wilma Crow?"

"Yes, ma'am. I am."

Emily extended her hand so the psychic obliged. "I'm so glad you could make it down here today. I was afraid it was going to take a week or something."

"Eh. Things are slow right now, and I had a spot open up."

Emily guided her. "Here. Let me show you—"

Wilma pulled back and interrupted. "Please. No." She gazed all around the property. "Don't tell me anything else. I need to feel it speak to me on its own."

Emily shrugged. "Okay. That sounds good. I'll just... stand here in case you need me."

Wilma cautiously walked up around the garden, around the house and pool construction, down by Fuzzy's house, and out to the horse barns. From time to time, she delayed and lifted her hands out.

When she got to Jim's workshop, she moved hesitantly until she approached where the explosion had taken place which was now a mound of freshly-turned soil. She chanted loudly and was overcome with emotion.

Emily stayed back, as promised, but was concerned about whatever Wilma was experiencing. She fought the urge not to run to her side.

Shortly, Wilma waved for her to come over. She hovered her hands over the burn area and mound of soil. "Somebody died right here."

Emily confirmed, "Yes."

"More than one."

"What do you mean?"

"I sense a native ancestor died here and was buried in a hurry. I also sense another person that died right here, in the same spot."

Emily listened carefully. "Go on."

"My ancestor says this land is cursed. As long as white people live here, there will be death on top of death. Fighting and trouble will find you every day."

Emily's eyes grew wide. "Oh no."

Wilma looked off in the distance. "Someone moved the Indian's bones far away. But they didn't get them all. Some are still here."

"I don't know what you mean."

The woman looked Emily dead in the eye. "You can't live here. There will never be peace for you or your family here. Your ancestors led many Indians to their death through this corridor and north of here at the Benge route. Even before then, some died right here on this land because of the white man. It is cursed."

"Oh no! We can't just move! We have to live here! Is there anything we can do?"

Wilma walked back toward the driveway. "I have some things in my car. I can pray and say blessings, but you'll have to make offerings and pray too, every day. Even then, it might not work."

Emily followed her. When they reached the car, Wilma pulled out a bag and started tossing things into it.

She handed it to Emily. "Take this."

They walked back to the burn area where Wilma dug a small spot in the soil with a gardening spade and buried a few small items. She then lit smudge over a weathered tortoiseshell, waved the smoke with a feather, and started chanting.

After a while, she put the smudge out and handed it and the shell to Emily. "You do that every day."

"I don't know how to chant."

"Then pray or sing. Ask forgiveness. Ask for peace."

"Can I call you if I need to?"

"Sure. But right now, I need to get back to Eureka Springs. It's a long drive. Can you pay me now?"

"Oh sure." Emily sat the items down on the ground and dug in her pocket. "I've been saving this for a little habit of mine, but we needed to have this done. Here you go." She handed the cash to her. "Thank you."

Wilma bent her shoulders forward in gratitude. "Thank you." She mulled things over. "Now move off this land."

Emily was shaken as Wilma drove away. Nevertheless, she picked up her things from the ground and started toward the house.

Then, she heard a hearty laugh. "Hey, there, good-lookin'!"

Emily swayed around and saw Luke peering out of Fuzzy's barn. "Hi, Luke!"

"Why don't ya come over here for a minute and show me your tortoiseshell? I'll show ya my smudge stick!"

She giggled as she trotted toward Fuzzy's barn.

***

At Bobby Joe's house, Mary sat on the floor with Hope, Faith, Gunner, and Mauser. Her words were soft and kind as she helped the twins dress their dolls and set up plastic army men with the boys.

Faith asked, "Gramma, are you alright?"

"What do ya mean, sweetheart? Yes, I'm alright."

"You just act different since Levi died."

Mary became teary-eyed. "Well, he was my little boy, Faith. It hurts my heart real big."

Hope gave her a hug. "My heart hurts real big too, Gramma."

Gunner said, "How about none of us die no more."

Mauser smarted off, "That's the stupidest thing I ever heard. We all gotta die someday."

Mary advised, "Okay. Enough of that talk. How 'bout let's just all think about livin' today and love each other as much as we can."

Hope agreed, "Good idea. Better than Mauser's lame-ass suggestion."

Mary snickered, "Now! Where did you learn how to talk like that?"

"Mauser."

Mauser shouted, "Not just me! Ya ever listen to the family we live in! Damned sailors!"

Mary attempted to get the conversation under control. "Mauser. Stop. Right now."

"She started it."

Hope flicked her neck in sarcasm. "Did not."

***

In the meantime, on the back deck, Bobby Joe, Rhett, and Georgia sat, drinking coffee.

Bobby Joe said, "If you're ready to get some help, I know someone who can get ya into a group. But ya have to decide when you're ready."

Rhett—still hungover—pleaded, "I'm ready. I'm sick of livin' this way. If I don't, I'm afraid I'm gonna lose Shelby and the kids. They already suspect somethin's goin' on."

Georgia informed him. "Rhett, they know. Your condition has elevated to red-hot, burn-my-ass, watch-me-crash level. Ya cain't hide that from your kids. They're not dumb. I saw how you were yesterday. Don't think they don't know it too!"

Rhett was ashamed to the point he couldn't look them in the eye. "I know."

Georgia challenged, "So, you're ready?"

"Yes."

Bobby Joe commended him. "Good. His name is Gene Collins. I'll tell him to give ya a call and set ya up. As a matter of fact, I think they have a meetin' tonight."

Rhett submitted, "Okay. I'll do it."

***

Willie sat in his living room listening to ol' Conrad on the radio. Catherine walked in, gave a dirty look, and walked back out.

The spew continued forth. "We're livin' in the darkest times, folks! There is no room for error here. Our plans, our motives, our awareness have to be top-notch, or else we will fall victim to these charlatans. God meant for us to keep our race clean, but liberals want ya to believe that mixin' is a good thing. They want to force us to change. We don't have to accept it. And that's not the only thing they're tryin' to power-grab out from under us. It's time for civil war, folks. We have to do it to protect our nation's interests and our allies' foreign interests. It is crucial for our survival!"

Catherine came back into the room. "I thought you weren't going to listen to that crap anymore."

Willie countered, "I haven't been, very often. But Catherine, I just think we need to listen to all sides, so we know what's goin' on. We had a tough meetin' the other day. I have to know what they're sayin'."

She started to leave the room. "Colton and I are going to the park."

"Catherine. Don't be mad. Please."

She walked out without another word.

He grabbed his head in exasperation. "I can't win."

After Catherine and Colton left the house, the phone rang. Willie turned down the volume on the radio.

"Hey, Dorene. What do ya need?" He paused. "Sure. I can help fix that water pipe. I'll be right over."

***

Out at Sand Gap, Curtis cooked bacon, eggs, and biscuits in a couple of cast-iron skillets over a well-constructed fire pit in his cave.

Bert said, "I gotta admire how ya ran solar down here to power your little refrigerator. I kinda admire the lockset you've got on it too."

Curtis cautioned, "Now don't go admirin' too damn much. Ya know, it'd be kinda hard to get away with it runnin' through these woods."

They laughed then ate a hearty breakfast. Bert thanked his gracious host then they joked and chatted for quite a while longer.

After a time, Bert asked, "Do ya know a good place to get a bath?"

Curtis laughed. "Boy, do I! Let's go! I need a scrubbin' myself!"

The long-haired mountain man led him through the woods to a spectacular turquoise pool of water fed by a natural stream and waterfall.

He put his arm out. "There ya go!"

Bert stood in awe. "This is just gorgeous."

"We don't use fancy words like that, but it sure is purty. Let's get 'er done."

The two men stripped naked and plunged into the pool, taking their soiled clothing with them. While they bathed, they rinsed out their clothes without wasting any time.

On the trek back to the cave, Curtis bragged about his trips to Colombia where he had a girlfriend. "Yeah, that chick, she was a real babe."

"How come ya don't see her no more?"

"Eh, it was too hard goin' back and forth. I had my mom here, who weren't doin' too good. So I figured it was best to stay here."

"I'm sorry. Your momma still around?"

"Nah. She died a while back. Dirty, rich brother of mine—not James—wouldn't help take care of her. Then he kicked me out on my ass when she died. So, here I am."

"Why don't ya go back to your girl then?"

"Dude. You sure ask a lot of questions."

"I'm sorry. It just seems like, well, you're livin' in a cave."

He laughed. "I like my little cave. I don't owe nobody shit! And cain't nobody find me if I don't want them to."

"Don't ya get lonely?"

Curtis gave him a sarcastic look.

Bert continued, "Hey, if your girl was that nice…"

He punched him in the arm. "She is nice. Cute, little ass and tatas that sit there like little Minuteman rockets. Damn. I admit I do miss her sometimes. She still sends me mail from time to time, up at the Pelsor Post Office. I got a mailbox there. Every once in a blue moon, she even calls and texts me and wants to send me a plane ticket. Chick's so well connected, she can get me there practically overnight if I wanted her to. Yeah, she's fine alright."

Bert was amazed. "And you won't take her up on it! Damn crazy man!"

"I ain't ready to jump back into that saddle just yet. I'm still grievin'."

Bert apologized. "Oh man, I'm sorry. I didn't realize."

Curtis elbowed him in the ribs. "Hey. No worries. Let's get back and watch a little YouTube on my phone. First, I gotta plug it up to the solar battery so it don't wear out on me. Meanwhile, you can tell me about your woman."

308.

**

    Still dressed in her bathrobe, Dorene sat on her sofa, nervously waiting for Willie to show up. When the doorbell rang, she and her little dog were spooked.

    She opened the door. "Hi, Willie. Thanks for comin' over. I tried and tried to get whatever it was to flush on through, but it didn't work."

    Willie walked in with his toolbox in hand and commented, "Aw, don't worry. I'll get it fixed. Which one is it?"

    She pointed to her master bathroom. "In there."

    "Gotcha," he said as he darted off.

    Dorene went into the kitchen to retrieve two cups of coffee. Then she followed him into the bathroom. "Here's some hot coffee."

    He took the cup and sipped from it. "Hmmm. Is this that fancy flavored stuff?"

    "No. Just regular."

    "Well, no matter. It tastes good. Thank ya."

    He got to work checking out the plumbing on the toilet.

    "Thanks for comin' over here so quick."

    He drank some more coffee. "Actually, it was fine with me. Catherine got all mad and took Colton out to the park so… so it was… I forgot what I was sayin'." He stumbled into the wall. "What the hell?"

    Dorene asked, "Willie, are you okay? Here. Sit down in here on my bed for a minute."

    He let her lead him to the bed. "That's weird. I wonder if I'm havin' a stroke or somethin'." He sat down.

    Dorene sat behind him. She began messaging his shoulders. "Maybe this will help."

    Willie got a strange look on his face. "Dorene? What… what are you doin'?" He muttered, "I really don't, uhm, feel comfortable with that." He mumbled, "Why don't ya call the doctor instead?"

Dorene lifted herself up and sat beside him. She began to cry with guilt.

Willie fell backward and passed out on the bed.

***

Hugh's old blue 1959 Cadillac Deville pulled up in the parking lot and parked by a small boat dock at Schroeder Lake, between Searcy and Beebe.

The two old war buddies laughed and ribbed each other while they unloaded their fishing rods and tackle. Then they leisurely walked toward the dock.

It had been years since either of them had felt so comfortable and so happy, being with someone who wanted nothing more than friendship. They were old friends with trust that no one could ever dissolve.

While one walked with a limp and a cane, the other scooted his boots along the ground. They wobbled, failed to walk a straight line, and occasionally bumped into each other.

"Dammit, Fuzzy! You're gonna knock me on my ass!"

"If you'd walk straight, I wouldn't have to bump into your sorry ass!"

"Okay, well, I've got fishin' 'quipment in one hand and a cane in the other. What's your excuse?"

"Head injury. I don't need those damned glasses no more since I quit takin' Searcy's pills, but I still got head injury."

"From what?"

"Masturbation."

Hugh coughed and laughed so hard that he swerved, twisted, and buckled to his knees. He couldn't get back up.

Fuzzy shouted, "I ain't lyin'! Stop laughin', you jealous heap of horse shit!"

Hugh couldn't stop laughing.

Fuzzy struggled to get him on his feet again. "You're just laughin' 'cause you ain't got no pickle to pour the dressin' on."

After five minutes of pulling and tugging, Fuzzy finally got him up and going again.

He was out of breath. "If you sit your ass down again, it better be in that damned boat, 'cause I ain't pickin' ya up again. I'm too old for that shit."

Hugh snorted.

Fuzzy shouted, "Stop laughin'! Or I'm fixin' to put this head injury to damn good use!"

Eventually, they reached the boat dock where Fuzzy pulled out his keys and removed the tarp.

Hugh asked, "This is your boat? You ain't stealin' it?"

Fuzzy waved the keys in front of him. "I got the keys, don't I? Why does everyone seem to think I don't have any money? I own the State's largest gun shop for cryin' out loud!"

"I'm sorry. I didn't realize you were so loaded."

Fuzzy poked his arm. "Shut the hell up and get in. And don't forget, you're drivin' me home after this."

After another couple of minutes of the two old guys getting into the boat and safely seated, Fuzzy finally put the key in and started the motor. Off they went into the middle of the small lake.

***

At the other end of the lake, Kyle and Annabelle strolled while holding hands. They hugged, kissed, and talked as they made their way around the bank.

She glowed like a woman in love. "It's so nice out here this mornin'."

"It is. This was a great idea."

"You know, Kyle... I don't think I've ever been so happy bein' with anyone. Sure, it's been hell with grievin' and missin' Levi, but there's something about bein' with you that calms my heart."

Chaotic yells echoed across the water.

Kyle and Annabelle looked out onto the lake. There, they saw Fuzzy and Hugh waving desperately for help.

Annabelle shrieked. "Grampa! Oh my God!"

Fuzzy shouted, "We're sinkin'! Help!"

Kyle swiftly kicked off his shoes and t-shirt and dove into the water. He swam as fast as he could toward the boat.

Annabelle dialed 911. She yelled, "Go, Kyle, go!"

When Kyle reached the boat, it was almost completely submerged. Hugh struggled to keep his head above water with a life vest. Primordial fear radiated from his eyes.

Kyle insisted, "Stay calm. But we have to hurry."

Fuzzy shouted, "Take him first!"

Kyle turned to Hugh. "Stay calm and do what I say, okay?"

Hugh gave a terrified nod.

Kyle rolled his body over. "Don't fight me. Stay on your back and breathe. Relax. I'll float you to shore."

He made his way across the lake with Hugh in tow. When he reached the shoreline, he pulled the old man onto the bank where Annabelle and EMTs took over.

With grave urgency, Kyle dove back in. He swam like a dolphin toward the boat, but it was gone, as was Fuzzy.

The swimmer was not deterred. He went under and found the old man struggling to get loose from the boat where his shirt was hung up. Kyle yanked hard and tore the shirt loose. At that instant, he pushed Fuzzy to the water's surface.

Fuzzy broke through the water with a huge gasp. He coughed and struggled to swim. He panicked.

Kyle held onto him. "Fuzzy. I've got you. You're fine. I'm not letting go of you. Trust me."

Fuzzy calmed somewhat.

Kyle reminded him. "Okay, same thing. Don't fight me. I'm going to roll you over on your back. You just float. I'll keep your head up, okay? Relax."

When they reached the shoreline, the EMTs scrambled to pull Fuzzy out of the water where they quickly treated him.

Annabelle was frantic. "Grampa! Breathe!"

Kyle quietly stepped away from the scene. An EMT came over, wrapped a blanket around him, handed him his clothes, and questioned if he was alright.

Kyle answered, "Yeah. I'm good. Please focus on those guys over there."

The EMT asked, "You're a swimmer?"

"Yeah. UCLA."

"Cool," the medic said as he rushed off.

They began to load Fuzzy into the ambulance, but he made them stop. He waved to Kyle to come to him.

Annabelle was still upset. "Grampa! I love you! Keep breathin'! Don't you die on me!"

Kyle walked over and bent down. "Yes, sir."

Fuzzy cracked a smile at him. "Take care of that young'un, would ya? Women."

Kyle promised as Fuzzy was lifted into the ambulance with his friend.

***

In Fuzzy's barn, Luke and Emily made love then hung out naked under the blankets on the hay.

Luke played with her hair and traced his fingers around her face. She giggled and ran her fingers—ever so lightly— over his skin, adoring every inch. He playfully kissed her neck and jawline, giving her the shivers. They played around for quite a while.

Then Luke's phone rang loudly. It made them both flinch. They laughed with carefree abandon.

Luke stood up, buck naked, and answered it. "Luke here."

Emily adored his body and his rugged manliness. She sighed with delight.

Luke's demeanor changed as he hurriedly put on his jeans and shirt. "Oh God, no! I'll be there as quick as I can!" He ended the call.

Emily sat up, concerned. "What's wrong?"

He rushed to put his boots on. "I'm sorry, Emily. There's been an accident. I have to go."

As he grabbed his hat and raced out the door, she began to dress too, but he was gone in a flash. Once she was fully clothed, she gathered her smudge and other things and went home.

***

Later in the day, Dorene watched over Willie as he awakened in her bed. He was groggy. His words were slightly slurred.

She handed him coffee. "Here. Drink this."

He glared at her. "Oh, hell no! What did ya put in that other coffee ya gave me? Tryin' to kill me?"

"No, Willie. This is good, fresh coffee. I promise."

He accepted it and drank. "So, what the hell did you do to me? And why? Good God, my head hurts!"

"Willie. I have to tell ya somethin', and it won't be easy."

"Goddamn. Just spit it out."

"You cannot tell anyone. Not a soul." She thought twice about her words. "Searcy wanted me to kill you but I can't do it."

"The fuck?"

She continued, "You're my cousin. I don't have much family, and none that like me. But you were always good to me. I couldn't do it. He swore if I didn't do it, he would kill Annabelle."

Willie rubbed his face. "Jesus."

Dorene warned, "We have to pretend you're dead, Willie. Otherwise, he will kill you, your family, and me and Annabelle."

He rubbed his head. "What did ya give me?"

"Date rape drug. It was supposed to knock ya out so I could kill ya. Then I hired a guy to come in and get rid of your body."

"You were really gonna kill me?"

"He said he would kill Annabelle! But I can't! I love you! I'm sick of the person he made me to be!"

Willie looked at her. "I'm sorry ya went through that, Dorene. But what are we gonna do now?"

She paced the floor. "I was thinkin' while you were sleepin'. We need to hide you and Catherine and Colton somewhere, where he can never find ya 'til it's safe to come out."

"And where do ya think you're gonna find a place that he doesn't know about?"

"I know the perfect place."

"Pray tell."

"One of Bert's bunkers that no one else knows about! And since they say he's somewhere over by Jasper, he'll never know."

"Why wouldn't he go hide out at his own bunker instead?"

"'Cause I know it's there! After what he did to Matthew, he's afraid I'll expose it. Trust me. He'd never go there now. His chances are better at Jasper."

"How did you know it was there?"

"Let's just say, we had a deal."

Willie lifted himself up. "Okay then! That sounds perfect. So now we need to get there fast. I need to get my family there too. How do we do that?"

Dorene picked Dolly up, paced her bedroom floor, and thought out loud. "You're supposed to be dead. So I'll tell the guy who's supposed to pick you up to put your body in the trunk of my car. Then he's done and won't know any different, so he can't nark."

Willie nodded. "Okay. That can work. I can play dead."

She continued, "Next step is that ya need to chat with Catherine by phone. Tell her that she needs to meet me away from your home, just in case he sent someone to watch out. The grocery store! That's a good spot! And no one will suspect her car sittin' there in the parking lot."

"You're good at this."

"I've had to be. So next, is that I will pick them up and bring them to the bunker where you are. Y'all will stay hidden there 'til I come to get ya."

"Let's get this started. Where do ya want me to lay down and play dead?"

She grabbed a heavy blanket off her bed and spread it out on the floor. "There! Lay down on that, and I'll wrap you up. Lay face down so he can't see if the blanket comes off your head and your face twitches. Matter of fact, let's just

316.

wrap this sheet all around your head really good so it's tight, but ya can still breathe. I'll call him to come over. You practice playin' dead and be completely limp. I mean absolutely and totally limp. Get busy. I'm callin' him now. Then you'll call Catherine."

***

Emily decided to go outside, smudge, and pray around the property. She thought, with bad things starting up again, it couldn't hurt to be safe.

As she walked around the land, waving smudge, and singing, she realized that there was some special part of the ritual that reminded her of smoking pot. She felt it was refreshing, renewing.

When she walked near the edge of the property line closest to Mandolin Road, she failed to notice something odd in the overgrowth. She continued on, waving and singing.

Then a sinister force overtook her from behind. She dropped her smudge stick and tortoiseshell to the ground. A large man in a black suit and ski mask covered her mouth, quickly dragged her into a van, and drove away.

On the way down the road, the van passed Jim returning home from having his truck maintenanced.

He did a double-take in his rear-view mirror. "Hmm. That's strange."

CHAPTER 17

The Rose family gathered in the lobby of the Sheriff's Department. Bobby Joe was in a baneful trance. Mary and Darcy were inconsolable.

Sheriff White entered the lobby with a sad posture. "I wish I had better news for all of you, especially Darcy, Mary, and Bobby Joe. But it is my job to tell ya what I can about the accident."

Mary pulled her hair. She wailed. "My God!"

Darcy flung her head from side to side, holding onto Mary's arm. "No. No. No."

The sheriff paused then continued. "Searcy and John Mark were out huntin' early this mornin' when John Mark fell from a bluff, approximately 100 feet. The coroner believes his death was immediate and he felt no pain. That is the belief at this time."

Luke wiped his eyes. "He wasn't just my cousin. He was my best friend."

Searcy sniffled and wiped his eyes too. "I'm so sorry. I tried to stop him from gettin' too close to the edge."

Darcy screamed, "John Mark wouldn't have done something so stupid! He's got four goddamn kids to raise! He would never do that! Besides that, just yesterday, he said someone was followin' him, and he was worried they might kill him. How ironic, don't ya think?"

Mabel blazed a stare at Searcy that could have scorched holes through a steel wall. He avoided looking back at her.

Bobby Joe's face was red and swollen. His thin body fluctuated. His head quaked. With a splintered voice of despair, he moaned, "I done lost both my boys now." He looked at Searcy. "You still got all your kids; my boys are dead." His body shivered violently. "How goddamn convenient for you, huh, Uncle?"

With tears in his eyes, Searcy fired back, "Bobby Joe, I tried to save him! You ain't even said 'thank you' for that!" He sniffled. "I ain't got no reason to do a thing like that. How dare you all accuse me of something so horrible! I would never do such a thing! I tried so hard to hang on to his hands!" He bellowed with grief.

Bobby Joe rose to his feet and faced off with Searcy. "I barely got one son buried in the ground, and now I'm gonna put another one six feet under! Fuck you! Fuck all of you!" He stormed out of the building.

Searcy followed on his heels.

When they got outside, Bobby Joe broke down emotionally as he sat on a parking berm. Searcy tried to touch his shoulder but he shoved his hand away.

"Don't fuckin' touch me."

Within moments, Cletus hoofed it out the door and interrupted. "I hate to bother you guys, but we've gotta get to the hospital asap. Fuzzy almost drowned. He may not make it! We've gotta go now!"

***

At the White County Medical Center, Annabelle and Kyle sat in a private room with Fuzzy as Dr. Tate told him he would be alright. He had no severe injuries but might suffer some anxiety or PTSD from the event.

As Dr. Tate headed for the door, Annabelle stopped him. "Doctor? I need to ask ya something."

"Sure."

She pulled Searcy's capsule out of her jacket pocket. "Can you tell me what is in this?"

Dr. Tate held it in his hand and studied it. "I can't be quite sure. We would need to send it to toxicology. Have them check it out."

Annabelle responded with a slight tremor in her voice. "Could you do that for us, please? It's urgent."

"Where did you get it?"

Annoyed, Fuzzy interrupted. "My goddamn, little brother was makin' me take those things for days! As soon as I stopped takin' 'em, I got better! My brain got better! I can see, and I can hear again!"

Dr. Tate cautioned, "You know I'm going to have to involve the authorities."

Annabelle affirmed, "Yes, please."

Fuzzy recalled Searcy's connections. "Wait! Hell, that boy has the authorities wrapped up in his back pocket. Maybe we better not."

Dr. Tate maintained, "Mr. Rose. I can personally guarantee you that he does not own the authorities that I intend to call."

Fuzzy concluded, "Then hell, let's do it."

***

Jim stood in his kitchen and finished tearing salad for his family's lunch. He announced, "Come on, everybody! Lunch is ready!"

Laura came into the dining room and grabbed a chair.

As Jim placed a bowl in front of her, he yelled, "Emily! Kyle! Come down and eat! Fresh homegrown salad right here!"

As they began eating, he asked, "Have you seen either of the kids? Are they here?"

Laura recounted, "Kyle went for a walk with Annabelle earlier. Emily was with an older, psychic lady this morning, walking around the property with, I don't know, a sage stick or something. That's the last time I saw her. She's probably in her room. I'll go get her."

"No. You go ahead and eat. I'll go up."

Just as he stood up, his cell phone rang with an unknown number.

He answered anyway. "Hello. Who is this?"

On the other end, Emily cried, "Daddy."

A visceral sense of foreboding flooded over him. "Emily! Where are you, honey?"

Then, a distorted male voice with a British accent answered. "Jim, I believe you took some bloody files from the shop that don't belong to you. We want those back immediately, or else little Miss Emily is going to die. All of the copies you made, including the original, must be put in a manila envelope and placed underneath the firewood box by the back door to the gun shop. You have until 10 p.m. tonight. Do not contact the authorities. We'll be watching you. Oh. And if you try to keep a copy or take them to the police, your daughter will most certainly die." The caller hung up.

Jim wilted into his chair. "That van."

Shaken, Laura shouted, "Where is she?! What's going on?!"

He clenched his face with his hands. "I have to explain something to you."

"What did you do now?"

He explained Bobby Joe's insistence that he help him by going in and getting the files off the computer. He stated that, now, someone had kidnapped Emily in exchange for those files. He paced around the dining table.

Laura reacted in horror. "Well, get them! Let's go do it now! I want my little girl back home! Let's go!"

Jim tried to settle her down. "Laura. It's not that easy."

She screamed, "Why not?!"

He faltered with remorse. "Because I gave them to the FBI."

Laura shrieked, "Oh, Jim! What are we going to do now?"

***

At the White County Medical Center, the Rose family gathered in the visitors' lounge. They waited to hear word about Fuzzy's condition.

Searcy was the last one to march into the place. "They won't let any of y'all go back and see him?"

Luke conveyed, "The doctors don't want a lot of people back there right now."

Soon, Annabelle and Kyle came out of Fuzzy's room, walked down the corridor, and joined the family in the lounge. Annabelle appeared heartbroken.

Cletus asked, "Is he alright?"

"Grampa is gonna be fine. But I'm heartsick about John Mark."

Searcy announced, "I'm goin' back to check on him."

Annabelle halted him. "No. He needs to rest."

Searcy puffed up and scowled. "Listen here, little girl. I will go back there if I want to."

Kyle, with his athletic, 6-foot-4 frame, went into protective mode and moved up closer to them. His look at

Searcy was intense and intimidating. Both men stared harshly at one another.

All of a sudden, there was a loud ruckus in the corridor that progressed toward the lounge. Then Fuzzy strutted around the corner in his hospital gown while battling off nurses trying to pull him back. At one point, he spun around to loosen their hold on him, and his ass shone brighter than a full-on supermoon.

"Y'all better let me go! I'm gonna sue ya for sexual harassment 'cause I know ya done went and grabbed my ass!"

The family and visitors nearby reacted with surprise.

Mabel shouted, "Fuzzy!"

Frustrated with the hospital staff, he threw his arms down. "If ya don't stop tuggin' on my junk, I swear to God, I'm gonna sue your asses! Now leave me be!"

The nurses finally ceased trying to pull him back to his room. They decided to just stand watch and keep an eye on him instead.

He snarled at them and arrogantly stretched out his neck, mocking them. "It's about damn time!"

Luke rushed over to him. "Fuzzy. Are you okay? Shouldn't you go lay back down?"

"Boy, I am just fine. Somebody tried to kill me and my buddy Hugh this mornin'. I aim to find out who it was! If it weren't for that neighbor boy, uhm… what's his name, Annabelle?"

"Kyle."

Fuzzy shouted, "Kyle! That boy saved our asses!"

Rhett questioned, "What makes ya think someone tried to kill ya?"

Fuzzy crouched his neck and shoulders and squinted his eyes. "'Cause somebody messed with the plug on the damned boat and bored the hole in it bigger so that once we got our weight in it, it sank, and wasn't no way to make it stop. An' I know damn good and well it wasn't that way already, 'cause I had Joey from the boat shop go over there and check it out yesterday!"

Mabel peered at Searcy, who tactfully avoided her stare again.

Dr. Tate crept up behind Fuzzy. "Mr. Rose. You seem to be catching a draft back here."

Fuzzy curled around. "And you keep lookin' because...?"

"Because it's hard to miss, sir."

All the visitors in the waiting area now had a clear view of his ass. Some snickered. Others covered their eyes.

Dr. Tate continued, "Mr. Rose, you seem to be just fine so I'm going to release you to go home. Your friend will also go on home today."

A nurse's assistant rushed over and put a blanket over Fuzzy's shoulders and backside.

Fuzzy smiled. "I'm goin' home! Yippee! But first, I have to go see how Hugh is doin'."

Dr. Tate said, "I'll go sign your discharge papers."

Fuzzy danced and shouted with glee. "I'm goin' home! Not no nursin' home! I'm goin' home!"

He eventually noticed that the family appeared glum. "Why ain't y'all happy I'm goin' home? Y'all don't want me there?"

Luke turned to Annabelle. "You didn't tell him?"

She nodded 'no' and put her head down.

Fuzzy looked at her with suspicion. "Didn't tell me what?"

Bobby Joe mumbled. "John Mark is dead."

There was a long, drawn-out moment of dead air.

Fuzzy made some awkward gestures, rolled his lips, furrowed his brows, and began to wobble. Then he collapsed on the floor in grief.

Quietly, Mabel cast a nasty, burning laser scowl toward Searcy. Then, she slowly approached him and leaned in to whisper in his ear. "Your war... is already here."

***

Kicking up dust clouds, Dorene's car barreled down a rural dirt road that was canopied on both sides with trees and heavy undergrowth. At last, the car slowed and stopped.

Dorene got out and opened a camouflaged, vine-covered metal gate. Then she got back in the car and carefully turned onto a hidden path. Once she drove the car through the opening, she closed the gate.

The car then proceeded down the path.

When the trail ended near a tree line where camouflaged solar panels peeked from their hiding place, Dorene put the car into park. She urged Catherine and Colton to quickly grab their personal belongings and rush toward a grassy mound.

Once there, Dorene picked up a sturdy stick. She hit it on the ground three times. Then she cleared away loose brush and tree limbs. The ground began to move. A secret door opened up.

Willie stuck his head out. "Hello."

Colton squealed with excitement as he leaped into his father's arms. "Daddy! There you are!"

Dorene placed her hand on Catherine's back. "Y'all need to get down there and get settled in before someone notices that we're here." She urged, "Go on. I'll get the groceries out of the car."

Catherine joined Willie and Colton in the elaborate well-prepared hideout.

Dorene grabbed the groceries from the car and handed them to the family below. "I've gotta go! Do not come out until I tell ya, Willie. There are phone chargers down there when you need them but remember, do not contact anyone! No one but me. And that, only if you absolutely have to! Got it?"

Willie answered, "Got it. Thank ya for doin' this, Dorene. You are my favorite cousin."

Dorene smiled as she lowered the door shut. Then Willie locked it from the inside.

***

Jim and Laura agonized over how to best deal with their situation in getting their daughter back alive. In between bouts of crying and angry fits of rage, they bickered. Calling the authorities could mean certain death for Emily, but the FBI already had the files.

Laura pondered, "So you can either give them what you have and hope they trust that you didn't make more copies? Or tell the FBI what's going on and hope they can find her before it's too late?"

Jim suggested, "I think it may take a little of both of those options. For now, we stall them for more time until I can figure out how to tell the FBI about the kidnapping without anybody else finding out about it. And if we can stall them for a little more time, that gives me a chance to narrow in on their whereabouts."

Laura's phone beeped with a text message from Kyle.

She read it aloud. "Hey, Mom. Going with Annabelle to take Fuzzy back to the nursing home. Wild day. Tell you later."

She peered at Jim.

He rocked his head and urged, "No. Don't tell him yet."

***

At dusk, the gun shop was quiet. The parking lot was empty, except for Bobby Joe's truck. A sign on the front door read: *Closed in honor of John Mark Rose. Open tomorrow.*

Bobby Joe sat alone inside the workshop portion of the shadowy gun shop. He wrestled with his thoughts as he sulked over a loaded handgun on the workbench in front of him. A tear rolled down his cheek.

Then, a loud engine roared outside. It shut off.

Searcy entered the back door and strolled into the workshop section. "I thought I might find you here."

Bobby Joe did not answer but continued staring at the gun.

"You're not thinkin' about doin' anything stupid, are ya?"

Bobby Joe was forlorn.

Searcy's boots clicked on the concrete floor as he paced around the work tables. "I hate to see ya so sad, Bobby Joe. It's horrible what has happened to your family. And I can't say that if it were me, I wouldn't be thinkin' the same thing right about now."

Bobby Joe stared at the gun—focus unbroken—tears flowing down his face. His chin quivered.

"Do ya want me to leave right now? I can leave you be if ya want me to."

Silence.

Searcy started for the door. "Okay then, I'll—"

The scraping of gunmetal across the workbench stopped him in his steps.

He swiveled around and saw that the distraught father held the gun pointed directly at him. "Now wait a minute, Bobby Joe."

Then the grief-stricken father slowly turned the gun toward himself.

Searcy walked over next to him. "Are ya sure you really want to do this?"

Bobby Joe trembled.

Then, ever so gently, Searcy slid his hand up on top of Bobby Joe's. "If you're scared, I can help you."

Bobby Joe's body convulsed violently.

The gun went off.

Stunned, Searcy stepped backward, as Bobby Joe's body slumped onto the hard floor. He then carefully positioned the gun in his nephew's hand and rushed out the back door.

His truck engine rumbled to life, and the truck sped away.

As soon as the mammoth noise was gone, Mabel raced out of the back room. She ran to Bobby Joe's side, placed a folded gun cloth underneath his head, and dabbed the fresh bloody wound on the side of it.

***

Jim got on his cell phone as Laura listened. He dialed and waited for an answer.

"Sheriff, I have an urgent situation and need your help. I need to meet with you and the FBI. It has to be a safe place though."

The sheriff warned, "If this has anything to do with Bert Black, I cannot help you. I'm sorry."

"No," Jim assured. "It's something different. Can you meet me with an agent at the air base in about an hour? I don't have much time."

"This sounds pretty urgent."

"It is. I can't talk about it on the phone. When you get to the front gate, tell them you're there to see me. They'll direct you where to go."

"Okay. I'll get Crowley. We'll be there."

***

At the church, the men's evening AA meeting began. Rhett sat next to Gene as the group went through all the normal formalities.

When it came Rhett's turn to share, he said, "There've been a lot of deaths in our family lately. Today, we lost my cousin." He wiped away a tear. "They told me I didn't have to come to this thing tonight, but the fact of the matter is, that after that, I wanted to drink more than ever. Gene said it might be a good idea to try. So here I am."

The leader said, "We're sorry about your losses but we're glad you're here. You can trust us."

Rhett continued. "I'm not supposed to talk about these things, but if I can trust y'all, it'd sure be good to get it off my shoulders."

He took a deep breath. "I've seen too much, know too much, more than I ever wanted to know. I've seen people killed, and I was too coward to say anything. I live in a culture where I'm expected to love guns, but I hate 'em. I'm expected to be a diehard Republican, but I'm not. Fact is, I loathe those ideas. There are so many more things to say, but I think that's enough to start. Baby steps."

Gene patted him on the shoulder as a gesture of support.

The leader smiled. "You can trust us, Rhett. Take all the time you need. No one here is permitted to talk about anything they hear in these meetings or they will be banned for life."

Rhett smiled. "Thank ya. I need a safe place."

***

Outside the classroom, Pastor Riley held his ear to the door, eavesdropping.

***

Jim met Sheriff White and Agent Crowley in a private room at the Air Force base. He told them the whole story about the files on the computer, including the *Year of Meteors* which laid out the family's plan for preparing for civil war. He gave the men all the files he had.

He then explained the kidnapping of Emily and the phone call he had received. He also described the van he had passed on the road home. He was exasperated. "I just don't know what to do."

Together, they came up with a plan to get Emily back safely. The first thing to do was that Jim had to put the flash drives in an envelope and deliver it, as instructed, before 10 p.m. that night.

***

Searcy entered his home from the back door and meandered through the kitchen. "Mabel? Where's dinner?"

He moved throughout the house. "Mabel!"

After a lengthy non-response, he threw himself into his recliner, turned on the lamp, put his readers on, and began reading a book.

He muttered, "Goddamn woman. Always out shoppin', spendin' my money."

He pulled out his phone and texted Toad. *There's a mess at the shop you'll need to clean up tonight asap. No questions.*

***

In Heber Springs, Mabel's car pulled up in the driveway of a breathtaking multi-million-dollar home.

Several members of the Carter family helped her and Georgia unload Bobby Joe from the back seat. The injured man tried to walk but wobbled sideways. The Carter men took over. They easily and quickly got him into the house.

Once inside, they took him into an oversized, beautiful guest bedroom where Mary waited in tears.

She ran to him. "Oh, Bobby Joe!"

They undressed him and made him comfortable in bed.

Mary would not leave his side. "Bobby Joe, talk to me, please."

He looked at her. "Mary. I've got a headache."

"Yes, I bet ya do. That bullet grazed ya pretty good. I'm just so glad you're alive."

He held her hand. "I love ya, Mary."

Mabel interrupted, "We would've got him here sooner, but Georgia had my car. She had to come pick us up. And we've got a doctor on the way over now."

In an emotional moment, Mary hugged her cousin. "Thank ya, Mabel. He might be dead if it weren't for you."

"Nah. Searcy's just a bad, damn shot. Why do ya think he's gotta use a machine gun to hit anything?!"

Bobby Joe added, "For that, I'm thankful. Thankful he didn't shoot me with one of those."

Mary exclaimed, "Oh! Can we not talk about that? You're alive, and that's what matters. My God. I just can't lose one more." She wept.

Bobby Joe squeezed her hand. "You won't. I'm here to stay. I won't leave you."

***

As Searcy read a book, his cell phone rang.

He answered, "Pastor?"

"Searcy. The men's AA group is here tonight."

"So. Are ya missin' out on a porn session, or what?"

"No, but ya might be interested to know that Rhett's here."

"He is?"

The pastor cautioned, "He is. And he's startin' to leak about a lot of things he shouldn't be discussin'." He paused. "Just curious. Did ya know he's a liberal?"

Searcy put his book down and removed his glasses. "You don't say." He rubbed his head in deep thought. With reluctance, he said, "Dammit. Well, ya know what ya have to do."

Pastor Riley surmised, "It'll take a little time and plannin'. I wanna be very careful. But you can consider it done. To preserve and protect God's callin'."

"You'll have to forgive me, Pastor. I have to go put my brother to bed at the nursin' home. We'll chat later."

***

After some time, Searcy arrived at the nursing home and scuffed across the entrance to the lobby. He paused only long enough to check for the capsule in his pocket. Then, he proceeded to clop across the tile floor.

Without knocking, he barged into Fuzzy's room.

Fuzzy, fully dressed, sat in his rocker, telling memories of Levi and John Mark. Kyle and Annabelle sat in lobby chairs, listening to him. They pondered at Searcy's brazenness and rudeness.

Searcy said, "I see ya have company."

Annabelle snapped, "Yes, he does!"

He sneered at Kyle. "And you're apparently not too picky."

Annabelle got in Searcy's face. "You know what! That's not very kind after he went and saved your brother's life today. You could say thank you!"

Searcy growled, "Shut up, little girl."

Fuzzy rose to his feet and moved toward them. "Searcy, that shit ain't called for. Git on out of here before I kick your ass. I'm already pissed off that ya made 'em bring me back here again. Don't push me."

"I just wanted to make sure you were tucked in for bed and got a good night's rest."

Annabelle's temper flared again as Kyle held her back. "He will be just fine! I'm stayin' here with him all night! So I think you should leave!"

Kyle tried to calm her. "Annabelle."

"No! I mean it! He hasn't got anything good to say, and I'm tired of it! I got two dead brothers! I ain't in the mood!"

Fuzzy chuckled, "She's got a bit of fire in her tonight."

As Searcy turned to leave, he mumbled, "Just like her daddy." He slammed the door and quickly left the building.

***

Dorene arrived home. She locked the door behind herself and tossed her handbag on the kitchen table. Then she let Dolly out into the backyard.

When she came back inside, she grabbed a plastic tub of pre-cut salad mix out of the refrigerator and placed it on the countertop. She took a bottle of Aleve out of the kitchen drawer, popped two into her mouth, and chased them down with a few gulps of Smartwater.

As she pulled a salad bowl out of the kitchen cabinet, her phone rang.

"Hi, Mabel."

"What are you doin'?"

"I'm grabbin' a salad and gettin' ready for Matt's funeral in the mornin'. Why?"

"Has anyone on my side contacted you today?"

Dorene poked a few leaves of salad in her mouth. "No. I haven't heard from anyone. What's goin' on?"

"John Mark was killed this mornin'."

Dorene spat out the salad. She fell into a dining chair. "What? How?"

"He went huntin' with Searcy. The old man swears that he just walked to the edge of the bluff and fell off."

Dorene seethed. "He did it. I know he did."

Mabel added, "I think you're right, but what makes you think that?"

"Because he assigned me to knock off Willie. He wants to own all of Fuzzy's empire."

There was a hollow moment of silence before Mabel quizzed her.

"Tell me you didn't do it."

"Hell no! I love Willie. I know you think I'm evil and, yes, I've done some bad shit. But only 'cause he made me do it, or else he said he would hurt Annabelle." She opined, "However, I will admit that I did kind of enjoy disruptin' Jim Barton's world 'cause he was so cocky and shit. He would've sacked anything that had a pussy. Cheatin' son of a bitch. He deserved it."

With a deeply sincere voice, Mabel asked, "Where is Willie?"

Dorene demanded, "Don't breathe a word to anyone." She said reluctantly, "I hid him and Catherine and their little boy where no one can ever find them."

"Good."

"Mabel, how are Mary and Bobby Joe holdin' up?"

"Not good, Dorene. Searcy shot Bobby Joe in the head."

Dorene yelled, "Oh my God!"

"Thank God, the bullet only grazed him. I was in the back cleanin' out the refrigerator. Searcy didn't know that though. So I brought him out to Heber Springs to hold out with my family. Searcy thinks he's dead, and I'm not answering his calls."

"Searcy has lost his everlovin' mind! Poor Mary! My God!"

"They've lost both their boys and nearly lost Bobby Joe too. Mary's especially a mess. She's so pissed off; she wants to kill that bastard. Darcy does too. And she's got those four kids. I don't know what they're gonna do without a daddy."

Dorene scratched her head. "I want him dead too." Her eyes became teary. "He's held me hostage all my life and made me do things I never wanted to do. He stole my baby from me. He stole my life. He had Bert kill the love of my life. And now he's killin' off the family, one by one."

"Well, when you live by the sword, you die by the sword. That's true, ya know. His time is comin'."

***

The deep woods at night can be a terrifying place. At Bert's secret bunker, it was no different. The darkness seemed impenetrable but for the pale glow of the waxing crescent moon pressing through a heavy fog moving in.

Near the bunker door, a coyote prowled for food, field mice scurried through the underbrush, and the soft foghorn call of a great horned owl echoed through the forest. The aroma of wildflowers, prairie grass, wild honeysuckle, and night jasmine filled the air, as did the loud songs of crickets, bullfrogs, and katydids.

Inside the bunker, a kerosene lantern burned dimly. Catherine rested next to Colton as he slept on the twin-size bed. With her forefinger, she rolled little twists of his hair and rubbed them between her fingers.

Willie rested on a makeshift pallet of blankets on the floor. He stared up at the low ceiling. "Is Colton asleep?"

"Yes. He's out. If you want to talk about Searcy coming after you, I think it's okay now."

"I have to apologize to you, Catherine. I've been an ass."

"Sometimes, you are. I still love you though, and God knows, I don't want anything to happen to you, even when you make me so mad I could spit nails."

"Cath, there are so many things I wish I could tell ya; I wish I could explain."

"Hey. We promised we would always tell each other everything. No secrets."

"I know, and I meant that. But, Jesus Christ, there are so many things that the family does that I cannot tell anyone about. We're sworn to secrecy. Besides, some of that shit would curl your toenails."

"Willie. I'm your wife. You can tell me."

"No, I can't. If one tiny nugget of it got out, they would not just come for me, they'd take you and Colton out first to punish me."

"I would never tell a soul anything. Do you not trust me?"

"It's not like that at all, hon. Please don't take it like that."

"Well, that's what it sounds like."

"It's not! I'm tellin' you!

"Shhhhh. You're gonna wake him."

Willie whispered, "I'm sorry." He paused. "I absolutely trust ya, but that's not even the issue. The issue is that I swore not to disclose. The issue is that once I tell ya shit, I put you and Colton in jeopardy. The issue is that no matter how much I trust ya not to say a word, human nature begs us to find someone to share it with. It's just how human beings are made."

"So you don't trust me."

He sighed with frustration. "No. I do. Jesus, aren't ya listenin' to me?"

"I'm listening to you, Willie. Even when you're listening to some crazy conspiracy theorist on the radio every morning, I'm listening to you. I'm watching. I am listening."

"Catherine. I made a promise to you, and I meant it. I'm not gettin' absorbed in it anymore. I have cut way back on it. The only reason I have to do it now, is that I need to know what is goin' on, what they are plannin'."

He sighed. "For God's sake, my own uncle tried to kill my ass today. And I wish that I could tell ya the bigger plan, but I can't."

He sat beside her and cupped her face in his hands. "I love you, baby. But ya have to trust me on this."

Catherine looked into his eyes. "Can't you at least tell me why he wants you dead?"

Willie leaned back against the wall. "He wants to take over my dad's business. All of it."

His cell phone beeped with a short alert. He picked it up and looked at it. "It's from Dorene."

The text message read: *I just found out. John Mark is dead. Fell off a bluff while hunting this morning with Searcy. Also, Bobby Joe got shot in the head but he's alive. Don't leave your hiding place. I am heartsick.*

Willie dropped the phone to the floor, grabbed his head, and tried to muddle the sound as he cried in agony.

Catherine read the text on his phone, heaved, and tried to comfort her husband. He was inconsolable.

Then Catherine found a bottle of Wild Turkey and a can of cola in the small cabinet by the portable electric cooktop.

She opened them, poured some into a plastic cup, and handed it to Willie. "Baby, here. Drink this."

Colton began to roll over and wake up. "Mommy? Why is Daddy cryin'?"

Catherine rushed to her son's side. "It's okay, sweetie. Daddy's heart is just so full of love."

Colton smiled. "I like that. Love is good." The young boy rolled over and went back to sleep.

Willie worked hard to suppress his emotions. He downed the drink and held the cup out for Catherine to fix another one. "Please."

***

It was 9:50 p.m. when Jim's truck pulled into the gun shop parking lot.

He noticed Bobby Joe's truck parked there but decided to ignore it and complete the mission at hand. He quickly got out, placed the envelope with the flash drives underneath the firewood box, returned to his truck, and drove away.

CHAPTER 18

Friday, July 19, 2013. Daybreak brought with it a sense of sorrow, grief, and fear. The sensitivity that hung in the air was equal to an unseen plague of epic proportions. The weight was heavy. The persistence was continual. It was like something that you really wished you could wipe away, but the impending residue just kept reappearing.

As Shelby and Rhett drove northwest on Highway 16 toward Heber Springs, Luke followed behind them in his own pickup truck. They drove cautiously due to the fog and the dozens of deer that grazed alongside the old rural highway.

While Rhett manned the steering wheel, Shelby watched Luke's truck in the side mirror. She asked, "Why didn't he wanna ride with us?"

"He said he had something important that he had to go do. He can't stay long."

Shelby ran her finger across her lower lip. "Does he know?"

"Yes. He does. I told him everything after Georgia called."

"Rhett, he's not gonna go try to do somethin' stupid, is he?"

"I don't think so. He's got a pretty good head on his shoulders, thanks to his mom."

She tried to smile. "I'm so scared right now."

He reached across the console and put his hand on her thigh. "It'll be alright. Somehow. It will."

***

In the bunker, Willie woke up with a vicious headache. "Aughhh."

Catherine wiped her eyes. "Are you okay?"

"What a headache. I haven't had a hangover like this in years."

"I'll get up and fix you something to eat."

"You don't mind?"

She patted his arm. "Don't worry about it."

As she rolled over out of the bed, he carefully put his head back on the pillow. Colton remained sound asleep.

Catherine made coffee and warmed bagels.

Willie stared at the ceiling. "Cath, I've been thinkin'. John Mark was an expert outdoorsman. On top of that, he was terrified of heights. He would never go right to the edge of a bluff like that."

"I didn't know he was scared of heights."

"Yeah, he was. It took all we had to get him up in a deer stand."

"Then what do you think happened?"

Willie speculated, "Searcy."

"You really believe that?"

"He tried to set me up to be murdered, didn't he? Didn't Dorene explain it all to you?"

"What? No. She didn't. You told me you thought Searcy was after you. She didn't want to talk about it. She said you and I had time to talk it through while we were hiding down here. I didn't want to bring it up last night after you got that text."

He sat up as she handed him a cup of hot black coffee. He carefully sipped from the mug. "He assigned Dorene to take me out."

"Dorene?"

"Yep. And I think he pushed John Mark off that bluff. And, furthermore, I think he had something to do with Bobby Joe gettin' shot."

Catherine handed him a warm bagel.

Willie took a bite and continued talking with his mouth full. "He wants to take over. Like I said. I wasn't jokin'."

"Oh my God. So you think he would try to kill off his own family, not just harm them?"

Willie had a horrible thought. He put the bagel down and swallowed his coffee. "I've gotta get back to town. You and Colton have to stay here. Don't make a peep."

"What's wrong?"

"Bobby Joe didn't die. Searcy will try to make sure he does. And he may go for Fuzzy too. I've gotta go."

"But Willie. Can't you just call or text him?"

"Dorene said not to contact anyone, but I tried anyway. There's no answer. I thought it might just be the reception out here but now, I don't know. Let's not take a chance. No more contact."

He quickly threw his clothes on and kissed her. "I'm sorry. I've gotta run. You stay right here. I mean it. Don't even poke your head out of here 'til I tell ya it's okay."

"Willie, I'm scared."

He grabbed his handgun and cell phone then unlocked the trap door and lurched out into the foggy darkness. He turned to her. "Lock this behind me. Don't make a sound. Don't come out."

She begged, "Please be careful!"

He closed the door and had only made it out a few feet when he stopped and vomited. Then he groaned and wobbled toward the camouflaged gate and the old dirt road.

***

At the nursing home, Fuzzy, all dressed for the day, finished brushing his teeth as Annabelle pushed the door open. She walked in with a tray full of biscuits and gravy, bacon, hash browns, orange juice, grits, and coffee.

Fuzzy patted her on the shoulder as she walked past. In a cheesy tone, he said, "Thank ya, sweetie."

"Oh my God. Where is all that nice comin' from, Grampa?"

"I love my young'uns, and I don't let ya'll know it enough."

"Thank you. That's real sweet. I love ya too. After all, you are my Grampa."

He patted the back of a chair. "Annabelle, sit down over here."

She obeyed, eyeing him with anticipation. "Okay. What's up? Breakfast is gettin' cold."

"Ya know, I'm thankful for Kyle. Good kid right there. And I went and misjudged him right off the bat. I'm sorry for that."

"That's good that ya realize that, Grampa. He really is a nice young man."

Fuzzy sat down at the end of his bed. "I know a lot of shit has been goin' on lately. It's hard to take it all in sometimes."

"Yep. Things have been tough."

"But I've got somethin' to tell ya, that I should have said years ago."

She wiggled in her chair. "What's that? Might as well come clean. Just lay it all right out there."

He hesitated and stammered. "I'm not really your grampa. I'm your great-uncle."

Annabelle was confused. "What?"

"I cain't lie to ya no more." He took a deep breath. "Ya know Dorene?"

"Well yes! She's my cousin, the blonde lady that comes to your house sometimes and always sits real quiet in the corner."

"Yes. That lady. She's your momma."

Annabelle's world just turned upside down. She jolted to her feet. "Her? That's my real momma? Not Mary?"

Fuzzy looked at the floor.

Her thoughts swirled in her brain like a riptide. "But wait! She's Searcy's daughter."

"That's right."

"So, you're tryin' to tell me, that Searcy is my real grampa?"

He swallowed hard and cleared his throat. "Yes, and no."

"Okay. I love ya real big, Grampa. But that's a crazy answer."

"He's your daddy too."

Shocked, Annabelle collapsed into her chair. "No fuckin' way!" Her eyes darted around the room. "How is that even possible, if she is my momma?"

Her eyes fell hard on Fuzzy. "Are you tryin' to tell me, that he did it with his own daughter? And I'm the product of that? Shut up!"

The old man reached out and took her hand. He smiled softly. "I love ya like my own, Annabelle. I almost died yesterday. I don't want to die livin' a lie, and lyin' about things I should-a made right."

She affectionately ran her finger over the top of his old, wrinkled, leathery hand.

He continued. "Long ago, Searcy met a woman he fell head over heels in love with. She got pregnant and had Dorene. Then, for some reason, none of us know, she ran off and left the baby with Searcy."

Annabelle was gobsmacked. She focused attentively on every word.

Fuzzy tried to unravel more of the tale. "Ever' time he looked at his little girl, hurt ran through his veins. The more Dorene tried to get his affection, the more he turned on her. Poor ol' Mabel tried to help, but there was only so much she could do."

Annabelle's face twisted with emotion.

He continued. "Then, when Dorene was in high school, her boyfriend broke up with her. It ripped her heart out, and she needed her daddy's attention."

Annabelle pulled a tissue out of a cardboard box. She dabbed her eyes and blew her nose.

"The hard part is, we don't know if it was out of anger or what, but it happened. He crawled on top of her and gave her his attention alright. About nine months later, you came into the world."

Annabelle murmured, "I almost can't find any words. Poor Dorene." She twirled a long strand of her hair. "How did I get to be with Mary and Bobby Joe?"

Fuzzy's voice lightened up. "They always wanted a lil' girl, but they had two boys. And Mary couldn't have no more kids. So they took you in and adopted you."

"What about Dorene?"

"Searcy ripped you right out of her arms and took you to an adoption agency. But Bobby Joe and Mary wanted ya real bad. That, and they felt bad for Dorene. She wanted to keep ya, but Searcy wasn't gonna let that happen. He didn't want to ever see ya again. I'm guessin' Bobby Joe gave the agency so much money, they couldn't say no. Searcy never got over that."

Annabelle wiped her eyes. "That is such a sad story. I had no idea."

Fuzzy winked at her. "Well, hell. I figured you'd find out when you got old enough and saw your birth certificate or somethin' that said you were adopted."

Annabelle waved her arm. "I never asked to see it and didn't need to! Mom always handled our paperwork for everything, even college! She's such a sweet lady."

"Now that both of your brothers are gone, and things are pretty dire, I just had to tell ya."

Annabelle's phone rang.

"Hello, Mabel."

"Annabelle. I've been tryin' to get a hold of you."

"Oh. I've had my phone turned off 'cause I stayed the night at the nursin' home with Grampa."

Mabel said, "Listen to me carefully. I need you to drive out here to Heber Springs as quickly as you can and bring Fuzzy with ya."

"Okay. What's up?"

"I'll explain it when ya get here. Don't mess around. Leave right now. Get here quick."

Annabelle looked at Fuzzy with great concern. "Okay. We will."

***

A few minutes later, Annabelle and Fuzzy rushed out of door number 45. They were going through the lobby when Dr. Tate walked in.

"Hey. Mr. Rose and Annabelle. How are you?"

Annabelle answered, "Hi, Doctor Tate. We're doin' fine, but we're in a hurry. We've got family stuff to do."

"Okay. But I got the toxicology results on the capsule you gave me."

Fuzzy asked, "What is it? Poison?"

The doctor theorized, "Might as well be. It's mercury. Not enough to kill you outright, but over time, it sure could. It usually doesn't go through the digestive tract like that but if you already have some issues, like you do, it could cause problems. Probably what caused you to have some eyesight and hearing problems, as well as confusion and mental issues."

"I'll be damned. He thought he could cover it up with the mercury I was around in 'Nam."

Annabelle pulled Fuzzy's arm with a sense of urgency. "Come on, Grampa. We've gotta go. Now."

As she pulled him out the door, Dr. Tate added, "I've already handed this over to the authorities!"

Annabelle shouted, "Great! Thank you, doctor!"

***

Laura and Jim sat in the living room, staring at a blank TV screen.

Kyle hurdled down the stairs, flew through the kitchen, grabbed an apple, and then pranced into the living room. He stopped and studied his parents' composure. "Hey! You guys look like you're havin' one of those wild and crazy parties! How about tone it down a little?"

Laura gave him a glare that pierced through her swollen and darkened eyes. He was bewildered. Jim's countenance was not any better.

"Wow. I was just joking. What happened?"

Jim answered. "Your sister has been kidnapped."

Kyle dropped his apple. "What?! That's why the lame undercover dude is back outside again?!"

Laura's raspy voice broke down as she spoke. "Someone took her yesterday."

Kyle exploded. "Yesterday?! Why didn't one of you tell me?!"

Jim explained, "The authorities told us to wait until you got home. They didn't want us to contact you while you were with Annabelle or her family."

"Why?"

"Because they are suspect."

Kyle tromped around the living room. "Okay. Maybe one of the fanatics, but not Annabelle!"

Laura begged, "Calm down, Kyle. This isn't helping."

Kyle picked up his apple and threw it against the wall. "I want you to tell me everything. I'm going to find my sister since you guys obviously aren't out looking for her!"

Laura fell apart. Jim moved over, sat beside her, and put his arm around her.

He looked up at Kyle. "Please sit down."

After a few minutes of angrily pacing through the house, Kyle calmed down and sat on the sofa. "I'm sorry. I'm angry. I want my sister back."

Jim acknowledged, "So do we."

"Do they have any idea where she is?"

Jim ran his hand over Laura's arm. "The FBI is working on it now."

Kyle roughly wrung his hands together. "How and why did this happen? Any ideas?"

Jim went into some detail about the favor he did for Bobby Joe and that somehow he must have been caught leaving the gun shop. Emily's kidnapping was to force him to return the files.

"So return the damned files! How hard can that be?"

"Because it's not that easy, Kyle. Electronic files can be easily copied and distributed, stored away, whatever. I gave them the drives, but they are not going to believe that it wasn't copied."

"What are you saying?"

"The authorities don't believe they have any intention of letting Emily go, alive."

Laura sobbed.

Kyle slammed the wall, running his fist through it. "Dammit!"

Jim scowled, "Kyle, I know you are pissed. I am too. But you are scaring your mother."

Kyle finally sat back down. "I'm sorry, Mom." He sighed. "What do we do now? Just sit here and wait?"

"Yes."

Kyle's face flushed red with anger. He ran up to his room and slammed the door.

***

On a lonely rural country road, the morning sun began to burn through the fog.

Willie walked along the shoulder, stopping from time to time to rest. "Why didn't I think to bring a water bottle and gum with me?"

When an old, rust-colored 1967 Ford pickup rolled up to him from behind and stopped, Willie looked in the window with caution.

The driver was an overweight, 80-year-old bearded man wearing a worn plaid shirt; Dickie's, hickory-striped overalls; and a red-white-and-blue ballcap that read: *Mike Beebe for Arkansas Governor!*

The man leaned over and rolled the window down. "Hey there, fella! Ya need a ride into town? It's about to git real hot out here! Too hot for walkin'!"

"Yes, sir. I'd be grateful."

The man waved his arm. "Well git on in there then!"

Willie piled onto the seat bench. "Thank ya, sir."

***

At Rest Hills Memorial Park in Sherwood—just outside
of Little Rock—it was a clear morning. The sun was
beginning to raise the mid-July temperatures toward the
normal midday 90-degree average.

A canvas canopy on aluminum poles stood over a closed
silver coffin laden with flowers as it hovered over an open
gravesite. Underneath the canopy, several people sat in
folding chairs while a pastor meditated in prayer near the
coffin.

In the front row, Dorene—dressed in black with a veil
covering her face—sat next to Florence. The rest of the
crowd included the Toller family, Matt's military friends,
and his church family.

Florence whispered to Dorene, "Shelby and Georgia
really wanted to be here but they got a call to go out to
Heber."

Dorene tried to smile but grief demanded her emotions.

The pastor finished his silent prayer and faced the
crowd. "Greetings to you all. I am Pastor McKenzie. I am
Matthew's pastor at the Church of Christ. Let me say, he
would be so happy to know, that all of you have come here
today to show your respects for him and his passing. Matt
was a special soul. He wouldn't hesitate to give his life for
any one of you."

A woman in the crowd cried out with grief.

Pastor McKenzie took a moment out of respect, then
continued. "There was a time, I witnessed him literally take
the shirt off his back and give it to a homeless man. In honor
of his giving spirit, you'll want to notice that the Church of
Christ and Rest Hills Memorial Park have set up a tent over
here in the parking lot. This is where we're handing out food

and clothing to migrant workers who toil endlessly in our fields so that we have plenty to feed our families. We want to make sure we take care of them too. God does love all His children. We should too." He lifted his arm toward the tent in the parking lot.

Someone in the crowd yelled, "Amen!"

Pastor McKenzie went on. "Matthew worked for the Air Force, trying to fight the good fight. He had a heart of gold, and we will miss him dearly. But let's take comfort in knowing that we will meet him again. This life is only temporary. But what lies beyond is eternal."

Florence glanced at Dorene. She saw a tear fall from underneath her veil. She put her hand on Dorene's to show comfort and support.

Dorene dabbed her face with a tissue that she held tightly.

Pastor McKenzie announced, "Now Miss Callee from our church wants to sing a tribute song to Matt and all of you."

A young woman stepped up by the coffin, holding a microphone. The pastor stood aside as she faced the coffin and sang "I'll See You Again."

***

Emily sat quietly, tied to a folding chair in a murky, cryptic room. She was blindfolded and tied at the wrists.

A tall British man named Arnold Corbin sat down beside her with a hot bowl of plain oatmeal. He scooped up a partial spoonful and put it to her mouth. "Open your mouth. Here's your bloody breakfast."

Emily refused so he forcefully shoved it into her mouth.

A Russian named Ivan Chernov stood nearby and warned, "Hey. Don't be so rough."

Arnold scoffed, "What does it fucking matter to you?"

Ivan snapped, "She hasn't done anything to you, idiot!"

Arnold reared up and angrily shouted, "Maybe she hasn't, and maybe she has, asshole!"

With that, Arnold turned around and shoved another heaping spoonful of oatmeal into Emily's mouth, breaking off part of a front tooth.

She coughed and spat it out.

Arnold was disgusted. He threw the bowl of oatmeal across the room and slapped her in the face with all his might, knocking both her and her chair over onto the floor.

Emily screamed and wept.

Ivan walked over and slugged Arnold in the face. A terrible fight ensued.

Immediately, a Colombian man named Pedro Moreno entered the room. He stopped the fight by wedging himself between the two men. "What the hell are you doing?"

Emily whimpered on the floor, afraid to move a muscle.

Arnold gathered himself together. "The girl started it."

Ivan disagreed, "She did nothing. He is trying to beat her up and kill her."

Emily shrieked in fear.

Pedro looked at both of the men, raised his finger, and warned them with a heavy Colombian accent, "If either of you touches her again, I will kill both of you *malparidos* myself. Do you understand?"

They arrogantly nodded as they started to sit down.

Pedro reacted angrily. "No! Don't sit down! Get the fuck out of here!"

When they were gone, he compassionately sat Emily upright in her chair. Then he tenderly touched her hair as she trembled and cried. "I'm so sorry for you. You remind me of my daughter. You should not be here."

**

In Heber Springs, the Carter women fried catfish and okra, baked cornbread, boiled cabbage, and sliced dozens of garden-fresh tomatoes. A couple of the men cooked a brisket, chickens, and a pork loin on the massive barbecue grill outside. The flavorful aromas drifted sweetly upstairs where several visited with Bobby Joe in his room.

After entering the front door, Luke, Rhett, and Shelby sniffed the air that made their mouths water. Yet they quietly proceeded upstairs and lightly knocked on the bedroom door then quietly went on inside.

Mary and Georgia sat on the bed while Bobby Joe sat in a rocking chair with white gauze wrapped around his head.

He greeted the visitors. "Hey, there."

Rhett asked, "How ya doin', big guy?"

"Oh, I'm alive, I reckon."

Luke added, "Well we're all glad for that!"

Shelby asked, "What exactly happened?"

"Searcy shot me in the head. Grazed me, but he don't know that. He thinks I'm dead."

Luke said, "I just can't believe it. I mean, I know he's done bad shit, but his own family?"

Bobby Joe stressed, "Believe it. He did it. He killed Levi and John Mark too."

Luke wondered, "But why?"

Rhett advised, "Luke. Not here."

Bobby Joe barked, "Why not here? It's time this young man knows the truth! Both my boys are dead! I don't care who hears it anymore!"

Shelby proposed, "Should us women leave?"

Bobby Joe quipped, "What the hell for? If it weren't for you women, us men would have already killed everyone off the planet by now."

Then he turned to Luke. "Boy, you been raised with guns and God and family in your life. It taught you good morals and respect. You been blessed with a good life. You also know that we've been preparin' for civil war if it becomes necessary. But for God's sake, we shouldn't be hopin' for it to happen. You can't lose sight of the morals and respect we all taught you. I say 'we all' because it takes a village, son."

At that moment, Fuzzy and Annabelle walked into the room. Annabelle rushed over and hugged and kissed her parents. Fuzzy acknowledged Bobby Joe and vice versa, but Bobby Joe wasn't finished talking yet.

"What you seen happen to Charlie the other day, that ain't right. That's not who we are. It wasn't just wrong; it was pure evil. You need to realize that now before you start thinkin' that's how this family operates. We don't turn on each other. We don't kill each other either. We're family, goddamnit. Remember what we taught you about morals and respect. Never forget that."

Luke informed, "I didn't like what I saw, Uncle. It made me sick. I threw up for two days. But I didn't say anything 'cause I didn't know what to do."

Fuzzy interrupted, "I don't know what y'all are talkin' 'bout, but I want to say that I'm so glad to see you alive, Bobby Joe. I gotta apologize for my goddamn brother. He's lost his mind. He even tried to kill me too."

Mary leaned back. "What?"

"Tried to drown me and Hugh by sabotagin' my boat, and then he was feedin' me those fuckin' pills. Annabelle had 'em check it out. They said it was mercury. Needless to say, I revoked my Power of Attorney."

Rhett said, "No shit."

Luke stepped back. "Goddamn!"

Annabelle's phone beeped with a text message. It was from Kyle.

She read it aloud: *Dad downloaded some files for Bobby Joe at the gun shop. Now they kidnapped Emily. I don't know what to do.* She shrieked.

Bobby Joe groaned. "Oh shit. What the hell did I do?"

Luke shouted, "No! Just no!" He looked at Bobby Joe. "What files? Why would you do that?"

Bobby Joe explained, "I was onto Searcy about havin' Levi killed. He started watchin' me all the time so I asked Jim to help me 'cause he's my friend. I had no one else to turn to. He agreed and did it for me."

Mary asked, "What's in those files that's so important?"

Bobby Joe revealed, "Mostly correspondence between Searcy and Bert about their plans to make the lawnmower blow up. If Bert got caught, the cover was that it was meant to get Jim. But it was meant to take out Levi, all along. The kicker was that Searcy couldn't lose because he wanted them both out of the way, one way or another."

Annabelle yelled, "Oh my God! So what about Emily? She's my best friend! We've gotta go find her!"

Luke shouted, "Right now!"

Annabelle ran to the door. "Quick! Let's go, Luke!"

Mabel stood in the doorway. "Hold on. We're all goin'."

***

An Uber pulled into Bobby Joe's driveway. Willie vaulted out. The car quickly drove away.

Willie rang the front doorbell and knocked loudly. "Mary! Bobby Joe! It's Willie! Let me in!"

He ran to the back of the house, found the hidden key under the back deck, unlocked the door, and replaced the key.

Once inside, he locked the door behind himself. "Mary! Bobby Joe! Where are ya? Are y'all alright?"

After searching through the house and not finding a soul, he prepared to go back out onto the deck when he heard the familiar roar of Searcy's truck engine. Without delay, he hid in the laundry closet and readied his pistol.

When the engine shut off, it was only a couple of minutes before the back door lock turned, and Searcy walked in.

"Mary? Are ya here?"

He peered into each room then returned to the back entryway. "Well, shit. Where did she go?"

He pulled out his cell phone, made a call, and put it on speaker. "Toad. She's not here. Neither is Mabel, and they're not answering their phones. You heard anything?"

"No, sir."

"Did ya clean up that mess at the shop last night?"

"I did. No questions, just like you requested."

"Good man."

Toad asked, "But sir, what do you want to do about Jim?"

"I want him taken care of, but first I want those files back even if they may have been copied. It's the principle of the thing."

"The flash drives were delivered last night. What about the girl?"

"Don't do anything with her yet. Wait 'til I get there."

"Just double-checkin'. You still want Bert dead?"

Searcy kicked a dining chair. "Without question. He stole a Colombian deal from me. That kind of betrayal is not tolerable."

"I think I should tell ya, Earl came into the shop today."

"What did he want?"

"Cletus helped him. Sold him a Dual Glock 17."

Searcy brooded. "Oh. He bought a gun, ey?"

"Yes, sir. And Mr. Rose, I think I need to tell ya one other thing."

"What's that?"

"The sheriff came in today looking for ya. Then Halp called after they left. They want ya for attempted murder on Fuzzy."

Searcy paced the entryway floor. "Tell Ivan to prepare for me. I'll be comin' there earlier than planned."

"Yes, sir."

"Hey… and Toad. Tell the core to meet me at ground zero as soon as they can. You'll have to give them directions since they don't all know where it is. Leave Earl and Rhett out of it. Also, don't worry about texting Willie and Bobby Joe. They're all four out of the picture."

"Yes, Mr. Rose. Consider it done."

Searcy disconnected the call and rushed out the back door, locking it behind himself. After replacing the key under the deck, he scooted into his truck, fired it up, and sped away.

Willie, stunned, stumbled out of the laundry closet, sweating profusely.

CHAPTER 19

As Searcy sped down the two-lane road, he had an epiphany. He pulled over in the ditch and put his flashers on. He then picked up his cellphone and dialed.

Pamela answered, "Hello, Searcy."

"Buy me a first-class plane ticket to São Paulo. I'm leavin' on business asap."

"Sure thing. When do ya wanna pick it up?"

He thought for a moment. "I'll pick it up at the meetin' this afternoon."

"What meetin'?"

"You'll know very soon. Just get the ticket."

***

Suddenly, members of the core group—including several of the Roses—received an urgent text message from Toad.

It read: *To the core, critical mtg at ground zero @4:00 today. Mandatory. E Red Barn Rd, Cave City. Delete this text ASAP.*

***

A while later, in Heber Springs, Mabel, Mary, and Bobby Joe looked on as the Carter family loaded 12 ATVs into their pickup trucks and onto trailers.

Fuzzy and Annabelle slid into the truck with Luke and took off.

Shelby and Georgia joined Rhett in his pickup and followed Luke down the road.

***

An Uber pulled up into Fuzzy's driveway. Willie got out, and the car drove away. He then frantically checked inside Fuzzy's house and horse barn but found no one. He walked over to the Bartons' and rang the doorbell.

Kyle answered. "Hi, Willie. How are you?"

"Hi, Kyle. I was just wonderin' if you guys seen any of my family around here today."

Jim and Laura joined the two in the foyer as Kyle continued, "Come to think of it, no. I haven't. I was with Annabelle and Fuzzy at the nursing home last night, but I left around nine. Is everything okay?"

Willie asked, "Is Emily here? Maybe she's talked to Annabelle."

Jim said, "Why don't you come on inside? We need to tell you something."

Willie sat with the family in their living room as they told him everything that had happened. He appeared grieved and weary.

He rubbed his head. "I don't know what to do next. My wife and son are hidin' in a bunker out in the boondocks. I'm not supposed to contact anyone 'til I get the okay to do so. I'm tired. I'm hungry. And I'm mad as hell."

358.

Laura hopped up with a purpose. "Let me get you some food. Kyle, set him up for a shower, please."

Willie thought out loud, "I could go over to Fuzzy's and shower but, dammit! You never know when or where Searcy's gonna show up."

Kyle beckoned, "Come this way. I'll show you where the bathroom is."

Willie followed. "Thanks."

Jim looked out the living room window toward Fuzzy's house. "Where did everyone go?"

***

As Luke drove down the narrow rural road toward Beebe, Fuzzy got an idea.

"Hey, Luke. I need to go by the nursin' home first. I need to pick somethin' up."

Luke claimed, "We got plenty of guns at the house, ya know."

"It ain't no gun I need from there. Besides, they wouldn't let me keep it there. Nah, I gotta pick up somethin' else. Real important."

"You got it. We'll go straight over there."

***

At Cotham's Café in downtown Little Rock, Duvall, Henry, Lisa, Earl, and Conrad sat together at a table as they ate and visited. When the meeting text came, they all looked at their phones at the same time.

Conrad said, "Well, look at that."

Earl remarked, "I didn't get it yet. What does it say?"

Lisa commented, "Oh, you'll probably get it in a minute. Sometimes texts get hung up in outer space, I think."

Henry read it aloud but in a whisper.

Duvall suggested, "It doesn't make much sense to take five separate cars. Why don't we all ride together?"

Conrad agreed, "Sounds good to me."

Earl looked at his phone. "I still haven't gotten it yet."

Henry said, "Probably your service provider. Why don't you ride along with them? I have another important meeting at the Capitol so I'm sittin' this one out."

Lisa advised, "Henry. It says 'mandatory.'"

"Yeah. And so is this other one. Y'all want these gun laws shot down or not?"

Earl leaned back in his chair. "No. I think I'll drive myself. I actually have some other things to do up that way."

Duvall brushed it off. "Suit your fancy."

The group finished eating and chatted about gun laws and other things. Then, they paid their checks and threw tips on the table. They left the café and casually walked toward the Capitol building together.

***

At the nursing home, Luke and Annabelle waited in the truck with the air conditioning on while Fuzzy went inside. They listened to country music on the radio and tried to stay upbeat while they waited.

Luke asked, "How is it that Fuzzy can now come and go as he pleases?"

"I had a talk with the administrator. Searcy may have Grampa in this place, but there is nothin' sayin' he can't take little excursions just like everyone else here. Threaten them with a lawsuit; they'll straighten up pretty quick."

They didn't notice when Fuzzy returned so when he pecked hard on the window, it jostled them both out of their seats.

Luke turned down the radio and opened his door. There stood Fuzzy and Hugh with his cane.

Luke was confused. "Um. What are you doin'?"

"Hugh's goin' with us!"

Annabelle asked, "Grampa, ya know this is gonna be a fight, right?"

"Goddamnit, I know it! And I'm takin' Hugh with me! Ain't nobody knows how to fight better than Hugh! He's goin'!"

***

Rhett dropped Shelby and Georgia off at his house. "I'm goin' over to Fuzzy's and wait on 'em to get there. Y'all take care of the kiddos."

Shelby asserted, "Rhett, you don't have to do this. You don't have to go."

"Yes, I do. I've been a failure at fightin' back. Now is my chance to prove it to myself." He kissed Shelby and hugged Georgia. "I'll see y'all tonight. Let's have dinner together."

***

Catherine sat in the cool, dark bunker with Colton. As he played on the floor with his G.I. Joe action figure, she rested comfortably on the bed and read *We Were the Lucky Ones* with a small bedside reading lamp.

Then there was a huge crash as the lock on the door burst off, and the door flung open.

Catherine and Colton screamed.

Five heavily armed special ops soldiers—dressed in black and wearing ski masks—dove into the bunker.

Catherine held Colton tight as he bawled. "We're just hiding! We haven't done anything wrong! You're scaring my baby!"

The soldiers removed their masks and put their guns down.

The leader said, "I'm sorry Catherine. We didn't mean to scare you. We're here to rescue you and make sure you're safe. We weren't sure you were alone."

Confused, she asked, "You're here for what?"

"To rescue you, ma'am. We're not here to harm you."

"How did you find us here?"

"We got a ping from Willie's phone."

She wavered. "Oh. So you knew we were here all the time?"

"Yes, ma'am." His eyes searched around the room. "Ma'am, do you know if there are any illegal firearms here?"

Catherine grinned. "You know what, I do! May I give them to you personally?"

"That's a little bit unusual, but I guess—"

Without wasting a second, Catherine sat Colton aside. He dropped his G.I. Joe on the floor, breaking the gun from its hands.

Catherine then grabbed a hammer, pulled a curtain open along the back wall, and smashed the glass on a locked gun cabinet.

Unsure what to do, the soldier stammered, "Um, ma'am."

She quickly began passing rifles, AR-15s, and AK-47s to him, one by one until they were all gone. She took a deep breath and smiled. "That felt good."

***

Willie sat at the Bartons' dining table, scarfing down his food. Then, in the short distance, he heard two trucks rumble down Fuzzy's driveway. He sat upright. "I really want to thank you for the food, Mrs. Barton. I hate to run, but I've gotta go."

Jim stood up. "Willie. Would you mind if Kyle and I join you?"

Willie hesitated as he cleaned food from his teeth. "I guess that's alright. I'm not sure what's goin' on, but I'm about to find out."

Jim signaled to Kyle. "Let's go!"

Laura called out, "Jim! What am I supposed to do?"

"Stay here in case you hear anything from Emily. We'll be back soon."

The men hurried out the front door, leaving Laura standing in the doorway.

She shouted, "Good luck! Call me!"

***

Willie, Jim, and Kyle ran across the property toward Fuzzy's horse barn where the two trucks were parked. They barged into the barn as Luke, Annabelle, Fuzzy, Hugh, and Rhett were discussing their plan.

Luke exclaimed, "Willie! Where have you been?"

"Long-ass story. Where have y'all been?"

Rhett pulled rifles out of a hidden gun cabinet. "Out at the Carters' place in Heber with Bobby Joe."

Willie exclaimed, "Oh, thank God! I was so worried about him. Searcy's tryin' to pick us all off."

Fuzzy added, "You ain't shittin'."

Willie asked, "So what's goin' on? What's the plan?"

Luke explained, "The core got a text to meet out at Cave City at 4 o'clock. We're gonna arrest his ass ourselves. The family ain't got no tolerance for betrayers. He's done gone past that point."

Jim claimed, "The sheriff and authorities know too. They know about the cave, thanks to Bobby Joe's files, and they're listenin' to everything. I'm sure they'll be there."

Fuzzy glared at Jim. "How did you get Bobby Joe's files?"

"He kinda gave them to me. Then... Oh, never mind. Ask him yourself. I can't go all through that again."

Fuzzy looked at Annabelle. "Okay. I will." He kicked his left boot off and rearranged his sock. "And we was just tellin' Annabelle, it ain't no place for a lady."

Annabelle insisted, "Oh, I'm goin' alright! I want a shot at that bastard."

Hugh muttered, "Rose blood right there."

Willie squinted and slanted his head at Fuzzy. "Does she know?"

Annabelle shouted, "You can talk straight to me, Willie! Yes, I know! And yes, I can shoot! And yes, I'm goin'! End of conversation!"

Kyle pleaded, "But, Annabelle—"

"No, Kyle!"

"I just don't want you to get hurt."

"You better worry about your own ass gettin' hurt! I'm goin'! Now, let's go! Who's hitchin' up the horse trailers?"

Rhett, Fuzzy, and Hugh hitched up the two trailers to the two pickup trucks.

Luke, Annabelle, Willie, Kyle, and Jim saddled up eight horses.

Annabelle threw on the saddle scabbards. Luke gathered up handguns, rifles, and ammo.

Then they quickly loaded the horses into the trailers, squeezed themselves into the two trucks, and took off.

***

Outside of Cave City, Searcy's ground zero was a huge, limestone cave located 100 feet below the surface of the earth. Above the surface, it appeared as any other 120-acre tract of pastureland with grassy knolls, lots of trees, ponds, dirt paths, and wildlife. In fact, if one didn't know it was there, they never would, but for the occasional big rig entering the driveway located almost a quarter mile away and the heavily armed security guards who monitored the entry.

The cave itself was a massive, open space with 20-foot ceilings, integral structural-support pillars, electric lighting, an enormous dehumidification system, and an elaborate ventilation system.

In the center was the main operational hub that had windows 360 degrees. There were five wooden picnic tables with several silk ficus trees just outside. About 30 feet from the hub was a large section of walled-off rooms and offices. This was where Emily was being held.

Throughout the cave were hundreds of floor-to-ceiling, heavy-duty pallet racks where thousands of pallets of firearms and ammunition were stored. Security cameras watched up and down the aisles as big rigs delivered their loads and forklifts worked the pallets.

The things that weren't so easily seen were the emergency escape tunnels that began in the ceiling and rose at a spiraling angle—with ladders inside—the full hundred feet to the ground's surface. Once they reached the top, the escape hatch was then covered with a camouflaged, weather-proofed coating, making them very difficult to see from the wooded landscape above.

On this day, there were many high-profile visitors to ground zero. Besides the employees, security personnel, truck drivers, forklift drivers, and office staff, there were also gun dealers, traffickers, and foreign players from Europe, Brazil, Colombia, Russia, China, South Africa, and Venezuela. Surprisingly enough, there were also politicians, religious leaders, media moguls, and TV/radio hosts.

Near the walled-off area, Arnold, Ivan, and Pedro waited outside, sitting in plastic patio chairs. Each was heavily armed.

When Searcy arrived, his core was already there with the other visitors. The core list was familiar: Dorene, Conrad, Duvall, Lisa, Pamela, Pastor Riley, Cletus, Toad, and Deputy Halp. Henry was a no-show.

Searcy grinned from ear to ear as he arrogantly strutted across the cave toward them. He rocked his head as he approached. "Y'all are amazin'! Thank ya for gettin' here on such short notice! We already had this meetin' planned for our foreign business partners, but it was a good time for all of y'all to meet and get acquainted! As y'all know, we have a civil war comin' and we need to be prepared! It won't be long now!"

The old man smirked and nodded at Dorene as if to question if her assignment was executed. She smirked and nodded back at him.

***

Above ground, the posse on horseback barreled down the narrow two-lane path leading to the cave entrance. Annabelle, Luke, Rhett, Willie, Jim, and Kyle rode proudly with rifles in hand as they searched for other entries into the cave.

Fuzzy and Hugh grimaced as they struggled to get comfortable in their saddles. The bandage on Fuzzy's nose reflected the sunlight like a beacon, while Hugh's walking cane stuck out from his scabbard in an awkward manner.

Fuzzy laughed, "Rackin' you up?"

Hugh grunted, "It has been a while. Ain't rode a horse in 40 years."

Luke reminded them, "There was a pond back there a-
ways! It's damned near 100 degrees right now! Don't forget
to water your horses!"

As they continued moving forward, the wind blew
Annabelle's hair away from her stern face. She rode with
precision and a mission. Her rifle was ready to fire at a
moment's notice.

The posse's demeanor was serious and deliberate. This
team was out for justice. Nothing else would do.

***

Near the cave's entrance, Earl parked his car in the
underground parking lot and met the security guards by the
door. They took one look at him and waved him on through.
Earl, with his brand-new gun in his pocket, strolled right on
inside.

***

Not far behind Fuzzy's posse, roaring ATV engines
were heard. The horses became jittery at the noise.

Within minutes, they turned around and saw Mabel,
Mary, Bobby Joe, and the Carter family bearing down on
them quickly.

Mabel wore a fierce look. She was the lioness who
sought to kill.

Mary, although exhausted, glowered like a wild panther.

Bobby Joe, with his head bandage flapping in the wind,
furrowed his brow and gnashed his teeth.

When they reached Fuzzy's gang, those on horseback
moved the horses aside, off the pathway. The ATVs stopped
there.

Mabel said, "Fuzzy, why don't you guys hold up and
keep watch above ground? I don't want my gang goin' down

there either. They'll shoot all of you, sure as shit. I need to go down there alone. They won't shoot me."

Fuzzy ripped the bandage off his nose and asked, "And what are you gonna do down there by yourself?"

"I have a plan. I'll go down and turn Emily loose. I'll shut down all the electricity and lights. Then they'll start bailin' out of there like fleas on a fresh-dipped hound. I'll flush 'em out."

Fuzzy cheered, "Good plan! We'll scatter about up here! There's gotta be some escape tunnels here somewhere!"

Bobby Joe hollered, "Right! Let's go!"

As Mabel drove her ATV toward the cave entrance, the other ATVs and those on horseback scattered throughout the property, each person with a rifle in hand.

***

Mabel met the guards at the entrance and, as with Earl, they waved her on through.

She smiled and acted cool, "Have a good day!"

"You too, Mrs. Rose!"

"Oh, I will!" She hurried off into the cave.

***

Once Earl made it through the entryway, he dodged behind some pallets and held his breath.

The camera monitors failed to notice him. The staff was eating pizza and laughing in the hub while Searcy proudly gave his speech about preparing for war and other conspiracy ideas.

**

Mabel, unafraid and unnoticed by nearly everyone, trekked right up to the walled-off area. Arnold, Ivan, and Pedro bowed their heads in her presence and did not say a word.

Mabel snapped, "I'm assumin' this is where the girl is?"

Ivan nodded 'yes.'

Mabel went in and rushed to her side. "Emily, are you okay?"

The matriarch pulled off the blindfold and untied her wrists. She noticed the left side of Emily's face was red, swollen, and severely bruised and that her front tooth was broken in half.

"Oh my God. What did they do to you?"

Emily rubbed her right eye and looked at Mabel with terror. Unable to speak, the young woman grabbed her by the neck, hugged her, and wouldn't let go.

When Mabel finally loosed Emily's grip, she spun around with fury. All three men stood there, looking on.

In a low, commanding voice, Mabel raged, "Which one of you fuckers did this to her?"

All three men put their heads down.

Mabel proceeded to walk over and slap all three of them in the face. She threatened, "Next time, I'll fuckin' kill you myself, every last damn one of you."

Then Mabel took Emily by the hand, led her outside the walled-off area, down a darkened aisle, and hid her in a dark space behind some pallets. She ordered, "You stay right there and don't move 'til this is over. It's about to get nasty in here."

Emily whimpered, "Okay."

Across the way, Dorene quietly observed Mabel go into the walled-off area and noticed again when she exited the room with Emily. She smiled to herself.

***

Above ground, Fuzzy's gang and the Carter family scoured the property for hidden entrances to the cave.

Then vehicles from the Sheriffs' Departments of Independence County and Sharp County, accompanied by State Police, FBI, and ATF vehicles, rushed onto the property.

The posses looked on as the authorities bypassed them and sped toward the cave entrance.

***

Alone, Kyle rode cautiously through a wooded area, looking for anything that would signify an opening. As he rounded a turn, a heavily armed man wearing dark clothing and a ski mask, stepped out from behind an enormous tree.

The man yelled, "Stop!"

Spooked, Kyle put his rifle down. "I won't shoot. Who are you?"

The man walked closer and studied Kyle's face. He removed his ski mask. It was Walter Kingsman.

Kyle fell off his horse and landed on his ass.

Walter laughed. "Son, you're no fighter."

Kyle stuttered, "You. You're..."

"I'm your dad. Yep."

"But why? Where did you come from? Why are you here? Where have you been?"

Walter laughed as he extended his hand to help Kyle to his feet. "I do owe you an explanation, and it won't be easy. The easiest way to tell it is that I had to leave you and your momma because I got called away to a special assignment. It was dangerous and was gonna put your lives in jeopardy, so I left, and pretended I didn't have a family."

"But Mom—"

"I know. It wasn't fair to either of you, but better than bein' dead. Don't ya think?"

"Why did you come back?"

"I watched you and your momma for years, decades. I kept track of you. Makin' sure you were alright. When I learned about what was shakin' out here in this area, I wanted to try to protect you the best I could."

Kyle couldn't take his eyes off him. "I have so many questions."

"I'm retiring after this job. We'll have plenty of time."

"But at the grocery store, why didn't you say anything? Why were you there?"

"Actually, I needed to confirm who the officer was that was with you. There are a couple you wouldn't want to mess with. And I also kinda wanted to see you up close, see your face, make sure you were alright. I honestly didn't think you would recognize me at all."

"Oh."

Their conversation was interrupted as gunshots rang out in the distance.

Kyle's eyes grew wide. He yelled, "Emily! We've got to go save my sister! Let's go!"

Both men mounted Kyle's horse and rode off.

***

A loud roar was heard as Army trucks and special ops' vans hurtled onto the property and toward the cave entrance. Then a low rumble rippled through the earth while helicopters advanced and a Stealth bomber flew overhead.

Jim pumped his rifle in the air and shouted proudly, "Hell yes! That's my guys!"

***

Fuzzy and Hugh rode their horses slowly through a wooded area, carefully searching for any secret passageway. They methodically worked their way along. When they reached an immense, long-dead oak tree that had been uprooted and fallen, Hugh stalled.

"Big-ass tree right there. What do you reckon killed it? I don't see no lightnin' burn on it."

"Termites. Beetles. Disease. Poison soil. Who knows."

As they worked their way around it, Hugh took the opportunity to unsnap his short-sleeved western shirt and take it off. He left his wife-beater on.

"Shoo! It's hot out here! Humid! Don't this kinda remind you of 'Nam?"

"Ya shouldn't-a said that, Hugh. Now, I'm waitin' for goddamn bombs to start fallin' on my head."

***

Inside the cave, the power shut off abruptly. Immediately, everyone scrambled for shelter. Even Arnold, Ivan, and Pedro scampered into the darkness.

The "tat-tat-tat tat-tat tat-tat-tat" of multiple assault weapons firing was heard on the other side of the structure.

Earl took advantage of the chance and ran toward the area where he had last seen Searcy. Then he remembered several escape routes bored in the ceiling of the cave, so he ran for one, assuming Searcy would try to get away.

In fact, Searcy did run to an escape tunnel. He hurried to open the hatch and crawl inside. He was almost through when Dorene grabbed his leg and pulled him partly back down. He kicked her hard with his boots.

They fought and struggled for a couple of minutes until she threw all her weight onto his legs and pulled him down to where his head and face were exposed. Only his arms held him to the tunnel entrance.

Earl saw Searcy hanging from the tunnel, trying to escape. He fired a shot.

Dorene squeezed her eyes and hung on with all her might in spite of him kicking as hard as he could.

Pamela and Lisa stood side by side as people scattered throughout the cave.

Pamela drew her gun and yelled, "Freeze! ATF!" She then fired a shot toward Searcy.

Earl walked out of the darkness with his arms held high. He walked toward Pamela. "I surrender! I'm not a bad guy!"

At the same time, Lisa drew her gun. She screamed, "Freeze! FBI!"

Then another shot rang out closer to the escape tunnel where Searcy struggled to get away. Startled, Dorene dropped to the floor.

Yet another shot rang out. Searcy scurried like a cockroach up into the hole. Blood dripped from the escape tunnel entrance, but the man himself was gone, no longer to be seen.

Dorene looked over and saw Mabel standing several feet away, with a handgun pointed toward the tunnel. She looked at Dorene and shrugged her shoulders.

As the shooting died down, the two women then sneaked their way over to Emily's hiding place. With guns drawn, they wrapped their arms around her, protected her, and led her toward the cave entrance.

***

Once they neared the entrance, Dorene and Mabel laid down their weapons and surrendered. Authorities, including FBI Investigators Lage and Crowley and ATF Investigators Wilk and Shook, greeted them with military firearms drawn.

Deputy Halp, Pastor Riley, Cletus, and Toad also went toward the entrance, laid down their weapons, and walked out with their arms held high. They quickly surrendered to authorities on the spot.

Among the many folks in the cave who exited and surrendered, Jim spotted Emily, Dorene, and Mabel. He noticed how the older women were protecting his daughter. He ran toward them. "Emily!"

The authorities stopped him. "You know them?"

"Yes! That's my daughter!"

They let him go. He and Emily fell into each other's arms. They hugged and cried. He carefully studied her wounds and attempted to kiss her face.

Then he told the authorities, "You should let Mabel and Dorene go too."

As they walked away from the area where the authorities were arresting folks, Annabelle and Luke ran over to hug Emily as well. It was a tearful reunion.

Emily beamed at Mabel and Dorene. She held their hands. "Thank you for saving my life."

Annabelle pointed and asked, "They did?"

Emily nodded 'yes.'

Annabelle faced the two women. Dorene grew nervous, but her daughter's sweet smile was endearing.

"You're my momma?"

Dorene broke into tears and smiled. They first shook hands and then embraced with a hug long-overdue.

Mabel threw her arms in the air. "Yes!"

Her laugh was infectious. Her joy spread like a wave over those who stood nearby.

Kyle and Walter finally arrived on the scene.

Kyle bolted off his horse, put his rifle down, ran to Emily, and held his sister with strong arms.

Investigator Crowley shouted, "Hey, Walter! Good to see ya! I hear this is your last assignment!"

"Hi, Crowley! I heard you were on this one too! Small world!"

Jim stepped back and eyed Walter. He walked over to shake his hand. "Hi there. I'm Jim. That's my son, Kyle, over there. I saw you ride in with him. Do you know him?"

"It's been a long time, but yes, I do know him. He's my son too."

Jim smiled nervously, then coughed.

In the near distance, a gunshot rang out. All heads turned to look in that direction.

***

In the woods, off to the side of Red Barn Road, Fuzzy and Hugh led their horses up to a dead body laid slumped over, face down, halfway out of an escape tunnel.

Fuzzy rolled it over to see the face. He squinted his greenish-blackened eyes as he peered at it.

It was that of Searcy Winston Rose, with a single gunshot to the head.

Fuzzy frowned.

Hugh shook his cane, "Well, goddamn."

Twenty feet behind Fuzzy and Hugh, Mary, Bobby Joe, Rhett, Willie, and the Carter clan gathered with guns drawn. Slowly, they lowered their weapons as they crept closer to get a good look at Searcy's body. It appeared that everyone wanted to make certain that he was dead, indeed.

Within moments, the thunderous crashing sound of dozens of military weapons being drawn fell upon the vigilantes. They were surrounded by county deputies, state police, and military soldiers who demanded they lay down their weapons and surrender with hands raised high.

They complied.

Hugh yelped, "Gawwwd damn! Talk about some cardio!"

***

Duvall and Conrad escaped and were never found inside the cave.

***

Meanwhile, at the Arkansas State Capitol, Henry greeted a gaggle of constituents in the lower rotunda. While some kneeled in prayer over their Bibles, the majority of the crowd clapped, whistled, and cheered.

"Way to go, Henry! Constitutional Carry is finally the law! God bless you! Protect our Second Amendment!"

Henry basked in the limelight. "Thank you! Thank you, everybody, for your support! We will continue to defeat the anti-constitutionalists that want to take our guns and our rights! Please continue to support us in this fight and donate whatever you can to help us out! Thank you!"

As he shook their hands and moved through the crowd, they shouted, "Whatever you need! You have our full support! Arkansas loves you, Henry Shoemaker! God bless you!"

He threw his arms high into the air. "This fight isn't over yet!"

***

Sunday, July 21, 2013. At dusk, a Boeing 747 touched down in Bogotá, Colombia.

At the arrival gate, people greeted their friends and loved ones who deboarded the plane. Music, laughter, and friendly chatter filled the air as the passengers filed out one by one.

Then, Bert deboarded with his backpack and a smirk that stretched from ear to ear. He quietly and casually strolled through the crowd and disappeared into the fading light.

THE END.